# THE BLOOD CROWS

By *Simon Scarrow*

The *Roman* Series
Under the Eagle
The Eagle's Conquest
When the Eagle Hunts
The Eagle and the Wolves
The Eagle's Prey
The Eagle's Prophecy
The Eagle in the Sand
Centurion
The Gladiator
The Legion
Praetorian
The Blood Crows

The *Wellington and Napoleon* Quartet
Young Bloods
The Generals
Fire and Sword
The Fields of Death

Sword and Scimitar

*Writing with T.J. Andrews*
Arena

The *Gladiator* Series
Gladiator: Fight for Freedom
Gladiator: Street Fighter
Gladiator: Son of Spartacus

# SIMON SCARROW

## THE BLOOD CROWS

headline

First published in Great Britain in 2013
by HEADLINE PUBLISHING GROUP

1

Cataloguing in Publication Data is available from the British Library

ISBN 978 0 7553 5380 4 (Hardback)
ISBN 978 0 7553 5381 1 (Trade paperback)

Typeset in Bembo by Avon DataSet Ltd, Bidford-on-Avon, Warwickshire

Printed and bound in Great Britain by Clays Ltd, St Ives plc

Headline's policy is to use papers that are natural, renewable and recyclable
products and made from wood grown in sustainable forests. The logging and
manufacturing processes are expected to conform to the environmental
regulations of the country of origin.

HEADLINE PUBLISHING GROUP
An Hachette UK Company
338 Euston Road
London NW1 3BH

www.headline.co.uk
www.hachette.co.uk

Ad meus plurimus diutinus quod optimus amicus,
Murray Jones

# THE ROMAN ARMY
## CHAIN OF COMMAND

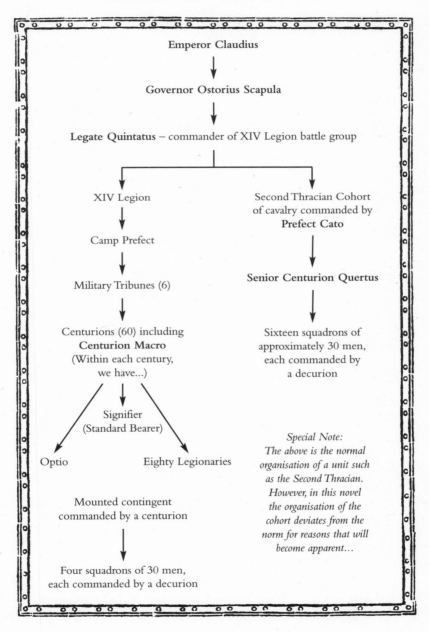

**Emperor Claudius**

**Governor Ostorius Scapula**

**Legate Quintatus** – commander of XIV Legion battle group

XIV Legion

Camp Prefect

Military Tribunes (6)

Centurions (60) including
**Centurion Macro**
(Within each century,
we have...)

Signifier
(Standard Bearer)

Optio                    Eighty Legionaries

Mounted contingent
commanded by a centurion

Four squadrons of 30 men,
each commanded by a decurion

Second Thracian Cohort
of cavalry commanded by
**Prefect Cato**

**Senior Centurion Quertus**

Sixteen squadrons of
approximately 30 men,
each commanded by
a decurion

*Special Note:*
*The above is the normal*
*organisation of a unit such*
*as the Second Thracian.*
*However, in this novel*
*the organisation of the*
*cohort deviates from the*
*norm for reasons that will*
*become apparent...*

# A BRIEF INTRODUCTION TO THE ROMAN ARMY

The Fourteenth Legion, like all legions, comprised five and a half thousand men. The basic unit was the *century* of eighty men commanded by a *centurion*. The century was divided into eight-man sections which shared a room together in barracks and a tent when on campaign. Six centuries made up a cohort, and ten cohorts made up a legion, with the first cohort being double size. Each legion was accompanied by a cavalry contingent of 120 men, divided into four squadrons, who served as scouts and messengers. In descending order, the main ranks were as follows:

The *Legate* was a man from an aristocratic background. Typically in his mid-thirties, the legate commanded the legion for up to five years and hoped to make something of a name for himself in order to enhance his subsequent political career.

The *Camp Prefect* would be a grizzled veteran who would previously have been the chief centurion of the legion and was at the summit of a professional soldier's career. He was armed with vast experience and integrity, and to him would fall the command of the legion should the legate be absent or *hors de combat*.

Six *tribunes* served as staff officers. These would be men in their early twenties serving in the army for the first time to gain administrative experience before taking up junior posts in civil administration. The senior tribune was different. He was destined for high political office and eventual command of a legion.

Sixty centurions provided the disciplinary and training backbone of the legion. They were handpicked for their command qualities and a willingness to fight to the death. Accordingly, their casualty rate far exceeded other ranks'. The most senior centurion commanded the first century of the first cohort and was a highly decorated and respected individual.

The four *decurions* of the legion commanded the cavalry squadrons, although there is some debate whether there was a centurion in overall command of the legion's mounted contingent.

Each centurion was assisted by an optio who would act as an orderly, with minor command duties. Optios would be waiting for a vacancy in the centurionate.

Below the optios were the legionaries, men who had signed on for twenty-five years. In theory, a man had to be a Roman citizen to qualify for enlistment, but recruits were increasingly drawn from local populations and given Roman citizenship upon joining the legions. Legionaries were well paid and could expect handsome bonuses from the emperor from time to time (when he felt their loyalty needed bolstering!).

Lower in status than the legionaries were the men of the auxiliary cohorts. These were recruited from the provinces and provided the Roman Empire with its cavalry, light infantry, and other specialist skills. Roman citizenship was awarded upon completion of twenty-five years of service. Cavalry units, such as the Second Thracian Cohort, were either approximately five hundred or a thousand men in size, the latter being reserved for highly experienced and capable commanders. There were also mixed cohorts with a proportion of one third mounted to two thirds infantry that were used to police the surrounding territory.

# BRITANNIA 51 AD

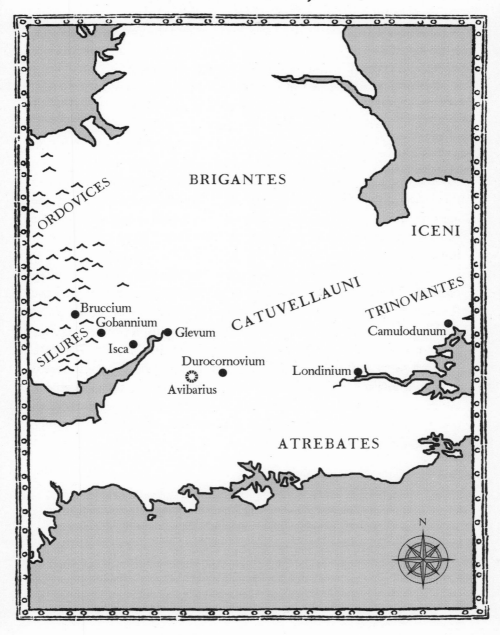

ORDOVICES

BRIGANTES

ICENI

CATUVELLAUNI

TRINOVANTES

Bruccium
Gobannium
Glevum
Camulodunum

SILURES
Isca

Durocornovium

Londinium

Avibarius

ATREBATES

N

# CHAPTER ONE

*February,* AD *51*

The column of horsemen struggled up the track to the crest of
the hillock and then their leader raised a hand to halt them as
he reined in. The recent rainfall had turned the surface of the track
into a pitted and rutted expanse of glutinous mud and the cavalry
mounts snorted and wheezed as their hoofs were sucked into the
quagmire. The chilly air was filled with the sound of the wet slap of
the horses' hoofs as they slowed and then stood at rest, snorting jets
of steamy breath. Their leader wore a thick red cloak over his
gleaming breastplate, across which ran the looped bands that signified
his rank. Legate Quintatus, commander of the Fourteenth Legion,
entrusted with maintaining the western frontier of the empire's
recently acquired province of Britannia.

That was no easy task, he mused bitterly. It had been nearly eight
years since the army had landed on the island that stood at the limits
of the known world. At the time, Quintatus had been a tribune in
his early twenties, filled with a sense of mission and a desire to win
glory for himself, Rome and the new Emperor, Claudius. The army
had fought its way inland, defeating the mighty host that had been
gathered by the native tribes, under the command of Caratacus.
Battle after battle had ground down the natives, until finally the
legions had crushed the warriors as they made their final stand in
front of their capital at Camulodunum.

That battle had seemed decisive at the time. The Emperor himself
had been there to witness the victory. And claim full credit for it.
Once the rulers of most of the native tribes had made treaties with
the Emperor, Claudius returned to Rome to claim his triumph and
announce to the mob that the conquest of Britannia was complete.

Only it wasn't. The legate frowned. Not by a long way. That final battle had not broken Caratacus's will to resist. It had merely taught him that it was foolhardy to pit his brave, but poorly trained, warriors against the legions in a pitched battle. He had learned to play a deeper game, luring the Roman columns into ambushes and sending fast-moving bands to raid the legions' supply lines and outposts. It had taken seven years of campaigning to drive Caratacus into the mountain fastness of the tribes of the Silures and the Ordovices. They were warlike, spurred on by the fanatic fury of the Druids, and determined to resist the might of Rome until their last breaths. They had accepted Caratacus as their commander and this new centre of resistance had attracted warriors from across the island who nursed a resolute hatred of Rome.

It had been a hard winter and the cold winds and icy rain had forced the Roman army to limit its activities during the long, dark months. Only towards the end of the season the lowering clouds and mists lifted from the mountainous lands beyond the frontier and the legions were able to renew their campaign against the natives over the winter. The governor of the province, Ostorius Scapula, had ordered the Fourteenth to push forward into the forested valleys and establish a chain of forts. They would serve as bases for the main offensive that would come in the spring. The enemy had responded with a speed and ferocity that had surprised Legate Quintatus and attacked the strongest of the columns he had sent into their lands. Two cohorts of legionaries, nearly eight hundred men. The tribune in command of the column had sent a rider to the legate the moment the attack had begun, urgently requesting support. Quintatus had led the rest of the legion out of its base at Glevum at first light and as they approached the site of the fort, he had ridden ahead with an escort to reconnoitre, his heart heavy with dread at what they might find.

Beyond the hillock lay the valley leading deep into the lands of the Silures. The legate strained his ears, striving to filter out the sounds of the horses behind him. But there was no sound from ahead. No dull rhythmic thudding of axes as the legionaries felled trees to provide timber for the construction of the fort, and create a wide cordon of clear land around the perimeter ditch. No sound of voices echoing off the slopes of the valley on either side. Nor any sound of fighting.

'We're too late,' he muttered to himself. 'Too late.'

He frowned irritably at his failure to keep his concerns to himself and glanced round quickly in case his words had been overheard. The nearest men of his escort sat impassively in their saddles. No, he corrected himself. Not impassive. There was anxiety in their expressions, eyes flickering over the surrounding landscape as they searched for any sign of the enemy. The legate drew a deep, calming breath and swept his arm forward as he eased his heels into the flanks of his mount. The horse walked on, dagger-like ears twitching, as if sensing its master's nervousness. The track levelled out and a moment later the leading horsemen had a clear view down into the mouth of the valley.

The construction site lay half a mile in front of them. A wide open space had been carved out of the pine trees and the stumps looked like broken teeth scattered across the churned earth. The outline of the fort was still discernible, but where there should have been a deep ditch, rampart and palisade, there was just a ruined jumble of burned timber piles and wagons and the remains of tent lines where the goatskin shelters had been torn down and trampled into the mud. Many sections of the rampart had been destroyed and the soil and the log foundations tumbled into the ditch. There were bodies, too, men and some mules and horses. The bodies had been stripped and the pale flesh reminded the legate of maggots from this distance. He shuddered at the thought and hurriedly thrust it aside. He heard his men sucking in their breath at the sight and a handful mumbled curses as they surveyed the scene. His horse slowed to a halt and Quintatus angrily jabbed his heels in and snapped the reins to force it into a trot.

There was no sign of any danger. The enemy had finished their work many hours ago and left with their victory and their spoils. All that remained was the ruins of the fort, the wagons and the dead. That, and the crows feeding on the carrion. As the horsemen approached down the track, the birds lurched into flight, their raucous cries of alarm filling the air as they were forced to abandon their grim feast. They swirled overhead like strips of black cloth caught in the wind of a storm and filled the ears of the legate with their ugly sound.

Quintatus slowed his mount as he reached the ruin of the main gate. The timber towers of the fort had been the first structures to be built. Now they were reduced to charred frameworks from which thin trails of smoke still rose up against the background of rock and tree covered hillsides before merging with the grey clouds pressing down from the sky. On either side, the ditch ran out to the corners of the fort where the remains of the towers stood. With a click of his tongue the legate steered his horse past the ruined gatehouse. On the far side lay the rampart and the cordon of open ground inside of the defences. Beyond that lay what was left of the tent lines, and the first of the bodies heaped together in a small knot. Stripped of their armour, tunics and boots, they lay twisted, bruised and streaked with blood that flowed from the dark mouths of the wounds that had killed them. There were smaller cuts and tears in their flesh where the beaks of the crows had been at work and several of the corpses had bloody sockets where the birds had plucked out their eyes. The heads had been hacked off some of the corpses and the stumps were caked with dried, blackened blood.

As Quintatus stared at the fallen legionaries, one of his staff officers edged his horse alongside and nodded grimly.

'At least it looks like some of our men put up a fight.'

The legate did not acknowledge the remark. It was easy to visualise the last moments of these men, fighting back to back as they stood their ground to the last. Afterwards, when the last of the wounded had been finished off, the enemy had stripped them of their weapons and equipment. What could be used by Caratacus and his warriors would be kept, the rest hurled into the nearest river or buried to prevent the Romans from returning it to the stores of the Fourteenth Legion. Quintatus lifted his gaze and looked round the fort. More bodies lay amid the destroyed tents, singly and in small clusters that told of the chaos that had ensued once the enemy warriors had broken through the half-completed defences.

'Shall I order the men to dismount and start burying the dead, sir?'

Quintatus looked round at the tribune, and it took a moment for

4

the question to penetrate his gloomy thoughts. He shook his head. 'Leave them until the rest of the legion comes up.'

The younger officer looked surprised. 'Are you sure, sir? I fear it will damage the men's morale. It's at a low ebb as it is.'

'I know the mood of my men well enough, thank you,' the legate snapped. At once he relented. The tribune had only recently arrived from Rome, all gleaming armour and keen to put into practice the military wisdom he had learned at second and third hand. Quintatus recalled that he had been no different when he had joined his first legion. He cleared his throat and forced himself to speak in a calm tone.

'Let the men see the bodies.' Many of the soldiers had only just joined the Fourteenth, replacements who had arrived on the first ships to sail from Gaul after the winter storms had passed. 'I want them to understand what their fate will be if they ever allow themselves to be defeated by the enemy.'

The tribune hesitated a moment before he nodded. 'As you command.'

Quintatus gently spurred his horse into a walk and continued towards the heart of the fort. Destruction and death sprawled out on either side of the broad, muddy track that cut through the ruins, intersected by a second way that crossed at a right angle. He came across the shreds of what had been the command tent of the cohort. There was another heap of bodies next to it and the legate felt a cold shiver trace its way down his spine as he recognised the face of Salvius, the senior centurion of one of the cohorts. The grey-haired veteran lay on his back staring sightlessly into the overcast, his jaw hanging slack and exposing his uneven yellowed teeth. He had been a fine officer, Quintatus reflected. Tough, efficient and courageous, and highly decorated, Salvius had no doubt maintained the highest standards of the centurionate to the very end. There were several wounds to his chest and stomach and the legate felt confident that there would be none on his back if his body was turned over. Perhaps they had left him his head as a mark of respect, the legate mused.

That still left the tribune Marcellus, the commander of the construction party. Quintatus raised himself up on the saddle horns, slipped his leg over the back of his mount and dropped to the ground with a loud squelch. He approached the corpses and searched for any sign of the young aristocrat whose first independent command had proved to be his last. There was no point in looking amongst the headless corpses and the legate avoided them as he searched. He could not find Marcellus, even after turning some of the bodies lying on their front. Two of the dead had been badly cut about the face, mangled flesh, shattered bone and flaps of scalp making immediate identification impossible. Finding Marcellus would have to wait.

Then the legate froze, struck by a sudden realisation. He straightened up and swept his gaze around the remains of the camp, roughly estimating the number of bodies that lay scattered in the mud. There was no sign of any fallen enemy. But there wouldn't be. The natives always took their dead away to be buried secretly, where the Romans would not find them and so know how many casualties they had suffered.

'What is it, sir?' asked the tribune, anxious at his superior's sudden reaction.

'There's too few of our men here. From what I can see I'd say a quarter of them are missing.'

The tribune looked about him and nodded. 'Then where are they?'

'We have to assume they have been taken alive,' Quintatus said coldly. 'Prisoners . . . The gods have mercy on them. They shouldn't have surrendered.'

'What will happen to them, sir?'

Quintatus shrugged. 'If they are lucky they will be used as slaves and worked to death. Before that they will be taken from tribe to tribe and shown to the hill people as proof that Rome can be beaten. They'll be abused and humiliated all the way.'

The tribune was silent for a moment and then swallowed nervously. 'And if they are not lucky?'

'Then they'll be handed over to the Druids and sacrificed to their gods. Flayed, or burned alive. That is why it is best not to permit yourself to fall into their hands.' Quintatus caught movement out of the corner of his eye and turned to look up the track leading from the main gate. The leading century of the main body had crested the hill and begun to descend the slope, struggling to maintain the pace as the ground became steadily more muddy. For a moment there was a brief break in the clouds and a thin shaft of light fell on the head of the column. A shimmering glitter showed the position of the eagle standard of the legion, and the other standards bearing the image of the Emperor and the insignia and decorations of the lesser formations. Quintatus wondered if that was supposed to be a good omen. If so, then the gods had a strange sense of timing.

The tribune enquired, 'What now, sir?'

'Hmm?'

'What are your orders?'

'We finish what we started. As soon as the legion gets here I want the ditch and rampart repaired, and then work can continue on the fort.' Quintatus stiffened his back and looked up at the dark forested slopes of the valley. 'Those savages have won their small victory today. There's nothing we can do about that. They'll be celebrating in the hills. The fools. This will only harden the resolve of Rome to crush the last vestige of resistance to our will. No matter how long it takes, you can be sure that Ostorius, and the Emperor, will not allow us any rest until the job is done.' His lips flickered in a brief, bitter smile. 'Better not get used to the comforts of the fort at Glevum, my boy.'

The young officer nodded solemnly.

'Right, I'll need a headquarters tent set up here. Have some men clear the ground and get to it. Send for my secretary. The governor will need a report on this as soon as possible.' Quintatus stroked his jaw as he stared back towards the bodies of Centurion Salvius and his comrades. His heart felt heavy with grief at the loss of his men and the burden of knowing that the coming campaign was going to be as hard and bloody as any Roman had known since setting foot on this accursed island.

This was a new kind of warfare. Rome's soldiers would need to be utterly ruthless if the enemy's spirit was to be broken. And those soldiers would need to be led by officers who would pursue the enemy with a merciless sense of purpose and no pity in their hearts. Fortunately such men existed, Quintatus reflected. There was one man in particular whose very name froze the blood of his enemies.

Centurion Quertus. With a hundred officers like him, Rome's difficulties in Britannia would be over very quickly. Such men were needed in war. But what would become of them in peace? That, Quintatus said to himself, was somebody else's problem.

# CHAPTER TWO

*The River Tamesis, two months later*

'By the gods, this place has changed.' Centurion Macro gestured at the sprawl of buildings on the northern bank of the river. The cargo ship had just tacked round a wide sweeping bend in the Tamesis and now the bows turned directly into the steady breeze and the sail began to flap against the dull, grey overcast.

The captain cupped his hands to his mouth and bellowed across the broad deck, 'Hands aloft! Take the sail in!'

As several men scrambled up the narrow ratlines, the captain turned to the rest of his crew. 'Unship the oars and make ready!'

The sailors, a mix of Gauls and Batavians, hesitated for the briefest of moments before going about their duty with sullen expressions. Macro could not help a grin as he watched them, seeing their mute protest for what it was: a matter of form rather than substance. It was the same with the soldiers he had known for most of his life. His gaze returned to the low, rolling landscape that spread out on either side of the river. Much of it had been cleared of trees and small farmsteads dotted the countryside. There was also a handful of larger buildings with tiled roofs, evidence that the stamp of Rome was making its mark on the new province. Macro broke off his musing to glance at his companion a short distance away, resting his elbows on the ship's side rail as he stared blankly at the ruffled surface of the river gliding past. Macro cleared his throat none too subtly.

'I said, the place has changed.'

Cato stirred and then looked up and smiled quickly. 'Sorry, miles away.'

Macro nodded. 'Your thoughts are turned towards Rome, no doubt. Don't worry, lad, Julia's a good woman, and a fine wife.

She'll keep it warm for you until you get back.'

Despite the fact that his friend outranked him, an easy familiarity had been forged between them over the eight years they had served together. Once Macro had been the senior officer, but now Cato had surpassed him and risen to the rank of prefect and was ready to take up his first permanent command of a cohort of auxiliaries: the Second Cohort of Thracian cavalry. The Second's previous commander had been killed during the last campaign season and the imperial staff back in Rome had chosen Cato to fill the vacancy.

'And when will that be, I wonder?' the younger man responded, his voice edged with bitterness. 'From what I've heard, the Emperor's triumphant celebration of the conquest of Britannia was somewhat premature. Like as not we'll still be fighting Caratacus and his followers until we're old men.'

'Suits me.' Macro shrugged. 'Better some honest soldiering back with the legions than all that cloak and dagger stuff we've had to put up with since we were last here.'

'Thought you hated Britannia. Always going on about the bloody damp, the cold and lack of decent food. Couldn't wait to leave, you said.'

'Did I say that?' Macro feigned innocence, and then rubbed his hands together. 'Still, here we are. Back where there's a decent campaign on the go and a chance for more promotion and awards and, best of all, a chance to top up my retirement fund. I've been listening to reports as well, my lad, and there's talk of a fortune in silver to be had in the mountains to the west of the island. If we're lucky we'll be sitting pretty once the natives have been given a good kicking and come to their senses.'

Cato could not help smiling. 'Kicking a man seldom induces him to be reasonable, in my experience.'

'I disagree. If you know where to kick a man, and how hard, he'll do whatever you need him to.'

'If you say so.' Cato had no wish to enter into a debate. His mind was still troubled by the prospect of being parted from Julia. They had met a few years earlier, on the empire's eastern frontier where her father, Senator Sempronius, had been serving as the Emperor's ambassador to the King of Palmyra. Marriage into a senatorial family was a considerable advance in status for a junior legionary officer like Cato, and the cause of some anxiety at the prospect of being sneered at by those from old aristocratic families. But Senator Sempronius had recognised Cato's potential and had been pleased for him to marry his daughter. The wedding had been the happiest day of Cato's life, but there had been little time to become accustomed to being a husband before he had received his marching orders from the imperial secretary. Narcissus was under growing pressure from the faction which had chosen the young prince Nero to succeed Emperor Claudius. The imperial secretary had sided with those supporting Britannicus, the Emperor's natural son, and they were steadily losing influence over the doddery old ruler of the greatest empire in the world. Narcissus had explained that he was doing Cato a favour in sending him as far from Rome as possible. When the Emperor died, there would be a scramble for power and no mercy would be shown to those on the losing side, nor to anyone associated with them. If Britannicus lost the struggle, he was doomed, and Narcissus with him.

Since both Cato and Macro had served the imperial secretary well, albeit unwillingly, then they, too, would be in danger. It would be better if they were fighting on some far-flung frontier when the time came, beyond the vengeful attention of Nero's followers. Even though Cato had only recently saved Nero's life, he had crossed the path of Pallas, the imperial freedman who was the brains behind the prince's faction. Pallas was not inclined to forgive those who stood in the way of his ambitions. Nero's debt to Cato would not save him. So, barely a month after the marriage had been celebrated in the house of Julia's father, Cato and Macro were summoned to the palace to receive their new appointments: for Cato, the command of a Thracian cohort, and for Macro the command of a cohort in the Fourteenth Legion, both units serving with the army of Governor Ostorius Scapula in Britannia.

There had been tears when the time came for Cato to depart. Julia had clung to him and he had held her close, feeling her chest shudder as she buried her face in the folds of his cloak, the dark tresses of her hair falling across his hands. Cato felt his heart torn by her grief at separation, which he shared. But the order had been given, and the sense of duty that had bound Rome's citizens together and made it possible for them to overcome their enemies could not be denied.

'When will you return?' Julia's voice was muffled by the folds of wool. She looked up, her eyes red-rimmed, and Cato felt a rush of anguish flow through his heart. He forced himself to smile lightly.

'The campaign should be over soon, my love. Caratacus cannot hold out for much longer. He will be defeated.'

'And then?'

'Then, I shall await word of the new Emperor, and when it is safe to return I will apply for a civil post in Rome.'

She pressed her lips together for a moment. 'But that could be years.'

'Yes.'

They were both silent for a moment before Julia spoke again. 'I could join you in Britannia.'

Cato tilted his head to one side. 'Perhaps. But not yet. The island is still little more than a barbaric backwater. There are few of the comforts you are used to. And there are dangers, not least the unhealthy airs of the place.'

'It doesn't matter. I have experienced the worst of conditions, Cato. You know I have. After all that we have been through we deserve to be together.'

'I know.'

'Then promise to send for me as soon as it is safe for me to join you.' She tightened her grip on his cloak and stared intently into his eyes. 'Promise me.'

Cato felt his resolve to shelter her from the dangers and discomforts of the new province dissolve. 'I promise.'

She eased her grip and shifted half a step away from him, with an expression of pained relief, and nodded. 'Don't make me wait too long, my dearest Cato.'

'Not one day longer than necessary. I swear it.'

'Good.' She smiled and stood on tiptoe to kiss him on the mouth and then stepped back and gave his hands a last squeeze before straightening her back. 'Then you must go.'

Cato took one long last look at her and then bowed his head and turned away from the senator's house and marched along the street that led in the direction of the city gate where he would take one of the boats down the Tiber to join Macro at the port of Ostia. He looked back when he reached the end of the street and saw her there, standing at the door, and forced himself to turn and stride out of sight.

The pain of their parting had not dimmed over the long journey across the sea to Massillia and then overland to Gesoriacum where they had boarded the cargo ship for the final leg to Britannia. It felt strange to return to the island after several years. Earlier that day the cargo ship had passed the stretch of riverbank where Cato and his comrades in the Second Legion had fought their way ashore through a horde of native warriors urged on by screaming Druids hurling curses and spells at the invaders. It was a chilling reminder of what lay ahead and Cato feared that it would be some years yet before he considered it safe to send for his wife.

'Is that it ahead? Londinium?'

Cato turned to see a slender, hard-faced old woman picking her way across the deck from the direction of the hatch leading down to the cramped passenger quarters. She wore a shawl over her head and a few strands of grey hair flickered in the breeze. Cato smiled in greeting and Macro grinned a welcome as she joined him at the side rail.

'You're looking much better, Mum.'

'Of course I do,' she said sharply, 'now this wretched boat has stopped lurching all over the place. I thought that storm would sink us for sure. And, frankly, it would have been a mercy if it had. I have never felt so ill in my life.'

'It was hardly a storm,' Macro said disdainfully.

'No?' She nodded at Cato. 'What do you think? You were throwing up as much as me.'

Cato grimaced. The tossing and pitching of the ship the previous night had left him in a state of utter misery, curled up in a ball as he vomited into a wooden tub beside his cot. He disliked sea voyages in the Mediterranean at the best of times. The wild sea off the coast of Gaul was pure torture.

Macro sniffed dismissively. 'Barely blowing a gale. And good, fresh air at that. Put some salt back into my lungs.'

'While taking out absolutely everything from your guts,' his mother replied. 'I'd rather die than go through that again. Anyway, best not to remember. As I was saying, is that Londinium over there?'

The others turned to follow the direction she indicated and gazed at the distant buildings lining the northern bank of the Tamesis. A wharf had been constructed with great timber piles driven into the river bed, supporting the cross-beams packed with stones and earth and finally paved. Several cargo ships were already moored alongside and as many others were anchored a short distance upriver, waiting for their turn to unload their freight. On the wharf, chain gangs were busy carrying goods from the holds of ships into the long low warehouses. Beyond them other buildings spread out, many still under construction as the new town took shape. A hundred paces back from the riverbank they could make out the second storey of a large complex rising above the other buildings. That would be the basilica, Cato realised, site of the market, courts, shops, offices and administrative headquarters of towns that Rome founded.

'That's Londinium all right,' the captain answered as he joined his passengers. 'Growing faster than an abscess on the backside of a mule. And just as vile.'

'Oh?' Macro's mother frowned.

'Why yes, Miss Portia. The place is a rat-hole. Narrow streets, filled with mud, cheap drinking joints and knocking shops. It'll be a while yet before it settles down and becomes the kind of town you're used to.'

She smiled. 'Good. That's what I wanted to hear.'

The captain frowned at her and Macro let out a laugh.

'She's come here to go into business.'

The captain scrutinised the old woman. 'What kind of business?'

'I intend to open an inn,' she replied. 'There's always a need for drink, and other comforts, at the end of a sea voyage, and I dare say that Londinium sees plenty of merchants, sailors and soldiers passing through its gates. All good customers for the kind of services I will offer.'

'Oh, there's plenty of business, all right,' the captain nodded. 'But it's a hard life. Even harder in a new province like this. The kind of merchants who make their fortunes here are tough men. They won't take kindly to a Roman woman trying to compete with them.'

'I dealt with tough men at the inn I owned in Ravenna. I doubt the locals here will cause me any difficulty. Particularly when they find out my son happens to be a senior centurion of the Fourteenth Legion.' She took Macro's arm and gave it an affectionate squeeze.

'That's right.' He nodded. 'Anyone messes about with my mum and they mess with me. And that hasn't worked out well for anyone who has tried it in the past.'

The captain took in the muscular physique of the stocky Roman officer and the scars on his face and arms and could believe it.

'Even so, why would you come here, ma'am? You'd be more comfortable setting up back in Gesoriacum. Plenty of trade there.'

Portia pursed her lips. 'This is where the real money can be made, by those who get stuck in quickly. Besides, this boy is all I have in the world now. I want to be as close to him as I can. Who knows, when he gets his discharge, he could join me in the business.'

Macro's eyes lit up. 'Ah, now there's a thought. All the wine and women that a man could want, under one roof!'

Portia swatted his arm. 'On second thoughts . . . You soldiers are all the same. Anyway, I will make my fortune here in Londinium, and this is where I will stay until the end of my days. It's up to you what you do with your life, Macro. But I'll be remaining here. This is my last home.'

With a steady rhythm the cargo ship approached the wharf. As they neared the town, those on board caught their first whiff of the place, an acrid, peaty, sewage smell that mingled with the odour of woodsmoke and caught in their throats.

'There might be something to be said for sea air after all,' Cato muttered as he wrinkled his nose.

There was no mooring space along the wharf and the captain gave the order to steer for the end of the line of vessels anchored further upriver. He turned apologetically to his passengers.

'It'll be a while before our turn comes. You're welcome to stay on board, or I'll have some of my boys row you ashore in the skiff.'

Cato eased himself up from the side rail and adopted the military manner he had learned from Macro, standing tall and being decisive. 'We'll go ashore. The centurion and I need to report to the nearest military authority as soon as possible.'

'Yes, sir.' The captain knuckled his forehead, instantly aware that the informalities of the voyage had passed. 'I'll see to it at once.'

He was as good as his word and by the time the anchor splashed down into the current and the crew shipped the oars, the kitbags of the two officers and the chests and bags belonging to Portia had been carried up from the hold. The skiff, a small blunt-bowed craft with a wide beam, was lowered over the side and two oarsmen nimbly leaped down and offered their hands up to assist the passengers. There was only space for the three of them; their belongings would have to be ferried ashore separately. Cato was the last and as he stepped down into the flimsy craft he frantically waved his arms to retain his balance, before sitting heavily on a thwart. Macro shot him a weary look and tutted and then the oarsmen pulled on their blades and the skiff headed towards the wharf. Now that they were closer to Londinium they could see that the surface of the river was streaked with sewage running from the drain outlets along the wharf. In the still water trapped by the wharf lay lengths of broken timber amid the other flotsam, and rats scurried from piece to piece, scavenging for anything edible. A set of wooden steps rose from the river at one end of the wharf and the oarsmen made for them. When they were alongside, the nearest man snatched his oar in and reached to grasp the slimy hawser that acted as a fender. He held on while his friend slipped a looped line over the mooring post.

'There you are, sirs, ma'am.' He smiled and then handed them ashore. With Cato leading the way, they climbed the steps to the top of the wharf and looked along the crowded thoroughfare between the ships and the warehouses. A cacophony of voices filled the cool spring afternoon and in amongst them were the brays of mules and the crack of whips and the shouts of the overseers of the chain gangs. Though the scene looked chaotic, Cato knew that in every detail it was proof of the transformation that had come to the island that had defied the power of Rome for almost a hundred years. For better or worse, change had come to Britannia and once the last pockets of

16

resistance had been crushed, the new province would take shape and become part of the empire.

Macro joined him and glanced round briefly before he muttered, 'Welcome back to Britannia . . . arse end of civilisation.'

# CHAPTER THREE

Once the boat returned with their belongings, Macro approached a small group of men gathered outside the nearest warehouse.

'I need some porters,' he announced, addressing them in his loud, clear, parade-ground voice. At once they hurried forward and he chose several of the burliest-looking men, one of whom had a strip of leather about his head to clear his brow of thick, wiry blond hair. A brand was visible on his forehead, beneath the leather. Macro recognised the mark at once. The brand of Mithras, a religion from the east that was steadily spreading through the ranks of the Roman army. 'You, a soldier once, if I'm not mistaken?'

The man bowed his head. 'I was, sir. Before I took a Silurian spear through the leg. Left me with a limp, I couldn't keep up with the rest of the lads. Army had no choice but to discharge me, sir.'

Macro looked him over. The man wore a threadbare military cloak over his tunic and his boots were held together by strips of cloth. 'Let me guess. You pissed away your discharge bonus and this is what you've been reduced to.'

The ex-soldier nodded. 'That's about the size of it, sir.'

'What is your name and unit?'

'Legionary Marcus Metellius Decimus, Second Legion, Augusta, sir!' The man straightened to attention and winced before stretching a hand down to steady his thigh.

'The Second, eh?' Macro stroked his jaw. 'That's my old mob. Or, I should say, our old mob.' He jerked his thumb towards Cato. 'We served under Legate Vespasian.'

Decimus tilted his head regretfully. 'Before my time, sir.'

'Pity. Very well, Decimus, you take charge of these men. Our

18

baggage is over there on the wharf by my friend there, and the woman.'

Decimus glanced across the thoroughfare and sniffed. 'She's a bit old for him. Unless she's got money . . . Then they're never too old.'

Macro gritted his teeth. 'The woman in question is my mother . . . Now move yourself!'

Decimus quickly turned away and gestured to the other men to follow. As they hefted the chests and kitbags, Cato tried to get his bearings. 'Which way to the local garrison?'

'There's no garrison, sir. No fort. Not even any fortifications, for that matter. There was a fort a few years back, but the place was growing so fast it got swallowed up. That's where they're building the new basilica, on the site of the old fort.'

'I see.' Cato sighed in frustration. 'Then where can I find someone on the governor's staff?'

Decimus thought about it. 'You could try the governor's quarters, sir. They're to the side of the building site. Anyway, that's where you'll find him.'

Cato was surprised. 'Ostorius is here in Londinium?'

'Yes, sir.'

'But the provincial capital is Camulodunum.'

'Officially, sir, yes. After all, that's where Caratacus came from, and that's where Emperor Claudius has pledged to have a temple erected in his honour. But it's too far east. Despite what they may want back in Rome, it seems that everyone here has chosen Londinium as the main town. Even the governor. And that's why you'll find him here.'

Cato took in the information and nodded. 'Very well, take us to his headquarters.'

Decimus bowed his head and then, shouldering one of the kitbags, and grunting under the weight of the armour it contained, he limped off into a side street. 'Follow me, sir.'

Londinium proved to be every bit as unpleasant as the captain of the cargo ship had warned them. The streets were narrow and crowded and, unlike Rome, there were no restrictions on wheeled vehicles in daylight hours. Cato and the others had to fight their way

19

up the narrow thoroughfares crowded with carts, horses and people. Familiar with the streets, Decimus and his companions hurried on and Cato feared that he might lose sight of them. He gestured subtly to Macro to chivvy his mother through the throng. From the dress and features of those they passed, Cato could see that most were from elsewhere in the empire, no doubt in search of easy money in the new province. Portia was going to face stiff competition, Cato reflected, and he hoped that the rank of her son would indeed be enough to protect her interests from the con men, thieves and gangsters who were already preying on Londinium.

'All right, Mum?' asked Macro.

Portia stared coldly at a group of tribesmen passing in the street, wrapped in furs and with swirling tattoos down their arms. 'Savages . . .'

Cato smiled to himself and then frowned. There was still a way to go before the people of the island accepted Roman rule. Caratacus and his followers might be far to the west of Londinium, but the spirit of the tribesmen living in and around the town was clearly far from broken. If the legions ever suffered a serious setback then it was sure to encourage more than a few of the natives into open revolt against Rome. If the main weight of the governor's army was concentrated at the frontier, there would be little to stop the rebels sweeping across those parts of the province that the officials back in Rome had already labelled as pacified on their maps.

'Where the hell's that Decimus and his crew?' Macro growled, craning his neck, but unable to make much out due to his short stature.

'Twenty paces or so ahead,' Cato replied.

'Don't lose sight of the buggers. Last thing we need is to have all our kit nicked the instant we step ashore. I'll not go back to the legions looking like some green recruit mummy's boy if I can help it.'

Portia snorted. 'If there's one thing you are definitely not, my son, it is a mummy's boy.'

They pressed on, struggling to keep up with the porters ahead of them. As they emerged into a crossroads filled with carts carrying amphorae packed tightly together, there was no sign of the porters on the far side of the junction. Cato felt his heart sink in despair and a sharp anger at Decimus for having tricked them.

'Hey! Prefect! This way.'

He turned towards the voice and saw Decimus and his companions just over to their left. The former legionary shook his head mockingly. 'There's me with my limp, and the officers still can't keep up. What's the world coming to?'

Before Cato could cut in and tell him to mind his tongue when speaking to a superior, the other man raised his hand and pointed towards a large gateway a short distance along the other side of the street they had just turned into. Beyond the wall Cato could see scaffolding and the tall timber frame of a crane rising up against the smoky sky.

'There you go, Prefect. That's the basilica. Or what there is of it.'

Without waiting for his customers to respond, Decimus set off again and this time the flow of traffic was such that the new arrivals were able to keep up. When the convoy of wine carts had passed, they made their way across to the gateway and approached the two legionaries standing guard. The surface of the arch had been plastered and whitewashed, but the brickwork on the wall surrounding the building site was unfinished.

'State your business,' one of the guards said evenly as he ran his eyes over the two men and the older woman, hurriedly assessing their status. The two officers were dressed in neat, new tunics and military cloaks purchased in Rome before their departure. Although there were no insignia to show rank, nor any ornate rings to indicate wealth, the bearing of the two officers and the visible scars told their own story. Particularly the long white line that stretched across Cato's face from forehead to chin. The sentry cleared his throat and moderated his tone. 'How may I assist you, sir?'

'Prefect Quintus Licinius Cato and Centurion Lucius Cornelius Macro.' He nodded towards Macro before continuing. 'Just arrived from Rome to take up our commands. We wish to report to the governor's staff and find accommodation for ourselves.'

'You won't find much of that here, sir. They knocked the fort down two months back.'

'So I gather. I assume that Ostorius and his staff are not working out in the open?'

'Fat chance of that, sir!' The sentry turned and lowered the tip of his javelin and indicated the scaffolding surrounding a large, single-storey complex. 'That's the start of the governor's palace. He ordered the builders to finish up the ground floor and get out. Still, they managed to get the hypocaust in before they left so they're all nice and cosy inside. Unlike those of us seconded to escort the governor. Sleeping in tents outside.'

'That's what soldiers do, lad.' Macro clicked his tongue. 'If it's too tough for you then perhaps you should have joined a pansy troupe of actors or something.'

'Come on!' Cato waved his arm forward and made his way along the path that had been cleared through the building site. On either side, piles of timber, stacks of bricks and roof tiles and cement-mixing troughs stretched out. The foundations for several large structures had been completed and walls, waist-high, demarcated the first great civic building of the new province that would dominate the landscape and inspire awe in the heart of every native who set eyes on it. Hundreds of men were labouring across the site, with a handful of chain gangs being used to carry materials where they were needed. The sounds of their grunts, the sawing of timber and sharp clatter of stones being cut to size mingled with shouted instructions from the overseers.

Macro nodded approvingly as they passed through. 'Should be quite a place, once it's finished.'

On the far side of the site a gap had been left in the scaffolding to give access to the half-completed building beyond, which served as the headquarters of Governor Ostorius and his staff. Two of his escort stood guard at the entrance. Once again Cato explained their purpose and then turned to pay off the porters who set their burdens down just inside the makeshift entrance. He reached for his belt purse and loosened the drawstrings.

'That'll be a sestertius, sir.' Decimus tapped a finger to his forehead by way of an informal salute. 'Each.'

Macro arched an eyebrow. 'By the gods, that's a bit steep.'

'It's the going rate in Londinium, sir.'

Cato turned to one of the guards. 'Is it?'

The legionary nodded.

'Very well.' He delved into the purse for a few coins, counted them out and handed them over to Decimus and the others. 'Seems like Londinium's going to be an expensive town to live in. You may leave us . . . Decimus, a word.'

The ex-legionary waved his mates on and turned to Cato. 'Sir?'

Cato stared at him, trying to see beyond the ragged soiled clothing and unkempt hair to the man who had once been a legionary. If Decimus was speaking the truth then his army career had been cut short by the fortunes of war. The same fortunes that had seen fit to spare Cato and Macro through all the campaigns and desperate battles they had endured over the years. It sometimes felt to Cato that he was sorely testing the luck that had been apportioned to him. Sooner or later a spear, or sword thrust, or arrow would find him, just as it had Decimus and countless others.

'How many years have you served in Britannia?'

Decimus scratched his chin. 'I came over five years ago from the training depot in Gesoriacum. Served with the Second against the Decangli before being sent up with a detachment to reinforce the Fourteenth at Glevum. Then two years campaigning against the Silures before this.' He patted his lame leg.

'All right, then.' Cato nodded and thought a moment before he continued. 'How do you like working as a wharf rat?'

'Fucking hate it, sir.' He hurriedly turned to Portia. 'Sorry, ma'am.'

Portia looked back levelly. 'I spent the best part of fifteen years living with a marine. So keep your fucking apology to yourself.'

Macro stared at his mother in shock; his mouth sagged open and then shut quickly as he decided it was best to ignore what she had said.

Decimus turned back to Cato. 'But what's an invalid soldier to do? I was lucky to get a partial pay-out of the discharge bonus. Enough to set me up in digs here, but not enough to live on.'

'I see,' Cato responded. 'Well, I may have work for you. Nothing too onerous, but there might be some danger. If you're interested, come back here at first light.'

Decimus looked surprised for a moment before he bowed his head and limped away.

Macro watched him until he was out of earshot and then turned to Cato. 'What was that all about?'

23

'Things have changed since we were last here. Sure, we're going to get a briefing from the governor, but he'll paint the scene from his perspective. The usual blend of confidence and underplaying the threat posed by the enemy. Ostorius is like any other governor. He'll want to make out that his period in office was a great success and he'll want any letters or reports that we write home to reflect that. So, it might be useful to hear the views of one of Marius's mules. Besides, I'll need a servant in camp to take care of my kit. Someone I hope I can trust.'

'Trust?' Portia sniffed. 'That vagabond? He looks like a common crook to me.'

Cato wagged a finger. 'Don't rush to judgement. Appearance is not everything. If it was, everyone would run a mile from your son.'

'They already do,' Macro growled. 'If they know what's good for them.'

'Oh, you!' His mother lightly slapped his shoulder. 'You're a pussycat in tiger's clothing. Don't think I can't see that. Cato too.'

Macro flushed with embarrassment. He hated talking about feelings and the idea that he even had a sensitive side to his nature filled him with disgust. Feelings were for poets, artists, actors and other classes of lesser mortal. A soldier was different. A soldier was required to put his heart and brains in check and get on with doing his duty. When he was off duty, he should play as hard as he could. Of course, he admitted to himself, some soldiers were different. He stole a glance at Cato, thin, sinewy and, until recently, youthful-looking. Now there was a certain hardness to his gaze and the gawky awkwardness of earlier years had largely gone. He moved purposefully and with an economy of effort that was the hallmark of a veteran. Yet Macro knew his friend well enough to know that his mind was ever restless, steeped in the works of the philosophers and historians that he had studied so earnestly as a boy. Cato was a very different kind of soldier, Macro reflected, and he grudgingly accepted that the younger man was all the better for it.

He cleared his throat with a deep rumble of irritation before addressing Cato.

'Well, it's your decision. But why not just buy yourself a slave?

24

You can afford to. And there'll be bargains to be had in Londinium with the prisoners the army has taken.'

'I don't want some tribesman. Last thing I need is a resentful native cleaning my sword and having to guard my back day and night, while I'm dealing with the enemy. No, it has to be someone who chooses to be there. If Decimus was a soldier then who better? He'll be a useful gauge of the men's spirits.'

Macro thought a moment and nodded. 'Fair enough. Now let's find ourselves somewhere to put the kit.' He turned to his mother. 'You'll be all right for a bit?'

'I have been for over fifty years now . . . Run along boys.'

One of the sentries pointed them towards the administration block being used by the governor and they strode across the courtyard towards the entrance. The thick walls of the structure slightly muffled the sounds of construction but there was a thin patina of dust and grime over the flagstones, and building materials were piled around the margins of the courtyard. A handful of clerks were moving from office to office clutching waxed slates or bundles of scrolls. Inside the headquarters, braziers provided warmth and scores of men worked at the long desks filling the main hall. Cato approached a junior tribune bent over his desk reading a document and tapped his knuckles on the desk. The man looked up with a knitted brow.

'Yes?'

Cato briefly made the introductions. 'Just landed. I need to report to the governor and we need quarters until we leave for our commands. And a room for a lady as well.'

'Quarters? There's not much to be had. We had to convert the stable block at the back for accommodation. There's a few places free. It's dry enough and the stalls have proper cots.'

'What about a place to stay in the town?'

'You can try that. It'll cost you and they are pretty grim. Most rooms rent by the hour, if you see what I mean, sir.'

'We'll take the stable,' Cato replied. 'Our kit is by the entrance. Have some of your men see to it that it's taken to our, er, stall. Centurion Macro and I need to report to Governor Ostorius at once. If you would be so kind as to take us to him . . .'

The tribune sighed and lowered the report he had been reading

25

before scraping his chair back and rising to his feet. 'This way, sir. I'll see to your baggage when I return to my desk.'

He led them to the rear of the hall and into a corridor lined with small offices. Some were packed with yet more clerks while others were occupied by officers and civilian officials assigned to the governor's staff.

The door at the end of the corridor was ajar and the tribune gestured to Cato and Macro to wait while he stepped forward and rapped on the wooden frame. 'Sir, there's two officers to see you. Just arrived from Rome.'

There was a pause before a thin, weary voice replied, 'Oh, very well. Send 'em in.'

# CHAPTER FOUR

Governor Ostorius sat behind his desk wrapped in a thick scarlet cloak. A brazier added to the heat of the hypocaust system and made the air inside the room sweltering. He sat on a stool close to the fire, hunched over several piles of papers and slates. He looked up wearily as the two officers strode inside and stopped a short distance away to salute. Cato saw that the governor's face was heavily lined and his eyes were deep-set and rimmed with wrinkles. He knew that Ostorius had won a good reputation as a soldier and administrator and was a tough and hard-driving commander. It was difficult to square that with the frail-looking individual sitting before them.

'Introduce yourselves,' the governor snapped, then coughed, raising a loose fist to his lips until the irritation in his lungs passed. 'Well?'

As the ranking officer, Cato spoke first. 'Prefect Quintus Licinius Cato, sir.'

'Centurion Lucius Cornelius Macro, sir,' Macro added.

The governor looked his new arrivals over in silence for a moment. 'You'll have to pass your service records to my chief of staff. I'll read them later. I like to know the calibre of my officers. Given the problems I'm facing here I can't afford to carry any lightweights. I take it you have been assigned specific commands in my army?'

'Yes, sir,' Cato replied. 'I'm to command the Second Cohort of Thracian cavalry.'

'A good unit, that. One of my best. Has been ever since the temporary commander took charge. Centurion Quertus has been hitting the enemy hard, by all accounts. I'll expect you to do the same when you take charge.' Ostorius turned his gaze to Macro. 'And you?'

'Appointed to the Fourteenth Legion, sir.'

'I see.' The governor nodded slowly and then continued, 'Then you'll both be joining the main column commanded by Legate Quintatus. He's a fine officer, but he doesn't tolerate those who fail to come up to the standards he sets. Be that as it may, I need every man I can get now. Officers more than ever, given the rate at which we have been losing them. I dare say there'll be a vacancy amongst the senior centurions of the Fourteenth for you, Macro. In fact, I imagine you'll be one of the most experienced in the legion, for as long as you survive.'

Macro felt a surge of irritation at the governor's comment. He did not deserve to be spoken to as if he was some no-hoper, rear-echelon outpost commander.

'I intend to survive long enough to get my discharge and the gratuity that's coming to me, sir. No barbarian is going to stop that. Many have tried in the past, and paid the price.'

'Bold words, Centurion.' A faint smile flickered across the governor's lips. 'And tell me, exactly what makes you such a dangerous proposition to our enemies in this cold, forsaken island that Rome insists on adding to the empire?'

Macro was momentarily stuck for an answer as his mind flashed back over recent years. The street fighting in Rome, then the campaign in the sweltering heat, glare and dust of southern Egypt. Before that, the suppression of the slave revolt in Crete and the defence of Palmyra against a horde of Parthians. And earlier, dealing with fanatical Judaean rebels, a secondment to the imperial navy in a campaign against a nest of pirates plaguing merchant ships in the Adriatic Sea. That was after a long period of service with the Second Legion which had guarded the Rhine frontier, before being assigned to join the army that had invaded Britannia and crushed the native armies led by Caratacus. It was a notable period of service by any standard and Macro had won his promotion to centurion on merit – unlike some, who owed their position to powerful family connections. Yet Macro was not prepared to make a song and dance about it in front of the governor. He cleared his throat.

'I've been on detached service for the last few years, sir. Before that I served with the Second, on the Rhine, and afterwards here in Britannia.'

'Detached service? That is something of a euphemism for spying these days. What exactly was the nature of your, ah, detached service?'

'I am not at liberty to tell you the details, sir.'

'Then at least tell me who you were working for.'

Macro felt uncertain, and glanced quickly at Cato, but his friend's expression was fixed and unreadable as he faced forward. Macro took a deep breath. 'The imperial secretary, Narcissus.'

'You worked for that snake?' Ostorius's eyes narrowed. 'Are you here on his orders?'

Macro was angered by the suggestion and sucked in through gritted teeth, but before he could respond Cato spoke up.

'If that were the case, sir, then we'd hardly divulge that inform-ation. In any case, I give you my word of honour that we no longer serve Narcissus. We are here as soldiers. To serve you, the Emperor and Rome. Nothing more.'

'Your word of honour, eh?' Ostorius sniffed. 'There's precious little of that commodity being traded in Rome these days.' He leaned back on his stool and rubbed the small of his back. 'I have little choice but to take your word for it. But I warn you, if I get one hint that either of you are here for any reason other than soldiering, I'll throw you to the natives and let them deal with you. The Druids have some very interesting ways of disposing of their prisoners.'

'We know that, sir. We've seen it with our own eyes,' Cato responded, resisting the urge to shudder as he recalled his encounter with the Druids of the Dark Moon, back in the early days of his life in the legions when he served as a lowly optio in Macro's century. Brief visions of the sacrificial victims and the wild appearance of the Druids flitted before his mind's eye and Cato hurriedly thrust all thought of them aside.

'And what about you, Prefect?' The governor stared at Cato. 'How much action have you seen? That scar on your face tells part of the story, but you seem a little young to have reached the rank you hold. Is your father a senator? Or some wealthy freedman, anxious for his family to have a leg up the path of honour? How old are you?'

'I am in my twenty-sixth year, sir.'

'Twenty-six? Younger than I thought. And who in your family has influenced your rapid promotion to prefect?'

Cato had long since accepted that he would be a victim of his humble birth throughout his life. No matter how good a soldier he was, no matter that his father-in-law was a senator, he would never be allowed to shake off the stigma of being the descendant of a freedman who had once been a slave at the imperial palace.

'I have no family, sir. Other than my wife, Julia Sempronia, whom I married when I achieved my present rank. Her father is Senator Sempronius. But I have never approached him to seek preferment.'

'Sempronius?' The governor's eyebrows lifted briefly. 'I know him. He served as my tribune in the Eighth Legion. A good man. Hard-working and, more to the point, trustworthy. Well, if he's prepared to let you wed and bed that precious daughter of his then you must have some quality. But do you have the experience to go with the rank of prefect, I wonder?'

'I have had the honour of serving at the side of Centurion Macro ever since I joined the army, sir. My friend is inclined to be modest about his experience. Suffice to say that we have fought German tribesmen, Britons, pirates, Judaeans, Parthians and Numidians in our time. We know our trade.'

Ostorius nodded thoughtfully before he responded. 'If that is true then you have a truly enviable record, Prefect Cato. I welcome such men. They are needed more than ever if we are to settle our affairs here in Britannia and turn this bloody wilderness into something that bears a passing resemblance to civilisation.' He waved a hand. 'At ease, gentlemen.'

Cato and Macro relaxed their postures as the governor collected his thoughts and then addressed them again. 'It's important that you are aware of the situation here. I don't know what they told you back in Rome, but any notion that we are merely engaged in a mopping-up operation before the conquest of Britannia is complete is – how shall I put it? – a little wide of the mark. It's been seven years since Emperor Claudius had his Triumph to celebrate the conquest. Seven long years . . . In all that time we have pushed forward the frontier one painful step at a time. Even those tribes we have conquered, or made treaties with, can't be trusted any further than you can comfortably spit a rat. Just two years back, when I was about to launch an offensive against the Silures and Ordovices, I gave the order for the Iceni to be disarmed to make sure our backs would be safe from treachery. A reasonable request to make of someone who calls themselves an ally, you might think. But those bastards rose up in rebellion the moment I led my army into the mountains. I had no choice but to abandon the campaign and turn back to deal with them. The fools had holed up in one of their ridiculous earthworks. They soon gave in after we broke into their defences. It was all over soon enough, but I was forced to spend the rest of the campaigning season constructing forts and roads across their territory to keep watch on them.'

Cato pursed his lips as he recalled the proud but touchy Iceni warrior who had acted as a guide when he and Macro had undertaken a mission deep into enemy territory for the commander of the army that had invaded Britannia. Cato could well imagine how Prasutagus might have been outraged by the order to hand over his weapons. The native tribes of the island were ruled by a warrior caste who would consider being disarmed the gravest insult to their prickly sense of pride. No wonder there had been an uprising.

'While I dealt with the Iceni,' Ostorius continued, 'Caratacus took full advantage of the respite to win over the mountain tribes and become their warlord. By the time I could turn my attention back to him he had gathered an army large enough to defy me. Which is why I had to send a request to Rome for reinforcements. Now that I have them it is time to deal with Caratacus and his followers once and for all.'

Macro nodded approvingly, relishing the prospect of the coming campaign, and the chance to win some booty and possibly further promotion. Though he was reluctant to speak of his ambition, Macro, like many soldiers, dreamed of becoming the senior centurion of a legion, a rank that conferred many privileges and much honour on its holders. With it came social elevation to the equestrian class; only the senators were more exalted, apart from the Emperor, Macro conceded. If there was much fighting in the months ahead then the ranks of the centurionate were bound to be thinned out, as they always were, since they led from the front and suffered a disproportionate casualty rate as a result. If Macro survived, he might achieve command of the First Cohort of the legion one day, and after that the post of camp prefect, and take direct command of the legion if the legate was absent, or badly wounded or killed. The very thought of assuming such a responsibility filled him with hope.

The governor sighed and stroked the grey stubble on his chin. He seemed to shrink in on himself even further as he pondered the situation in silence for a while before speaking again.

'I am getting too old for this. Once my period of office is over I shall retire.' The corners of his lips lifted slightly. 'I'll return to my estate in Campania, tend to my vineyards and grow old with my wife. I have served Rome long enough, and well enough to earn that at least . . . Still, there is work to be done!' He forced himself to sit up and return his attention to the two officers standing before him. 'Even though I am preparing for the new offensive, there is still some small hope for peace.'

'Peace, sir?' Cato puffed his cheeks. 'With Caratacus? I doubt he will agree to any terms that Rome offers him.'

'Oh? And how would you know, young man?'

'Because I know the man, sir. I have met him and talked with him.'

There was a tense silence as the governor stared wide-eyed at Cato. Then he leaned forward. 'How can this be true? Caratacus is consumed with hatred for Rome, and all those who serve in her legions. He rarely takes prisoners, and those that are captured are never again seen by their countrymen. So how is it that you were accorded such a dubious honour?'

The governor's tone was scathing, but Cato ignored the slight when he replied. 'I was captured by Caratacus, along with a handful of my comrades, in the second year of the invasion, sir. Once we reached the enemy's camp, I was questioned by him.'

'Why?'

'He wanted to know more about Rome. About what motivated her soldiers. He also wanted to impress on me that the native tribes were proud and their warriors would never bow their heads to those who invade their lands. He vowed that they would rather die than accept the shame of submission to the Emperor.'

'I see. And how is it that you lived to tell me this?'

'I escaped, sir.'

'You escaped from the enemy camp?'

Cato nodded.

'Then the gods must favour you, Prefect Cato, for I have never heard of another Roman who can claim to have done the same.'

Macro chuckled. 'You don't know the half of it, sir. Fortuna has a full-time job keeping the prefect out of trouble.'

Cato cocked an eyebrow at his friend. 'You don't do so badly yourself.'

The governor cleared his throat irritably. 'I was talking about peace, gentlemen. It's several years since you last encountered Caratacus. Years of continual warfare. Both sides have been worn down by the struggle and I suspect that our enemy's appetite for conflict is as exhausted as mine. And there are those in Rome whose impatience with the situation in Britannia is growing by the day. Most notably, Pallas, one of the Emperor's closest advisers. I don't suppose you know the fellow.'

'I know of him, sir,' Cato replied cautiously, before the governor continued.

'From what my friends in Rome say, Pallas is the rising star. He's close to the Emperor's new wife and her son, Nero, who may well be the next Emperor when Claudius dies. It seems that Pallas is all for pulling the army out of Britannia and abandoning the province. To be sure, it has been an expensive exercise and there's precious little return on Rome's investment of gold and men. Nor is there much prospect of deriving anything of lasting value from Britannia once we've exhausted our supply of prisoners of war for the slave market. The silver, tin and lead we were led to believe the island was awash with have proved to be far less in reality. As far as I understand it, there's only two reasons why we still have boots on the ground. Firstly, some of the wealthiest men in Rome have lent rather large sums to the leaders of the tribes who have allied themselves to us. As it happens, Narcissus is amongst them, which is probably why he is so keen to have our armies remain here, at least until his loan has been repaid. The other reason is to do with simple pride. If Rome was seen to retreat from Britannia, it would be a humiliation for the Emperor, and our enemies in other frontier provinces would be bound to take heart from our failure here. Of course, with a change of regime, the next Emperor could justify a withdrawal in terms of correcting the mistakes of his predecessor. So, gentlemen, as you can see, Rome's grip on Britannia is far from certain.'

The governor lowered his gaze and reflected a moment before he continued. 'Many of our comrades have shed blood here, and many have fallen. If we are ordered to abandon Britannia then that sacrifice will have been for nothing. As I see it, I have two courses of action open to me, if the sacrifice of our comrades is to have had a purpose. I must utterly destroy the remaining tribes who oppose us here, or make a lasting peace with them. Either way, it must be done as swiftly as possible, so that there is peace in the province before a new Emperor ascends the throne. Only then will there be no excuse to pull out of Britannia. That is why I have invited the kings and chiefs of every tribe as far north as the Brigantes to a meeting to discuss terms to end the conflict. I have given my word that safe passage through our frontier will be granted to the tribes that have not already allied themselves to us.'

Macro hesitated before he asked the obvious question. 'Do you intend to keep your word, sir?'

'Of course.'

'Even if Caratacus himself turns up? If we bag him, and the others who are causing us trouble, we could put an end to the native resistance as quick as boiled asparagus.'

Ostorius sighed and shook his head. 'Or, we could outrage all the tribes and provide them with a cause to unite them against us – as swiftly as the culinary cliché you suggest. Perhaps it would be best if you kept such thoughts to yourself, Centurion. Leave the thinking to wiser heads, eh?'

Macro pressed his lips together and clenched his fists behind his back as he nodded curtly in response to the put-down. There was an uncomfortable silence before Cato turned the conversation in a different direction.

'When and where is this meeting to take place, sir?'

'In ten days' time, at one of their sacred groves, some sixty miles west of Londinium. I will take a small bodyguard with me.' He suddenly looked at Cato and smiled. 'There's no immediate rush for you two to join your units. In any case, it's only a small diversion from the road to Glevum.'

'Us?' Cato could not hide his surprise. 'But we're soldiers, sir. Not diplomats. Besides, we hoped to join our new commands as soon as possible. If the coming campaign is going to be tough then I want to get to know the men I am leading as well as possible before we go into action.'

'That won't be necessary, if we can make peace with our enemies. And since you have met Caratacus before, you may prove to be useful during the negotiations. You're both coming with me.'

'Very well, sir. As you command. There's just one thing. What makes you think the enemy will be prepared to make peace with us?'

Ostorius replied in a cold tone, 'Because if they don't, then I shall make it perfectly clear that before the year is out, every last village in every tribe that still opposes us will be razed to the ground, and those natives that are spared will all be sold into slavery . . .' The governor yawned. 'And now I must take some rest. That will be all, gentlemen. I suggest you enjoy the few delights that Londinium has to offer while you can. I'm sure they'll have some suggestions in the officers' mess. Dismissed.'

Macro and Cato stood to attention, saluted and then turned to leave. Ostorius stared down at the piles of records and reports at his feet for a moment and then rose slowly from his stool and walked stiffly to the narrow campaign cot that had been set up by the wall. Easing himself down, he lay on his side, still wearing his boots, and pulled his cloak over his body as best as he could before he fell into a troubled sleep.

★ ★ ★

35

'What do you make of him?' Macro asked when they were a short distance down the corridor outside the governor's office.

Cato glanced round and saw that there were no clerks near enough to overhear his remarks. 'He's at the end of his tether. Worn out by his duties. But I've heard that he's as tough a commander as any.'

Macro shrugged. 'Being tough does not make you immune to age. I know that well enough. I ain't as fast in a fight as I used to be. Comes to us all in the end.'

Cato shot him a look. 'Just don't let it come to you while you're fighting at my side. Last thing I need is some old codger guarding my flank when we get stuck into the enemy.'

'That's pretty ungrateful, given how I had to nursemaid you through your first battles when you were a green recruit.' Macro laughed and shook his head. 'I'd never have guessed then that you'd turn out to be quite the soldier.'

Cato smiled. 'I learned from the best.'

'Shut up, lad. You'll make me cry.' Macro chuckled. Then his expression hardened. 'Seriously though. I have my doubts about our new general. The way he looks now, a few months in the field will kill him off. Right in the middle of the campaign.'

'Not if he can negotiate a peace with Caratacus. Or at least with enough tribes to islolate him.'

'What chance do you think there is that Caratacus wants peace?'

Cato thought back to the small hut in which he had been questioned by Caratacus. He remembered all too vividly the determined gleam in the Briton's eyes when he said that he would die rather than bow to Rome.

'If I was a betting man, I'd give you odds of a hundred to one against.'

'And I'd say those are generous odds, my friend.' Macro clicked his tongue. 'We're in for a tough time of it, Cato. Just for a change.'

'Nothing we can do about it.'

'Oh yes there is!' Macro grinned. 'You heard the man; there's all the delights of Londinium awaiting us.' His expression became a little anxious. 'Just as long as you don't let on to my mother, eh?'

# CHAPTER FIVE

'Well, boys, what do you think of this place?' Portia asked as they took a table close to the inn's fireplace. It was the evening of their third day in Londinium and she was accompanied by her son and Cato. Just for a change it was raining again, a steady downpour angled by a stiff breeze that lashed the streets of Londinium, pattered off the few tiled buildings and ran off the thatched roofs of the rest. The inn had once been a large barn before it had been extended with outbuildings that formed a modest courtyard in front of the entrance. A gate opened out on to a wide street that stretched from the quay on the Tamesis up to the site of the basilica complex. Despite the weather the street was busy and the rattle of cartwheels and the braying of mules could be clearly heard over the hiss of the rain.

Macro drew back the hood of his military cape and ran a quick glance over his surroundings. The inn was warm and dry and the floor was paved and liberally covered with straw to absorb the filth on the boots and sandals of those coming in from the street. There was a bar counter to one side, inset with large jars to hold the stew and heated wine that was served to customers. Several long tables with benches on either side filled most of the open space. Despite all the renovations, there was still a faint tang of horse sweat in the air, but Macro did not mind. There were worse odours.

'Nice enough,' he conceded. 'Compared to most in this town.'

Cato nodded. While waiting for the order to join Ostorius and his staff on the ride to the meeting with the tribal leaders they had spent the time in the inns recommended by Decimus. There was little else of note to see. Despite her earlier misgivings about the discharged legionary, Portia had found his guidance useful as she inspected a number of inns and subtly sounded out their owners to discover who might be willing to sell their business to her.

Cato gestured to a serving girl behind the bar and she hurried over to take their order. She was young, barely into her teens, and was dumpy with a poor complexion but at least she spoke reasonable Latin.

'Jar of wine for the three of us. What's in the stew today?'

She shrugged. 'Same as every day. Barley and onion gruel.'

Cato forced a smile. 'Sounds fine. Three bowls then, with bread. I take it that's fresh?'

'Baked just the other day, sir. Fresh enough.'

Without waiting for further comment she turned and hurried back towards the counter to prepare a tray for their order.

'Nice enough?' Portia said flatly as she stared at her son. 'Is that all you have to say?'

'What do you want me to say?' Macro growled. 'It's an inn, like any other.'

'No, as it happens.' She wagged a finger. 'This is the one I want to buy. Thanks to Decimus, I learned that the owner is a veteran of the Second Legion who has had enough of Britannia and is selling up to return to Rome. I've made an offer and he's accepted.'

Macro took another, longer look round the premises. 'Why this one?'

Portia swiftly marshalled her arguments and counted them off on her fingers as she replied. 'Firstly, the location. Plenty of passing customers and a lot of them work at the governor's headquarters so they can afford to pay more for their wine and food. Second, there's eight rooms in the courtyard that are already rented to travellers. I can have more accommodation added to the rear. As the province is settled, this town is bound to grow in size and there's a small fortune to be made from those passing through Londinium. And third, there's some small storerooms on the opposite side of the courtyard that we could rent out to the prostitutes' guild. An extra service that some of the customers would welcome, I'm sure. There's plenty of potential here and the price is very fair.' She paused. 'There's only one snag. What's left of the money I got from

38

selling my place in Ariminum is not going to cover what I offered.'

Macro cradled his head in his hands and groaned softly. 'I can see where this is going, Mother. You want me to give you the rest from my savings.'

'Not give, as such. Think of it as a loan or, better still, a sound investment. I can cover half the cost. You pay for the rest and I'll make you a sleeping partner, and you can take four-tenths of the profits,' she added quickly.

Macro looked up sharply. 'Four-tenths? Why not half?'

'Because I'll be doing all the hard work. Four-tenths. That's my final offer.'

Cato sat quite still, watching the exchange and somewhat in awe of Portia's sound business sense and ruthless approach to getting her way. It was clear which of those qualities Macro had inherited in abundance.

'Wait a moment!' Macro held up his hands. 'What if I decide I don't want to lend you the money?'

Portia folded her slender hands together and pouted slightly. 'Would you really do such a thing to your mother? Force me to buy some grotty little chop house, which is all I could afford without your help. Work myself to the bone for a pittance and then die old and alone?'

'For fuck's sake, you know it won't come to that!' Macro said crossly. 'I'll see to it that you're taken care of. It's the least I owe you.'

'Quite.' She nodded. 'So?'

Macro breathed in deeply and let out an exasperated sigh. 'Very well. How much do you need?'

'Five thousand denarii. That's all.'

Macro's jaw sagged. 'Five thousand! That's . . . that's . . .' His brow creased in concentration. 'Several years' pay.'

'You can easily afford it.'

'What makes you think that?'

'I had a little look in that chest of yours that you keep at the bottom of your kitbag.'

'But it's locked.'

She gave him a sympathetic look. 'I spent fifteen years working in a bar in Ariminum, my boy. There are many useful tips and skills

I picked up from my customers. Lock-picking is the least of them. The more interesting point is how a centurion managed to come by such a large fortune.'

Macro exchanged a quick glance with Cato and both men felt a tremor of anxiety trace its way down their spines. When they had been in Rome they had helped to unmask a conspiracy in the ranks of the Praetorian Guard. The silver was part of a convoy of bullion that the conspirators had stolen from the Emperor, and was still unaccounted for as far as the imperial palace was concerned. Cato had argued that it should be handed back but Macro had fervently insisted that they had earned the silver and refused. So they had split the proceeds. Cato had left his share with a banker in Rome while Macro, who regarded bankers as corrupt parasites, changed the silver into gold coins to make his fortune more portable and kept it in his possession. His little secret, until now. He looked round hurriedly in case anyone had overheard his mother's remark. Then he turned back to her.

'All right then. Five thousand. For a half share of the profits.'

'Four-tenths, I said.'

'Split the difference,' Macro said desperately.

'Four-tenths.'

He gritted his teeth and glared at her before he eventually nodded. 'Shit. I give in. But keep your hands off my things from now on.'

His mother smiled sweetly and patted his cheek. 'I knew you'd see sense. And you'll do very nicely out of it in due course, I promise you.'

Macro wondered about that. His mother, like most small business owners, was as adept at cooking the books as she was at cooking cheap meals for her customers. Still, at least Portia would have the means to make an independent living and that suited Macro, who would rather not have to worry about her when he marched off to fight the enemy. In any case, if she was right then he would earn a tidy profit from his investment.

The serving girl came over with their order, steam curling up from the wine jar and the bowls of stew. She set the tray down with a rattling thump and ungraciously set their bowls before them, together with the plain clay cups and bronze spoons. She sniffed and wiped the cuff of her long-sleeved tunic on her nose.

'Nine sestertii.'

Before Cato could reach for his purse, Macro interrupted. 'I'll pay. Might as well, since it seems to be my day for being fleeced.'

He fumbled in his purse for a handful of coins and slapped them into the grubby hand of the serving girl, who counted them quickly before returning to the counter. Portia watched her closely with cold eyes.

'It would seem,' she spoke softly, 'that there are going to be a few changes when I take over this place. That girl, for one, needs some lessons in how to mend her appearance and her manner.'

'Let's eat,' said Cato, lifting his spoon, anxious to put an end to the carping between Macro and his mother. They were hungry and ate in silence and Cato's thoughts inevitably drifted back to Julia in Rome. It would be years before he was released from his duties in Britannia. At some point he would have to ask her to give up the comforts and pleasures of her life in Rome to come and join him. He was under no illusions about the basic conditions of life in a frontier fortress, or a provincial town. It would not worry him, but he feared that it would not be good enough for Julia.

His thoughts were interrupted by the sound of voices outside in the courtyard and a moment later two officers entered. He recognised them from the governor's headquarters. Junior tribunes serving with the Ninth Legion. He swallowed the stew still in his mouth and dabbed his lips on the back of his hands before calling out to them.

'Care to join us?'

The two young men hesitated and Cato chuckled. 'The drinks are on me.'

The taller of the two, with fine dark hair, smiled. 'Well, since you put it like that!'

They came over and sat down while Cato introduced Macro and his mother.

'Tribune Marcus Pellinus,' the taller one announced and nodded towards his companion. 'And Caius Decianus. I've seen you up at headquarters, haven't I? You're the new commander of the Thracian cavalry cohort attached to Legate Quintatus.'

'That's right,' Cato replied. He caught the eye of the serving girl and indicated his new companions. She stirred reluctantly and bent down behind the counter to get some more cups. 'And my friend here will be taking on a cohort in the Fourteenth.'

'I bet I know which one that'll be,' Pellinus chuckled. 'Looks like you two have been hand-picked for the job.'

'And what job would that be?' asked Macro.

The serving girl set down two more cups and Tribune Decianus helped himself to the jug as he spoke. 'There's a forward outpost, some distance inside Silurian territory, where the Thracians have been brigaded with a cohort from the Fourteenth. All part of the governor's plan to have strong columns pushed as far forward as possible to keep an eye on the enemy and nip in the bud any attempt by Caratacus's lads to break out into the province. Only, we've had reports about trouble with the garrison at the fort.'

'What kind of trouble?' asked Cato.

'You know how it is. There's never much love lost between legionaries and auxiliaries. Routine name-calling and punch-ups are fine, but the soldiers in those two units really have got it in for each other.'

'Seems to me the idiots just need someone to knock their heads together,' Macro grumbled.

Decianus smirked. 'The temporary commander seems to be doing a good job of restoring discipline while waiting for a replacement to take over. Clearly the garrison will continue to need a firm hand. Which is why I imagine you two have been sent to do the job, judging by your record. I saw the documents today. Very impressive. Sounds like you are just what they need. Especially as your column is going to be one of those at the sharp end of Ostorius's offensive.'

'Assuming that he fails to win over the locals at that meeting he's called,' said Pellinus.

'I think we all know that's not going to end happily,' his friend responded. 'The only thing the locals seem to want is to fight. When they're not doing in Romans they're at each other's throats. Ostorius is wasting time when he should be waving the stick about. A damn good caning is the only thing that'll get the message through their thick skulls.' Decianus paused and his eyes widened. 'And since we're talking about thick skulls, did you see that one in the courtyard just now?'

Portia leaned forward anxiously. 'What's that? A barbarian here, on the premises?'

'Too right, ma'am. Him, his woman and a handful of his brutes. Just arrived. Since they're armed they must be on their way to the governor's meeting. Bloody great giant of a man. Wouldn't want to face him in battle.'

Macro sniffed. 'I find the bigger they are, the harder they fall.'

'Well, you'd need a great big felling axe to take that one down. There's been quite a few of 'em passing through Londinium in the last few days. Caused quite a stir since many of the locals we have here haven't worn woad in years. Some of 'em have taken to our dress and customs quite well actually.'

Cato doubted it. While they might look the part, and do their best to pick up as much Latin as they could, they would consider themselves to be Britons first and foremost for many years yet. Especially while the tribes of the province were still regarded as separate kingdoms, fiercely proud of their heritage and their independence. That would change the moment their client kingdom status elapsed. It was the same technique Rome used in every new province: strike deals with the local rulers which guaranteed them Rome's protection in return for the peaceful annexation of their kingdom once the current ruler had died. That might work well enough in other parts of the empire, but Cato suspected that the arrangement would not proceed so easily when applied to the bellicose warriors of Britannia. He finished his stew and washed it down with a draught of warm wine before he spoke to Pellinus.

'How are preparations going for the new campaign season?'

The tribune's expression became weary at the prospect of talking shop but Cato outranked him and therefore could direct the course of their conversation as he wished.

'Almost complete, sir. The forward depots are fully stocked with supplies, the last of the reinforcements are moving up to join their units and the cavalry mounts are being brought to hard condition. The governor wants us ready to march on the first good day of spring, assuming the attempt to get a peace treaty falls through. Which it will. After that, we're in the lap of the gods. The ground over which we'll be fighting is mountainous and heavily forested. Only a handful of tracks have been discovered by our scouts. Ideal terrain for ambushes. If Caratacus plays it smart he'll just wear us down with hit-and-run tactics. Our only hope is to find their villages and lay waste to enough of them so that we force them to face us on the battlefield. Then, if we're lucky, we can do for Caratacus and his army.'

'You don't sound very optimistic,' said Macro.

'Oh, I'm optimistic enough. Because that's what the governor has told us to be in his standing orders. Doesn't want us to unsettle the reinforcements who are joining our happy little band. No more defeatism is his line and he'll come down hard on any of his subordinates who even suggests that we won't have the beating of Caratacus this time round. So yes, I'm an optimist. But before that, I'm a realist. And I'd say anyone who really thinks this is going to be just a stroll in the forum is in for a great big fucking surprise. Pardon, madam.'

Portia sighed with exasperation and waved the apology aside. Then she froze and looked towards the doorway of the inn. Cato turned to follow the direction of her gaze and saw that two large warriors had entered the room. They wore heavy capes woven with a checked design in brown and white. Their hair was tied back and braided in a thick queue that hung down their backs. Swirling tattoos covered their hairy arms and long swords hung from baldrics. The native warriors slowly shuffled inside, followed by several more of their companions, including one huge man who had to bow his head to avoid the beams that stretched across the interior. At his side was a woman, her head covered with the hood of a cloak. The serving girl took one look at the giant and hurried through a doorway behind the counter, calling for her master.

As the newcomers made their way to the counter, the leader of the party looked round the room until his gaze rested on the small party of Romans. His expression was fierce, but then a look of puzzlement worked its way through as he stared directly at Macro and Cato.

'I don't fucking believe it . . .' Macro grasped Cato's arm. 'Look who it is! Recognise him?'

'Of course,' Cato replied quietly. 'Prasutagus.'

There was a scraping as Macro rose from his bench and called across the room. 'Prasutagus! It's me. I mean us. Macro and Cato!'

Decianus nearly choked on his wine. 'You mean you know that brute?'

Macro ignored the tribune and took two steps towards the native leader and held out his hand. Prasutagus stood still for a moment before he smiled faintly and nodded without offering his hand in return. Macro lowered his and shook his head in wonder. 'I don't believe it . . . Prasutagus.'

'Hello, Centurion,' a woman's voice interrupted the startled silence of the inn. Macro turned and saw that the woman had lowered the hood of her cloak to reveal thick tresses of coppery red hair. Her eyes twinkled as she smiled a greeting.

The power of speech failed Macro for an instant before he swallowed nervously and cleared his throat. 'Boudica . . .'

# CHAPTER SIX

'Queen Boudica, as it happens.' She affected an aloofness that was betrayed by the smile that she could not suppress.

'Queen?' Macro frowned. 'I don't understand.'

'I am the wife of Prasutagus, and so queen of the Iceni nation. I assume that you, too, have risen in status since we last saw each other. No longer the centurion we once knew.'

Macro shook his head. 'Centurion Macro still, though I am more senior than I was.'

Boudica stepped away from the bar and made for the side of her husband and took his hand. 'We are pleased to see you again.'

The two Roman officers exchanged looks with the rulers of the Iceni tribe, and for a moment no one spoke as memories of shared hardships and dangers flooded back into their minds. Macro felt a deeper pang of loss as he gazed at the woman whose affections he had once known, when Boudica had been no more than the wayward daughter of an Iceni nobleman. At length Prasutagus could maintain his regal aloofness no longer and let out a hearty bellow of mirth, before surging forward and throwing his arms round Macro in a rib-cracking embrace of friendship.

'Hah! It is good to see you again, Roman! Too many years have passed.'

Macro clasped the giant's arms and eased himself free of the powerful grip. He took a deep breath before he responded. 'I see you've picked up a bit more Latin since last time.'

'It is well to speak the tongue of your friend,' Prasutagus responded, his accent heavy but his words readily comprehensible. He turned to Cato and grasped his hand and smiled warmly. 'And you, Cato. Still as cunning and brave, I think.' He tapped the scar that ran down from Cato's forehead. 'The mark of a warrior, eh?'

'The mark of a man who did not get out of the way of a blade in time, more like,' Cato replied with a smile.

His wife approached and looked Cato over with a slight expression of concern. 'You were little more than a youth when last we met. Now you look more like Macro did then.'

'What?' Macro interrupted. 'Then what do I look like now?'

Boudica scrutinised him. 'Your face is more lined, and there is grey in your hair, but you are still the same Macro I knew. Which is as well. It is good to see an old friend . . .' Her tone became more serious. 'Friendship is needed now more than ever. Relations between Rome and the Iceni are fragile. I take it you are aware of our recent history?'

'We heard about the rebellion,' said Cato. 'It is a pity.'

'Pity?' Prasutagus's eyebrows knitted together. 'It was a tragedy. A betrayal of the bond between our people and Rome. Ostorius demanded we surrender weapons, even after I gave my word of honour that we hold true to our alliance with the Emperor. Some gave up weapons. Others did not and died with sword in hand.' Prasutagus lowered his gaze. 'They were fools, but brave fools. Perhaps . . .'

'You did the right thing.' Boudica squeezed his hand. 'You survived and now you serve the Iceni people. They need you.'

Prasutagus shrugged. Cato sensed his wounded honour but could not help the urge to discover the full story. 'So, how did you come to be King?'

'I was one of the few who had no part in the rebellion. I was too sick to fight alongside my brothers. So when it was over, the governor chose me to replace the old king. He was killed in the battle.'

'I see. I am sure that Ostorius's choice was wise.' Cato turned and gestured towards their table. 'Would you care to drink with us? That is Macro's mother, and the others are comrades from the army.'

'Macro's mother?' Boudica cocked an eyebrow. 'Now there's someone I would be fascinated to talk to.'

But Prasutagus was staring coldly at the two tribunes and shook his head. 'Another day, my friends. When we can speak freely to each other.'

Pellinus flushed at the words and stood up. He addressed Cato. 'Thank you for the drink, sir. We are expected back at headquarters and have to beg our leave of you now.'

The other tribune looked surprised, but then caught on and nodded in agreement. They bowed their heads to Portia and left the inn, without acknowledging the Iceni rulers. There was a strained silence before Boudica spoke again.

'You know about the assembly of the tribes, I take it?'

'Yes. We'll be part of the governor's retinue.'

'I see.' Some of the warmth had drained from her voice. 'Then we shall see you there, or perhaps somewhere on the road.'

'We look forward to it. Now, how about that drink? We've a lot to catch up on.'

Boudica was about to reply when her husband broke in with, 'Another time. Somewhere less . . . Roman. Come.' He took Boudica's arm and gently steered her towards the door. Prasutagus growled a command to his warriors and they withdrew across the inn to join them before the small party quit the inn and closed the door behind them.

Macro shrugged sadly. 'Is that the way it has to be between us? So soon after we meet them again?'

'Time takes its toll in many ways, old friend,' Cato said kindly.

Macro glared at him. 'Old? Fuck off. Let's get back to our wine. Least we don't have to share it with those freeloading tribunes now.'

They returned to the bench and sat down opposite Portia. Cato raised the jug, frowned at its lightness and shook it. A faint slop of liquid sounded from inside. He refilled Macro's cup and tipped what was left into his own before raising it in a toast in an effort to restore some cheer to the atmosphere.

'Here's to your new business. I'm sure it will be a great success from the amount of passing trade that seems to come through the door.'

Portia raised her cup half-heartedly. 'It would be more of a success if some of the trade actually stayed for a drink.'

Cato glanced into the dregs of his cup. 'Or even bought a round or two.'

'So where are these troublemakers, then?' a voice called out from the direction of the counter and Cato turned to see a burly, grey-haired man emerge from the door leading to the store-room. The serving girl anxiously peered round from behind his back. The innkeeper glanced round the room where his customers were drinking peacefully, then turned on the serving girl. 'Well?'

She flinched back towards the door and he cuffed her hard about the head. 'Stop wasting my time, you stupid bitch! Get in there and stoke up the cooking fire!'

The girl reeled from the blow and then hunched down and scurried away to do her master's bidding.

Cato nodded towards the man. 'The owner, and vendor, of the inn, I take it?'

'That's him.' Portia beckoned to the innkeeper when she caught his eye. 'Time, I think, to settle the deal, now that my dear son has agreed to invest in my new business.'

'Invest?' Macro echoed wryly. 'It feels more like I've been mugged.'

Portia ignored her grumpy son and smiled as the innkeeper made his way over to their table. He moved with the self-assurance of one who was used to command and did not tolerate any subordinate who caused even the least bit of trouble. His hair was thinning but the well-toned physique that had seen him through many a battle was still there. Cato had little doubt that he could swiftly sort out any customers who got out of hand on his premises. As he came close enough for his features to be clearly recognisable, Cato gave a small start of surprise and then called out a greeting.

'Centurion Gaius Tullius!'

The innkeeper slowed his pace and squinted at his customers, then his expression changed abruptly and he beamed happily.

'Bugger me, if it ain't Cato and Macro! What on earth are you two doing here? Thought the Second Legion had seen the back of you years ago.'

'So it had.' Macro grinned. 'But it seems like you lads have been having a little difficulty with the locals and need to call on the

49

services of some real soldiers to sort 'em out.'

'Ah, get away with you!' Tullis swatted Macro on the shoulder. 'We managed well enough without you two troublemakers. Anyway, this is a turn-up, and I'm always glad to see old comrades. The gods know there are few enough of us about.' He turned to Portia. 'Oh, it's you, ma'am. You with them?' He winked. 'Or are they with you?'

Portia regarded him coolly. 'If that's supposed to be amusing, then I fail to see why. As it happens, Centurion Macro is my son.'

Tullius turned to stare at Macro with a look of astonishment. 'You have a mother?'

He pulled up a stool and sat down. 'Tullia!' he shouted. 'Bring another jar of wine. The good stuff! Wait . . . That Gaulish stuff'll do! Anyway, what's the story, lads? How come you're back in this shithole? Can't be because you like the weather.'

'Shithole?' Portia fixed him with a stare. 'Is that why you're selling up? I might have to knock a thousand or two off the price.'

Tullius dipped his head in acknowledgement of his clumsy remark. 'I'm selling up because I want to retire to some place warm in Campania, miss. There's nothing really wrong with Londinium. There's good money to be made here. I'm hardly likely to try and put one over the dear old mother of one of my former comrades in arms, am I? Besides,' his tone hardened slightly, 'I thought we made a deal.'

'No. I made an offer. You said you'd think about it. And now, I'm having a rethink about the offer I made, in view of your eagerness to sell. I think nine thousand is a more reasonable price.'

Tullius could not hide his surprise at the sharpness of her tone. 'Fuck me, but you've got a hard and ruthless streak. She's your mum all right, Macro . . . The price is still ten.'

'Nine.'

'And five hundred.'

Portia chewed her lip briefly. 'Nine thousand, five hundred.'

He frowned. 'Well, since you're kin of Macro, it's a deal. But I'm robbing myself.' He spat into the palm of his hand and held it out. Portia took it at once, before there was any chance of him changing his mind, and sealed their business. The serving girl arrived with a fresh jar of wine and set it down on the table and hurriedly withdrew. Tullius poured them each a cup, filled right to the brim, and raised his. 'To the Second Augusta!'

'To the Second!' Macro and Cato chorused and drained their cups. The wine was better than Macro had expected and at once he reached for the jug to refill their cups.

'Go easy on that,' Portia said firmly. 'That's part of my stock now. You pay for the next jug, you hear?'

Tullius smiled ruefully. 'Hard as nails. Anyway, I take it you two are here to beef up the ranks of the legions for Ostorius's new campaign.'

'That's right,' said Cato. 'Macro's going to the Fourteenth as a senior centurion.'

'Pfftt! Fourteenth, bunch of pansies. Not fit to lick the boots of the Second, I reckon.'

Macro was cautious about knocking the reputation of his new unit as he was sure to develop pride in the Fourteenth as a matter of course. He pursed his lips and poured himself some more wine as he muttered, 'We'll see.'

Tullius turned to Cato. 'And what about you? Going to join Macro's lot? I'm sure he could use a good centurion like you.'

Cato felt a moment's awkwardness. 'No. I'll be going to a different unit. Thracian cavalry cohort. I've been given the command.'

Tullis looked surprised. 'You? Then . . . you must have made prefect. Fuck me, that's a turn-up for the books. You were just a junior centurion when we last knew each other . . .' He paused and shuffled sheepishly. 'Bloody hell . . . Well done, lad. I mean, sir.'

'There's no need for that,' Cato responded. 'We're off duty. I mean . . . you're out of the army now.'

'Maybe so, but I still have respect for the rank. And the man that bears it. Prefect Cato. Now that's something. Really something. By the gods, you must have seen some action and covered yourself in glory to be promoted to prefect. That or you've gone and shagged the Emperor's missus. Or perhaps been shagged by Claudius. Randy old dog, from what I hear.'

Macro drained his cup and raised a finger. 'That's enough. Cato

51

won his rank the hard way. I know. I watched him do it.'

'Fair play to him then,' Tullius conceded. 'And now you've both fetched up here, the graveyard of ambition, or so they say.'

'Meaning?'

'Meaning that there's no glory to be won here. Not any more. The big battles are over. Caratacus and his mob have taken to the hills. Most of our lads are stuck in small forts keeping a wary eye on the natives and trying not to get themselves bumped off when they go out on patrol. Once in a while we manage to chase a few of the painted bastards to ground and stick it to 'em. But the rate things are going I dare say Rome will still be struggling to tame these Britons long after anyone has forgotten there ever was an invasion. You want my advice? Apply for a transfer as soon as you get the chance.'

Macro replied, 'You're wrong. Ostorius is about to give them one last chance to bend to Rome, then he's going to hit them with everything he's got.' His voice was beginning to slur.

Tullius chuckled. 'Is that right? You think it's the first time a governor's tried to wipe the floor with the bastards? What makes you think he's got any more chance of finishing the job than Aulus Plautius before him?'

Macro waved a finger at Cato and slapped himself on the chest. 'Because this time we're going to be doing the fighting for him. That's what!'

Cato folded his fingers together and gently shook his head.

Macro had warmed to his theme and raised his fist. 'We'll give Caratacus what for, you'll see! Bloody his nose and whip him like the cur he is. It'll all be over by Saturnalia.'

'Care to place a bet on that?' Tullius asked slyly.

'Course I will.' Macro nodded vigorously.

'Macro!' Portia snapped. 'Don't!'

Before her son could respond there was a cold draught as the door opened and a headquarters clerk came into the inn. He looked round until he spied the table at which Cato and the others were sitting, just as Macro glared over his shoulder and bellowed, 'Put the bloody wood in the hole!'

'Sorry, sir.' The clerk pushed the door to and the latch clicked home then he made his way over to the table and stood to attention. 'Begging your pardon, Prefect, but the governor sends his compliments and says that you are both to be ready to join him tomorrow morning when he rides to Durocornovium.'

'Very well.' Cato nodded. 'We'll be there. You may go.'

The clerk bowed his head and departed. Cato stood up. 'Come, Macro. We must find Decimus and have our packs made ready. Then an early night is in order.'

'Stuff that. I'm enjoying a drink with Tullius here. I'll be along when I'm done.'

For an instant Cato considered ordering his friend to join him. But he knew that would only put Macro in a sour mood. Better to let him drink his fill and roll back into their quarters happy and drunk. Besides, the inevitable hangover the next morning would give Cato some peace and quiet on the road to Durocornovium.

# CHAPTER SEVEN

Portia came to see them off shortly after dawn the following day. Cato had provided Decimus with enough silver to buy three mules, two to carry their baggage, and one for the servant to ride. The governor had authorised the provision of two horses for Cato and Macro. There was no tearful parting scene at the gates of the town because they had not been constructed yet and Londinium merely petered out amid a shanty town of shelters either side of the road leading west. Fearing for his mother's safety amongst the barbaric-looking denizens of this fringe community, Macro stopped his horse, waited until the last men in the small column had passed by, and briefly kissed her on the forehead. He wished his own head was not pounding so. Nor did he like the raw nausea in his guts that threatened to humiliate him in front of his companions should he have to throw up.

'It's best that we part here,' said Macro. 'I'm not sure how far I trust this lot.'

He nodded to some of the inhabitants who had risen early and watched the Romans leading their horses down the rutted roadway.

'I'll be fine.' She lifted her cloak aside to reveal a cosh hanging from her tunic belt. 'A souvenir from my Ariminum days.'

'Try not to kill too many of the natives,' Macro joked, attempting to lighten the mood at their parting. 'Leave some for me. That's my job.'

She smiled weakly then cupped her son's cheek in her hand and stared intently at him. 'Take care of yourself, and that boy, Cato. Don't do anything stupid. I know you. I know what you're like. Just don't take unnecessary risks. Understand?'

Macro nodded.

She sighed and shook her head. 'Maybe one day you'll have a son of your own. Then you'll understand. Now go. Before you make me cry.'

'That'll be the day,' Macro drawled. 'Tough as old boots, you are.'

'Just go!'

Without another word, or any lingering hesitation, Portia dropped her hand and turned to walk back down the road towards the heart of Londinium. Macro watched her briefly, but she did not look back.

'Tough as old boots . . .' he repeated under his breath. Then, tugging on the reins of his mount, he strode forward to catch up with the rest of the governor's escort while the natives, their curiosity sated, turned away and went back to their rude huts. Once they had passed beyond the last of the huts and emerged into open countryside, the governor gave the order for his men to mount.

Cato had been taught to ride as a recruit and had had some practice in the following years, but he still did not feel wholly comfortable in the saddle and the horse he had been given had a tendency to nervous jerks and twitches at the slightest flicker of movement in the periphery of its vision. Ostorius rode a length ahead of his men and glanced over his shoulder once in a while at Cato, and the latter understood his intent well enough. The governor was testing his new cavalry commander to see how he handled a difficult mount. Accordingly, Cato concentrated on keeping the beast in check and trying to anticipate its reactions to its surroundings to make sure that it did not bolt, or rear, or cause any embarrassment to him.

The road was a rough affair, often no more than a muddy track, and where the ground was particularly soft the army's engineers had constructed corduroys of logs packed with earth to provide a stable surface for marching columns, riders and wheeled traffic. Although there was no rain, the sky was overcast and pockets of mist filled the hollows of the landscape. With no sun to burn them off they were set to remain there through most of the day and Cato could well understand why that was the prevailing impression of the island in

Roman minds. The country-scented air was cool and a relief after the cloying stench of Londinium. It was late in April and the bare limbs of trees and shrubs were budding and hardy flowers provided a splatter of bright colours across the landscape. Soon, the town had fallen behind them and only a faint brown hue on the undulating horizon marked its presence.

Cato soon came to master the idiosyncrasies of his horse and could give some attention to his comrades. There had been a brief round of introductions at the governor's headquarters before setting out but Cato had forgotten most of their names. He was familiar with the types, though. Aside from Ostorius, there were ten picked legionaries who acted as his personal bodyguard. Tough veterans with good records who could be trusted to give their lives to protect the governor. Then there were the tribunes. Six junior officers who would go on to a succession of appointments in civil administration and who might one day be rewarded with promotion to the Senate. From there, the select few would be awarded the post of governor of one of Rome's provinces. Ostorius Scapula was such a man. He had devoted his life to the twin ideals of Rome and to adding lustre to his family name. No doubt he had hoped to tame Britannia as a fitting end to his long career, Cato reflected. Too bad the native tribes had different ideas about being tamed.

The last member of the party was a native translator, though with his neatly cut brown hair, red tunic and cape he could easily be taken for a Roman. It was only the gleam of the ornately patterned torc round his neck that indicated his true heritage. Marcommius, the latinised version of his native name, was in his thirties, slender and well-groomed. It was clear that he had abandoned the ways of his people.

Cato rode behind the tribunes while Macro had slipped back to join the bodyguards and engage them in conversation. Their cheerful chatter mingled with the rumbling clop of hoofs as the small column followed the track across the green downs of the lands of the Atrebates. There was heavy cultivation and small farms, and a handful of villas with their more regular pattern of fields lay scattered amongst the remaining woodlands of ancient oaks and smaller trees. Now and then they passed some of the natives working their land; Ostorius smiled a greeting, and his officers followed his example, Cato noted approvingly. He could never understand the haughty, high-handed attitude of many Romans to the peoples they had conquered. The swiftest way to Romanise a population was to encourage good relations. The quickest way to antagonise them was to beat them down and treat them as inferiors, a policy that only caused bitter resentment where it did not result in outright revolt.

Five miles or so down the road Ostorius gently tugged on his reins and fell into step alongside Cato. The road had dipped down into a shallow vale filled with mist which closed in around the riders and made vague shapes of the trees and bushes on either side. They exchanged a nod before the governor began speaking.

'I briefed my tribunes and the bodyguard before we left, but just wanted to ensure that you, and Centurion Macro, were put in the picture. As you can appreciate this is very much a make or break occasion. Our last chance to secure peace with Caratacus and his followers. Of course, there's no guarantee that he will put in an appearance. But there will be some there who share his views and will doubtless report back to him. The vast majority are already firm allies. Some, admittedly, are more grudging. Even so there will be more voices raised for peace than war and, if nothing else, this meeting will serve to emphasise the isolation of those who still resist. That said, I am taking nothing for granted. You, and your subordinate, will at all times treat the native delegates with courtesy and respect. Is that clear?'

'Yes, sir.'

'And that goes for any Druids that are present as well.'

'Druids? I thought they were our most implacable foes, sir. That was certainly the case when Macro and I last served here.'

'Oh, they still hate us with a vengeance, and it is official policy not to take any of them alive, but if we don't allow them to attend then there is no chance of peace. I hope that they can be persuaded to see reason.'

Cato clicked his tongue. 'The Druids I knew were fanatics, sir. They would gladly die rather than give an inch to Rome.'

Ostorius turned to him with an irritated expression. 'As I told you before, Prefect, that was several years ago. Men change. Even the most determined of enemies can grow tired of killing each other and desire peace.'

'Most men, yes. But Druids?'

'This is the kind of thinking that you must put aside. That is why I am telling you this. There can be no misunderstanding between us, Prefect Cato. You will behave as I have said, to all who attend the meeting, including the Druids. No, especially the Druids. And that goes for the centurion as well. I will not have either of you cause any trouble. That is an order.'

'Yes, sir.'

'Good. The same applies to Caratacus, if he shows up. Or any who represent the Silures or the Ordovices.'

'I understand, sir.'

'Then be so good as to make sure that Centurion Macro does as well.'

With that the governor urged his horse forward to resume his position at the head of the small column. Cato watched him with a sense of misgiving. It seemed that Ostorius might be staking too much on his desire for peace. Even if he could persuade Caratacus to lay down his arms, Ostorius must know that the terms of such a peace would be unacceptable to Rome if they could be construed as a humbling of the Emperor and his legions. However much Cato shared the governor's desire for an end to hostilities, he feared that the most likely outcome was the continuation of the bitter struggle. Which would suit Macro nicely, Cato reflected with a grim smile. His friend thrived on it. Battle was as much his element as water was to a fish. It would be interesting to see how his friend coped with the governor's orders.

Cato reined in and waited for Macro and the legionaries to catch up. Macro seemed to have recovered from his hangover and was telling a story as he clutched a wineskin that one of the men had handed him.

'. . . and I said, "That's just too bad if she's only got one leg." And he didn't get it!'

The others roared with laughter as Cato fell in alongside his friend. 'That's an old one. Must be at least the tenth time I've heard it.'

'Jokes are like wine, they only improve with age,' Macro replied, and hitched his reins over the saddle horn so that he could lift the wineskin and have a quick swig.

'Is that wise?'

Macro smacked his lips and shrugged. 'Hair of the dog and all that.'

'I wonder what your dear mother would say.'

'You can't imagine. So what are you doing, slumming it back here with the squaddies?'

'Passing on orders from the governor. He wants us on our best behaviour in front of the locals. So I'd go easy on the wine if I were you.'

'Not a problem, I can handle it when I want to. Right now I'm just having a laugh with the lads. You can trust me to play my part when the time comes. Have I ever let you down before?'

'Not let down as such. You've got me involved with a few brawls in your time. There's a time and place for that. For now we have to be good boys. Model citizens.'

'If I wanted to be a model citizen I'd never have joined the army.'

'We're under orders, Macro. That's all there is to it.'

Macro nodded sullenly and dropped back to return the wineskin to its owner before he rejoined Cato, who was glancing warily from side to side as the column clopped through the eerie mist. Macro could not help an ironic snort.

'I just hope the tribes are as keen to win prizes for good behaviour. This would be a fine spot for an ambush. They could hit us from all sides before we knew it.'

'Thanks for the comforting thought.' Cato's eyes and ears were straining to pick up any suspicious movement or sound but there was nothing apart from muted conversation between the tribunes and the bodyguards and the steady, dull clopping of the horses. Above them the sky cleared a little and the sun appeared as a pale disc, providing light but little warmth.

Some hours passed and the sombre ambience was only briefly lifted as the road crested a low ridge before descending back into another valley and more mist. As the sun reached its zenith, the governor halted the column to rest the horses and allow his men a brief break from their saddles. Two of the legionaries trotted forward to hold the reins of the officers' horses while they stretched their legs.

Ostorius smiled at Cato. 'How does it feel to be back on British soil? There's no place in the empire like it for making the hairs stand up on the back of your neck, eh?'

Cato recalled that the mists and fogs of Britannia could wreath the landscape for days at a time, playing havoc with the imagination of some of the men. Not something that plagued Macro, of course, but it left Cato feeling tense and anxious. He was about to respond to Ostorius when he heard it. The faint sound of hoofs pounding along the track.

At once Ostorius's smile disappeared and he stepped off the road and looked back past his bodyguards standing silently by their mounts.

'Centurion Macro, get those men off the road. And that servant of yours. Half on each flank, fifty feet out, and wait for my order before you move. The rest of you, mount up and form up across the track.'

As the soldiers moved into position, Cato and the others swung themselves up into their saddles and formed a line across the track. Ostorius stood listening, and was the last man to mount, easing his horse forward so that it stood in the middle of the track a short distance in front of his officers. Cato saw the governor's left hand slip down to rest on the pommel of his sword as he waited. The sound of the approaching horses was much more distinct now and one of the junior tribunes at Cato's side cleared his throat nervously.

'How many of them, do you think?'

Cato was unsure who the question was aimed at but knew that the young officer needed reassurance. He had heard enough cavalry in his time to hazard a guess. 'No more than ten, I'd say.'

The tribune nodded and, following the example of his commander, he rested his hand on the pommel of his sword. Cato noticed the nervous tremor in the officer's fingers. He recalled his own fears in the early days of his army service when combat seemed imminent. The fear had gone, but he still suffered from the gnawing anxiety of letting his comrades down, Macro foremost. That and the terror of a crippling wound that would leave him as an object of pity and ridicule. Then his thoughts were distracted as his mount shied and tried to retreat from the line. He dug his heels in firmly and gritted his teeth as he struggled to still the brute and get it back into position. By the time that was done the sound of hoofs was much closer and then a shadowy form emerged from the gloom, and there was a shout an instant later, in a tribal tongue. The rider reined in abruptly and then there were several more, forming up on each side, and others behind.

A challenge sounded, in the same language, and Ostorius raised his left hand in greeting. 'Romans!'

There came a gruff muttering in response and then stillness and silence. A faint metallic scraping sounded close to Cato and he glanced aside to see the tribune's sword emerging from its scabbard.

'Put that back, you fool!' Cato hissed. 'We do nothing without an order from the governor.'

The tribune eased his blade down and the fingers of his hand clenched and unclenched.

'Advance and be recognised!' Ostorius called out. There was a tense pause before one of the Britons urged his horse forward and emerged from the mist, revealing a large man in a fur-trimmed cloak, beneath which mail gleamed dully. His hair fell across his shoulders and as he drew nearer, the governor lowered his hand and bowed his head in greeting. 'King Prasutagus.'

'Governor Ostorius,' came the deep, rumbling reply. 'I thought that it was maybe an ambush, for a moment.'

'Who would ambush you here, in territory we control?'

'We all have our enemies.' Prasutagus turned and beckoned to his retinue and they trotted forward to join their leader, as Ostorius called out to Macro and his bodyguards to return to the road. The Iceni riders looked round suspiciously as the legionaries appeared from both sides. The governor edged his mount forward and clasped arms with Prasutagus.

'I'd be honoured if you joined us for the rest of the journey to Durocornovium.'

'As would I, if you joined us.'

Ostorius was silent for an instant before he nodded. 'Very well, I should be pleased to accept your invitation.'

The tension eased and Cato heard the tribune next to him let out a long, low breath as he relaxed in his saddle.

Shortly afterwards the enlarged party of riders emerged from the mist as the track climbed gently up towards a more heavily used track running along the top of the chain of low ridges stretching away to the west. The overcast began to break up and the sun shone intermittently from patches of blue sky, causing shadows to glide across the landscape. The governor rode beside Prasutagus, occasionally attempting conversation. The Iceni warriors followed behind. Then came Queen Boudica with Cato and Macro on either side, and then the rest of the Romans.

'I had hoped we would catch you up,' she admitted. 'After last night's touchy atmosphere I wanted a chance to clear the air.'

Unlike her husband she had been taught the Roman tongue from a young age, by a merchant hired by her father who had foreseen the need to be able to converse with the great power that had reached the coastline of Gaul and stood poised to invade Britannia for so many years before taking the plunge.

'It's been such a long time,' she continued. 'But you've not changed much, Macro. Still the same handsome rogue.'

The centurion gave a non-committal grunt. It was a hard thing to re-encounter someone he had once had a physical relationship with. There had been affection too, but mostly it had been about raw desire. The situation was made more difficult by the presence of Prasutagus to whom Boudica had become betrothed the last time Macro had seen her. Now she was his wife, and he was a king. It was a bloody awkward situation and Macro was not sure how he should deal with it. There was no question of a return to their old ways. Equally, it was hard to treat her formally as befitted her new rank. Boudica's friendly approach now was not making the situation any easier.

'But you, Cato, you look every inch the seasoned veteran now, and that scar is quite fetching. It gives you a rather savage look.'

'That's what my wife says.'

'Married too! I shouldn't be surprised. Who is the lucky girl?'

'Her name is Julia.'

'And where is she?'

'In Rome.'

'Oh dear. That can't be easy for either of you. Why not bring her with you?'

Cato paused before he replied. He wanted to explain, to say that Julia was used to the comforts and luxuries provided by her father and that, in truth, he feared that she would resent being obliged to live in Britannia, with its inhospitable climate and even more inhospitable tribes. He cleared his throat. 'I would prefer Julia to remain where she is most content.'

'Really?' Boudica shot him a curious look. 'I would have thought that a wife would be most content at her husband's side.'

'It's different for Roman women.'

'Not so much fun, you mean.'

'They have a profound sense of duty. They are prepared to wait for their husbands to return from active service and keep the home ready for them.'

'Oh yes.' Boudica nodded. 'I can see why your Julia would prefer to do that. I mean, she wouldn't want to endure too much excitement in her life, would she?'

Cato bristled. He did not like this prying into his marriage. There were enough doubts already plaguing him on that front. He decided to turn the tables. 'So, what about you? Are you happy in your new role? Is Prasutagus?'

Boudica's smile faded and she turned to look ahead, at the broad shoulders of her husband riding at the head of the party. 'He became King only two years ago.'

'Lucky Prasutagus,' said Macro.

'Hardly. It was a choice between exile or accepting the title. Apart from being the placeman of Rome, Prasutagus has had to accept the presence of a line of forts along the frontier of our lands and give free passage to Roman patrols. Worse still, Ostorius has insisted that Prasutagus honour the debts of the old King, Bodominius, who had borrowed a fortune from Roman money-lenders. Now our people are taxed to the hilt to pay them back, and we are obliged to provide five hundred young men a year to serve in your auxiliary cohorts. I tell you, if this is how Rome means to treat the tribes of Britannia, it is only a matter of time before there is an all-out revolt.'

'The Iceni paid the price of defying Rome,' Macro said evenly. 'They were only one tribe. What could they hope to achieve?'

'The only tribe to rise up, yes. But not the only one with a sense of grievance. Our neighbours, the Trinovantes, have it even worse since the governor founded a veterans' colony at Camulodunum. Your men have been given the surrounding land and they have taken even more for themselves. Anyone who tries to complain is given a beating. Some have even been killed. Then there's the temple dedicated to Claudius that is being constructed in the heart of the town. I had no idea he was a god,' she sneered. 'He didn't look like much of a god when I saw him during his brief visit to Camulodunum.'

'Careful,' Cato warned. 'That kind of talk is dangerous if word gets back to Rome. Immortals have rather unpleasant ways of reminding others of their mortality.'

'That may be so, but threats tend to lose their sting if you push people too far. The Trinovantes are already aggrieved about having their land taken from them. But to make matters worse they are being taxed to pay for the construction of the temple. Can you imagine? Being bled white to provide the silver to pay for a monememt to your own oppression? If this is the Roman peace, then I fear your governor is going to have a hard time persuading the tribes of its value. I can see nothing good coming of this meeting.'

'Then why are you here? Why has Prasutagus accepted the invitation to the gathering of the tribes?'

'Invitation?' Boudica let out a bitter laugh. 'A summons is more the term I would use. As a master summons his slave, or his lapdog. We are here because the cost of not being here would earn the Iceni the further displeasure of your governor. I would imagine it is the same for the other tribes who are fortunate enough to be allies of Rome.'

'He seeks peace,' Cato insisted. 'Ostorius wants to put an end to the conflict in this province.'

She rounded on him with a glare. 'Don't you understand? I've just told you what peace means to those tribes already under the Roman yoke. And if that is, by some perversion of the meaning of the word, peace, then tell me, Cato, would you welcome it, if you were a native of this island?'

# CHAPTER EIGHT

As dusk gathered at the end of the third day's ride, the small company of Romans and Iceni left the road to Durocornovium and approached the outpost at Cunetio, some five miles from the sacred rings, where the gathering of the tribes was to take place. The small garrison comprised a half century of Gauls under the command of an optio who made his meagre quarters available for the governor while the rest of his men were ordered out of their barrack blocks to make way for the other visitors. The soldiers would be obliged to spend the night in the storerooms, or in the open. The optio had been briefed about the gathering and told to remain in the outpost and avoid any contact with any passing natives. Ostorius was leaving little to chance in his pursuit of an alternative to yet another season of bitter campaigning.

'We've done as ordered, sir,' the optio confirmed. 'The men haven't been out of the gates for the last five days.'

'Good. Have you seen any of the tribal delegations passing by?'

'Yes, sir. Plenty of 'em. And some of them as might be Druids.'

'You can tell?' Macro queried.

The optio thought briefly and nodded. 'The tribesmen wore bright colours. The others were in plain cloaks. Not many of 'em, mind. But they looked different, and kept themselves apart from anyone else on the road.'

Macro turned to Cato. 'Druids? Can't say I'm pleased at the prospect of another run-in with their kind.'

Ostorius rounded on them. 'There will be no run-in with the Druids, or anyone else. Is that clear? All who attend have been given free passage to and from the rings at Avibarius for a period of ten days. I'll have the head of anyone who causes any trouble for the duration of the truce.'

'Yes, sir.' Macro bowed his head in acknowledgement. 'But what if the other side doesn't abide by the arrangement? What are the rules of engagement?'

'None of our weapons are to be drawn except in self-defence, and only then if they draw theirs first,' Ostorius said firmly, staring round at all his officers. The Iceni had already occupied the barracks allotted to them and only a handful stood outside, looking on in silence as the governor addressed his men. 'If it should become necessary for us to fight then you will await my order before acting. The gods help any man who fails to obey my orders on this.'

He let his threat sink in before speaking again in a more moderate tone. 'All parties should have arrived by now. My translator, Marcommius, will ride on and confirm that is the case. If so, then the first meeting should take place tonight. As the site is sacred to the natives, we will wait here for word that they are ready for us to attend. After that, we are in the hands of the gods, gentlemen.'

Macro leaned closer to Cato and whispered, 'Yes, but whose gods, ours or theirs?'

'Until then,' Ostorius continued, 'I suggest you get some rest. You will need your wits about you tonight. Dismissed.'

While Ostorius strode towards the optio's quarters the tribunes and bodyguards moved away towards the entrance to their barrack block.

'Coming?' Macro asked. 'One of the bodyguards has a decent jar of wine. I said I'd play dice for it. Want to join me?'

Cato was torn. It would be a pleasant diversion to while away a few hours with Macro and the others, but at the same time he was a prefect, a difference in rank that neither he, nor the legionaries of the governor's bodyguard, could overlook, even off duty. He shook his head. 'I need a little time to think.'

Macro smiled. 'You're missing your woman again.'

'I miss her all the time, Macro. I suspect I will for a while yet.'

'You'll have plenty to distract you soon enough.' Macro punched him lightly on the shoulder and turned away to make for the door to the barracks. Once his friend had disappeared within, Cato climbed the outpost's watchtower and gazed west to where the sun dipped towards the rolling horizon. A few miles away, in that direction, lay the sacred stone rings, and close by, the encampments of those who had travelled from their tribal homelands. In amongst them, some Druids. Cato felt a shiver ripple down his spine as he recalled the Druids of the Dark Moon. He and Macro had fought against them the last time they were in Britannia. Fearsome and fanatic, there was no extreme of cruelty they did not embrace in the war against Rome. If they had chosen to join the meeting of the tribes then Cato was certain that they would be tireless in urging the others to destroy the legions, even those tribes who were presently allied to Rome. That was the real danger of the coming days, the possibility that Ostorius's bid for a peaceful settlement might end in a general uprising against the outnumbered and hard-pressed legionaries and auxiliaries of the army in Britannia. Most dangerous of all was the outside chance that Caratacus himself would appear before the tribes and talk them into joining him in the war against the invader. He shivered.

'Cold?'

Cato turned quickly and saw Boudica smiling at him from the top of the ladder. 'A bit. It's been a long day and I'm tired.'

Boudica continued up the last two steps and entered the watchtower, by which time Cato was in command of his nerves once more. She made her way to his side and followed the direction he had been looking at a moment earlier.

'It's going to be longer still, I think,' she said. 'And more tiring. I think Governor Ostorius is making a mistake. He should never have agreed to this. There are no promises he can make that will satisfy those tribes who are hostile to Rome, and certainly no promises which his masters in Rome will be willing to keep.'

Cato feared that she was right, but he did not doubt the sincerity of the governor's efforts to avoid further bloodshed. 'That may be so.'

'Then why are we here?'

Cato glanced round to make sure that his words would not be overheard. 'Because Ostorius is an old and sick man, worn out by the burdens of his office. What he wants more than anything is to go home to his family and enjoy the last measure of his life in peace and comfort. He may not survive another campaign season. I fear this place has broken him.'

'Then he should leave. And take his legions with him.'

Cato was surprised by the vehemence in her tone. There had been a more cordial atmosphere between the Iceni and the Romans over the last two days. 'You know that cannot happen.'

'Then we must all live with the consequences,' she responded quietly, then forced herself to smile. 'But enough of that. Old friends, old comrades, must put such thoughts aside. We have shared dangers, and pleasures, and that is a bond that is not lightly broken. Tell me, does Macro still resent my taking Prasutagus for my husband all those years ago? I tried to tell him at the time that I had little choice in the matter.'

'Macro is Macro. It is not in him to bear those sorts of grudges. He had a strong affection for you, certainly, but you pledged yourself to another man and he felt a passing sorrow and anger, and then put the matter behind him. That is how he chooses to live. So I doubt he harbours any ill will towards you, or Prasutagus.'

'I wish I could be so philosophical.'

Cato chuckled. 'I doubt it's a question of philosophy as far as Macro's concerned. If you really want to rub him up the wrong way, then call him a philosopher to his face.'

Boudica laughed briefly, then grew reflective. 'Still, I would like to think that his fondness for me was not cast aside quite so readily as you imply.'

Cato detected the regret in her voice and with a stab of guilt realised that he had never considered the prospect that his friend might inspire such feelings in Boudica. Macro was as fine a soldier as ever lived, and as loyal a friend. But he possessed few other qualities that Cato could imagine being of any attraction to a woman who did not earn her living on her back. He winced at the ignoble thought. Macro was his closest friend. He felt as close to him as a brother, or son.

A flare of light drew his attention towards a low ridge on the horizon where the molten glow of the sun was brilliant against a clear sky.

'Quite beautiful,' Boudica muttered.

'It is.' He nodded, but his mind was still working. The basis of a close friendship was impossible to define. And the same was true of love, it seemed. There was in Macro some ineffable quality that appealed to Boudica. Perhaps it was true of every person; they all possessed some quality of character that called out to its mate in another being . . .

'Look!' Boudica raised her hand and pointed to the west.

Cato thrust his introspection aside and saw a bright flicker in the gloom not far from the ridge behind which the sun had set. Then another appeared, and more until the wavering flames seemed to form a shallow ellipse, with a line leading off to the side. The fires had been seen by one of the garrison's sentries and he sounded the alarm, clattering the point of his javelin against a small bronze cauldron hanging beside the outpost's gate. A moment later the optio roused himself and bellowed at his soldiers to man the palisade. The door to the nearest barracks crashed open as Macro raced outside, crested helmet in one hand and mail armour hanging over his other arm. Behind him came the rest of the Romans, the last of them making way for Ostorius, just as Prasutagus and his warriors burst out of their quarters and scrambled up the turf inner wall and on to the boarded walk behind the sharpened stakes of the palisade. The sentry continued sounding the alarm a moment longer before Macro shouted to him.

'Shut that fucking racket up!'

As the last tuneless note died away, Macro lowered his helmet and struggled into his chain-mail vest. 'Make your report, man! What did you see?'

Before the sentry could reply, Cato drew a breath and called from the watchtower, 'Fires to the west!'

As the last of the men lined the palisade, Ostorius struggled on to the walkway, breathing heavily. The fires, scores of them now, were well enough established to be clearly visible and there was a hush before one of the junior tribunes spoke up. 'What is that? It looks like an army on the move.'

Ostorius coughed to clear his throat. 'That's Avibarius, I imagine.'

'Aye, Roman,' said Prasutagus, his deep voice carrying clearly. 'It

70

is.' He glanced up to the watchtower and frowned as he caught sight of his wife. A moment later the structure swayed slightly as the giant Iceni warrior climbed the ladder and then squeezed on to the platform alongside Cato and Boudica. There was a terse exchange in the Iceni tongue before Prasutagus eased himself between his wife and the prefect and stared towards the distant fires.

'The fires mark the boundary of sacred stones. As the sun dies, the fire gives light to the world. When priests give the order.'

'Priests?' Cato took in a sharp breath. 'You mean Druids.'

Prasutagus nodded.

Cato unconsciously raised his hand to touch his chest where a Druid had wounded him seven years before. There was only a scar there now, but suddenly he felt a chill on the flesh beneath the cloth of his tunic. 'What does it mean, Prasutagus?'

'They prepare the ground for the meeting. There are rituals they must perform, and sacrifices. To appease spirits and please our gods.'

'What kind of sacrifices?' Cato asked quietly but Prasutagus did not reply. He strained his eyes to try and make out more detail. At length he continued in his broken Latin.

'They send for us soon.'

'Already?'

The Iceni king shrugged. 'Why not? You have something else to do?' He glanced meaningfully at his wife.

Boudica scowled. 'We were talking about the last time we were together. The four of us, my King.'

'That was long time ago. Long time. Much has changed. You are my wife and Queen of the Iceni.'

'And what of friendship?' Cato asked. 'Has that changed?'

'Is a man a friend if he takes and takes, until he leaves nothing?'

Cato smiled. 'You are talking about Rome. What about Macro and me? What have we ever taken from you? Why should we not be friends, as we once were?'

Prasutagus raised his eyebrows in surprise as he answered. 'Because you are Romans.'

'There's some movement over there!' the junior tribune who had spoken earlier piped up. 'Horseman approaching.'

71

'Thank you, Tribune Decianus,' the governor replied tersely. 'I may be getting old, but I'm not blind.'

The outpost commander turned to him. 'What are your orders, sir?'

'Have your men stand to along the palisade. Let's look smart and alert, eh? The kind of soldiers who will never be taken by surprise.'

The optio smiled. 'Yes, sir.'

The governor turned to look up at Prasutagus. 'It might be a good idea if you and your retinue stayed out of sight, rather than looking as if you are here under my protection.'

Prasutagus gritted his teeth and growled, 'The Iceni need no protection.'

'Of course not,' Ostorius replied soothingly. 'It's just a question of form. Best not have any of your peers jumping to conclusions.'

Prasutagus hesitated a moment, then issued an order to his warriors and swung himself on to the ladder and began to descend from the tower. After a brief apologetic look, Boudica followed him. The tribesmen scrambled down to the base of the turf rampart and out of view of the horseman approaching the outpost. The soft thud of hoofs carried to the ears of those standing on the walkway and then the pace of the rider slowed. There was a tense silence as he made his way close enough to the outpost to address those within. Then the dim shadow stopped, fifty feet from the ditch, and a voice called out to them in a native tongue.

'Where's my damned interpreter?' Ostorius demanded in a low voice. 'Marcommius, on me, damn you. Quickly!'

The interpreter thrust his way past the tribunes to join the governor.

'What did he say?'

'He asks for you, sir.'

'Ask him how he knows that I am here?'

There was a brief exchange before Marcommius relayed the words. 'He says that we have been watched closely since we passed through Calleva, sir. Us and the Iceni contingent. The others have been waiting for us to arrive before the ceremonies began, sir. Now he asks us, and King Prasutagus, to follow him to the sacred rings.'

'Who is he?' Ostorius demanded. 'What is the fellow's name?'

Cato had a better view from the watchtower and could easily make out the dark robes and wild flowing hair of the rider. He already knew the answer even before the translator could reply to the governor.

'He's a Druid, sir. And he says his name is known only to his followers, as is their custom. And he, uh, requests that you bring your men and follow him now.'

'Requests? I suspect that he put it more forcefully than that. I need you to interpret as accurately as possible. Tell me the precise words he used and let me deal with the nuances.'

'Yes, sir.'

'Then tell him we will come at once.' Ostorius turned to his officers. 'Don't forget what I said. No man does, or says, anything without my express order.'

'What if anything happens to you, sir?' asked Tribune Decianus.

'In that event, I think you can rely on instinct.' Ostorius smiled wryly. 'The line of command is clear. If I fall, Prefect Cato will be the senior officer present. Look to him.'

Several of the men glanced up at Cato who was climbing down from the watchtower. Although he understood his duty well enough, the prospect of being thrust into command in what could only be a desperate situation caused him some anxiety.

The horses, used to the routine of being unsaddled at the end of the day and given their feed, whinnied and snorted in protest as their saddlecloths were replaced and then the heavy saddles and the rest of their tackle. Decimus saw to the mules, relieved that he would not have to ride out with his two masters. Night had fallen by the time the gates of the outpost opened and Ostorius led the column out to meet their Druid escort. The latter had not moved and now waited until Ostorius reined in a short distance from him. There was a pause, then the Druid clicked his tongue and walked his horse forward. Cato and Macro sat in their saddles a short distance behind the governor and his interpreter and could just make out the features of the Druid as he stared haughtily at Ostorius. Up close he appeared even more wild, and unworldly with his unkempt hair and dark robes.

'If he thinks that staring routine is going to scare me, then he'd better think again,' Macro said under his breath. 'If it weren't for orders, I'd have the bastard.'

'Early days, Macro,' Cato whispered. 'If I'm any judge of the situation, you'll get your chance.'

The Druid turned his attention from the governor and slowly rode down the column. Ostorius stared fixedly ahead, not willing to let the Druid's scrutiny unsettle him. As the latter passed beside Macro and Cato, Macro gave a broad wink and the Druid growled what sounded like a curse back at the Roman officer. He continued, passing the tribunes who were taking a lead from their commander and striving not to look anxious. Then the Druid stopped in front of Prasutagus and his retinue. There was a long silence and the Druid sniffed the air, before his nose wrinkled with distaste and he spat on the ground in front of the Iceni King. Then he spoke.

'What did he say?' Ostorius asked calmly.

'He said that the Iceni have been spending too long in the company of Romans. They are, ah, beginning to stink like Romans.'

Macro chuckled softly. 'That's rich. Coming from a bog-hopping, hairy-arsed barbarian.'

Cato glanced at him. 'Shhh . . .'

With a sudden, harsh cry the Druid wheeled his shaggy mount round and rode back to the head of the column. He gestured to Ostorius to follow him as he trotted away from the outpost towards the distant fires. The night air was filled with the thud of hoofs and the chink of the bits of the horses and the armour of the riders.

'He's going too fast,' Tribune Decianus complained. 'It's madness in this darkness.'

'If he can do it, then so must we,' Cato called back to him.

Soon the grass beneath gave way to the packed earth of a track and Cato realised they must have rejoined the route from Calleva, and his concern for the safety of their horses abated a little.

Ahead of them the track passed through a small wood before climbing to the crest of a low ridge. The Druid, more familiar with the track, had stopped to let them catch up and as Cato's mount slowed and crested the rise, he saw the sacred stones of Avibarius in the shallow vale below him. The spectacle caught his breath. An avenue of fires, half a mile long and some fifty feet wide, stretched across a levelled strip of ground. On either side he could make out the pillars of stone, lit a lurid red by the fires spaced between them. At the end of the avenue was a ring of earth, within which stood yet more stones, and more fires blazed from the top of the earth embankment. An open gateway stood at the point where the avenue pierced the earthworks and on the opposite side of the ring stood two monumental obelisks with a slab laid across their tops. Before it lay a large stone altar, barely visible even by the light of the flames, due to the blood that had stained it across uncounted years. A steady stream of figures was making its way down the avenue towards the gateway. The Druid gestured towards the near end of the avenue where hundreds of people and horses milled in an open area and urged his mount on.

They rode down a gentle slope and soon reached the throng, which instantly drew aside at the sight of the Druid, and those that followed him. As they made their way through the natives, Cato was aware of hundreds of eyes watching them pass. But there was no shout of greeting, or any cries of hostility hurled at the Roman governor and his retinue, just a silence that surrounded them as they rode towards the start of the avenue. There the Druid halted and slipped down from the back of his horse. Several boys darted forward to take the reins of the new arrivals and once the Roman governor and the others were ready, the Druid waved them on with a curt word of command and entered the avenue.

Most of those attending the meeting had already entered the ring and only the tail end of the earlier procession remained in the avenue of stone and fire. The Druid walked quickly but Ostorius led his men at a more sedate pace, refusing to hand the initiative to the Druid. As he looked back, the Druid saw that a gap had opened up and his teeth bared in anger. He stopped and waited, and then led at the pace set by the Romans. Cato was aware of figures on either side of them, barely visible as they watched from the fringe of the loom cast by the fires. The silence, and the spectacle of the setting, filled him with a sense of foreboding.

'I don't like this,' Macro muttered, his hand moving towards the handle of his sword before he was aware of it. He forced it back to his side. 'If there's trouble we'll be a long way from the horses, even if we did manage to fight our way out.'

'If there's trouble we won't even make it out of the ring,' said Cato.

'Thanks. You're going to be a real inspiration to the men of your cohort.'

'A bitter truth is better than the sweetest lie, my friend.'

'Pffftt!' Macro spat scornfully and then marched on in silence, keeping a wary watch on each side. At length they approached the gates to the ring and Cato saw that it was studded with what looked like large pearls. It was only as they got closer he realised that they were skulls hanging face down from nails.

'Oh, sweet Jupiter . . .' Decianus muttered. 'What is this place? A temple or a slaughterhouse?'

'A bit of both actually,' Marcommius answered him in an undertone. 'Our gods demand blood sacrifices from time to time.'

Decianus looked at the interpreter with a disgusted expression. 'Barbarians.'

'No one asked you to come here, Roman.'

'Then it's as well we did. Time to put an end to these atrocities.'

Ostorius looked back angrily. 'Quiet there! Keep your tongues still.'

They passed between the gates, fifteen feet high and made of oak. There must have been over a hundred skulls fixed to the timbers, Cato estimated, and he could almost sense the spirits of the dead looking on, sinister and hostile to those who came to Britannia unasked. The ring opened out before them, a hundred paces in diameter. The tribesmen who had already arrived had taken their places round the perimeter. The Druid pointed across the ring, to the left of the altar, where there was open ground, and spoke briefly to the interpreter.

'He says we are to stand there, sir. The Iceni are to stand by you.'

Ostorius nodded. 'Very well.'

Every face turned towards the last arrivals and watched them as they crossed the beaten earth at the heart of the sacred site.

'Are the mountain tribes here?' Cato asked Marcommius. 'The Ordovices and the Silures?'

76

The interpreter scanned the tribesmen lining the ring. Cato had noted the subtle differences in clothing and hair styling between the groups.

Marcommius shook his head. 'And no sign of Caratacus either. Hardly surprising, given how badly you Romans want to get your hands on him.'

'The governor gave his word that all would be given safe conduct. Even Caratacus.'

'Such guarantees are easily broken.'

Cato looked at Ostorius. 'Not by some Romans, at least.'

A figure emerged from between the stone pillars behind the altar. Robed in black from shoulder to toes, the Druid wore a leather headpiece from which a set of antlers protruded like the bare branches of a tree in winter. As the Romans and the Iceni took their places, the Druid who had brought them here hurried to join the others standing beside the altar. There was a silence before the antlered figure stepped up to the altar and slowly raised his hands into the air, fingers spread so that his untrimmed nails looked like claws in the red hue of the fires burning on top of the earth rampart. Then he spoke, or rather chanted, in a high-pitched sing-song, and at intervals the other Druids joined in.

'What are they saying?' Macro whispered to Marcommius.

'It is a prayer that all who are gathered here show wisdom, and do the will of the gods of their tribes. The High Druid asks that the spirits of the gods speak through us . . . He asks this in return for the offering.'

Cato turned to him. 'What offering?'

Before Marcommius could reply, another figure emerged from between the pillars, a boy, barely into his teens, clad in a white robe with a garland of mistletoe about his neck. His eyes were wide and his lips trembled as he walked slowly towards the altar.

# CHAPTER NINE

Behind the boy walked a man in a richly patterned cloak. He rested one hand on the boy's shoulder and the other hung limply at his side. He struggled to contain his grief. When the boy reached the altar, the man stepped forward and kissed him tenderly on the top of his head and was still for a moment before the High Druid snapped a word of command. The man shrank away in fear, his mouth opened to cry out to the boy. But no sound came, and then two Druids took him by the arms and held him in place.

'What in Hades' name is going on?' Macro growled. 'This better not be what I think it is. Marcommius, tell me.'

'This is the sacrifice demanded by the gods. An unblemished child. The man is his father.'

'What? What father would play any part in this fucking horror show?'

'It is an honour to be chosen, Roman. See, the boy goes quite willingly. And the father will be held in respect by his people when it's all over.'

'How could any man be respected for leading his son to the slaughter?'

There was genuine anger and outrage in Macro's voice and Cato knew his friend well enough to fear that he would charge forward at any moment to put a stop to the ritual, with no thought to the consequences.

'Macro, for pity's sake, control yourself.' Cato clamped his fingers round the wrist of the centurion's sword arm. 'There's nothing we can do. We cannot change what is going to happen.'

'We'll see about that!' Macro snarled, shaking off his grip.

'No.' Cato stood in front of his friend, blocking Macro's view of the altar. 'Stand your ground. That is an order.'

Macro looked at him with a shocked expression. 'An order? Cato . . . lad, you can't be serious.'

There was a sick feeling wrenching at Cato's guts as he heard the pleading tone in his friend's voice. Part of him wanted to tell Macro he understood – he shared – his revulsion and a desire to stop this macabre ceremony. But there was also the soldier in him, the man who obeyed orders. But it was the need to protect Macro that decided him. He turned to two of the bodyguards.

'Hold him. If he struggles, or shouts out, knock him senseless.'

One of the legionaries shook his head. 'Sir?'

'Do as you are ordered!' Cato snapped fiercely. 'Do it! Before he gets us all killed.'

The legionaries quickly grabbed Macro and held him firm, though he was too shocked to react at first. Instead he stared at Cato. 'Why?'

'We cannot save the boy.'

'What's going on here?' Ostorius demanded as he edged through his men towards the commotion. The legionaries' attention was broken and Macro pulled himself free. The governor ordered in a low voice, 'Shut your mouths and stand still, damn you. Prefect, speak up, man. What in Hades' name is happening?'

Cato turned towards his superior. 'It's sorted out, sir. Isn't that right, Macro?'

Cato's eyes pleaded with his friend and Macro glared back for a moment before he lowered his head and his shoulders drooped in despair. Cato turned about, so that his back would be in Macro's way. The boy was struggling to climb on to the altar, whether because he was too scared or too weak, Cato could not tell. The High Druid stepped forward, grasped the boy by the waist and heaved him on to the top of the altar before forcefully pressing him down, his arms outstretched. The Druid turned the boy's head to the side so that he was facing into the heart of the ring, and then raised his own arms to the heavens, tilting his antlered head back as he chanted. The sound of his voice was rich and melodic and he delivered his words with a steady cadence. A phrase was repeated, and the other Druids joined in, and then the rest of the tribesmen followed – even the boy as he lay on the altar, eyes wide as his lips moved as if they had a will of their own. The volume steadily rose until the chant was deafening and Cato felt as if his ears were being assaulted by the din driving into his skull, his body and his bones until he felt almost consumed by the rhythm.

Then, when it seemed that the chant could not get any louder, the high priest bent and rose up with a narrow-bladed dagger clutched in both hands. He raised it slowly and the polished steel of the blade reflected the glitter of the flames. All eyes were fixed on the spectacle being played out at the altar. Cato glanced at Macro and saw the clenched jaw and his left hand tightly clutching his right fist as if to stop it creeping towards the handle of his sword. As Cato's eyes turned back towards the altar, the chanting stopped abruptly, as if the breath had been torn from the lungs of every one of the natives at precisely the same instant. The silence was as awe-inspiring as the sound had been a moment before and there was only the soft distant rustle of a light breeze and the faint crackle of the fires.

With a shrill, inhuman scream the High Druid stabbed his blade down with all his savage strength. The point plunged into the white tunic over the boy's heart with such force that his arms and legs jerked wildly and the air exploded from his lungs with a half cry, half grunt. Then his head snapped back, jaw agape as he screamed briefly and writhed beneath the dagger that pinned him to the altar. The blood quickly soaked through the cloth and pooled on the stone surface before a dark stain began to trickle over the edge and streak down the side of the altar. Then the boy was still and the natives whispered a sibilant sound to mark his death. 'Sa . . . sa . . . sa.'

'Sick bastards,' Macro groaned through his teeth. 'Sick, savage fucks.'

Cato hissed a warning. As the people round the ring looked on, the High Druid set to work with his knife, opening up the dead boy's chest, and Cato could see wisps of steam curling into the chilly air. Then the Druid leaned forward and dipped a hand in and wrenched out a bloody lump of flesh and examined it closely. The boy's heart, Cato realised, and his throat tightened with nausea. After a lengthy delay, the Druid lowered the organ and looked round his audience before he made an announcement. There was an audible sigh of relief from the tribespeople.

'The High Druid says that the heart is good and strong and will make a fine offering to the gods,' Marcommius explained to the Romans in a hushed voice. The Druid turned to a small brazier burning close by the altar and tossed the heart into the flames. The fire instantly flared brightly and a large cloud of smoke billowed into the night sky. Some sleight of hand, Cato reasoned. The Druid had somehow thrown something in with the heart. Still, the effect was impressive and certainly had an impact on the audience who had instinctively flinched at the brief burst of light. Then he realised that the High Druid had disappeared at the same time, just as if the ground had swallowed him up. There was an anxious muttering before the Druid who had escorted the Romans and Iceni to the rings stepped forward and raised his hands to quiet the crowd.

'He says the meeting of the tribes can begin.'

The governor nodded and stood ready as the Druid continued to address the crowd and Marcommius interpreted.

'He says that you have asked them here to discuss terms for a lasting peace between Rome and the tribal kingdoms of Britannia. Some tribes have already pledged their allegiance to Rome, while a handful still offer resistance. Even without Rome, there are grievances between a number of tribes that had been the cause of long feuds and conflicts. He reminds those who have gathered here that this is the consecrated ground of the Druids and only they have the right to shed blood within the ring. Furthermore, Rome has pledged to give free passage to all who gather here, ally and enemy alike, and there are to be no fights or honour challenges for the duration of the meeting. Any who break these terms do great dishonour to themselves and their people and will surely reap the wrath of the gods as a result. If any of those present refuse to accept these conditions, they are free to go . . .'

The Druid fell silent and waited for a response, but none came, and no one moved.

'Very well. Then I welcome the governor of that part of our lands presently called the province of Britannia to address the tribes.'

The Druid bowed his head to Ostorius and backed away to the side of the altar. The governor gestured to his interpreter to attend him and walked steadily into the centre of the ring. There was no sound as he reached his position and stopped, and stared round at the faces watching him. There were no cries of support or jeers or shouts of anger. Just silence. Ostorius cleared his throat and began to speak, and his interpreter broke into the rhythmic delivery of the Celtic tongue to convey his meaning to the gathering.

'I am Ostorius Scapula, praetor of Rome, governor of Britannia and commander of all land and naval forces currently based on the island. I bid you welcome. All of you. Even those who represent the Silures and the Ordovices, sworn enemies of Rome and all that Rome stands for.' The governor paused for a moment. 'It has been nearly eight years since the legions landed on these shores. Within the first months we had defeated the most formidable army that the tribes could concentrate against us under the command of Caratacus. Not just once, but three times. Since then nothing has stood before the might of Rome. Not your armies, brave as your warriors are. Nor your hill forts, formidable as they must once have seemed to your eyes. You cannot beat us in battle, no matter how courageous you are. Our soldiers are better trained and better equipped. They have triumphed over the finest warriors of Carthage, Greece and Gaul. We have fought across the tallest mountains, penetrated the darkest forests of Germania and no river has been so fast flowing or wide that we have not thrown a bridge across it in a matter of days. Nothing stands in our way, however long it may take. Once our emperors have given the order, there can only be one outcome: victory. That is the way it is. Rome is good at war. The cost of defying us is to have your towns, villages and farms burned to the ground. Your warriors slaughtered, your women and children led off in chains to become slaves . . . Yet, as we are good at war, so we are good at peace. Rome brings order and wealth for those who embrace us as allies and accept our protections. Yes, there are taxes. But that is the price of living in peace. Accept our laws, our ways, and in time you will come to understand that the Roman way is your future and in your best interests.'

A warrior stepped forward from one of the tribal contingents, a tall, powerfully built figure. He spoke bitterly, stabbing his finger at the governor to drive home his point.

'That's Venutius, of the Brigantes,' said the interpreter. 'Husband of Queen Cartimandua.'

'Then he's the king?'

'No, sir. The queen rules the tribe. He is her consort, and does not share her liking of Rome.'

'I see. And what does the consort have to say?'

'He is angry at the effrontery of your words. That you should tell the tribes to adopt Roman ways, here on the ground that has been sacred to the tribes from time beyond memory. He accuses you of forcing us to give up our gods.'

Venutius's words had provoked angry muttering and Ostorius raised his hand and called for silence. Once the muttering died away he spoke again through his interpreter.

'Rome has no intention of taking away your gods, or your sacred sites. You are free to hold to your beliefs. Or choose ours, as you will. You can embrace our ways or live much as you do now. That is your choice. But you must learn to live under our rule and our laws. It is a small price to pay for an end to the bitter conflict of recent years. And before that, the continual raids and small wars that raged between your tribes.'

Venutius listened to the words and responded immediately, in the same angry tone as before.

'He says that is the way of the tribes. How else is a warrior supposed to prove himself? He must show his courage and his skill in battle. If you take that away from him then you take away his purpose in life.'

Ostorius replied firmly. 'Then the warriors must find a new purpose. They must learn to be farmers, or they can volunteer to serve Rome in the ranks of our auxiliary forces. That is their only future. You must accept the truth. Your warriors must give up the old ways, or die in battle against the legions.'

Venutius laughed harshly.

'He says you give him no choice.'

'On the contrary. I am offering him the choice between life or certain death.'

When the governor's words were translated there were cries of protest and angry shouts from around the circle and Cato feared that his superior was in danger of pushing the tribal leaders too far. Then another man emerged into the open. He raised his hand and commanded the attention of the others. He was solidly built but had run to fat and his jowls hung heavily, fringed with a neatly trimmed beard. Though he was clad in a woven cloak and leggings, beneath he wore a Roman-style tunic and his hair was cut much shorter than the other natives. He strode confidently into the middle of the ring and waited until he had silence before he addressed the gathering.

'Who in Hades' name is that clown?' asked Macro.

'I can guess,' said Cato. 'Cogidubnus, of the Regni.'

'The one who sold out to us even before the first boot was planted on British soil?'

'That's the one.'

Macro saw the looks of contempt on the faces of many of the other natives. 'I can't help wishing he wasn't speaking up for our side.'

The man in the centre of the ring spoke with a clear, deep voice as his words were translated. 'First I would like to offer my sincere gratitude to the governor for offering us this chance to make a lasting peace . . . You all know me. I am King Cogidubnus. I wish to speak plainly, to speak the truth. I too was raised as a warrior, and have led my men into battle. I have no need to prove my worth to back up my words. I come here to support the arguments of Governor Ostorius Scapula. Rome has indeed proved a mighty friend and ally to me and my people. I can swear to the fact that we have profited from the coming of Rome and what is true for the Regni can be true for any tribe that accepts the hand of friendship extended by the governor.'

'Traitor!' a voice called out in Latin, and then repeated the cry in the native dialect.

Cogidubnus frowned as he, and everyone else, turned towards the source of the accusation. There was movement in the native ranks and then a large warrior thrust his way to the front. He wore a hooded cloak and drew it back to reveal his long fair hair. At once there was a chorus of excited muttering. Marcommius shook his head in surprise.

'Caratacus . . .'

# CHAPTER TEN

The old enemy of Rome strode forward and stopped a sword's length from Cogidubnus. He scrutinised the King of the Regni with contempt, his fists resting on his hips. Then he spoke, his voice carrying clearly to the fringes of the crowd as Marcommius translated for the Romans.

'You have profited all right. All of us know about the fine palace the Romans are building for you. A luxury kennel for the Emperor's favourite lapdog. That's what you are. A mongrel, half Briton and half Roman, begging for fancy tidbits from the table of your master. You have sold your honour for fripperies, Cogidubnus, to your eternal shame.'

Cogidubnus opened his mouth to protest, but the other man took a menacing step towards him and he wilted, backing away towards his contingent. Caratacus glared at him for a moment, before making a sweeping gesture with his hand, as if swatting away an irritating insect before he addressed the crowd.

'You all know me. You all know that I have fought against the Romans from the first. I have never given in to the enemy, *our* enemy. It is for our freedom that I have fought so long. While the eagle standards of the legions fly over our lands we can only be slaves. That is the way of it. The Roman governor says that we must change. We must forget who we are and become part of the Roman empire. Is it so easy to give up all that we are?' He pressed his hand against his chest. 'I am Caratacus, King of the Catuvellauni. Even though my kingdom no longer exists, I carry it here in my heart. My people, our history, all the honour that we have won in battle, all here in my heart, and I live for the day when the Romans are thrown back into the sea, as they were before when their great general, Julius Caesar, first attempted to steal our land. That day will come, I believe it as surely as I believe in our gods.' He thrust his finger at Ostorius. 'The Roman governor tells us we must give up the old ways, or die in battle. He offers us a simple choice between saving our honour or submitting to slavery, like dogs. I have chosen honour and freedom!'

He paused to let his words have their effect. Some in the crowd cheered him, but many looked on in silence as he continued.

'The governor tells us that our struggle can only end in our defeat. It is true that we were defeated in the early battles, but our will to resist lives on. For long years we have defied Rome. We have forsaken the battlefield for a different kind of warfare. We have attacked their outposts, burned their supplies and picked off their patrols. Slowly but surely we are eating away at the mighty Roman legions, consuming them a piece at a time. All the while, we have been gathering our strength and taking ever more bold action against our common enemy. In token of which, I give you this.'

He turned and waved a signal to the Silurians. Some men came forward, two holding a third who had the hood of his cloak up. The man stumbled, as if he was drunk, and the others held him up and half dragged him across to the centre of the ring amid the silence of all watching. The three men stopped before Caratacus, who leaned forward and flipped the hood back to reveal a mop of dark curly hair above a thin, drawn face within which there were two darkened and scarred patches where the eyes had been. As he felt his hood being removed, the man shuddered and opened his mouth and let out a guttural animal moan of panic.

'They've cut his tongue out,' said Macro. 'Whoever he is.'

Cato swallowed. 'We'll know soon enough.'

Caratacus gave the order for the man to be released and then he thrust him forward so that he staggered a few steps and fell on to his hands and knees with a muffled squawk of pain and then felt his way forward across the hard-packed soil, crawling away from the harsh laughter of Caratacus and his companions. The enemy leader turned to face Ostorius and his retinue and made a flourishing gesture.

'I return him to you. We took him prisoner a few months ago,

86

along with some others who have since been disposed of. This man was passed from village to village and sorely abused in the process. A pity, since I am certain he would have had a promising future. But it was necessary to prove that the men of the legions are flesh and blood like the rest of us, and just as easily broken. Even men like your Centurion Quertus who we will deal with in due course. For now, we have grown tired of using this tribune for our amusement and it is time for him to rejoin his comrades. Isn't that right, Tribune Marcellus?'

He strode up behind the helpless captive and with his boot he shoved the man towards the governor so that he collapsed on to his face. A ripple of cruel laughter sounded from certain sections of the gathered tribes. Others looked on in shock, fearing the inevitable wrath of the Romans when they reacted to this outrage. Governor Ostorius pressed his lips together as he fought to control his anger. Then he turned back to his men and spoke in a quiet cold voice. 'Pick him up. Get him out of here.'

Macro was the first to move, striding forward, jaw clenched, and Cato followed him. The centurion leaned down and gently took the tribune's arm. The other man flinched and instinctively recoiled with a meaningless croak.

'Let's get you up on your feet, sir,' Macro said evenly, even as he felt sick to his core at the ruined features of the face that turned blindly towards him. Cato took his other arm and between them they lifted Marcellus up and led him towards the other tribunes and the bodyguards, who looked aghast.

'It's all over now, sir,' Macro continued. 'You're back with your own kind.'

Cato gestured to two of the bodyguards. 'Over here. Take care of the tribune. Get him to the outpost at once and see that his wounds are treated and he is fed.'

The legionary nodded as he and his comrade took over from the two officers and led the tribune away round the periphery of the circle. Macro watched them for a moment before he muttered, 'If that ever happens to me, then swear you'll cut my throat.'

'And answer to your mother?'

Macro turned to his friend with a dark expression. 'You'll be sparing her as much as me, Cato. Promise me.'

Cato nodded. 'As you wish.'

'Swear it!'

Cato was surprised by the intense glare in Macro's eyes. 'I swear it, on my life.'

Macro let out a deep breath. 'And I'll do the same for you.'

Cato cocked an eyebrow at Macro's readiness to end his life. Then the image of the tribune's ruined face filled his mind and he felt an icy squirm in the pit of his stomach as he imagined himself in the tribune's place, returning home crippled and useless, and the looks of horror, disgust and pity that would distort Julia's face when she saw him. Not that he would see it. But he would hear it in her voice. Perhaps there was a woman waiting for Marcellus in Rome, he reflected, doomed to endure for real what he was only imagining.

Caratacus had allowed his moment of theatre to play out, standing to one side. Now he occupied the centre of the circle again and continued to address the gathering.

'The tribune was in command of nearly a thousand legionaries. All were killed or captured in just one raid. If such a powerful column can be overwhelmed then I find it hard to share the governor's certainty that Rome will win this conflict. There is not one outpost on the frontier with the lands of the Silures and Ordovices that is safe from my army, not one supply convoy; nor are any of the roads safe for Romans and their allies to travel on. This is how it will be from now, until the day that we have worn away our enemy's will to continue the fight. Even mighty Rome cannot endure steady losses of men and morale forever. And I say to you all that our will to defend our homeland and fight for our liberty is greater than their will to conquer! In the end victory will be ours . . .'

He glared defiantly at Ostorius as those who followed him cheered. Looking round, Cato could see that, in addition to the mountain tribes, some of the Brigantes were joining in, as well as warriors from the other northern and western tribes of the island. The governor stepped forward to confront Caratacus and the cheering slowly died away. When Ostorius spoke, there was no trace of the reasonable tone he had used earlier. His voice was cold and ruthless.

'Your torment of one of my officers will not go unpunished. From now on, I will execute ten of your followers for every man of mine that you kill or take prisoner. The same holds true for any other tribe foolish enough to join your ill-fated cause. I can see now that my offer of peace was a wasted effort. The time for talking is over. Instead I swear an oath now, on my life, and by all the gods that I worship, that I will not rest until you are defeated and taken, together with your family, to Rome, where the humiliation you visited upon Tribune Marcellus will be repaid tenfold upon you and those who share your blood. Furthermore, I swear that I shall not rest until the mountain tribes are crushed. The Ordovices and Silures will be utterly erased. Only memory of them will endure, as a reminder to every other tribe on this island of the cost of defying Rome.'

'That's told the bastard,' Macro nodded approvingly.

Caratacus laughed. 'Swear what you like, Roman. It changes nothing. We will continue to defy you, and kill your men, until your spirit breaks.'

Before Ostorius could respond, another figure entered the debate. Prasutagus stepped forward and waited for silence before he spoke. Marcommius listened to the opening phrase and translated for the Roman officers.

'The Iceni King says that there has been enough bloodshed already. Too many have died on both sides. It is time to put an end to conflict. He says it is true that the Roman peace comes at a price, but that price, onerous as it is for the present, is better than the continued suffering of those caught up in the struggle against Rome. He knows from personal experience the quality of the men of the legions. He has fought at their side and knows they cannot be beaten, and they will never give in until they have achieved victory.' As he interpreted, Marcommius shifted his words to the first person. 'I beg you, Caratacus, to seize this chance to put down your sword and embrace peace, and follow the example of the Iceni.'

'Follow your example?' Caratacus snorted with derision. 'You, who became King only after the last noble with the balls to resist Rome had been cut down? And how long did it take the brave Iceni to turn on the Romans in the first place? Years after they had sold their souls to the Emperor in exchange for his silver coin. Too late did your people learn the cost of their perfidy. Too late to help us when we first faced the legions. Too late to make a difference when it counted. And now you live under the heel of the Roman boot. Just like the spineless Trinovantes who now play unwilling host to a veterans' colony and are squeezed for every last coin in tax to pay for the cost of a temple in honour of Emperor Claudius. So much for leaving us free to worship the gods we choose to!' He lowered his voice marginally. 'Prasutagus, your people suffer from the same burden. Your warriors have been forced to surrender their weapons. You stand defenceless before the will of Rome. What is to stop them treating you like slaves? You think the Iceni will endure the situation forever? One day they will have had enough and they will rise up. On that day they will see your treachery clearly. You say that you want to save lives and have peace. The truth is that you had to choose between dishonour and war. You chose dishonour . . . and you will have war. As surely as night follows day.' He turned to point his finger accusingly at all the rulers and their tribes who had made treaties with Rome. 'When your warriors and tribesmen have had their fill of Roman peace they will sweep you away like chaff. You will perish in the flames, alongside your Roman friends. Think on it! If you come to your senses, then seek me out in the mountains.'

He stared defiantly at the assembled rulers and then approached Ostorius and his officers and spoke in Latin. His accent had much improved since he had summoned Cato to his hut many years before.

'The war continues. You cannot defeat us. Save yourselves and quit this island. Only then can we have peace. The peace that exists between equals.'

Ostorius shook his head. 'I have my orders. The Emperor has spoken and his word is law. Britannia will become a part of the empire.'

'Then there is no more to be said.' Caratacus looked at the officers standing behind Ostorius. 'Take heed, you will end up like your governor. Old and exhausted in pursuit of the impossible. Britannia will be your grave.' He paused as his gaze fell on Cato and frowned. 'I know you . . .'

'We met once before, sir. When I was your prisoner. Back when we fought in the marshes to the west.'

The enemy commander thought a moment and then his eyes widened as he recalled. 'Yes! You seemed much younger then. Now you are scarred and marked by the years of war you have endured.'

'As are you.'

Caratacus smiled briefly. 'You can't imagine. As I recall, when you were my prisoner we talked at length.'

'We did, sir. I hoped to persuade you to give up the struggle.'

'And here we are, years later. You are older but no wiser, it seems.'

It was Cato's turn to smile. 'I was thinking the same thing about you, sir.'

Caratacus's expression was fixed for a moment before he smiled sadly. He clasped Cato's forearm. 'Well said. It is a pity that we should be enemies.'

'Then let us not be enemies, sir.'

'It is too late for that. Rome should have treated us as partners, rather than try to be our masters. If we ever meet in battle, I shall kill you without pity or regret.'

Cato pursed his lips. 'Perhaps. Or maybe the next time we meet, you will be my prisoner.'

Caratacus's expression darkened. He released Cato's arm and strode back across the ring towards the gateway, summoning his followers. Macro watched him leave and then muttered to his friend, 'It seems that the time for talking is over. Now we've got a fight to the finish on our hands.'

Cato said heavily, 'There was never going to be any real negotiation. It was already too late. Caratacus wants a war, and Ostorius is all too willing to give him one. This was all a waste of time. Now it's about to become a waste of good men.'

# CHAPTER ELEVEN

As soon as the governor and his party returned to the outpost he dismissed his bodyguards and retired into the optio's cramped quarters to confer with his officers. The meeting with the tribes had been far shorter than Ostorius had anticipated and there was no prospect of it being resumed the following day. After Caratacus and the Romans had withdrawn, several other contingents had followed suit, some setting off immediately for their homelands even though night had fallen. It was clear that any attempt to agree terms for peace across the island had failed.

'If Caratacus wants to continue the war then he shall have it,' Ostorius announced to his officers as they crowded round the small table which, together with a stool and bed, constituted the only furniture. 'I shall not be returning to Londinium but making for the army headquarters at Cornoviorum at first light. Decianus, you will ride back to Londinium and inform the staff of my decision. They are to pack up and join me as soon as possible. Send word to the commanders of the Ninth and Second Legions that I shall be commencing the campaign as early as possible, and they will be responsible for ensuring the security of the province behind the frontier zone. Prefect Cato, you and Macro will ride to Glevum and report to Legate Quintatus.'

'Yes, sir.'

'Gentlemen, my plans are made, it only remains to put them into effect as swiftly and fully as possible. There will be no mercy shown to those who side with Caratacus. My orders are that there is no requirement to take prisoners. Such women and children as are spared will be marched to the rear and sold to the slave contractors at the depots. All hostile settlements we encounter are to be torched and razed. I meant what I said earlier. Those who take up arms against Rome are to be crushed. Is that quite clear?'

His officers nodded.

'Then you had best retire for the night and get what sleep you can. That's going to be something of a luxury in the days ahead. Dismissed.'

The officers saluted and filed out of the room into the darkness. Macro saw that the small garrison was under arms and spread out along the palisade. The optio must have spoken to some of the governor's bodyguards and heard what had taken place in the sacred ring. He was taking no chances and had ordered his men to keep watch through the night. The legionaries of the bodyguard had settled round the garrison's cooking fire and were warming themselves as they muttered in low, anxious tones about what they had witnessed. To one side Decimus was carefully bathing the wounds of Marcellus. The tribune had stripped to his loincloth and was carefully spooning gruel into his mouth and making a gurgling noise as he struggled to swallow. As he ate, the servant washed the grime from his pitifully emaciated body, revealing the bruises and cuts that told of the brutal treatment the tribune had been subjected to.

'What will become of that poor sod?' Macro wondered.

'I am sure he has family in Rome. They will care for him, as best they can.'

Macro stared a moment longer. 'It would have been kinder to kill him. Fucking barbarians. No better than animals.'

'Maybe, but they're clever. Everyone who sees Marcellus on his journey home is going to learn what happens to those soldiers captured by the enemy and it's going to shake them. Even more so back in Rome, far from the battlefield. A mutilated young aristocrat is going to be something of a talking point. It may add weight to the words of those arguing that we should not expand our territory in Britannia, and even abandon the province altogether. Caratacus knows how to make his point eloquently, and ensure that it is rammed home as deeply as possible. Killing Marcellus would have been a wasted opportunity.'

Macro stared at his friend. 'By the gods, you're as cold-hearted as he is.'

'No, I just understand the thinking behind his deeds. My only worry is that Ostorius may be playing into the enemy's hands. If he brings fire and sword to the mountain tribes, he may turn some of the others against us. There's a wider problem too. If our men get used to treating the natives harshly, it's going to be hard to rein them in when they are redeployed after the campaign. That's assuming we manage to hunt down Caratacus and force him to turn and fight.'

'I was under the impression that he was spoiling for a fight,' Macro replied. 'He made a bloody great song and dance about defeating Marcellus's column, and how it was only the beginning.'

'Yes, he did. So perhaps that's the impression he is keen to give us.'

Macro sighed irritably. 'And what exactly do you think he intends, then?'

'I'm not certain. If we strike deep into the mountains looking for his army, or his main stronghold, then we'll be stretching our lines of communication, and leaving them vulnerable to raids. Looks to me like he's reverting to his old tactics. Luring us on, only to strike at our rear. He's certainly succeeded in goading Ostorius.'

'Or he's getting over-confident and looking for a set-piece battle on favourable terms.'

Cato shrugged doubtfully. 'There's a further possibility.'

'Which is?' Macro queried with forced patience.

'The show he put on was as much for his own followers as us. He's fighting a long war. It's going to stretch the resources and will of his own followers as much as our side. And whereas our soldiers have discipline, the tribesmen need to be inspired to fight. I wonder how far Caratacus can depend on them. As long as he presents them with victories they will stand by him. If we grind them down then he's going to be forced to fight a battle while he still has enough men prepared to follow his standard.'

'Then let's hope that's what happens. I don't fancy spending the next few years chasing shadows through mountains and forests.'

'Quite.' Cato reflected for a moment. 'At least one of our officers appears to have the right idea. That centurion Quertus has made his mark on Caratacus. Sounds like a good man to have around when I take command of the Thracians.'

Macro scratched his chin. 'Quertus might not be so pleased about it. He's making a name for himself, and then you fetch up. Could be a difficult situation.'

'Not if he's half the officer you are, Macro.' Cato stretched his shoulders and yawned. 'Better get some rest.'

They retrieved their saddlebags from the stable and made their way across to their quarters. Inside the small barrack block a single oil lamp provided just enough light to see. The tribunes had already settled down on their bedrolls, wrapped in their thick military cloaks. A handful were still awake as Macro and Cato picked their way over to the far corner and laid out their thin rolls of coarse cloth stuffed with horsehair.

'I'm telling you,' Decianus was muttering to his companions. 'This campaign is going to be a disaster. These people are savages. No better than wild animals . . .'

There was a pause before another tribune replied, 'I don't want to end up like Marcellus.'

'We should leave the bastards to their mountains,' Decianus continued. 'Build a line of forts and hem them in. That would be best.'

Macro eased himself down on to his bedroll and cleared his throat. 'Tribune, if you don't mind, I'd like to get to sleep. It ain't easy if you're going to sit there all night scaring the women.'

In the gloom, Cato could just make out the tribune opening his mouth to respond, then thinking better of it. Instead he lay down and pulled his cloak up to his chin and fell silent. Macro tutted gently and then shuffled into a comfortable position and a moment later began to snore lightly. Cato knew that there would only be a brief opportunity to get to sleep before Macro began snoring in earnest. He had taught himself a trick on their journey from Rome to clear his mind and drift off. He imagined building a small villa in the Alban Hills close to Rome. Room by room. Before he got as far as the triclinium he was asleep. However, if he ever came to that part, then he knew that a troubled night lay ahead . . . A long day in the saddle and the nervous strain of the assembly took their toll and Cato was asleep even before he had completed the atrium, and thankfully, long before Macro's deep rumbling filled the room, disturbing the slumber of the more anxious of the tribunes huddled along the far wall.

It was more than half a day's hard ride to Glevum where the governor and his retinue continued north along the road to Cornoviorum. As they reined in at the top of a gentle slope, Cato, Macro and Decimus surveyed the scene below them. The Fourteenth Legion had constructed a large fortress on low ground close to the River Severnus and, as was usual, a large civilian vicus had established itself a short distance from the outer ditch of the fortress, just beyond bowshot. Most of the buildings were constructed in the native style, round huts of wattle and daub with thatched roofs. A small opening at the apex of the thatch served to let the smoke escape from the hearth inside. Some of the structures were more substantial affairs, erected by traders from Gaul who had followed their customers when the legions had been transferred to the army that had invaded Britannia. The vicus was where the off-duty soldiers could indulge their appetites for drink and women and, if the legion remained in the location, some of the men would take women for wives and raise families. Such arrangements were unofficial as common soldiers were forbidden to enter formal marriages whilst serving, but it was a long-established custom, and the men were only human after all.

In addition to the fortress, there were two smaller forts for the auxiliary, cavalry and infantry units attached to the Fourteenth Legion, and the entirety had the appearance of a modest town in the making as it lay beneath a thin skein of woodsmoke. On the far side of the river the landscape was open and flat, and in the distance Cato could see the grey mass of the line of hills that marked the boundary of Silurian territory. Clouds hung over the hills, obscuring the heavily forested mountains that lay beyond.

'Not the most cheery of prospects,' Macro commented. 'But at least we're no longer skulking around doing dirty work for Narcissus.'

'Given the situation, that's a small mercy, I think you'll find.' Cato clicked his tongue and urged his horse down the broad, muddy track that led to the eastern gate of the fortress. The route passed by a few small farms where the natives were sowing seeds in strip fields for summer crops of barley and wheat. They were so used to soldiers passing by that hardly anyone paid attention to the three riders. Only a small child, a boy, squatting in the muddy soil beside his mother, stared up from beneath a fringe of dark hair and smiled suddenly at Macro. The spontaneity of the infant's expression touched his heart.

'Look, Cato. Not everyone seems to hate us.' Macro smiled back and winked at the child.

Cato shook his head. 'Give 'em time. That one will reach for his sword soon enough.'

'Quite the little ray of sunshine today, aren't you?'

Cato didn't reply but spurred his horse into a trot and with a reluctant sigh Macro and Decimus followed suit. The servant edged his pony towards Macro and muttered, 'Excuse my asking, sir, but is the prefect often like this? You know, miserable?'

'Oh no!' Macro chuckled. 'Only when he's in a good mood.'

The child watched them for a moment longer before the smile disappeared and he turned his mind back to the simple straw figures clutched in his tiny fists. With a light growl he charged them towards each other and mashed them together.

As they made their way past the vicus, Macro gave it the once-over, a professional soldier's assessment of the kinds of pleasures the makeshift settlement might provide, and made a mental note to pay a visit at the first opportunity. Two legionaries stood guard at the ramp leading across the ditch to the fortress gates. Cato had put on his armour that morning, after Decimus had given the breastplate a quick polish, and the gleaming metal and the red ribbon tied round his midriff indicated his rank and the sentries instantly snapped to attention. Behind them, the optio in command of the watch hastily called out the rest of the section who fell in either side of the gateway as Cato walked his horse across the ramp and returned the optio's salute.

'Is Legate Quintatus in camp?'

'Yes, sir. Should be at headquarters.' He hesitated briefly before he asked, 'Your authorisation, sir?'

Cato reached into his saddlebag and brought out the small waxed slate bearing the governor's seal and detailing his name, rank and purpose of travel. The optio examined it quickly before handing it back.

'Very good, sir. You may pass.'

They rode under the gate and entered the fortress with its neatly ordered timber barracks stretching out either side of the broad avenue that led to the cluster of large buildings that formed the headquarters, senior officers' accommodation and stores of the Fourteenth Legion. Off-duty soldiers sat outside their section rooms cleaning their armour or playing dice. Others were kitting up ready for the change of watch, or heading out on patrol. Some of the barracks were empty, their former occupants already detached from the legion to garrison the advance outposts. The light plink of hammers sounded from the armoury and a detail of men on fatigues headed towards the latrines carrying buckets, brushes and shovels. Macro smiled at the surroundings that were as familiar to him as any home.

'Quintatus likes things nice and ordered.'

'A spit and polish merchant,' Decimus added sourly.

'Which is half of what the army is all about. Can't go out and kill barbarians in the name of Rome unless you look the part.'

The guards on duty at the gate passed them into the legion's headquarters where Cato and Macro left Decimus with the horses and mules while they went to report to the legate. Despite the pending campaign there was a calm, efficient atmosphere to the place as clerks bent over their records and carried messages to and from the senior officers. Legate Quintatus was with the Fourteenth Legion's quartermaster as his secretary announced their arrival.

'A moment,' Quintatus responded curtly from behind his desk and turned his attention back to the quartermaster, who stood stiffly before him. 'The granary should have been inspected daily. That's your responsibility. If you had done your duty then the rats would have been driven out before they ruined a thousand modii of grain. Now it needs making up.'

'The next grain convoy is due to reach us by the end of the month, sir. I'll send word that we need more to replace the losses.'

Quintatus shook his head. 'The end of the month is not good enough. I want it replaced within the next five days.'

The quartermaster's jaw sagged. 'But—'

'No excuses. See to it. If you can't cut a deal with a reserve unit, then you'll have to buy it from the natives. Dismissed.'

The quartermaster saluted and turned to leave the room, an anxious expression on his face. Quintatus let out a frustrated sigh, then fixed his penetrating gaze on the two officers standing just inside his office. 'Well?'

Cato made the introductions and they handed over the slates detailing their service records. The legate looked at his visitors curiously for a moment before he read their records and nodded his satisfaction. 'Glad to see you've served here before. And plenty of combat experience besides, though there are one or two gaps in the record.'

'We were waiting for reassignment, sir,' Cato replied. 'On half pay in Rome.'

'A waste of your talents. Sitting on your hands while some fat-arsed imperial clerk takes his time finding you a new job. Bloody bureaucrats, eh?' A sympathetic smile flickered on his lips and then it was gone. 'Now you're here. No doubt itching to take up your posts and get stuck into the enemy.'

Macro grinned. 'You're reading my mind, sir.'

'If that's what you weren't thinking then you're no use to me. I won't tolerate anyone who doesn't pull their weight, gentlemen. No matter what their rank. We're up against tough opposition and I want results. Clear?'

Cato nodded. 'Yes, sir.'

'As it happens, I've been fortunate . . . very fortunate to have Centurion Quertus on hand to take command of the outpost at Bruccium while we waited for you to arrive. Quertus has been taking the battle to the enemy at every opportunity. He's burned more villages and killed more Silurians than any other man in the army. And the enemy have come to fear him. According to some of the prisoners we've taken, they call him the Blood Crow, and even the name strikes fear into their hearts.'

'The Blood Crow . . .' Macro repeated and cocked an eyebrow at Cato. 'Did the prisoners say why, sir?'

'It's straightforward enough. The Thracian cohort have a crow on their standard. I imagine the blood part is down to the methods used by Quertus and his men. It seems that the cohort has adopted the name for the unit. They call themselves the Blood Crows now.'

Cato felt a cold tingle at the base of his spine. 'What methods do you mean, sir?'

The legate hesitated for a moment before he replied. 'Centurion Quertus has risen from the ranks. He was recruited in Thrace, though his family comes from the mountains in Dacia, far from anything we might recognise as civilisation. So some might consider his methods . . . questionable. But then the outpost is in the heart of Silurian territory and perhaps one needs to fight the barbarians on their own terms if we are to achieve victory. Speaking of which . . .' He reached to the side and drew out a long roll of parchment and spread it out across his desk. Cato saw that it was a map. The marks indicating the position of the Roman forces and the surrounding terrain were detailed, but large sections of the map were blank, beneath the inscription of the names of the Silurian and Ordovician tribes.

The legate tapped his finger on the map. 'Glevum. I have the Fourteenth and two cohorts of auxiliary cavalry and four cohorts of infantry under my command. A third of my column is garrisoning the forts we have built, or are in the process of building. Our job is to control the valleys and act as the anvil upon which the main weight of the Roman army will strike like a hammer. The hammer is the main column under the governor. He is based further north, here, at Cornoviorum, with the Twentieth Legion, and twelve cohorts of auxiliaries. When he is ready to march, Ostorius intends to strike hard against the Ordovices, and then turn south against the Silures. If it goes to plan, then Caratacus and his forces will be trapped between us, and crushed.'

Cato studied the map, and though the lack of knowledge about much of the terrain over which the Roman forces would march concerned him, he could see the sense of the governor's strategy. He nodded. 'Seems like a sound plan, sir.'

Quintatus arched an eyebrow. 'I'm so glad that you agree, Prefect. I'm sure that Ostorius would be pleased to know that he has your blessing. In any case, he has to find Caratacus first. The bastard's proved to be as slippery as an eel. All that we know for certain is that he is in the territory of the Ordovices at present.'

Cato flushed, thought about replying but decided it would be better to keep his mouth shut and not risk further opprobrium over his moment of hubris.

'Your task, assuming it meets your approval, is to control the valley in which Bruccium is located.' The legate indicated a symbol on the map. 'You are to patrol the valley and keep it free of the enemy. If you see fit, you may extend the scope of your operations somewhat further. The last report I had from Quertus was over a month ago. He said that he had burned several native villages further to the west and south and claimed that he has killed over a thousand of the enemy. He has suffered considerable losses himself and I will be sending a reinforcement column to the fort as soon as the latest batch of reinforcements arrive from Gaul.'

Macro clicked his tongue 'There's been no word for over a month, sir? Anything could have happened in that time. It's possible that the fort might have been overrun.'

'If that was the case, then I think the enemy would have let us know by now. Caratacus always insists on trumpeting any good news for his side. No, I think Quertus is still very much in the game.'

Cato was examining the map and saw that Bruccium was deep inside Silurian territory, over sixty miles from Glevum, he estimated. Forty miles beyond the nearest Roman-occupied fort of any size. It was too exposed, he decided. Far too exposed. Any supply convoy making for Bruccium would have to cross the passes through the mountains before marching through densely forested valleys: perfect terrain for setting ambushes.

'How often is the fort resupplied, sir?'

'It isn't.'

Cato frowned. 'How is that, sir? Surely they have to be supplied.

There must be several hundred men at Bruccium. Not to mention the horses.'

Quintatus shrugged. 'The first few convoys got through. Heavily escorted. Then the Silurians got stuck in and we couldn't get any more to the garrison. I sent word to Quertus that he had permission to fall back before his supplies ran out. He replied that he and his men would live off the land. That was his last word on the subject, so he must have found a way.'

'That's hard to believe, sir,' said Macro. 'He's surrounded by the enemy. Surely they could starve him out if they put their minds to it.'

'Well they haven't, as far as I know. However Quertus keeps his men going, it works. You'll see for yourselves once you reach the fort. You're going to find that there's a lot Quertus can teach you. If you are wise, Prefect, you'll pay heed to the man.'

The implied criticism angered Cato and he struggled not to let it show. He was a professional soldier who had served his Emperor loyally and effectively for many years. He knew damn well that it was wise to listen to his subordinates, especially one as evidently capable as Centurion Quertus. Cato swallowed his irritation. 'Of course, sir.'

'Good. Then you can leave at first light. I'll assign you an escort to get you to the fort. A squadron from the legion's mounted contingent should suffice. After you take command at Bruccium I want a more detailed report of the strength and condition of the two cohorts, as well as the progess they are making against the Silurians. That's if it is safe to send a rider back to Glevum. Now, if you'll excuse me, gentlemen, I am hard pressed to prepare the rest of my column for the coming campaign. Good fortune go with you.'

He gestured towards the door and Cato and Macro saluted and left the legate's office. Outside in the corridor, as they made their way back to the courtyard to rejoin Decimus, Macro spoke quietly.

'I'm not so sure about this Centurion Quertus. Sounds like he might cause us a bit of trouble.'

Cato thought a moment. 'He's playing by his own rules, that's for sure. But, as you heard, he is hitting the enemy hard. That's what the legate and the governor want. I just hope we can maintain the standard when I take command.'

Macro breathed in deeply. 'Somehow, I don't think Centurion Quertus is going to be very welcoming. He's run the show his way for some months now. What makes you think he'll be happy to hand over the reins to you?'

'Because he's a soldier and he does as he's told.'

Macro pursed his lips. 'I hope you're right.'

# CHAPTER TWELVE

It began to rain shortly after dawn and Glevum disappeared behind a grey veil of drizzle as the riders hunkered down inside their cloaks and urged their mounts along the track that led towards the distant line of hills. Macro and Decimus had visited the vicus the night before and shared a few jars of cheap wine in one of the simple inns. Cato had remained in headquarters, searching the records office for as much information as he could find about his new unit, and the officer temporarily in command of it. The Thracians had performed creditably in the years they had been posted to Britannia but in the last few months they had accounted for more of the enemy than they had in the previous eight years.

As for Quertus, there was nothing on record that revealed any more than Quintatus had already told him – except for one minor complaint from the previous commander of the Thracians. Following a skirmish on the banks of the Severnus, prefect Albinus had issued an order for Quertus to escort their captives to Glevum. They never reached the fortress. According to Quertus they had all attempted to escape on the first night of the march and were killed in the process. None survived. There was no mention of any disciplinary action and a few days later the prefect was killed when he was thrown from his horse and his skull was caved in when it struck a rock.

The cohort of legionaries that made up the rest of the garrison of Bruccium had an equally competent and unspectacular record up until their success of recent months. The only curious aspect was that neither unit had reported any breaches of discipline since Centurion Quertus had led them into the mountains. Normally, such infractions were part of the reports that were regularly sent back to the legion's headquarters. But after the first few reports, there were only brief outlines of the number of enemies killed and villages burned. And nothing more for over a month now.

Cato, his companions and the escort crossed the timber bridge thrown across the Severnus by the engineers of the Fourteenth Legion and followed the route along the riverbank. There were fewer signs of the natives here than at any point on their journey through the new province. A handful of small farmsteads dotted the landscape. The inhabitants, wild-looking people in furs and rags, tended a handful of goats and worked small fields in the rich soil beside the river. Every five miles, the riders encountered one of the small fortlets that had been built to guard the route. Each garrison of twenty or thirty auxiliaries sheltered behind a turf wall topped with a stout wooden palisade, and a sentry kept watch over the surrounding landscape from a small tower rising up above the meagre fortifications.

At the end of the day they reached a large fort at Isca, garrisoned by a cohort of Gauls. After the mounts and baggage animals had been stabled for the night, Cato and his comrades joined the decurion leading the cavalry escort in the cohort's mess. There was only one small room with two tables and a small counter where a skinny merchant sold bad wine for a premium to his captive market. This side of the Severnus was Silurian territory and none of the Roman army's camp followers had been brave enough to settle into a vicus outside the walls of the fort.

Macro and Decimus had worked off their hangover during the day's ride and Macro ordered some wine from the merchant with the begrudging attitude of a man who knows he is being exploited.

'Five sestertii for this piss?' Macro growled as his lips wrinkled away from the rim of the cup following his first sip. 'Fucking outrage is what it is.'

'It's not so bad, sir.' Decimus raised his cup and drank again.

Macro looked at him sourly. 'Never is so bad when you haven't had to pay for a drop of it. I ought to take deductions from your pay for the wine you consume.'

'Then you'd only go and have to drink more of this piss, sir.'

Decimus pretended to look hurt. 'Really, you should be thanking me for helping you out with it.'

'Really?' Macro narrowed his eyes a moment, then turned to Cato. 'What do you think?'

'Eh?' Cato looked up vacantly. 'Sorry, what was that?'

'The wine. Taste it and tell me what you think.'

Cato looked down into the Samian-ware cup and sniffed it. It was not unlike vinegar, but somehow suffused with a very ancient blend of goat's cheese and sewage. Still, for Macro's sake, he took a sip and as the foul liquid flowed across his tongue he winced. He set the cup down with a sharp rap. 'That's wine?'

'According to our friend behind the counter. The sewer brewer. I've a mind to have a word with him.'

'What good would it do? This is as good as it gets this far beyond the frontier.'

Macro looked shocked. 'By the gods, I hope not. What in Hades' name must they be drinking up at Bruccium?'

The comment stirred Cato's thoughts and he turned to the decurion who had been drinking quietly, clearly preoccupied. Cato cleared his throat.

'It's Trebellius, isn't it?'

The decurion looked round and nodded. 'Yes, sir.'

'You don't seem to be enjoying your little trip up into the mountains very much. At least the wine will keep your mind off it. Drink up.'

Trebellius dutifully took a sip, without any change of expression.

'Seems like someone has a taste for it,' said Macro.

Decimus chuckled. 'Like I said, sir. Not so bad. You get used to such things in Britannia. The worst of everything. Weather, wine and even the women are as rough as you'll find anywhere in the whole empire. It's a wonder that Claudius and his advisers think there's anything good to be had out of the bloody place. If you ask me, we should never have invaded and left the barbarians to themselves. If they want to live in mud huts, worship bloody Druids and fight each other all the time, then let 'em. If the Emperor had given Britannia a miss then I'd still have a good leg.'

Macro stared hard at him. 'And did I ask you? No. You knew the score when you signed up. You go where you're sent and don't stop to ask questions. You kill who you're told to kill and that's it. If the buggers get you first then that's the risk you take. Otherwise, you might as well be some shirt-lifting ponce who spends his life reading philosophy.' Macro shot a quick glance at Cato. 'Present company excepted.'

'Thank you, Macro,' Cato responded testily before turning his attention back to the decurion. 'How long have you served with the Fourteenth?'

'Twenty years, sir. Come summer.'

'And how long has the Thracian cavalry been serving with the Fourteenth?'

'That lot? Seem to be something of a fixture, sir. As long as I've been with the legion.'

Cato smiled. 'I've seen plenty of auxiliary units in my time. Some good, some bad. Never served with Thracian cavalry, though. So what are they like?'

The decurion sniffed. 'They don't stink, like some of them. Germans is worst. But at least with your Germans you know where you are. Them Thracians is different. Got a cruel streak in 'em, they have. Bloody good horsemen, though. Glad they're on our side, is all.'

'I see.' Cato reached for the jar and topped up the decurion's cup. 'And what about Centurion Quertus?'

The decurion answered warily. 'Can't really say. The Thracians tend to keep to themselves. I've come across him on the parade field when we've been on training manoeuvres. He's a big man. Built like a brick shithouse and has the guts to match.'

'You have to be so careful what you eat,' Macro chipped in.

Cato shot a frown at him before he spoke to the decurion again. 'What else?'

'Like I said. He's brave and the men would follow him anywhere.'

'Inspiring, then?'

'You could say that, sir. Depends what kind of inspiring you mean. He's a born fighter, the kind who would die rather than give an inch of ground. Trouble is, he wants the same from those who he leads. I saw him beat a man senseless on the parade field once because he wouldn't leap his horse over a ditch. Let's just say he takes discipline seriously. And loyalty. I've heard he's supposed to be some kind of prince in his homeland.' Decimus looked round and leaned closer. 'That, and some kind of priest. The kind who knows magic. The kind of magic that needs blood sacrifices.'

'Magic?' Cato repeated slowly. 'I've yet to see any genuine magic in my lifetime.'

Macro tilted his head to the side. 'Don't be so quick to pass judgement. After all, someone's put a curse on this bloody wine, that's for certain.'

The decurion scowled briefly, then drained his cup and pushed it away with a nod of thanks. 'Better see to the horses, sir. They'll need feeding before the second watch.'

He rose from the bench and left the mess. Macro stared after him and muttered wryly, 'Was it something I said?'

'Best not to make fun of someone's beliefs, sir,' Decimus suggested mildly.

'Oh, come on!' Macro chuckled. 'Magic? Priests? Sacrifices? That's a load of old bollocks. Anyone with half a brain knows that the only gods with any clout are Roman gods. That's why Rome rules the world.'

'I thought Rome ruled the world because our soldiers were better than everyone else,' said Cato. 'In any case, we clearly don't rule half the tribes on this island.'

Decimus made to reply to Macro but then closed his mouth and looked down into his cup. He was silent for a moment before he said quietly, 'Some gods are false. Perhaps most of them. But there's one who is powerful. One who comes from the east. And he promises a life in paradise to all those who choose to follow him.'

Macro laughed. 'I've heard that kind of rubbish before! Cato, you remember? Back in Judaea? The fools who called themselves servants of some wandering holy man. I hope that's not who you're talking about, Decimus.'

The former legionary shook his head. 'Never heard of no Judaean nonsense. I'm talking about Lord Mithras, sir. He's the one.'

'Mithras . . .' Macro scratched his stubbly jaw. 'Bit of a cult in some units, so I understand. Can't see the attraction myself. What's he got to offer that Jupiter hasn't, eh? Believing in Mithras is no better than that nonsense Trebellius was talking about our Thracian friend.'

Decimus pursed his lips. 'I think there's more to it than that, sir.'

Macro pointed at the brand on Decimus's forehead. 'I can see why. But you're wasting your time, I'm telling you. Jupiter, best and greatest, and the rest of our lot piss all over anyone else's gods.'

'Maybe that's what you believe now, sir. But I'll pray to Mithras that he shows you the righteous path all the same.'

Macro shrugged. 'Pray all you like. It ain't going to change a bloody thing. I'll personally put a curse on any man who says different.'

Cato sighed and turned his mind back to the matter of Centurion Quertus. It was evident the man had quality as a warrior and leader and was carrying out his orders to the satisfaction of his superiors. Such a man would not relinquish his position eagerly, or even willingly. Bruccium was far enough away from Glevum for Cato to have to rely on his own authority to take command of the fort and its garrison. It was an acutely uncomfortable prospect and the more he brooded over it, the more of a challenge it seemed.

The following morning the track entered the Silurian mountains and wound its way up the broad valley through which the River Isca flowed. The river was wide and glassy, swollen by the rain that had fallen during the early months of the year, and the snow on the tops of the mountains that had melted into the streams and tributaries of the Isca. The route was guarded by more of the fortlets, whose sentries peered anxiously from behind their palisades at the grim landscape around them. The engineers had felled trees either side of the track to remove the cover that could be used to ambush any patrols or supply columns travelling through the valley. Beyond the cleared ground the trees reared up, and the shadows beneath their boughs were dark and impenetrable. In the distance, as the ground rose steeply, the treeline gave out on to rocky slopes with long grass and shrubs, bent over in the wind that blew across the mountains.

The track began to twist and turn around the rocky outcrops and hills and the conversation of the riders died away as the oppressive landscape and the possibility that they were being watched by the enemy played on their nerves. Cato, having strapped his helmet on, rode beside the decurion at the head of the column and noted the anxious glances that Trebellius directed to each side.

'Do you think we are in danger here?' Cato asked quietly.

'There was a patrol ambushed not far from here several days ago, sir. Lost half their men before they could reach the nearest outpost. In any case, the enemy has become more bold recently. The Silurians have raided the frontier zone as far as the Severnus on several occasions.'

'Well, if they've set an ambush here once, they'd be foolish to do it again, where it might be expected. We should be safe.'

The decurion looked at him. 'I hope you're right, sir.'

Cato shrugged off the other man's fears. 'How much further to Bruccium, do you think?'

'Half a day's ride to the last outpost. Then another day should see us over the pass leading down into the valley. A few miles on from there is where you'll find the fort.'

'That's good.'

Trebellius smiled faintly. 'Good enough for me. I can't wait to get out of these accursed mountains and back to the arms of my woman in Glevum.'

'Oh? Lucky man.'

'I suppose. She's not some classy bit from Italy. Not even from Gaul. Garwhenna's a local girl, half Silurian. Not much to look at but strong and loyal. And she's taught me some of their tongue. Comes in useful when I'm trading with the locals for feed.'

'I can imagine.'

They fell silent for a moment before the decurion pointed to a bend in the track a quarter of a mile ahead, where a rocky cliff pushed out from the side of the valley. 'There's a fortlet just beyond there, sir. We'll stop to rest the mounts and I'll pick up the optio's report on his strength and supply situation.'

'Very well,' Cato responded absently. The rain had subsided into a misty drizzle and he was looking forward to enjoying a little shelter and warmth before they resumed their march. Then he heard a muffled noise above the sound of the hoofs clopping over the stony track. He was alert in an instant, straining his ears. For a moment he wondered if he was imagining it. The decurion's anxiety was starting to rub off on him. But better safe than sorry. Cato tugged on his reins and threw his right hand up.

'Halt!'

Beside him the decurion reined in and the rest of the column lumbered to a stop and the quiet of the surrounding landscape closed in around them. Macro edged his mount forward to join his friend and the decurion.

'What is it?'

'I heard something. Up ahead.'

Macro listened intently then shook his head. 'I don't h—'

Then it came again. The long deep blast of a horn, muffled by the drizzle and the mass of the cliff rising up in front of them. It had been a long time since Cato had last heard the sound, but it was quite unmistakable. The brassy blare came from a Celtic war horn.

# CHAPTER THIRTEEN

'It's an ambush!' Trebellius said, eyes wide with fear as he scrutinised the treeline on either side of the track, well within the throw of a javelin. 'We have to get out of here!'

'Wait!' Cato commanded. 'Compose yourself! You're a bloody officer.' He turned to Macro. 'Stay here. Have the men drop their packs and prepare to fight. Do it as quietly as you can. The decurion and I are riding ahead to see what's going on.'

'We are?' Trebellius looked shocked. Then, as Cato glared at him, the decurion fought to steady his nerves and nodded. 'Yes, sir.'

'Then let's go.' Cato spurred his mount into a canter. After a moment's hesitation the decurion followed and Macro turned towards the squadron and Decimus and drew a deep breath to bellow his orders. Then he caught himself and spoke in a husky undertone. 'Now then, lads, let's do this without too much noise, eh? Packs down . . .'

As the track began to bend round the foot of the cliff, Cato slowed his horse to a trot and then stopped. The sound of the horn was clearer now, and he could hear men shouting. He glanced at the cliff and saw that it was less than fifty feet in height at this point. Some rocks had fallen by the side of the road and it should be possible to climb to the top.

'Take my horse,' Cato ordered as he slipped from the saddle and began to scramble over the rocks and up the cliff.

The decurion watched his superior in alarm. 'Where are you going, sir?'

'To spy out the lie of the land.' Cato paused and looked down over his shoulder. 'Just make sure you stay there.'

He did not wait for a reply but continued up, carefully testing his grip on the handholds and the weight on his boots as he made his way towards the top. It was a short climb but he was breathing heavily as he hauled himself over the crumbling edge and slithered far enough away from it to be sure it would not give way beneath him. Then, rising cautiously to his feet, he looked in the direction of the horn as it sounded again. On the far side of the cliff the track continued straight down the valley, towards a small hillock on top of which sat a Roman outpost. Around it, in a loose circle, were a hundred or so figures armed with shields and spears. A handful wore helmets but the rest were bareheaded with long dark hair tied back. As Cato watched, some more emerged from the trees a short distance away, carrying a stout length of timber. They made directly for the fort and their intention was perfectly clear. Cato made sure that there were no more of the enemy visible before he climbed back down to Trebellius and took his reins and swung himself back into the saddle.

'The enemy are attacking the outpost. There's no time to lose if we're to save them!'

Cato turned back towards Macro and beckoned his friend forward. A moment later the men of the squadron had reached the cliff and stood waiting for orders. Freed of the burden of their saddlebags and feed nets the horses were lively and snorted excitedly as their hoofs scraped the ground. Decimus, on his mule, came up last, armed with a buckler and his old army sword hanging from its strap across his shoulder.

'The enemy are trying to take the outpost up ahead,' Cato explained, his mind racing ahead to form his plan. 'Their attention is fixed on our auxiliary comrades so they won't see us coming until it is too late. They'll be caught between the garrison and ourselves. When we get round the cliff I want you to form line and follow the pace that I set. We must hit them at the same time so the charge carries as much weight as possible. Anyone tries to overtake me and they'll be in deep shit. Specifically, latrine duty for a month.'

Some of the men laughed at his feeble joke, the rest, even Trebellius, smiled and Cato knew that they would not let him down. 'When I give the order to charge home, hit them as hard as you can.

113

Break 'em up and ride 'em down. Show no mercy until it's clear the fight's been knocked out of the enemy.' He glanced over the faces before him to make sure that they understood. The eagerness in their expressions told him all he needed to know. Cato turned his mount round and reached for the handle of his short sword. He intended to draw a longer cavalry blade from stores when he reached Bruccium.

'Ready weapons!'

Macro, Decimus, Trebellius and Cato drew their swords while the men hefted their spears. Slipping their shield straps from their shoulders they grasped the reins loosely in their left hands as the shields protected that side of their bodies. There would be little chance to use the reins in the fight ahead; the men made sure that they were seated securely between their saddle horns and prepared to control their mounts with their thighs and heels.

Cato lowered the tip of his blade. 'At the trot! Forwards!'

The column lurched forward with jingling bits, snorts from the horses and curt words of command from their riders. Macro spurred his horse on, until he was at the side of his friend. 'Here we go again.'

Cato kept his eyes on the track ahead. As they rounded the base of the cliff and the ground opened out he saw the enemy a few hundred paces away, surging towards the ditch surrounding the fort. Some hurled spears, others rocks, while the auxiliaries answered back with light javelins and slingshot. Already several of the enemy were down. But the party with the battering ram had reached the gate and a crash sounded as their weapon struck home against the timbers of the outpost.

'Form line!' Cato called out and the men behind him adjusted their pace so they caught up and moved out to the flanks until they were all in line, scarcely two hundred paces from the nearest of the native warriors. But already they had been seen. Faces turned towards them, and the triumphant shouts and taunts of a moment earlier turned to cries of alarm. The men with the battering ram stopped attacking the gate and lowered the ram and backed away from the fort uncertainly.

The moment of surprise was over. The leader of the enemy war band shouted orders to his men and they turned towards the oncoming Romans and began to form a line. Cato saw that the opportunity to crush the enemy in the first charge was slipping from his grasp. If they could form up in close ranks and present their spears then there was every chance that they would stand firm against the horsemen. Yet it was vital that Cato and his men charged at the same time to ensure the maximum impact. In less than two heartbeats he weighed up the options in his mind, calculating the remaining distance, the time needed to strike, and the likelihood of his men being dispersed as their mounts galloped at different speeds. Snatching a deep breath, Cato stabbed his short sword towards the tribesmen and bellowed the order, 'Charge! Charge!'

His cry was taken up by Macro, who gritted his teeth and drew his lips back in a feral grin as he waved his sword above his head and grasped his reins in his left hand. Trebellius and his squadron shouted their war cry and raised their spear arms ready to strike down at the enemy. Decimus brought up the rear, legs dangling almost to the ground as he urged his braying mule on, slapping its flank with the flat of his sword. Cato heard the roar of wind in his ears and the icy sting of the drizzle against his face and his heart pounded wildly as he clenched his thighs against the flanks of his horse and leaned forward slightly. The acrid tang of the animal's pelt filled his nostrils and stinking spittle spattered his cheek. Ahead he saw some of the tribesmen stand their ground, bracing their feet as they crouched and lowered the points of their spears and swords towards the charging horsemen. Others had clustered together in small groups and a handful were running for the cover of the treeline as their leader hurled angry insults after them before turning to face the Romans with an enraged expression contorting his features. The man with the carnyx horn was blowing for all he was worth to lend courage to his comrades, and the stout hearts amongst them answered with a loud cheer of defiance.

A swift glance to either side revealed that the extended formation of horsemen had become ragged and Cato snatched a quick breath and cried out, 'Hold the line!'

Only those nearest to him heeded, or heard, the order and tried to adjust their pace. But before Cato could do anything more about

115

it they were upon the enemy. There was a blur of faces, etched with rage and fear, some with woad patterns painted on their skin, then a thud from Cato's left as the first of the horses burst into a loose group of tribesmen, smashing into a shield. The horse let out a shrill whinny and its rider stabbed his spear down, piercing the neck of the man knocked down by his mount. Cato glimpsed the other tribesmen closing round the horse, thrusting with their swords and spears, then his attention snapped to the line of men directly ahead of him, and beyond them their leader, shouting encouragement to his warriors. These men seemed more disciplined than their companions, and were better armed with bronze-trimmed shields; some even wore helmets and armour, looted from the bodies of Romans.

One of Trebellius's men charged directly at their spears, but his horse shied away from the points, swerving aside, and the rider struggled to retain his seat. Cato just had time to pull on his reins and steer to the right side and avoid a collision. More of the Romans charged home, stabbing at the enemy while wheeling their horses from side to side to avoid becoming an easy target in turn. Macro's voice carried above the thud and clatter of weapons.

'Cut 'em down, lads! Kill 'em!'

Cato clamped his jaw shut and bared his teeth as he picked the man at the end of the line, a tall, sinewy warrior, with a stubbly fringe of dark hair above his snarling face. He carried a heavy spear in both hands and saw Cato at the same moment, swinging the point of his weapon round and bunching his shoulders as he braced himself. Cato kicked his heels in and his horse lurched forward, the sudden movement throwing the enemy off guard so that he instinctively took a step backwards as Cato swung his short sword down in a savage arc. He could not hope to reach the man and tried instead to strike at the shaft of his spear. The tribesman jerked his spear back and it caught just the end of Cato's sword with a sharp, harmless rap. At once both men made to recover and strike first. Cato was quicker, as he urged his mount on and hacked again. This time the edge cut through the knuckle and two fingers of the warrior's leading hand. He let out a howl of rage as blood sprayed from the stumps. He swept Cato's sword to the side and stepped inside the reach of the Roman as he thrust the point of his spear home.

Despite its battle training, the horse made to rear and the blow missed Cato's side and tore into the animal's flank instead. The front hoofs lashed out in pain and one struck the warrior, spinning him aside and throwing him on to his back. The spear was lodged between the horse's ribs and the animal reared again, tossing its head wildly. Cato felt a stab of terror as he struggled to control his mount, pulling hard on the reins as he shouted, 'Easy there!'

In its agony the horse ignored his desperate command and staggered on, blundering into the enemy line, before stumbling over the uneven ground and falling heavily to the right, driving the point further into its vitals before the shaft snapped with a loud report. Cato released his grip on the reins and tried to throw himself from the horse. He felt himself part company with the leather of the saddle, the ground rushed up towards him and he crashed on to the grass. The impact drove the breath from his lungs, he saw a flash of the grey sky and then his face was embedded in grass and mud. He just managed to raise his head enough to see the face of the man he had wounded no more than a foot away, contorted with pain and spitting a curse at his attacker. Then Cato felt a tremendous blow on his back that drove him deep into the ground. He fought for breath, the great weight of the horse writhing on top of him for an instant as the animal let out a long terrified whinny, hoofs lashing the air.

Cato knew the damage a wounded horse could do with its hoofs and hugged the ground, feeling the painful pressure on his right leg as the dying horse pinned him down. Then he realised that he no longer had his sword in his hand. Quickly raising his head, Cato saw the handle in the grass in front of his face, and beyond that the intent glare in the eyes of the warrior, who had also been trapped by the mortally wounded horse. The other man reacted first, snatching at the weapon with his injured hand. Cato thrust his left hand out, fingers clawing to get a firm grasp round the man's wrist before he could use the sword. Both were pinioned by the horse as they struggled desperately for control of the weapon. Twisting round, Cato managed to get his other hand into action and grabbed at the bloody stumps of the warrior's fingers and squeezed tightly. A scream of agony split the air and a moment later his remaining fingers loosened their grip and Cato tore the handle from his enemy and grasped it in his right hand. He stabbed at the man's chest and the warrior tried to fend the blow aside with his bare hands, incurring further wounds. Drawing the blade back, Cato braced himself on the ground and then rammed it home with all his strength, feeling the point drive into the man's chest. He tugged the blade free and thrust again. There was an explosive grunt from his enemy, who slumped back, feebly mouthing words as he stared up into the sky, the fingers of his good hand pressed over wounds that pulsed blood between his fingers.

Cato slumped down on to his elbow, breathing heavily, keeping the crimson-stained sword pointing towards the other man. It was clear that he no longer presented a threat. Cato tried to look round to see how the fight was going but the length of the grass and the trembling body of the horse obscured his view. The ring of blades, the crack of weapons on shields, and the softer thud on flesh and bone, punctuated by cries of agony, anger and triumph, sounded on all sides. There was a sharp pain in Cato's right leg. He looked down and saw that it was pinned under the heavy leather mass of the saddle. He tried to pull it free but the pain instantly became unbearable and he eased back on to his elbow with a bitter curse of frustration. The warrior's head rolled to the side and he grinned at Cato's discomfort, until a gush of blood spilled from his lips and he spluttered and coughed, spraying flecks of blood across the side of Cato's face. He struggled pitifully as the blood filled his lungs, drowning him.

'Fuck,' Cato muttered fiercely to himself. 'I am not going to die here.'

He tried to free himself again, bracing his left boot against the horse's rump as he strained his muscles to try and free his trapped leg. But it was hopeless, the weight of the dying animal bore down on the saddle and made the task impossible. At length Cato slumped back on to his elbows. 'Shit . . . shit . . . shit . . .'

There was nothing he could do, and he held his sword ready and waited for someone to come for him, friend or foe.

Macro slashed his blade down, grimacing as the edge bit deeply into his opponent's skull with a sound like the cracking of a large egg. The tribesman's body convulsed and his sword dropped from his nerveless fingers. A moment later the man collapsed beside his weapon, eyelids fluttering wildly as blood and brains spattered out of his shattered head. Straightening up in his saddle, Macro swept his gaze over the men fighting around him. None of the enemy was near enough to present a direct threat and Macro hurriedly assessed the situation.

The enemy's formation had broken and now a series of duels were being fought out across the ground in front of the fort. There were plenty of bodies lying on the ground, and Macro could see that perhaps a third of Trebellius's men were down. The rest were outnumbered and now that the initial impact of the charge had passed, the tribesmen were beginning to have the upper hand, as they heavily outnumbered the Romans. Even as Macro watched, several of the warriors, led by their chief, had surrounded the standard-bearer of the squadron. He held the staff close to his body while cutting at any native that came within reach of the long blade of his spatha. But there were too many of the enemy and one, more daring than his comrades, leaped forward and snatched the reins from the hand of the standard-bearer and savagely wrenched the horse's head round to unbalance its rider. The chief stepped in and thrust his sword into the Roman's side, while another man ripped the shaft of the standard away and held it aloft with a cry of glee. Macro could see the mortified expression on the face of the standard-bearer as he used what strength he had left to steer his horse round with his knees and slash his sword across the back of the warrior who had seized the squadron's insignia. The standard dropped to the ground as the native collapsed and then his comrades fell on the Roman, hauling him from his saddle before they butchered him on the ground.

Macro saw that Trebellius and four of his men were closer to the fallen standard and he cupped his left hand to his mouth.

'Decurion! Save the standard!'

Trebellius looked round and saw Macro, who stabbed his finger in the direction of the natives who had finished off the standard-bearer and were already making off with their trophy. Their success had encouraged their comrades and Macro saw that the fight was in the balance. He turned towards the fort.

119

'Come on, you bastards! Help us!'

The commander of the garrison had already correctly read the situation and even as Macro's words died on his lips, the gates opened and the auxiliaries quick-marched in tight formation towards the skirmish. Macro felt a surge of relief as he raised his sword again and looked round for a fresh opponent. Then it struck him: there was no sign of Cato. He felt an icy stab of anxiety at the base of his spine as he scanned the scene.

'Cato! Sir! Where are you?'

Then he saw the flutter of red in the grass fifty paces away, the thin horsehair crest of the prefect's helmet, and Macro pulled harshly on his reins to turn his horse towards his friend. Close by lay the bulk of a horse and Macro realised at once that Cato must be trapped underneath. A short distance away one of the natives had just finished off a legionary with his spear and pulled the bloodied tip free. He looked round and the same red crest now caught his attention. With a look of cruel intent he turned and paced towards Cato.

'No, you bloody don't!' Macro growled as he spurred his horse forward.

Cato sensed the man's approach before he saw him and turned to see the tall figure striding through the wild tussocks of grass towards him. He wore a thick brown cloak over a black tunic and strapped leggings. The ends of a silver torc gleamed at his throat and his hair, drenched by the drizzle, hung lankly across his shoulders. All this Cato saw in an instant, then he strained to free his leg again, groaning with the effort. The horse had bled out and lay still, a dead weight pressing down on the saddle and the leg caught beneath. He turned on his side and propped himself as best he could on his left elbow as he raised his sword and aimed the point at the oncoming warrior.

The man saw that he had an easy kill and grinned cruelly as he raised his spear and made to strike at the helpless Roman officer. Cato clenched his teeth and glared back, determined not to show any fear at his imminent death. There was only fleeting regret that it had to be this way, slaughtered like a tethered goat, so ignominious, so shameful. He hoped that when his death was reported to Julia back in Rome, the details would not be revealed and that she would grieve for him as the hero he wanted to be. Not like this.

The tribesman drew back his shaft to strike and Cato tensed his arm. Down flashed the head of the spear, tapering like a broad leaf to tear as great a wound as possible. Cato timed his parry well, not lashing out too soon and risking missing the strike; the edge of his sword connected with the head of the spear with a loud clang and the point deflected away from his throat, over his shoulder and whispered close to his ear so that he felt the brush of air on his skin.

With a frustrated grunt his opponent whipped the spear back for another attempt. This time he targeted Cato's sword, viciously cutting horizontally and knocking the blade aside so hard that Cato nearly lost his grip and pain coursed through his fist at the impact. Then the man swung the butt of the spear round and delivered a heavy blow to the side of Cato's helmet. Stunned, Cato slumped back helplessly and the warrior let out a roar of triumph and raised his spear a last time, to deliver the killing blow.

'No you don't!' Macro bellowed and the warrior hesitated and looked round. Then the horse was upon him and Macro threw himself from the saddle on to the spearman and they crashed to the ground side by side. It was a hard landing and both lost hold of their weapons. Macro snatched out the dagger from his belt and stabbed it into his enemy, tearing through the coarse material of the cloak. The thickness of the material saved the man as only the tip of the blade penetrated his flesh. By the time Macro stabbed again he was already rolling away and took a flesh wound in the shoulder. The centurion's stocky build gave him the edge in such close-quarter fighting and he quickly rose into a crouch and fell heavily on his opponent with his knees. At the same time he snatched at the man's hair to yank the head to one side and expose the throat. He drew his elbow back to stab his enemy under the chin.

'Macro! Wait!' Cato shouted.

The centurion snarled, 'What the fuck for?'

'I want him spared, for questioning.'

Macro drew a deep breath of frustration and nodded before he muttered, 'Lights out for you then, pal.'

Reversing his fist he smashed the pommel of his dagger against

121

the man's head and knocked him senseless. With a grunt his body went limp and his head thudded to the ground as Macro released his hair. He sheathed his dagger and then his sword and turned to Cato, hands on hips. 'What are you playing at down there? Sleeping on the job?'

'Funny,' Cato grunted. 'Actually, I'm in a bit of difficulty here, Macro. Would you mind?'

There was a rustle in the grass nearby as a section of auxiliaries, led by their optio, came trotting over to Macro. The optio stopped and hurriedly saluted.

'Caius Lentulus, sir.'

Macro looked at them sourly.

'Great timing, Optio. You missed the fight. But you can at least do something useful. Get this bloody horse off the prefect.'

The optio and his men downed their spears and shields and dragged the carcass away from Cato. He gritted his teeth as the movement caused fresh agony in his leg.

'Careful!' he snapped. Then his boot came free and Cato sat up to inspect his leg. The brass studs on the leatherwork had gouged the flesh below his knee where the hem of the breeches exposed his skin. Blood flowed freely and Cato swore as he struggled to stand up. His leg was numb and he staggered as he tried to take a step. At once Macro grabbed him by the arm and held him up.

'Sir, you all right?'

'Oh, fine, thank you. Next stupid question?'

Macro looked down at his friend's leg anxiously. 'Anything broken?'

Cato shook his head and straightened up to survey his surroundings. The enemy had been defeated. Scores of bodies lay sprawled on the ground, together with a handful of horses. Trebellius was reassembling the survivors of his squadron and Cato saw that barely half the number that had charged with him were still in their saddles. Several others were wounded, hunched over. A few mounts stood riderless, pawing at the ground. The last of the tribesmen could be seen disappearing into the shadows beneath the trees and Cato quickly estimated that the enemy had lost at least thirty men. The auxiliaries were picking their way over the bodies, finishing off any that still lived. Cato nodded with satisfaction. It had been a quick, violent struggle, but the outpost had been saved, and the enemy had been taught a sharp lesson.

Then he recalled that Trebellius's squadron had lost its standard. It would be foolhardy indeed to chase after the enemy into the woods to attempt to retrieve it. A pointless waste of lives. The loss would go hard with the decurion when he returned to Glevum. The army did not tolerate any excuse in relation to the loss of one of its standards, even from the smallest of its units. He would be disgraced and demoted to the ranks at the very least and the stain on his record would never be erased. But better that than lose what remained of the squadron in an attempt to rescue his honour. Perhaps in time the standard would be recovered – once the Silurians had been crushed and their lands added to the province of Britannia.

'Macro, tell Trebellius to get his men inside the fort before he does anything stupid.'

Macro nodded. 'I understand.'

Cato ordered two of the auxiliaries to help him to the gate, and two more men to carry the unconscious warrior. Once his leg had been seen to, and the wounded made comfortable, there would be plenty of time to see what information they could get out of their prisoner.

# CHAPTER FOURTEEN

Trebellius took a step back from the prisoner and wiped the blood from his knuckles with a rag. 'I think he's ready for questioning now.'

Cato nodded from where he sat on a stool in the outpost's mess. The minor wounds to his leg had been cleaned and dressed, but the knee joint had been badly wrenched during his brief fight with the spearman and made walking an agony. So one of the auxiliaries had fashioned a simple crutch for him to get about until his knee had recovered. It was inconvenient, Cato reflected, but he would recover in a day or so. Which was more than could be said for the spearman who was paying a heavy price for his attempt on the prefect's life.

Stripped to the waist, the Silurian's hands were chained together in front of him and a spear shaft had been passed through the crook of his elbows behind his back. A rope was tied to the shaft and the other end had been thrown over the sturdy beam running across the mess room. Trebellius had hauled the rope to drag the prisoner up on to his feet, then his toes, before tying it off on the beam. After that, he had administered a steady beating to the Silurian's stomach and face. Not so hard as to cause any disabling injury, but hard enough to cause considerable pain and fear. Trebellius had explained that he had been trained as a frumentarius, an interrogator, and watching him at work Cato could see that he had learned his craft well. Macro sat at a table nearby, hunched over a bowl of steaming barley stew as he watched proceedings. A jar of wine and two cups stood on the table, and another bowl for Cato, which he had not touched.

124

'Very well.' Cato cleared his throat. 'Ask him where his war party came from. I want to know where his settlement is.'

Trebellius translated the question as best he could into the native tongue. The Silurian looked up at Cato and spat a crimson gobbet of blood and spittle in his direction before he muttered briefly. Trebellius wrenched his head up with one hand and slapped him hard across the face.

'That'll do,' said Cato. 'What did he say?'

Trebellius released the man's hair and the Silurian's head slumped forward. 'He told us to go fuck ourselves, sir.'

Macro lowered his bronze spoon and made a shocked expression. 'Such incivility! I tell you, the prospect of putting a clean tongue in the mouths of barbarians like him makes it all worth while. Decurion, tell him that I'll go and fuck his sister if he doesn't show us a bit of respect. And his mother, and his daughters. Shit, I'll even fuck his prize hunting dogs within an inch of their lives if he doesn't start being a bit more cooperative.' Macro waved his spoon. 'You tell him.'

There was a brief exchange before the decurion grinned. 'He says, why would his dogs fuck you while there are still pigs in the world?'

Macro glared for a moment before suddenly laughing out loud and shaking his head. 'He's got balls, this one . . . For now at least,' he added in a harsher tone.

Cato gestured to his friend to stop speaking. 'Tell him that he's going to reveal what I want to know one way or another. He can make it easy on himself, or we can continue this for the rest of the day. For as long as we like, until we get what we want. There's no shame in speaking up now and saving himself a lot of pain.'

Trebellius translated and punched the Silurian in the guts for emphasis, but the tribesman groaned and gasped for breath and then clenched his teeth together defiantly. Cato ordered the decurion to continue and Trebellius laid into the prisoner methodically, a steady series of blows to his stomach, head and ribs. The Silurian endured it without saying a word, and merely groaned in pain and sucked in shallow breaths when his tattooed chest hurt too much to breathe normally.

'This isn't getting us anywhere,' Cato decided at length. 'We'd better try another tack. Decurion, let him down and bring him some water and bread.'

Trebellius wiped the beads of sweat from his brow. 'I could try applying a bit of heat if you like, sir. A hot iron to the arse can be effective.'

Cato shook his head. 'Not now. Maybe later on, if we need to. Let's just try to get him talking. Let him down. Find Decimus and tell him to bring some food and water, and some wine for myself and the centurion.'

Trebellius untied the rope and the Silurian collapsed on to the ground with a pained grunt as the impact drove the air from his lungs. While the decurion left the room to fetch some water and bread, Trebellius wrenched the spear shaft away from the prisoner, freeing his arms. The Silurian lay on his side, panting, until his breath returned and then he eased himself on to his backside and shuffled towards the wall and sat propped up, glaring at the two Roman officers.

Macro finished his soup and pushed the bowl to one side. He wiped his lips on the back of his forearm. 'You know, I don't think he likes us, Cato.'

Cato smiled thinly.

'We come all this way to share the benefits of civilisation,' Macro continued, 'and this is the thanks we get. Sometimes I wonder if these barbarians deserve us. What do you plan to do with him, once Trebellius has finished his work?'

Cato tapped the end of his crutch against the instep of his boot. 'I rather think this one's going to present a bit of a challenge to the decurion. He's a hard case, right enough. We'll have to take him on with us. Tie him down over one of the mules and try questioning him again once we reach Bruccium. I'm sure Quertus has an interrogator in the garrison.'

The Silurian looked up sharply and for an instant Cato saw the look of fear in his expression before the prisoner clenched his jaw and glared back at him.

'You see that, Macro?'

'What?'

'How he reacted when I mentioned Quertus's name. Seems the centurion's reputation amongst the local tribes is as infamous as we've been told.'

The door to the mess opened and Trebellius held it ajar as Decimus entered carrying a sturdy wooden tray bearing a jug, three plain Samian cups, a canteen and a small hunk of bread. He set the tray down on the table and poured wine into the cups and passed them to each of the officers.

'Give him some water,' Cato ordered. 'And feed him the bread.'

Decimus nodded and approached the prisoner warily before he knelt at his side. He pulled the stopper from the waterskin and held it out for the prisoner to see. The Silurian hesitated a moment before nodding curtly and opening his lips so that the Roman could angle the nozzle into his mouth. He gulped greedily, spilling water down his front. Once he'd done, he drew back and waited for Decimus to press the bread into his hands. He strained to reach up to his mouth and tore a chunk off to chew. Cato let him eat a moment before he turned to Trebellius.

'Ask him what his name is.'

'His name?' Macro frowned. 'What do you need to know that for? You're not planning on being his best mate.'

'Macro, let me deal with this.' Cato indicated to the decurion to translate his question. The Silurian viewed the prefect suspiciously for a moment, weighing up the pros and cons of giving his name, and then he made his decision and gave his answer.

'Turrus, he says.'

'I see.' Cato nodded and then tapped his chest. 'Prefect Cato. The surly one there is Centurion Macro.'

Given that Trebellius had been beating the prisoner for the last hour or so, Cato decided there was no profit to be had from introducing the decurion's name. Instead he continued with his attempt to find a crack in the prisoner's tough veneer. The man looked to be in his late twenties and Cato hazarded a guess.

'Do you have a woman, Turrus? A family?'

After the decurion had translated, the Silurian deliberately took another mouthful of bread and chewed slowly to buy himself a little

127

time. Cato indulged him, while Macro leaned back against the wall and folded his arms. At length the man swallowed the final morsel of bread and nodded.

'*Sa . . .*'

Cato smiled slightly. 'I have a wife, back in Rome. She worries about me. Can't wait for this campaign to be over so that I can return to her. Or she can join me here, once the new province is settled and we have peace.'

Turrus listened to the translation and then replied.

'He says that if the Romans returned across the sea and left this island to its people then everyone could return to their families.'

Cato shook his head sadly. 'Alas, it's not so simple. Most of the tribes have already become our allies, and accepted the rule of Rome, along with all the benefits that come with that. Benefits that come at a price, admittedly. We can't abandon our new friends to the ravages of Caratacus and his warriors. Moreover, the reputation of the Emperor depends upon bringing peace to Britannia, no matter what the cost, or how long it takes. And you should know that when Rome sets her mind to achieving something, it will be achieved and no one can stand in the way. Tell him, Trebellius.'

The Silurian listened and then nodded thoughtfully before he responded.

'He says that Romans and Silurians have much in common. Neither is prepared to give way to the will of the other. It will be a long war.'

Cato shrugged. 'That may be so. But I doubt it. Our soldiers are the best in the known world. The result is not in doubt, Turrus. Believe it. If the Silures continue to follow Caratacus then they will be led down a path that ends in destruction. Along the way, there is only suffering, for both sides. It would be far better to face up to realities and for the warriors of the Silures to seek peace with Rome. Then I can return to my wife, and you, Turrus, can return to your family. Surely that is for the best?'

The prisoner smiled and replied in a regretful tone.

'Even if I agreed with you, our desires would never sway those of our leaders. Your Emperor and Caratacus will continue this conflict until the last drop of our blood. So we must fight on.'

'Not you,' Macro growled. 'The fighting's over for you, sunshine. One way or another.'

Cato ignored his friend and focused his attention on the prisoner. He felt a small thrill of satisfaction at the Silurian's last comment. So, he was disenchanted with his leader. No doubt there were others like Turrus, many others, tribesmen who had answered the call to arms with full hearts, thinking that it would be a more glorious cause than the usual round of tribal feuds and minor conflicts. Caratacus knew how to inspire the hearts of warriors and the proud tribes of the mountains would have responded eagerly. But instead of marching to battle they had been dragged into a drawn-out war of attrition that had become more bitter with each passing month. Unlike the soldiers of the Roman army, the Silurians were farmers and herders. They would surely long to return to their families and the warmth of their hearths, rather than stalking the Romans through the icy winds and rain of the mountains. It was time to press home his advantage, Cato decided. He forced a smile as he spoke to Trebellius.

'Ask him why he's afraid of Centurion Quertus?'

The decurion seemed surprised by the question but shrugged and turned to the prisoner and translated. At once Turrus stopped chewing, then swallowed nervously and stared down at the ground.

'That got his attention,' said Macro. He made his way across the room and dug his boot into the man's thigh. 'Speak up.'

The tribesman drew his legs close to his body and hunched down, like a whipped dog, and he began to speak in a low, haunted voice.

'He says Quertus is a devil. That he has burned many villages and slaughtered every living thing in his path. Right down to the last infant, dog and lamb. He is evil and cruel and he worships dark gods and makes blood sacrifices in their name. There is no black deed that he does not inflict upon the Silures. When he rides into battle, he wears the skins of the greatest of the warriors he has defeated. He drinks the blood of those he kills and eats their flesh. Those that follow him are slaves to his will, and follow his example. Wherever they go, they leave death and devastation in their wake. They are . . .'

Trebellius asked the man to repeat his final words and there was a brief exchange before he turned to the two officers. 'The nearest Latin word for it is barbarians.'

'Barbarians?' Macro burst into laughter. 'Barbarians! Our side? The cheeky fucking sod! Here, Trebellius, stand aside. I'll show him fucking barbarians.'

'That's enough, Macro,' Cato interrupted. 'Leave him be.'

The prefect regarded the prisoner thoughtfully. Centurion Quertus clearly had earned himself a frightening reputation amongst the Silures. That was all to the good. If you could strike fear into an enemy's heart before they faced you in battle then the fight was half won. Of course, the man was exaggerating the details. That was to be expected when rumour fed on rumour. No doubt the centurion's methods were harsh and he made full use of surprise to achieve his victories over the enemy, but the rest of it was nonsense. The stuff of nightmares. Still, it gave Cato an edge over his prisoner. He glanced at Trebellius and spoke in a harsh tone.

'Ask him where his village is again. Tell him that if he does not give me the location we'll take him with us to Bruccium and let Quertus continue the interrogation there.'

As he heard the translation Turrus flinched, as if he had been kicked, and Cato saw that he was genuinely terrified by the prospect of falling into the hands of Centurion Quertus. The Silurian clasped his hands together and shuffled slightly towards Cato and pleaded with him.

A cold look of satisfaction was on the decurion's face as he conveyed the prisoner's words. 'He begs you to spare him. Don't take him to Bruccium. Send him to Glevum instead. He'd rather be a slave than face Quertus . . . Then there was some stuff about begging his gods to save him.'

Cato leaned forward and prodded the end of his crutch into the prisoner's chest. 'Then tell me where your village is! Tell me that and you have my word that you and your people will be spared. Slaves you will become, but you will escape sword and fire. Now tell me!'

Turrus made a keening noise in his throat and shook his head, torn between the dread of facing the enemy who haunted his darkest nightmares and the shame of betraying his tribe. He gritted his teeth and bowed his head as he shrank back into himself.

Trebellius clicked his tongue. 'Want me to continue with the interrogation, sir? Another beating might break him, now that you've gone and put the frighteners on him.'

Cato thought a moment. Despite the man's terror, he would not give up his family. There was a chance, however remote, that the Romans might be set upon before they reached Bruccium. No doubt he would cling to that hope. Until they reached the fort. Then there would be no escaping the choice Cato had forced upon him. The prefect shook his head.

'No. Pick him up. Take him outside and tie him up securely for the night. Make sure he can't do any harm to himself. You'd better tell the optio to have the men on watch check him from time to time. All right, we're done here.'

Trebellius saluted and then hauled the prisoner up on to his feet. 'Come on, my little beauty, it's time for some shut-eye.'

The decurion bundled Turrus out of the mess room and shut the door behind him.

Cato nodded to Decimus squatting in a corner chewing on a strip of dried beef. 'I want to speak to the optio in command of this outpost.'

Decimus struggled to his feet and limped out of the room. There was a brief silence before Macro gestured to the bowl of stew that had been prepared for Cato. 'Do you mind?'

The stew had cooled and congealed into a glutinous mass, with a thin film of fat across the surface. Cato shook his head again. 'Be my guest.'

As Macro tucked into his second helping his friend stroked his jaw and considered their situation.

'The nearer we get to Bruccium, the stranger things seem to be. Even if half of what our friend Turrus said is true, then we're really going to be out on a limb. Doesn't it strike you as very convenient?'

Macro looked up, spoon dripping small brown clods as he held it in mid-air. 'Convenient, how?'

'We didn't exactly win many friends in Rome before we left.

131

Indeed, that's why Narcissus was doing us a favour getting us posted to Britannia as soon as possible.'

'And here we are, so what's the problem?'

'It's just that "here" happens to be on the road to an isolated fort as far forward as it's possible to be, surrounded by enemy warriors and commanded by a man who seems to be a bloodthirsty maniac. It feels to me like we've been set up for a fall, Macro.'

'Set up by who?'

'Who do you think? Pallas, it has to be.' Cato recalled the oily Greek freedman who served as an imperial adviser. With the Emperor growing old and infirm, his servants were positioning themselves to take advantage of the situation when Claudius's successor took the throne. Pallas had sided with the Emperor's new wife, Agrippina, and her son Nero. The latter might already be Emperor but for Cato and Macro saving the life of Claudius in an attempt on his life. Cato sighed. 'We put an end to Pallas's plot against the Emperor and he wants his revenge, as well as to tidy up any loose ends.'

'Shame that none of the mud stuck to him.' Macro sniffed. 'That sly Greek bastard got away with it.'

'True, but we know what he did. As long as we're alive then Pallas sees us as a potential threat. He can't afford for us to reveal what we know, even though few people are going to believe us. What could be better for him than sending us into danger?'

'Aren't you forgetting something? I doubt the fort was even built when Narcissus sent us on our way. And your predecessor died shortly before that. There's no way the news could have reached Rome before we set out.'

'It doesn't matter. The specifics are of little account. My guess is that after Pallas learned that we were bound for Britannia he sent a message to one of his agents here with orders to make sure we were put in harm's way. My guess is that Pallas has a man inside the governor's staff, if not the governor himself. They would see to it that we were sent somewhere there is a good chance we'll be killed off. Bruccium fits the bill nicely and the death of the previous prefect meant there was no need to get him reassigned to a new posting. So far it's worked out well for Pallas.'

'If that's what is going on,' Macro said doubtfully. 'But frankly, Cato, I think you're jumping at shadows. Our being sent to Bruccium is just the luck of the draw.'

Cato looked at him. 'You really think so? After all the scheming we've witnessed over the last few years? You know how things work inside the palace.'

They were interrupted by Decimus as he returned with the optio. They stepped into the mess room and the optio closed the door behind him before saluting his superiors. 'Optio Manlius Acer, sir. You wanted to see me.'

Cato nodded. 'At ease, Optio. Take a seat.'

The optio looked briefly surprised at the informality shown to him by someone as senior as a prefect and then sat on the bench opposite.

'This is the last outpost before the fort at Bruccium, right? There's nothing beyond here. Not even a signal post.'

The optio nodded.

'The thing is, there's been no report from Bruccium in over a month. Have you heard anything?'

'Heard, no. But I saw a patrol towards the head of the valley ten days ago, sir. A squadron of Thracian cavalry. They looked on for a moment and then disappeared into the trees.'

'But no message? No request for supplies?'

The optio shook his head.

'Peculiar, don't you think?' Cato pressed him.

'Peculiar doesn't begin to describe it, sir. Before Quertus took command the prefect used to send two squadrons and two centuries of legionaries back to the depot to escort the supply convoy up to the fort every ten days, regular as anything. After the prefect died the routine continued for a while, then many days would go by between supply runs. Eventually the resupply requests and the escort stopped coming.'

Macro looked at the optio. 'Why didn't you send a patrol to investigate?'

'Not my job, sir. My orders are to guard this side of the pass and report back to Glevum on any sightings of the enemy.'

'That's not really good enough, is it?' Macro asked caustically.

'You were pretty slow to come to our aid earlier today, and now this. I'm not impressed.'

Acer folded his hands together and rubbed a thumb across the knuckles of the other hand. 'Sir, I've less than forty men here. We're in the heart of enemy territory. If we take unnecessary risks then we die.'

'That's what you signed up for, Acer. What we all signed up for. That's no excuse.'

The optio opened his mouth to protest but saw the cold glint in Macro's eyes and looked down in shame instead. There was no profit in undermining the optio, Cato decided, and he returned to the subject at hand.

'If there's been no request for supplies then it means that Quertus and his men are living off the land.'

'Or they've been wiped out,' Decimus suggested anxiously. 'If there's been no word from them, then what else could have happened?'

Macro corrected him. 'The optio says he saw one of their patrols ten days ago.'

'Quite,' Cato agreed. 'So we must assume the fort and its garrison are intact. We'll know soon enough in any case. If we start out at first light we should reach the fort by dusk.'

'You're continuing, sir?' asked Decimus.

'Of course. I have orders to take command of the fort.'

'But things ain't right, sir. Not by a long way. It would be madness to continue. Not before you know what you're leading us into.'

'Nevertheless, we will continue to Bruccium.'

'Not me, sir. I ain't going another step. Come the morning, I'm heading back to Glevum, and then Londinium.'

Macro smiled. 'All by yourself? On foot, with that gammy leg of yours? Sounds like more of a risk than continuing to Bruccium.'

'I'll take one of the mules.'

'One of *our* mules? I don't think so, Decimus.'

The veteran turned to Cato. 'You can spare me one, sir.'

Cato shook his head. 'We've got a prisoner to carry, as well as our baggage. But if it'll help change your mind, I'll give you a hundred denarii bonus if you stay with us until the autumn.'

Macro looked startled. 'A hundred? Are you mad?'

Cato raised a hand to silence him, his attention fixed on Decimus. 'If it's as dangerous as you think, then I'll need you at my side. And that hundred denarii should set you up nicely in Londinium when this is all over. What do you say?'

Decimus looked distraught, his fears warring with his greed. In the end he stared bitterly at Cato. 'Seems I ain't got any choice anyway. I can't stay here. I can't get back to Londinium. The only way is forward. All right, a hundred denarii it is. I accept.'

Cato smiled thinly. 'Very big of you. Now, you'd better see to our bed rolls. Centurion Macro and I will be sleeping in here. Then get some rest. It'll be a long day tomorrow.'

Decimus nodded unhappily and left the mess room. Once he had gone, Macro let out a sigh and muttered, 'Glad to see that Decimus is willing to stand with us . . . The hundred denarii helped, though.'

'You know how it is. Money talks.' Cato cocked an eyebrow. 'Actually, it practically screams.'

Optio Acer looked up at him. 'Perhaps your servant is right to be nervous, sir.'

'How so?'

'I don't quite know how to put it, sir.'

'Well, try putting it into words, man,' Macro growled. 'Before I lose my patience.'

The optio winced but then took a sharp breath and steeled himself to speak. 'I don't know what they've told you about what's been going on at Bruccium, sir, but it's never been quite right to my mind, since the fort was built. The last prefect was, well, a bit on the weak side. Left most of the running of the garrison to Quertus.'

'How do you know this?' asked Cato.

'I heard it from the men passing through here on the way to the supply base. That, and more.' The optio lowered his voice. 'They said that Quertus rules the fort with a rod of iron and hands out the harshest punishments for the smallest of infractions. They said he had ordered one of the optios beaten to death for questioning his order not to take prisoners following a raid on a local village.'

135

Macro sucked in a breath. 'Good discipline is one thing. But that's going too far.'

Cato shot him a look. 'You think? Carry on, Acer. What else have you heard?'

'The prefect looked the other way for a while, but in the end he confronted Quertus. Told him that he had put in a request to have him transferred to another unit. That was shortly before the prefect's accident.'

Macro narrowed his eyes. 'What are you suggesting, Optio?'

Acer swallowed nervously. 'I'm just telling you what I know, sir. You can draw your own conclusions.' The optio stood up and faced Cato. 'I've said enough, sir. I should see to the sentries. After the attack this afternoon, I've doubled the watches. I don't want to be surprised again.'

'Very good.' Cato nodded. 'You may go.'

Once he had left, Macro puffed out his cheeks. 'Now they're all at it. Quertus has got our own side spooked as much as the enemy. Perhaps you're right. Maybe there's more to this than I thought.'

'We'll know soon enough. We should reach Bruccium tomorrow.' Cato stretched his back and yawned. 'And then we'll finally meet Centurion Quertus in the flesh.'

# CHAPTER FIFTEEN

'The top of the pass should be just ahead.' Trebellius spoke quietly, as if fearful that they might be overheard. Around them the mist was thick enough to conceal the rocky slopes rising up on each side. The clatter of their hoofs on the loose shale seemed unnervingly loud as the riders slowly made their way up the rise. Cato's replacement mount was a steady, mild-mannered beast by the name of Hannibal. Fortunately he did not take after his namesake and presented no trouble to his Roman rider. As near as Cato could estimate, it was mid-afternoon. A light drizzle filled the air and coated the cloaks of the riders in tiny beads of moisture. The prisoner had been tied over the back of a mule and his tattooed back glistened in the damp. The stillness and quiet of their surroundings made the men of the squadron nervous and they glanced warily from side to side as they walked their mounts up the track. Cato pulled his cloak more tightly about him and tried not to shiver.

'And what is beyond the pass?' he asked the decurion.

'The track leads down into the valley, straight to the fort, about five miles from here. You can't miss it.'

'You've been there before then?'

'Once, shortly after it was completed.'

'What's the layout?'

Trebellius paused a moment as he recalled the details. 'It's well-sited, above a small gorge with a swift current flowing through it. The cliff bends round the side and then there's steep ground in front of the other two faces which have the usual ditch and rampart. It's a pretty formidable position and you'd need an army and even a decent siege train to break into the place.'

'Does it command a good view of the valley?'

The decurion nodded. 'That too. Though in a mist like this that's of little use, and mists are commonplace in these mountains.' He shook his head. 'Why the fuck anyone, even barbarians like the Silurians, would want to live here is beyond me.' He turned to Cato. 'Once we reach the top of the pass, I'll be turning back to Glevum, sir.'

'I know.'

There was a brief pause before Trebellius continued. 'We've already escorted you further than my orders required, sir.'

'I know. You don't have to justify it to me, Decurion. We'll be fine.'

'Yes, sir.' The decurion nudged his heels in and urged his mount forward to resume his position at the head of the small column.

They rode on in silence until Macro edged his horse alongside Cato and muttered, 'I hope we will be fine. If laughing boy's Silurian friends are still around I don't give much for our chances when Trebellius and his lads about face.'

'If the enemy are as scared of Quertus as our prisoner seems to be then I don't think we're going to be in any danger once we enter the valley. Not from the Silurians, at any rate.'

Macro flashed him a searching look. 'What's that supposed to mean?'

'You heard what Acer said about the previous prefect. Seems that I might have to be careful I don't go the same way.'

Macro glanced round anxiously before he responded in an undertone, 'You really think Quertus would do something like that? Bump off his commander in the middle of a campaign?'

'Can you think of a better time to do it? With the enemy close at hand and casualties piling up, who is going to question one more death? As long as a killer is careful not to be too obvious he could get away with murder. From the sound of things, Centurion Quertus is a man with a pretty ruthless streak, who doesn't let anyone stand in his way.'

'That may be true,' Macro mused. 'But still.'

'But still, what?' Cato said tersely. 'We've known men do worse things, Macro. Far worse.'

'And there was me thinking that we only had to watch our backs when in Rome.' Macro swore under his breath. 'Fuck, what is it with us, Cato? Everywhere we end up we need eyes in the back of our heads. It's like we're cursed or something. I thought we'd left that all behind when we came back to Britannia.'

They continued in silence for a while as the track levelled out and then there was a shout from the man riding point. At once Trebellius gave the order to halt and called for the rider to make his report.

'Something ahead, sir, on the track!'

'What is it?'

'Can't quite make it out. There was a gap in the mist, now it's gone again.' The man's voice betrayed his nervousness and Macro flicked his reins to urge his horse forward.

'I've had enough of this nonsense. Come on.'

For a moment Cato felt a spark of irritation at his friend taking the initiative before he could react. Then Cato kicked his heels into Hannibal's flanks and set off after Macro. As they passed the decurion, Macro gestured to him. 'You too, sunshine.'

The three officers trotted along the track for a hundred paces before they saw the figure of the point rider emerge from the swirling mist, his spear already in his hand as he stared into the gloom beyond.

'What did you see?' Macro demanded as they reined in beside the soldier. 'Out with it, lad!'

'There was something on the track, sir.'

'Something?' Macro growled. 'Try being more specific. Something, or someone?'

The soldier swallowed. 'I thought I saw a man, sir, standing on the track. Just for a moment, before the mist thickened.'

'Did he see you?'

'I'm not sure. He didn't seem to move. Not even when I called to challenge him. He made no reply, sir.'

'I see.' Macro squinted ahead for a moment. 'And nothing since then. No sign of movement? No sound?'

'No, sir. Nothing.'

Macro turned to Cato. 'What do you think?'

Cato felt his heartbeat quicken and suppressed the urge to tremble that was building at the base of his spine. He swallowed before replying as steadily as he could, 'I think we should see for ourselves, Centurion.' He turned to the decurion. 'Trebellius, if you hear anything, come forward at once with your men. Understand?'

Trebellius nodded and made no offer to join his superiors as they walked their horses forward.

The mist hung across the landscape like a veil wafting in the lightest of airs. Thicker one moment and then thinning in patches before it closed in again. An eerie quiet and sense of menace pressed in from all sides. Then a fluke in the light breeze revealed the track before them and they saw a thin shape emerge from the mist fifty paces ahead. At once the two halted their horses.

'What's that?' Macro squinted. 'Your eyes are better than mine. Is that a man?'

'I think so, but he's not moving.'

If it was a man, there was something odd about his posture, Cato decided. He drew a deep breath and called out, 'Who goes there?'

There was no reply, and still no sign of movement, and after a short interval Cato walked his mount on, followed closely by Macro.

'I don't like it,' the centurion muttered. 'What if it's another ambush?'

'If it is then they're doing their level best not to catch us by surprise.'

Despite his calm tone, Cato's heart was pounding inside his chest and his hands felt clammy with anxiety as he led the way along the track. He glanced to each side, straining his eyes and ears for any sound of movement, but all was as before. Ahead, the figure slowly resolved into a firm outline as they approached. It was clearly a man, and at last they could see why he had made no movement nor responded to Macro's challenge. He was naked and impaled on a stout wooden stake that had been driven into the middle of the track. The man's pale, mottled skin was covered in painted native designs and his limbs and head hung lifelessly. As they drew closer, Cato could see that the stake had been driven up under his groin and the wood was covered in a dark stain that had also pooled on the ground around the base of the stake.

'What in Hades' name is this?' Macro asked softly.

'A marker, I should think. Quertus is setting out the boundary of his territory and warning those who dare to enter the valley.'

'Warning who? The enemy, or us?'

'Both, I should think. Why else put it here, where one of our patrols might encounter it?' As he spoke the last word, it caught in his throat as he spied another body on a stake, off to one side of the track, then another opposite, forming a line across the route leading into the valley beyond. 'There's more of them, Macro. Look.'

He pointed them out and his friend swore. They gazed at the bodies a moment before Macro turned back and cupped a hand to his mouth.

'Decurion! Bring your men on! It's safe.'

Cato shot him a surprised look. 'Safe?'

'These three aren't going to pose much of a threat, are they?'

Cato glanced at the bodies. 'No, not them.'

There was a dull rattle of hoofs on loose stones as Trebellius and the rest of the column emerged from the mist and reined in in front of the line of stakes. Even though most of the soldiers had experienced the horrors of war, Cato could see the ashen expression on the faces of the men nearest to him. The prisoner, hanging over the back of one of Decimus's mules, looked up and his eyes were wide in terror at the sight of the impaled men. He began to speak quickly, in a desperate pleading tone.

'Decimus!' Macro called out. 'Shut him up.'

Decimus tore his gaze away and nodded. He turned his mule back to the prisoner and raised his fist menacingly. Turrus flinched, and clamped his jaw shut, watching the Roman warily.

'Who are they?' asked Trebellius.

'Silurians, I'd guess.' Cato pointed to the markings on the nearest man. 'We can find out soon enough. Decimus! Bring the prisoner forward.'

The mules trotted up. Turrus's jaw sagged slightly at the sight of the three bodies and then he started to tremble.

'Ask him if these are his people?'

Trebellius translated the question and Turrus nodded anxiously.

'Then this is the work of Quertus, all right,' said Macro. 'Only thing that makes sense.'

141

He was about to continue when there was a soft groan from the man to the right. The heads of the riders turned towards the figure and Cato saw that he was moving feebly, his feet struggling against the rough wood of the stake.

'Dear Mithras.' Decimus's voice wavered. 'He's alive.'

Cato swung his leg over the saddle horns, slipped to the ground and strode through the tussocks of grass towards the man. Macro came after him as the others looked on. When they reached him, Cato could see that he was a young warrior, no older than twenty, thin-limbed, with his matted hair plastered to his head and straggling over his shoulders. His eyes were half open and rolled up as he let out a thin, keening groan of agony. Cato watched as he tried to press the soles of his feet against the stake and lift his weight up. But each time his feet slipped on the damp wood and his groin settled again on the point with a horrible sucking creak and he let out a moan. Then Cato understood. He was not trying to get himself off the stake, only hoping to put an end to his agonies by driving the point further into his vital organs. Cato felt his stomach knot tightly in disgust and nausea. He opened his mouth, ready to order Macro to put the Silurian out of his misery, but then stopped himself. If that was his wish, then he had no right to force it on his friend. Cato gritted his teeth and drew his sword. Hesitating briefly, he steeled himself to the task and then stepped forward and raised the point until it touched the bare flesh of the man, just below his ribcage. The Silurian's eyes opened wide and he glanced at Macro before fixing his gaze on Cato below him. The eyes were a piercing blue, Cato noted, desperately trying to focus his attention away from other details.

The Silurian mumbled something between his cracked lips, softly spoken words, in a pleading tone, and then he nodded and winced at the terrible pain that even such a slight movement caused him.

Bunching his muscle, and drawing the sword back a short distance, Cato punched it up through the soft skin, under the ribs, until the point fetched up against bone. The Silurian flung his head back and let out a sharp gasp. His body tensed as Cato twisted the blade, left and right, and then ripped it free. A rush of blood followed the blade and spattered down on to the ground below the stake, where a barely visible curl of steam licked into the air. The Silurian began to tremble violently and his breathing came in snatched, ragged gasps, growing weaker all the time until at length his body went limp and his head slumped down on his breast. The body hung in the cold air like a side of meat in a butcher's shop. Cato fought to keep his expression neutral as he bent down to wipe the blade clean on a tussock of grass. He removed as much of the blood as he could before straightening up and thrusting his sword back into its scabbard with a sharp snap. He looked round to see the other men watching him.

'We're finished here. Time to move on.'

There was a pause before Trebellius cleared his throat. 'Begging your pardon, sir, but this is where my men and I turn back.'

'What are you talking about?'

'This is where the valley starts, sir. Like you said yourself, these bodies mark the turf controlled by the fort. You'll be safe until you reach your new command now.'

Cato stared at the decurion and saw that he was doing a poor job of disguising his fear.

'You may be right, but I would prefer it if you and your men escorted us to within sight of the fort before leaving us. Just so that you can report back to the legate that we arrived in one piece and didn't disappear somewhere along the route. If you understand me.'

Trebellius nodded slowly. 'I understand, sir. But, as I said, I'm turning back.'

This was too much for Macro who turned on the decurion with a ferocious glare. 'Abandoning us, more like. You coward! What are you afraid of?' Macro gestured to the bodies hanging on the stakes. 'You think these cunts are going to jump down and give you a good hiding? Trebellius, for the gods' sake, grow a pair!'

The decurion gritted his teeth and answered in a cold, flat tone. 'I ain't a coward. I've been fighting on this cursed island for the last eight years, like most of my men here. I've got five years to go before my discharge. So I obey my orders, to the letter. And my orders say for me and my men to escort you and the prefect to this valley. That we've done.'

'Then I'm giving you new orders,' Cato interrupted. 'I'm ordering you to escort us to Bruccium.'

The decurion did not reply but stared back defiantly. Cato decided to try another tack. He continued in a more reasonable tone, 'Look here, Trebellius. You know what's waiting for you when you return to Glevum. You'll be held accountable for the loss of your standard back at the outpost. If you stay with us as far as Bruccium, I give you my word that I will put in a good word for you with the legate.'

The decurion considered the offer but shook his head regretfully. 'Sorry, sir. I am not going on. I doubt any of my lads would want to follow me even if I agreed to do as you ask.'

Cato stared hard at him for a moment, giving him a chance to change his mind, but Trebellius met his gaze steadily and kept his silence. With a sigh of frustration Cato resolved to make one last appeal to discipline. He strode over to his mount, took the reins and swung himself up into the saddle. 'Now let's get moving.'

His instruction was met with silence and stillness. Cato felt his pulse quicken and the cool air suddenly seemed colder still. Trebellius met his gaze flatly and his men sat in their saddles waiting to follow his lead.

'You heard the prefect!' Macro called out. 'Form column and prepare to advance!'

'No . . . sir,' Trebellius responded loudly enough for his men to hear. 'We take our orders from the legate. Not you. Either of you. Column! About face, and form up!'

'Oh no you don't,' Macro growled as he reached for his sword. There was a soft scrape as the blade began to leave its scabbard.

Cato hurriedly jerked his reins and moved his horse between Macro and the decurion and hissed, 'Don't, Macro. Trebellius and his men are terrified. You try and face him down and anything could happen.'

'But—'

'Leave it be. That's an order.'

Macro frowned for an instant and then gave a frustrated shrug and slid his sword back. 'At least someone is obeying orders around here . . .'

144

They watched as Trebellius and his men hastily formed a column of twos and when they were ready, the decurion turned in his saddle to salute his superiors. 'You should reach Bruccium before dark. Good luck.'

Cato nodded while Macro clenched his jaw and muttered, 'And fuck you too.'

Trebellius raised his arm. 'Column, forwards!'

The riders urged their mounts into a trot and moved off, back up the track through the pass. Soon the last of them had dissolved into the mist and only the sound of the horses' hoofs carried to Cato and the others for a while longer before there was silence and they were alone. Decimus looked around anxiously, then chewed his lip.

'What now, sir? It's not too late to ride after them.'

'Keep your mind on the reward,' Cato said gently. He looked at the body of the young Silurian. 'There's no point staying here.'

Macro nodded. 'Conversation's a bit limited. Just hope we find some live ones soon, and on our side. All this mist and quiet is starting to piss me off.'

Cato smiled. 'What better reason to get moving?'

He clicked his tongue and steered his horse on to the path, giving the body a wide berth, and Macro and Decimus urged their mounts to fall into place behind the prefect. Decimus tugged on the rope tied to the mules and with a muted bray they followed on. The prisoner mumbled some prayers to his gods as they continued into the mist. The track descended another mile to the valley floor. Gradually the grey shroud began to lift a little and they could make out the loom of the forested slopes on either side. It was Decimus who noticed first, and he used his crop on the mule's back to urge it closer to the two officers.

'Sir, there's someone behind us.'

Cato and Macro slowed to a stop and turned in their saddles. For a moment all three looked back, ears straining. Then Macro sighed heavily.

'You're imagining things, Decimus. Your only danger in this place is the prospect of frightening yourself to death.'

Decimus shook his head. 'Shhh! Just listen.'

'What do you think you heard?' asked Cato, after a brief silence.

'A horse . . . Horses. I'm sure of it, sir.'

'Well, I can't hear anything.'

'Like I said,' Macro sniffed contemptuously, 'he's jumping at shadows.'

A faint whinny sounded some distance behind them. All three froze, and Cato felt an icy tingle spread across his scalp.

'Shadows, eh?' Decimus muttered. 'I told you, sir. What do we do? Run for it? Find somewhere to hide? If they catch us, then they'll be sure to do to us what Quertus did to their mates. Or worse.'

Macro glanced at him and cocked an eyebrow. 'Worse? I think I must have underestimated your imagination . . . Should we turn and face 'em?'

'No. We've no idea of their number. Best to keep moving and let them think we're not on to them yet. Decimus, keep your ears open. If they sound like they're getting closer, tell me at once. We'll look for cover as we go. We can't be too far from Bruccium now. Might even run into a patrol. Let's go.'

The continued along the track, with Cato and Macro keeping watch on their flanks and the way ahead while Decimus nervously glanced over his shoulder every few breaths. The horsemen behind them seemed to make no attempt to draw any closer and aside from the odd soft whinny or the faint clatter of hoofs on stone, it was hard to believe they were not alone in this ethereal, menacing landscape of cold, damp and shadows. A half mile further on Macro edged his mount alongside Cato and spoke softly.

'There's more of 'em off to the left.'

Cato nodded. 'I noticed them a few moments ago.'

'And you didn't say anything?'

'Didn't want to scare you.'

'Ha . . . ha . . .' Macro intoned, deadpan, as they both faced ahead but swivelled their eyes to the left. The ground was more even now, as the valley spread out on either side in the thinning mist. A quarter of a mile to their left was the edge of a forest. Moving along the trees was a line of horsemen, ten of them. They were too distant to make out in any detail. With a sudden inkling Cato glanced to his right. A similar distance away another party of riders was tracking them.

'I fear we have walked, ridden I should say, into a trap, Macro. Look there.' He gestured subtly and Macro turned, and swore under his breath.

'Why don't they attack?' Macro asked. 'Surely they can see they have the drop on us?'

Cato was thinking swiftly. There was no way out but to continue forwards. Half a mile further on the route entered a wood that sprawled a good way across the valley floor. If they could reach the trees far enough ahead of their pursuers they might be able to turn off the track and hide amongst the trees.

'Sir!' Decimus called softly. 'Have you seen, they're all around us!'

'I see 'em,' Cato replied calmly. 'Just ignore them. Until I give the word.'

'What are you thinking?' asked Macro.

Cato did not answer. He calculated the distance remaining, and the angle the pursuers would have to take to continue following them into the wood. They would have to abandon the mules. The small beasts were too slow. Cato, as was his way, briefly considered all the alternatives, even ruthlessly abandoning Decimus to his fate in order to give himself and Macro a chance to escape. Just as typically, he instantly abandoned the notion. Whatever logic dictated, there was a code of conduct that embraced those entrusted with command, and it would be unthinkable to sacrifice Decimus.

Slowing his horse so that he dropped back towards his servant, Cato spoke quietly. 'When I give the word, Decimus, you get off the mule and climb up behind me.'

'What about the prisoner?' asked Macro.

'We'll leave him behind with the mules. If those are his people, hopefully they'll stop to set him free, and that'll buy us a little more time.'

'What are you planning, lad?'

'We'll ride hard for the treeline. They'll be forced to angle across country to follow us, and lose a bit of ground. If we reach the cover of the trees sufficiently far ahead of them, we can leave the track and lose them in the wood.'

'That's madness,' Decimus protested. 'They'll hunt us down.'

'Maybe. But with two on my horse, they'll catch us quickly in open country. We'll stand a better chance of getting away from them in the wood.'

Decimus clenched his jaw and said bitterly, 'I should have stayed in Londinium.'

Macro spat to one side. 'Beginning to wish the same thing.'

'Quiet!' Cato ordered. 'Just be ready when I give the signal.'

They were no more than a quarter of a mile from the edge of the wood when Cato noticed that the men on either side were moving closer. The time to act had come, he decided. Taking a deep breath, he reined in and spoke steadily to Decimus.

'Now is the time. Up you get!'

Decimus slipped from the saddle of his mule and Cato offered a hand to help him scramble up behind the saddle. As soon as the man had a firm grip on the rear saddle horns, Cato spurred Hannibal forward.

'Go, Macro! As fast as you can! I'll follow!'

The centurion slapped his hand on the rump of his mount before leaning forward and urging it on towards the distant trees. The mules, spooked by the sudden action, brayed and trotted after the horses for a short way before the burden of the baggage and the prisoner slowed them to a halt and they stood uncertainly, strung out along the route, abandoned.

As soon as they realised what their prey was up to, the riders on either flank gave chase, making for an opening in the trees where the track entered the wood in an attempt to cut the Romans off. Macro had already drawn a short distance ahead and Cato was tempted to call out to him so that he would not leave his companions behind. It was an unworthy thought and Cato banished it in an instant as he gritted his teeth and dug his heels in, forcing his mount to rush headlong down the track, kicking up small stones and divots of turf in its wake. The cold and chill of the day were lost in the anxious hot thrill of the chase and the details of the world around him were leaping before his eyes as the powerful muscles of the horse galloped for the safety of the trees.

'Come on, Cato!' Macro shouted over his shoulder. 'Keep up!'

The other men were close enough now for their shouts to be heard even above the din of the hoofs thrumming on the ground beneath Cato. But he could not make out the words, and leaned slightly further forward in his saddle as he and Decimus galloped on. Then the trees rushed up on either side and the track passed into the wood. Ahead, the route continued more or less straight, before bending around a clump of tall oaks and out of sight.

'Macro!' The driving impact of the horse made it hard for Cato to call out his instruction. 'Once we get – past those oaks – get off the track – to the right!'

Macro nodded and the two horses pounded down the narrow route. Risking a glance back, Cato could not see their pursuers. Then, a short distance from the bend, he heard an excited cry and saw that the first of their pursuers had already reached the forest track, barely a hundred paces away. They still had enough of a lead for his plan to work, Cato thought desperately, and urged his horse on. Ahead, there was a short distance to the bend, and already Macro was swerving round the fallen branches and brambles at the foot of the ancient oaks and disappearing from sight. Cato could feel the flanks of his horse swelling and falling like bellows against his calves as the beast struggled under the weight of two men. It was already slowing down, despite his desperate urging. Then they reached the oaks and Cato leaned to the side as the horse galloped round the bend. He saw Macro no more than ten feet in front of him, sword in hand, facing down the track while his horse snorted and pawed at the ground. Cato pulled hard on his reins and his horse swerved to the left and glanced off the rear quarter of the other animal with a frightened whinny. Decimus was thrown forward by the abrupt halt and knocked Cato so that the coarse hair of the horse's mane brushed his face.

He straightened up at once. 'Macro, what the—'

Then he saw them. No more than fifty feet ahead, the track was blocked by more riders, sitting silently in their saddles, staring at the Romans. They wore dark cloaks and their hair straggled on to their shoulders. Each man carried a spear and an oval shield. That was as much as Cato took in before his attention was drawn to the sound of hoofs rapidly approaching from behind.

'We're fucked,' Decimus groaned as Cato reached down and drew his sword.

'Shut up!' the prefect snapped, drawing his horse up alongside Macro.

'So much for the plan.' Macro smiled grimly. 'What now? Cut our way through?'

Cato nodded. 'That's all we can do. Ready?'

Both men tightened their grip on their sword handles and pressed their legs against the sides of their mounts as they prepared to charge. Cato heard a dull scrape as Decimus drew his blade.

Behind them there was a sudden rumble of hoofs and cries of alarm as their pursuers reached the bend, saw the confrontation ahead of them and drew up in confusion. This was the moment to strike, Cato decided, while at least some of their opponents were disrupted. He drew his breath, ready to let out his battle cry, when a deep voice bellowed through the air. A figure emerged from the ranks of the men blocking the way ahead. He walked his horse forward casually and turned it so that it stood across the track, neck raised, ears pricked, breath pluming from its nostrils. Cato's heart was beating so fast he felt sure that it must be heard by everyone around him. He stared hard at the man confronting them. Like the others, his hair was dark and tied back by a broad headband. His brow was prominent and his eyes dark and deep set above a thick beard that masked his jaw. Even though he wore a cloak, Cato could see that he was massively built and his bare arms were like hams, covered with dark bristles. The man stared at them impassively while his men waited on his command, spears poised to strike down the three Romans that had dared to ride into the heart of these wild mountains.

There was a pause that made every moment linger on Cato's heightened senses; he took in every visual detail, every sound, and smell in what might be the last few breaths of his life. Then the figure settled back in his saddle and he rested his left hand on his hip.

'Who are you?' he demanded in Latin.

'Romans,' Macro replied.

'You don't say.' There was a hint of amusement in his tone.

'Well, that's a shame. I had hoped to make an example of some more of those Silurian scum . . . What are you doing here?'

Cato eased himself up in his saddle and sheathed his sword. 'I'm Prefect Quintus Licinius Cato. This is Centurion Lucius Cornelius Macro. I've been sent to take command of the fort at Bruccium. I assume you're Thracians from the garrison.'

The man nodded.

'And who are you?' Macro asked as he lowered his sword but kept it tightly gripped at his side.

The man clicked his tongue and walked his horse towards the Romans. He stopped again, directly in front of them, and raised his head. His dark eyes bored into Cato.

'I am Centurion Quertus.'

# CHAPTER SIXTEEN

The mist had lifted by the time the horsemen emerged from the wood and followed the track across open land. The sky was still overcast and the sun was no more than a faint loom amid the grey shroud that hung over the landscape. A light drizzle added to the discomfort of Cato and his companions as they rode with the Thracian auxiliaries. Once he had examined Cato's authority to assume command, Centurion Quertus gave orders for the mules and the prisoner to be rounded up. Then he re-formed his men and led the column in the direction of the fort. As they reached open ground, he sent two riders to scout ahead while he dropped back and fell in alongside Cato and Macro.

'Mind telling me what all that was about?' said Macro. 'Back there when you and your men were hunting us down.'

Quertus pursed his lips so that they disappeared behind the bristles of his beard before he replied. 'This is Silurian territory. Or it was until we established the fort here. It's my job to take the war to the enemy. You were spotted by one of my patrols, even before you entered the pass. They couldn't get close enough in the mist to identify you as Romans. In any case, it's been a while since we've seen any Romans from outside the garrison.'

'So I understand,' said Cato. 'You've also failed to send any reports to Glevum for quite a while. I imagine that some of those at headquarters were on the verge of giving you and your men up for lost.'

'Not enough to stop you being sent out here, apparently.'

Cato and Macro exchanged a quick glance.

'Why haven't you been in contact with headquarters for so long?' Cato asked.

'We're surrounded by the enemy. If I send a man back with a report, then the chances are the Silurians would take him. In which case I lose a man, and the report fails to get through in any case. So there's no point. If I have anything significant to tell the legate I'll make sure he gets a report. Otherwise I'll carry on with my orders to harrass the enemy. Which is why I led one of my squadrons out to set an ambush for you, if you turned out to be the enemy. By the way, you fell into the trap nicely. Though I was under the impression there were more than three of you, not counting the prisoner back there.'

'Our escort turned back at the pass leading into the valley,' Cato explained. 'Where we found three Silurians that had been left out to die. That was your work, I take it.'

'I like to let the enemy know what they can expect if they dare to cross my path. There are others at every route into the valley. And we leave some behind every time we raid a village or clash with one of their war parties.'

'Why?'

Quertus turned to give him a withering look. 'It's obvious. It scares the enemy.'

Macro gave a dry laugh. 'Scares our lads as well.'

'Then they should stay out of my way.' Quertus scowled. 'I don't need anyone interfering with my work.'

'Your work? You mean your orders. You're supposed to be harrassing the enemy, not waging a private war.'

Quertus shrugged and looked ahead. 'My valley, my rules. As long as I do what the legate wants.'

'Yes, well, I'm in command now,' Cato responded warily. 'Things may change at Bruccium.'

'We shall see.'

'And while we're on the issue, since I am the new prefect, you will call me sir, Centurion Quertus.'

The other man looked at him, scarcely bothering to conceal his contempt as he replied, 'As you wish, sir.'

Cato felt an icy fist close round his heart. A dark cloud of menace seemed to surround the Thracian officer. Cato was cautious, and not a little afraid. He had no desire to provide this man with an opportunity to get rid of any new rival for control of his men. He decided it would be wise to make Quertus aware of the wider picture.

'I expect you have taken quite a few casualties since the fort was constructed.'

'Some. Mostly the weaker men.'

'Then you'll be glad to know that a column of replacements will be marching from Glevum to join us in a matter of days.'

Quertus looked at him sharply. 'More Romans?'

Cato nodded. 'Legionaries for the most part. Though those that can ride well can replace some of the men you lost, should I decide to do so.'

It was a subtle reminder that the Thracian officer would go back to his unit and surrender the overall command of the garrison to Cato.

'When we reach the fort I shall expect a full report from you on the period of your command, together with an inventory of supplies and up-to-date strength returns,' Cato continued. 'Then I shall want both cohorts paraded for inspection at dawn tomorrow.'

Quertus did not reply and Cato felt himself flush with anger. He cleared his throat and spoke clearly. 'Did you hear my orders, Centurion?'

'Yes, sir.'

'Then be so good as to acknowledge them in future.'

'Yes, sir,' Quertus replied flatly. 'If that's all, I need to check on my scouts.'

'I thought you said this valley was your turf,' Macro commented. 'That was the point of the men you impaled for the enemy to see. To warn them off.'

'It does that. And it unnerves them, and it serves to remind my men of the kind of war we are fighting. That is the fate of any men who allow themselves to be taken prisoner. A lesson I think even you two must learn. The sooner the better.' He glowered at Macro. 'Even so, there are some enemy warriors made of sterner stuff who we have to look out for.'

He spurred his mount forward, breaking into a canter as he rode ahead of the column towards the scouts, some distance ahead. Cato and Macro watched him recede, his cloak flapping around his body like a swirl of crows.

Cato glanced round. The Thracians returned his gaze steadfastly, as if not caring that they were under scrutiny from the new prefect in charge of the fort at Bruccium. Many of them bore tattoos on their faces, dark swirling patterns, unlike the ornate blue patterns favoured by the Britons. Their cloaks and tunics were heavily worn and stained and their equipment was a mixture of that issued to auxiliary troops, captured Silurian weapons and some examples of more exotic design that Cato guessed came from their native Thrace.

At the rear of the column Decimus was riding by the edge of the track where he could stay in sight of Cato and Macro and be reassured. Behind him, tied to the saddle horn of one of the other mules, was the prisoner, a look of acute misery etched on his face. Cato turned back to his companion and spoke quietly.

'What are you thinking, Macro?'

His friend replied in hushed tones. 'Centurion Quertus is not taking it well.'

'I'll say.'

Macro gestured discreetly in the direction of the men riding behind them. 'And I've never seen such a rabble before, even amongst some of the sorriest-looking auxiliary units in the army. They look like barbarians. It's hard to tell this lot apart from the natives.'

Cato nodded. 'Perhaps that's the intention. That, or Quertus is going one step further and making his men seem even more frightening than the Silurians.'

'They don't frighten me,' Macro said firmly.

'Not much does, I'm glad to say.'

Macro smiled at the compliment and then his expression hardened again. 'Even so, I don't like the situation. We'll have to watch Quertus closely. He's probably already thinking about how he can dispose of us without drawing too much attention from headquarters.'

'My thoughts exactly,' said Cato. 'And while he continues to strike fear into the hearts of the local tribes the legate is going to want to keep him at it. We shall have to watch our step.'

Macro nodded. 'Something else worries me. If this lot are typical of the men at the fort, what else are we going to have to deal with? They're not going to take kindly to a bit of spit and polish and some square-bashing.'

'No.'

Cato felt a drop of rain fall on the hand holding the reins and looked up at the sky. A band of dark clouds was blowing in across the mountains, bringing a downpour with it. He pulled up the hood of his cloak and hunched down inside the thick folds of the material. More drops fell and soon the rain closed in around the riders, hissing as it spattered off the ground and turned the surface of the track into a glistening stream of mud.

'You know,' Macro grumbled, 'it's times like this when I wonder if it might not be better to leave these particular Elysian fields to the locals. Why the fuck does Claudius want to add this miserable pit to the empire?'

'Macro, you know how it is. We don't get to ask the questions. We're here because we're here, and that's all there is to it.'

Macro laughed. 'Finally, you're learning.'

The rain continued to fall for the rest of the day without let-up. As the pallid light began to fade, the landscape of the upper valley gave way to what had once been cultivated land. Abandoned farms spread out on either side of the track. Some clusters of huts still stood, empty with no smoke rising from their hearths. Others had been burned leaving ugly blackened ruins rising up from the ground like the rotten teeth of an old hag. About them lay neglected fields, overgrown with weeds and wild barley. Close to the track, in the long grass, Cato spied the remains of animals, weathered pelts hanging over bone, lying where they had been slaughtered. There were the corpses of people as well, wizened, blackened faces stretched over skulls with empty eye sockets. More evidence of the handiwork of Quertus and his men.

The track reached the bank of a narrow river and followed its course as the rain exploded off the surface of the water like a shower of silver coins. A few miles further on, as the last of the daylight began to fade, the riders at last came in sight of the fort of Bruccium. Cato sat up in his saddle and stared ahead. From Trebellius's earlier description he already had some idea of what to expect and he saw that the site had been well chosen indeed. The course of the river ran around the low hill upon which the fort had been built, providing a natural defence along three sides. An attacker would have to abandon any notion of assaulting the turf ramparts overlooking the steep slopes that fell down to the riverbank. On the fourth side the fort was protected by a ditch in front of the rampart.

'Impressive,' Macro conceded. 'Caratacus hasn't much hope of taking Bruccium.'

Cato nodded. No matter how brave the natives were, they lacked understanding of siege weapons. That was why they had placed so much faith in the hill forts they had constructed on a lavish scale. But while they had proved effective in the conflicts between the tribes of the island, they stood little chance against the bolt-throwers and onagers of the Roman legions. The latter had battered down the palisades and gates of one hill fort after another, while the bolt-throwers had scourged the ramparts, striking down any warriors brave enough to stand their ground and show their defiance to their enemy. After that it had simply been a matter of forming a tortoise to approach the breaches in the defences and then charging home to overwhelm the remaining defenders.

As yet the native warriors were only beginning to discover ways to counter the superiority that the soldiers of Rome had on the battlefield or in siegecraft. It had taken Caratacus several defeats before he learned to avoid pitched battles with the legions and to use the ponderous pace of the Roman army against itself. For some years now he had devoted his energies to striking at the legions' supply lines, raiding deep behind the frontier and withdrawing before the Romans could react. It had proved an effective and profitable strategy and the raiders had returned to their tribes laden with the spoils they had taken from raiding villas and ambushes of supply columns and unwary patrols. For their part, having lost the initiative, the Romans could only respond to the raids by sending columns racing to the scene, too late to intervene. Inevitably, Governor Ostorius came to the realisation that the long war against the native tribes would only come to an end if there was no safe haven for Caratacus and his warriors. Without the defeat of the Silures and the Ordovices there would never be peace in the new province of Britannia.

Now that they were in sight of the fort, Quertus and his scouts reined in and waited for the rest of the column to catch up before continuing along the track to the approaches of the fort. There was no vicus, nor any bathhouse built outside the wall. Only the thatched haystacks that served as part of the stockpile of feed for the horses. These were protected by a modest palisade with two sentries on the gate. The track turned up towards the main gate of Bruccium.

'What are those?' asked Macro, pointing up the slope.

Cato turned in the saddle and raised a hand to shelter his eyes from the rain as he looked in the direction that Macro had indicated. From the gates of the fort a line of short posts ran down either side of the track at intervals of ten feet for a distance of perhaps two hundred paces. On top of each was a crude orb. Cato felt his stomach lurch as he guessed at once what they were. A moment later his fear was confirmed. Heads. An avenue of grisly trophies, their expressions frozen in pain and terror at the moment of their deaths, glistening in the rain as water dripped from the tendrils of hair hanging from their scalps.

Cato swallowed as he fought to control the wave of disgust that threatened to overwhelm him. Then, as he looked up at the fort, he saw more heads along the rampart, facing out over the valley as if to warn any onlooker that this had become a place of death and darkness. A darkness of the human soul as black as night itself, Cato thought as he rode beside Macro in silence, passing between the severed heads of the victims of Quertus and his men.

As they reached the narrow causeway across the outer ditch, an order was shouted inside the fort and the gates began to open, the hinges groaning and creaking under the burden of the heavy timbers. Quertus halted and turned his horse across the track so that he could face the two officers behind him. The rain had drenched his dark hair and cloak, which seemed to merge into one, slick with a dull gleam, like pitch. His beard parted as he grinned and waved a hand towards the gloomy opening beneath the gatehouse.

'Centurion Macro, Prefect Cato . . . welcome to Bruccium.'

# THE FORT AT BRUCCIUM

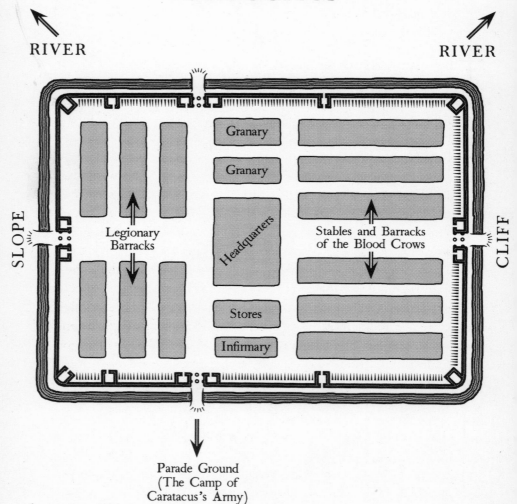

RIVER

RIVER

SLOPE

CLIFF

Granary

Granary

Headquarters

Stores

Infirmary

Legionary
Barracks

Stables and Barracks
of the Blood Crows

Parade Ground
(The Camp of
Caratacus's Army)

# CHAPTER SEVENTEEN

There was a knock on the door and a moment later Decimus entered and bowed his head in salute. 'Sir, the last of the officers has arrived. They're waiting in the hall.'

'Very well.' Cato eased himself up from the stool behind the desk. 'Help me with the armour.'

'Yes, sir.' Decimus crossed the commander's office to the wooden frame on which Cato's armour and weapons hung. Two hours had passed since they had reached the fort. The prisoner had been taken to the fort's guardhouse while Decimus had managed to unpack Cato and Macro's baggage in the quarters they had been assigned in the fort's headquarters block. There had been no need for Quertus to remove his kit since he had never chosen to occupy the rooms that had belonged to Cato's predecessor. The former prefect's meagre possessions had been left in place and Decimus had summoned the last two clerks from the headquarters staff to remove them to one of the storerooms. The clerks were aged veterans, grey-haired and too feeble to take their place in the ranks alongside their younger, fitter comrades. Earlier, they had explained to Cato that since Quertus had taken command, the rest of the headquarters staff had been plucked from behind their desks to join the ranks of the men that Quertus led against the surrounding tribes. There had been no attempt to maintain the records of the two cohorts in the garrison and the headquarters block had been largely abandoned. Only the two clerks remained, doing such tasks as their temporary commander deigned to give them.

Cato had changed out of the tunic and boots he had worn for the ride from Glevum. In their place he had put on a fresh tunic and a leather jerkin trimmed with shoulder strips, and calfskin boots which were more comfortable and practical than the sturdy soldier's sandals that he favoured in the field. He held his arms out as Decimus fitted the back and front plates of his cuirass and started fastening the buckles. Once he had finished one side, the servant shuffled round and started work on the other, clearing his throat as he addressed his superior.

'This ain't what I was expecting, sir,' he began cautiously.

'It isn't what either of us was expecting,' Cato replied wryly. 'Centurion Quertus has some rather individual notions about the duties of a garrison commander and officer in the Roman army.'

Decimus grunted and continued to the next buckle. 'I've never seen anything like this place before, sir. Never want to see anything like it again, for that matter. All those heads. And the bodies left in the ditch. It ain't right. And those men of his, it's like they're in a trance. None of them wanted to speak to me while we were marching to the fort. Just ignored me, though I did see a look in their eyes. Like they were too afraid to talk.'

'Really? Perhaps they were just observing good discipline.'

Decimus fastened the last buckle and took a step back. 'Is that what you think, sir?'

'I don't have to tell my servant what I think, Decimus. Nor do I think it is proper for you to voice such opinions about a senior centurion. Is that clear?' Cato did not want to dress the man down but he needed to know there were boundaries which had to be observed, unless permission was given to cross them. Cato relaxed his tone as he continued, 'That's the official line, in normal circumstances. But the situation here is far from normal. We must tread very carefully about Centurion Quertus for the moment. I need you to be my eyes and ears amongst the rankers of the garrison. Find out what has been going on here. See if anyone knows anything about the fate of my predecessor, Prefect Albinus. But be careful, Decimus.'

'I will be, sir. Since you left me with no choice about coming here, I aim to get out of Bruccium in one piece and get what you promised to pay me.'

'Assuming I live long enough to honour my debt.'

Decimus stared at him. 'Do you think we're in that much danger, sir?'

Cato looked at him with a surprised expression. 'Of course we are. These mountains and valleys are home to the toughest, most ruthless warriors in Britannia. They hate us with a passion, and they'll fight until the bitter end. And it's possible that we don't just have to worry about the enemy. I won't lie to you, Decimus. I've never seen anything like this place either. I'll have to be careful. So will you and Macro. Keep your wits about you at all times, understand?'

'Yes, sir.'

'Good. I hope I'm being overcautious and things aren't as bad as they seem. Maybe in a few days we'll have a laugh about it.'

'Somehow I doubt that.'

'We'll see. Now for the band.'

Decimus took the bright red strip of cloth from the stand and passed it round the midriff of the cuirass before tying it off at the front and tucking the loose ends in so that the slack hung in decorative loops.

'How do I look?' asked Cato.

Decimus pursed his lips. 'If it was anywhere else, I'd say fine. But here, you look out of place, sir.'

Cato did not respond but pointed to his sword and Decimus placed the strap over his shoulder and settled the scabbard to Cato's right, and then plucked up the collar of the tunic to ensure there was no point at which the neck of the cuirass would chafe against the prefect's skin. He stepped back to admire his handiwork and forced a smile. 'You look ready to present to the Emperor himself, sir.'

'One last thing.' Cato hated vainglory but considered that it would strengthen his position at the fort if the officers realised that their new commander was not just some chinless wonder straight from a comfortable household in Rome. 'Over there, in that chest. My medal harness.'

Decimus did as he was told and retrieved the set of polished discs fastened to the gleaming leather of the harness. Cato was gratified to see the frank look of admiration in the veteran's eyes as he placed the harness over the breastplate. Cato held them in place while his servant fastened the buckle at the back.

'You've seen quite a lot action then, sir. They don't hand these out just for showing up.'

'No, they don't.' Cato smiled briefly. 'As for action, I've seen more than enough. But I've got the feeling that I'll be seeing plenty more, and soon, if the gods have their way.'

'Don't know about the gods, sir. But I'm sure that's what Caratacus has in mind for us. And if not him, then Centurion Quertus.'

'That is for me to decide now,' Cato responded firmly. He took a deep breath and faced the door, pausing a moment to collect his thoughts and calm his troubled mind. Then he picked up the leather document holder that contained his authority to assume command of the garrison and strode towards the door. He stepped out into the corridor and made his way towards the main hall of the headquarters block, his boots echoing off the walls.

The centurions and optios of the Thracian unit and the cohort of infantry from the Fourteenth Legion were sitting on a series of benches as Cato entered the hall. The space was lit by tallow lamps set in iron brackets along the walls, and heated by a brazier burning at one end.

As soon as Cato entered, Macro shot to his feet and barked out, 'Commanding officer present!'

The other men hesitated until Quertus rose slowly to his feet and then they followed his lead. Cato made his way round the room to the space in front of the officers and indicated to Macro that he was ready.

'At ease!'

The officers sat down and Cato gave them a moment to make themselves comfortable, and to run his eye over the men he now commanded. He had assumed that there would be a marked difference between the appearance of the officers of the Thracian cavalry cohort and those from the legion. Instead he was shocked to see that nearly every man was unshaven, with uncut hair tied back in the manner of Centurion Quertus. Only two of the centurions from the Fourteenth and their optios were recognisably Roman, with cropped hair and standard-issue tunics and boots. Cato felt his

164

heart sink at the sight, and knew that he faced even more of a challenge than he had thought. He took a breath and clasped his authorisation in his hands behind his back.

'Good evening, gentlemen. If this fort is like any other then word will already have got round about my arrival, but, for the record, I am Prefect Cato, appointed to command the garrison at Bruccium.' He held the document holder up and flipped open the lid of the tube before extracting the authorisation bearing the Emperor's seal. He raised it so all could see and then returned it to the leather case. He indicated Macro. 'The other officer is Centurion Macro, taking up the command of the Fourth Cohort of the Fourteenth. Before I commence the briefing I wish to know more about the men I shall be commanding. One officer at a time.'

Before Cato could choose the first, Quertus was on his feet, arms folded. 'Very well. I am Centurion Sycharus Quertus of Dacia. I was a prince among my people before I was forced to flee after my father was murdered. I was raised in Thrace, where I was conscripted into the regiment and sent to serve on the Rhine. There I remained until the regiment was ordered to join the army gathering for the invasion of Britannia. In the following campaigns I was promoted to optio and then centurion and twice decorated for valour in battle. On the death of Prefect Albinus, I became commander of the cohort, and the fort, and since then we have carried the war into the heart of Silurian territory and burned scores of villages and slaughtered thousands of the enemy. I have made Rome a word to be feared in the lands between Glevum and the sea. The enemy know my name, and it strikes terror into the hearts of all who hear it.' He stretched out his arms and clenched his fists. 'I am Quertus, the destroyer of all who dare stand in my path! None can defeat me!'

The other officers stamped their feet in approval and Quertus basked in their praise until he lowered his arms and they instantly fell silent again. He turned to Cato with a cold smile of satisfaction. 'These officers are my brothers. They command my horse squadrons.' He indicated them each in turn. 'Fermatus, Cremax, Stellanus, Pindarus, Mithridates and Miro. Brave warriors all. Those others,' he nodded to the legionary centurions, 'they are infantry. Centurions

Publius Severus and Gaius Petillius. They are tasked with defending the fort, since that is all they are fit for.'

The two centurions flushed with anger and shame but dared not respond to the insult directed at them. Quertus glared contemptuously at them before he turned his gaze back to Cato and cocked his head slightly to one side.

'For months now we have waged our war against the Silurians, without interference from the legate at Glevum. I did not request anyone to replace Prefect Albinus. With respect, sir, you are not required, nor wanted here. You should return to Glevum. Tell the legate that I am carrying out his orders and will continue to do so until Silurians only exist in memory.'

Cato could see the blood draining from Macro's face as he listened to this torrent of insolence and feared that his friend would intervene. He stepped between them and faced Quertus.

'Centurion, you don't get to say who is required here and who is not. You, and I, are subject to the rules and regulations of the Roman army. We have both sworn an oath to the Emperor to obey those he places over us without question. I have been ordered to assume command here and you will recognise my authority to do so. We both know the severe penalties that are applied to those who refuse to obey their orders. In recognition of the success of your operations here, I will, on this occasion, overlook your insubordination and put it down to the consequences of the zeal with which you have taken the war to the enemy. But I will not tolerate such behaviour from you again. Is that understood?'

Quertus stared at Cato with a bemused expression that only angered, and alarmed, Cato even more. Quertus bowed his head mockingly.

'As the prefect wishes . . .'

'I do. Sit down,' Cato said firmly and, to his relief, the Thracian did as he was told. Cato waited a moment for the tension in the atmosphere to ease. 'Regardless of the success you have enjoyed in recent months, the aim of the governor's campaign must be kept in mind. The purpose of constructing forts like Bruccium is to restrict the movements of the enemy and to harass the tribes with a view to forcing Caratacus to concentrate his forces to deal with us. It is at that point that the main Roman army can advance against the enemy and try to force them into a decisive battle. If we crush the Silures and the Ordovices then Caratacus will be a spent force. No other tribe will be prepared to let him lead them to defeat. And since there is no more able commander amongst the natives, then the threat to Roman interests in Britannia will be dealt with, once and for all. My task is to see that the garrison of Bruccium plays its part in this overall plan. I will not tolerate any officer, or soldier, who does not understand and accept their duty. This garrison is part of the Roman army, and I will see to it that it conforms to the standards expected of Roman soldiers. The first step along that road will be a full inspection of every man in the garrison at first light tomorrow. I shall also want strength returns, inventories of kit, food supplies for the men and feed for the horses. Those records will be kept up to date and relevant copies sent to the headquarters staff. There will be changes in the way the garrison operates from now on and you would be wise to cooperate as fully as possible.' He paused briefly. 'Until tomorrow morning, gentlemen. Dismissed!'

Once again there was a pause while the officers waited for Quertus to provide the lead. He stood up and turned to them. 'You heard the prefect. Dismissed!'

They rose obediently and began to file out of the hall. Meanwhile, Cato fought hard to suppress the humiliation that burned in his veins. He waited until there were only a couple of officers remaining, and Quertus, before he called out to him.

'Centurion Quertus. A word, if you please.'

Quertus shrugged and turned back and sat on one of the rearmost benches while the last of the officers disappeared into the corridor outside, casting curious looks over their shoulders. Macro remained where he stood.

'Want me to remain behind as well, sir?'

'No need, Centurion. You may go.'

'Yes, sir!' Macro saluted smartly and marched from the hall.

As the door closed, Cato turned his attention to the thickset Thracian. Now that he had removed his cloak and sat in his tunic, Cato could see that he was even more powerfully built than he had thought. The man had a physique to match the best of the wrestlers in the arena at Rome and his glowering features were enough to arm him with an irresistibly intimidating demeanour. Cato had to forcibly remind himself of his superior rank, and the need to ensure that it was honoured. He narrowed his eyes a fraction as he stared at the Thracian.

'What is going on here?'

'What do you mean, sir?'

'Don't play the fool with me, Quertus! The men look like savages, and the bodies, and heads, you have put on display... It's beyond any notion of what is acceptable. It is not civilised.'

'Spare me your fine sentiments, Prefect. We are at war. We are not playing at war.' He gestured contemptuously at Cato's polished armour and medals. 'There is no place for civilised values here. Rome has been fighting the mountain tribes for the last six years with precious little result. I have lost many comrades in the struggle, men I was close to. The people who live in these lands are the real savages. They are fanatical in their hatred of Rome and they are driven on by the Druids. Until they are wiped out, and their Druids with them, there will be no Roman peace in the province. I've fought them long enough to know that they will keep on fighting Rome until the last drop of their blood. Every defeat only hardens their resolve. There is only one way to break their spirit and bring this to an end.'

'And what would that be?'

The Thracian leaned forward and his eyes bored into Cato's. 'You have to show them no mercy. Show them that we can be even more savage, cruel and ruthless, than the darkest of their Druids. I make them afraid. So afraid that they will think of me in their every waking thought with dread, and I will be there haunting their dreams with visions of blood and fire.'

'That is the reason for the gruesome displays that surround the fort?'

'Of course, and also the reason why I encourage the men to adopt an even more barbaric look than the enemy.'

'On that, I congratulate your achievement,' Cato responded acidly. 'But there is more to it than that, isn't there?'

Quertus did not reply for a moment, and then smiled thinly

168

at Cato. 'Very good. You're right, Prefect. My tactics and the appearance of my men is only part of the plan. What's more important is that the men think and act like savages when the time comes. That's something you can't simply order them to do. They must do it without thinking. They must become more barbaric than the barbarians they are fighting. Only then can we win. And we are winning. Every village we destroy, every man, woman and child we slaughter, every mutilated body we display serves to weaken the resolve of our enemy.' He paused and lowered his voice. 'When we first built this fort the Silurians would attack us every night. They ambushed our patrols, massacred our forage parties and taunted us with the heads of our comrades. When I took command we put their farms to the torch, destroyed their villages and drove every last one of them out of the valley – those we didn't put to the sword. Then we moved on to the surrounding valleys and made sure that they understood who was responsible for their suffering. Word of our actions spread and soon we began to encounter entire villages that had been abandoned. Fear is like any other contagion, it spreads from man to man and weakens the resolve, and the ability, to resist. We are close to breaking their spirit. I know it. Another month is all it will take. Then they will come to us on their knees, begging for peace on any terms.'

Cato listened in silence, taking it all in. It made sense of what he had seen, he reflected, but there was something that Quertus was holding back. And besides, it did not excuse the challenge to his authority. Above all, there was still the matter of the circumstances surrounding the death of the previous prefect.

'This . . . success of yours has come at a cost, I should think. How many men have you lost since taking command here?'

'No more than Rome can afford.'

'How many?'

'I haven't been keeping strength returns.'

'But you must have some idea,' Cato insisted.

Quertus folded his hands. 'There is a price for success in war. A price that is paid in men's lives. It has cost my cohort over half of its men. I made good the losses from those legionaries who volunteered to take their places. And there are many who freely volunteered. And some who did not. Men like Petillius and Severus who did not have the stomach for such work. They were left to defend the fort when I led the rest to fight the enemy. But now we are short of legionaries. It is good that we can expect reinforcements. Enough men to finish what I started.' His eyes gleamed at the prospect.

'Quertus, I am in command now. I will decide what happens next.'

The Thracian regarded him coolly. 'You would be wise to let me continue my work . . . sir.'

'Is that a threat?' Cato asked, resisting the urge to let his hand rest on the pommel of his sword.

Quertus was still for a moment before he shook his head. 'We are on the same side. We work for the same ends. It is simply a question of method, and I believe that mine works. Let me show you. Come on the next raid and judge for youself. I understand that you witnessed a Silurian war band attacking the outpost in the next valley.'

'Yes. And how exactly did you come to understand that?'

'One of my scouts saw it. He reported it to me and we set out to hunt down the Silurians. Instead we found you. And your prisoner. Once I have questioned him and we have the location of his village we can make an example of them.'

'I'd prefer to have Centurion Macro interrogate him.'

'Has he been trained in interrogation techniques?'

Cato allowed himself a light smile. 'He, uh, got his training on the job. Macro can loosen a man's tongue if anyone can. But that can wait until tomorrow.'

Quertus nodded thoughtfully. 'As you wish, sir.'

'I'll be honest with you, Centurion. I am not sure what to make of your activities in the last few months. I need to consider the situation. We'll talk more tomorrow, after the inspection.'

'The men don't need inspecting, sir.'

'I'll be the judge of that.' Cato yawned.

The Thracian stood up. 'Will that be all?'

'Not quite. I want the heads removed from the fort's walls, by tomorrow.'

Quertus inclined his head in the slightest of salutes before he turned and left the hall. Once he was alone, Cato slumped down on the chair and lowered his head into his hands and closed his eyes. He instinctively disliked and distrusted the Thracian officer. Yet the man had made a reasoned case for his extreme methods and perhaps there was some merit to them. The strains of the long ride from Glevum were beginning to tell and it was hard for Cato to think. He needed rest. A decent sleep to ready his mind for tomorrow, which was sure to be a testing day.

Stifling another yawn he stood up and stretched his shoulders, feeling a satisfying crack in one of his joints. He left the hall, and saw no sign of Macro in the corridor. He felt vaguely uneasy about going to his quarters without knowing that his friend was safe in this strange fort with its garrison of soldiers intoxicated by Quertus's thirst for war. But Macro was tough enough to look after himself, Cato decided. He walked slowly to his quarters and shut the door behind him. He hesitated a moment before slipping the bolt into place, locking it shut. Then, for good measure, he dragged a document chest against the inside of the door before heading for the sleeping chamber.

Cato removed his sword, struggled out of his harness and unbuckled his armour before setting it all down on the floor beside his cot. Then he eased himself down on to the cot and lay on the thin mattress stuffed with horsehair and closed his aching eyes with relief. For a moment he reviewed the conversation he had had with Quertus, before his mind started drifting. The last image that filtered through his thoughts was the young Silurian impaled at the head of the pass leading into this valley of death. Cato frowned at the image, and knew it was a harbinger of worse sights to come. Then at last he fell into a troubled sleep.

# CHAPTER EIGHTEEN

'Hey!' Macro called out to the other centurion as he followed
him out of the building into the darkness of the small courtyard
at the front of the fort's headquarters. A single torch flared in a
bracket above the entrance gate, though the other officers had
already left. 'Severus!'

The man stopped and turned to face Macro, who grinned.

'I knew it was you! By the gods, man, how long has it been?'
Macro strode up to him and clasped him by the shoulders. The
centurion was thin and his face looked drawn. A thin fringe of wiry
grey hair ringed his head and his bald crown gleamed dully in the
light of the torch flame. 'You've changed, Severus. I almost didn't
recognise you. What happened to that athletic legionary with
the fine head of blond hair? The one who broke the hearts of all the
local women in the vicus outside the Second Legion's fortress?'

'He grew old, and fearful,' Severus replied quietly. He glanced
past Macro towards the corridor leading to the hall. 'Will the prefect
be keeping Quertus for long?'

'If I know Cato, they'll be talking for a good while yet.'

Severus looked relieved and he offered Macro a tired smile. 'Well,
at least you haven't changed that much. Still the same bull of a man
with coarse curly hair you could brush your boots with.'

'So you recognised me too then?'

'The moment I saw you in the hall.'

'Then why didn't you say? I doubt there's any of the original
training section left these days. Fuck, it's good to see a familiar face
in this nightmare of a place.'

Severus's smile faded. 'It's a nightmare all right.'

172

'And that Quertus is a piece of work. A regular cold killer.'

Severus stared back at Macro. 'You don't know the half of it. That's why I didn't say anything about recognising you back in the hall. I'm in enough danger already without drawing any more attention to myself.'

'Danger? What do you mean, Severus?'

The other man looked around anxiously, but nothing moved in the shadows of the courtyard. They were alone. 'Look here, Macro, we need to talk. But not here. Let's get over to our side of the fort, away from these Thracian bastards. I've still got a few jugs of Gallic wine. I'll share a cup with you.'

'Fine. Let's go!' Macro clapped him on the shoulder. 'There's a lot to catch up on. Be good to have a drink before I take charge of the cohort.'

They left headquarters and turned into the main thoroughfare that bisected the interior of the fort. To their left Macro could see some of the other officers making for the long barrack blocks where the troopers had their quarters on one side while their mounts were stabled on the other. They turned right, towards the smaller barracks of the legionary cohort. As they made their way through the fort Macro could see signs of neglect. Weeds were thrusting up in the alleys between the timber and daub buildings. Some of the drains had blocked and small pools of foul-smelling water were backing up. There were none of the usual sounds that Macro associated with the forts he had known for most of his life. The barracks were silent – no raucous laughter from men sharing a drink as they played dice. There were no men sitting on stools outside the section rooms cleaning their kit. There were few men to be seen at all. As they reached the quarter assigned to the legionary cohort they passed a high timber cross frame with a footplate nailed into the riser. Macro glanced at it, but said nothing as he made small talk with his companion.

'Good to see that we both made centurion,' said Macro. 'It took me a fair amount of time, and the usual helping of good luck. How about you? You were transferred out of the Second fairly quickly, as I recall.'

Severus nodded. 'They were stripping men from the Rhine to fill out the ranks of the legions earmarked for a campaign across the Danuvius into Scythia. Where our commander hails from originally. As you can imagine, I keep quiet about that part of my career.'

'He's not the commander any longer. The fort has a new prefect now.'

Severus shot him a quick look. 'You think so? I doubt that Quertus is going to hand over control of the garrison that easily.'

'He has no choice. Chain of command.'

Severus laughed bitterly. 'I think you'll find that things operate a little differently at Bruccium.' He changed the subject. 'So what happened to the rest of the lads in the section after I left the Augusta?'

Macro scratched his jaw as he recalled their old comrades. 'Postumus was drowned when his boat capsized on a river patrol. Lucullus was bitten by a hunting dog. The wound went bad and killed him. Barco, the big bastard, you remember? He got picked for the legate's bodyguard, then caught the eye of Caligula and was transferred to the Praetorian Guard. Last I heard he'd got a promotion to centurion in the fleet at Misenum. Aculeus became a clerk at headquarters and was discharged for fiddling the books. Piso was killed in a skirmish with some Germans who had refused to cough up their taxes, and Marius, well, you'll find this one hard to believe: Marius was kicked to death by a mule.'

They both laughed before Severus looked at his companion curiously. 'I heard something about your promotion to centurion. I gather you were summoned to Rome to be decorated and promoted by Claudius himself.'

'Yes,' Macro replied quickly. 'Just a bit of a ceremony, a few months' leave in the city and back to the Rhine.'

'Oh.' Severus looked disappointed. 'I heard rumours there was more to it than that.'

'So how did you end up here?' Macro clumsily redirected the conversation. 'Bruccium, the absolute arse end of the empire.'

Severus shrugged. 'You go where you are sent. Ostorius is determined to push on and crush the last centre of resistance to Rome. So he's been constructing a number of big forts like this, strong enough to hold off any attacks and with enough men to make life difficult for the surrounding tribes. The forts are out on a limb, but that was a risk the governor was prepared to take, with our lives.'

Macro glanced round. 'Some forts are more out on a limb than others.'

'Tell me about it.'

'I was rather hoping you'd tell me.'

Severus said quietly, 'Not out here.'

He raised his hand and pointed out the end of a barrack block twenty paces ahead. 'That's mine. Home to the Second Century, Fourth Cohort, Fourteenth Legion. Or what's left of my century. The cohort commander's quarters are there at the end of the street.'

'Who is the ranking centurion at the moment?'

'That would be me. It should be Stellanus but he's gone over to the Thracians. As it is, only Petillius and I are left. And we've barely enough men to fill out the ranks of two centuries.'

'Two centuries?' Macro raised his eyebrows. The full complement of a legionary cohort was four hundred and eighty men, organised into six centuries of eighty soldiers. Barely a third of that number remained. 'What happened to the rest?'

They had reached the door to Severus's quarters and he ushered Macro inside. An orderly had been sitting by the small fireplace warming himself and he jumped to his feet as the officers entered.

'Titus, build the fire up, then fetch me a jug of wine from my stores.' He turned to Macro. 'Have you eaten?'

Macro shook his head.

'Then bring us some bread. Any of the cheese left?'

'No, sir. You ate the last of it two days ago. Same with the bread. There's biscuit, sir.'

Severus sighed. 'Biscuit then, and more bloody dried mutton.'

The orderly bowed his head and then turned his attention to the fire, carefully stacking some split logs on to the low flames.

'Trouble with food supplies?' Macro queried.

'Not if you like salted or dried mutton and biscuit. Quertus has resorted to living off the natives as part of his effort to cut himself free from Glevum. It means we eat what Quertus and his men pillage from their villages. Since their crops have only recently been planted that leaves only what they set aside for winter.'

'Well, I'm hungry enough to eat anything. And not a little thirsty.'

'Happily, in that regard I can provide you with something a little more interesting than the native beer which would otherwise be all that is on the menu.'

'Beer?'

'That's what they call it. Frankly, I've smelled more appetising horse piss. But Quertus is happy for the men to drink the stuff. Reckons a plain diet helps them keep their minds focused on killing.'

The orderly finished building the fire and left the room. Macro was keen to press Severus on his earlier question. 'Seems like there's been a lot of that on both sides. So what happened to the rest of the Fourth Cohort?'

'We started losing men as soon as we arrived in the valley and began work on the fort. Nothing serious, just the usual skirmishes when the natives had a crack at our lumber parties. Then, when the fort was ready, the prefect began to send patrols out into the valley. We were under orders to take the fight to men under arms only. The rest were to be left unharmed. We were even encouraged to trade with them.' Severus smiled. 'Seems the prefect had some quaint notion that there's more ways to build an empire than simply using force.'

'Yes, I've come across his kind myself.' Macro sighed. 'Bloody odd notions of how to go about the business of being a soldier.'

'Quite. Anyway, the Silures were happy to stage ambushes and harass the patrols, and then hide their weapons and slip back into their villages as if nothing had happened, and we had to go along with it. Except for Quertus. He refused. His unit had been fighting the Silures for years, and he argued that he knew their mind, and that the prefect's approach was futile. Maybe he's right. He should know. A few years earlier, before he was promoted to command the unit, he was captured, along with the survivors of a squadron he led. It seems the Silures held them for some months, and killed a handful off, before handing the rest over to the Druids to sacrifice. Quertus managed to escape, after he'd seen his companions burned alive. So I guess he has some grasp of the way the Silures live and think. In any case it convinced him that they could never be won over. More than that, he thinks that they can only be defeated if we turn their barbarism on them, and make the Silures as afraid of Romans as we are of the Druids.'

Macro puffed his cheeks. 'So that's his strategy?'

Severus lowered his voice as he continued. 'It's only half the story. Quertus knew that those who follow him need to be committed to his way of waging war. That's why he's encouraged his men to change their appearance and go back to the old ways of Thrace. He began to change their training, making them concentrate on killing, and absolute obedience to his will. One day he brought back some prisoners from a village at the far end of the valley. Twenty or so men, women, and a handful of kids. He had them tied to stakes on the training ground below the fort and then ordered his men to use them for spear practice. One of the men refused, and Quertus took his sword out and killed him on the spot. I didn't see it happen, but I'm told he showed no emotion when he did it, and simply told his men that the same would happen to them if they ever refused an order.'

'Shit . . . That's taking things a bit too far.'

'That's what Prefect Albius thought.'

They were interrupted by the return of the orderly who set down a jar, two cups and a wooden platter on which he had arranged a few strips of dried mutton and a handful of barley-flour biscuits. He bowed his head and left the room, closing the door behind him. Severus waited until he heard the man's footsteps receding before he continued.

'The prefect summoned Quertus and, so I heard, warned him not to do it again. If he did then he would be reported to the legate for disciplinary charges. So Quertus took to killing his victims on the spot, but word of that got back to the prefect, who announced that he would accompany Quertus on patrol from then on.'

'Let me guess,' said Macro. 'That's the patrol the prefect didn't return from.'

Severus nodded. 'The official version is that they charged into a village and the prefect was killed in the fighting when he fell from his horse. That was the first of the villages to be burned to the ground and every living thing in it put to the sword, in revenge for the death of the prefect, Quertus said. That became the pattern afterwards.

177

Village after village, farm after farm. Until the only living people in the valley were here at Bruccium. Then, earlier this year, he started work on the surrounding valleys. Of course, he lost men in the process, but then he offered the legionaries a chance to join the Thracians. By that time food was running short, and since the legionaries were left behind to protect the fort, Quertus said that they did not need as much food as the auxiliaries. Then the reason was that they did not deserve it, since they took no risk. A man can only go so far on an empty stomach, and our lads went to him willingly. The only conditions were that they obeyed his will completely, and that they take on the appearance of the Thracians. That's what happened to Stellanus and Fermatus.'

Macro's eyes widened. 'They're Roman officers?'

'They were. And a third of the Thracian cohort used to be legionaries. There was one other requirement before men could count themselves as followers of Quertus.' Severus poured them both a cup of wine and then looked down into the dark liquid in his cup. 'Quertus told them they had to take the head of one of their enemies and drink his blood.'

Macro stared at him. 'You are fucking joking . . .'

'I wish I was. By all the gods, I wish I was joking. But it's true.'

Despite the horrors he had seen in the campaigns he had fought across the years, Macro felt his guts clench tight, and cold, with fear.

'It can't be true.'

'You'll see for yourself, soon enough. You, and the new prefect. He won't last long, though.'

Macro stared across the table. 'Is Cato in danger?'

'Of course he is. If he tries to take any action against Quertus then he's as good as dead.'

'But he's the bloody prefect!' Macro protested. 'Appointed to the command by the Emperor himself. What he says goes. The moment Quertus tries anything on, Cato will have him disciplined. Or arrested.'

'Really? And who will do that?'

Macro shook his head disbelievingly. 'This is the fucking army. An order is given and the men jump to it.'

'Oh, this is the army, all right. But in this fort it belongs to

Quertus. Who do you think the Thracians will obey if there is a confrontation between your prefect and Quertus? And what goes for them goes for most of the surviving legionaries as well. None of them dares to step out of line. Not any more. You remember that cross we passed earlier? After the last prefect died, there were some officers and men in this cohort who refused to accept Quertus as their new commander. They confronted him in front of the whole garrison. He had his men arrest them for mutiny, and they were crucified and left to die, one by one. No one has dared to challenge him since then. Worse still, there is a reward promised to anyone who brings word of someone plotting mutiny. You can imagine how that might still any tongues.' Severus drained his cup. 'You should never have come here, Macro. But you weren't to know. No one does outside of this valley, except those poor Silurian bastards.'

Macro was silent for a moment. 'Why hasn't anyone attempted to inform the legate what is going on at Bruccium?'

'None of the legionaries is allowed to leave the fort, except as part of a Thracian patrol. When he took over, Quertus announced that anyone who tried to leave would be regarded as a deserter and executed.'

'And has anyone attempted to reach Glevum?'

'One of the optios. He got no further than five miles from the fort when one of the Thracian patrols ran him down.'

'What happened?' Macro asked quietly.

'Quertus was as good as his word.' The centurion reached for a strip of mutton and chewed on the end until he separated a chunk. As his jaw worked he looked across the table at Macro. 'You rode past the optio when you reached the fort. His head is on one of those stakes and what's left of his body is in the outer ditch.'

There was silence as Macro took it all in and then shook his head in disbelief. 'This is madness. Complete madness. The legate must be told.'

Severus looked doubtful. 'As long as we're carrying out his orders to take the fight to the Silures, why would he worry? As far as Quintatus is concerned, everything is going to plan and there are no problems at Bruccium. Why else would he send you and Prefect

179

Cato here? You can forget about any help from that quarter.'

'Then we must act. Someone has to do something about it.'

'You're welcome to try, Macro. Just don't involve me in it. I've given you fair warning of what has been going on here, for the sake of an old comrade. But that's as far as I'm prepared to go.'

'You won't back me?'

Severus sat still for a moment and shrugged helplessly. 'There's nothing I can do. Not now, at least. I'm hoping that Caratacus will throw in the towel. That's the only way I'm getting out of here alive. If Caratacus defeats Ostorius and forces the Romans out of the lands of the Ordovices and Silures, then he'll turn his attention on us. Given what Quertus has done to the tribes around Bruccium you can be sure there will be little pity in the heart of Caratacus when he deals with any survivors of the garrison.'

Macro sat back and took a deep breath. He could never have imagined a situation like this. His next thought was for Cato and he felt his heart leap in panic. He had left Cato alone with Quertus. He made to rise and knocked the edge of the table. Severus had to thrust out a hand to steady the jug.

'Oi! Careful, Macro. That's my bloody wine!'

'Sod your wine,' Macro growled. 'The prefect's in danger!'

'No . . . No, he's not. For the moment. Think it through, Macro. Sit down and think about it.'

He waved at the stool Macro had been sitting on and the latter hesitated a moment before he allowed himself to resume his place. 'Go on.'

'At first Quertus will try to win the new prefect over. If he can do that, then he will avoid any conflict, and be free to continue as before. His men follow him because he took command of the garrison by the book when Albinus was killed. If he tries to murder Cato, or seize his position, then it will divide the men. That's not to say that he won't try to stage an accident. Particularly if the new prefect tries to wrest control of the garrison from Quertus's hands. As long as Cato's back is covered he will be safe. But he's going to have to be very careful about how he deals with Quertus and his Thracians. The same applies to you, my old friend.'

Before Macro could respond, the door opened revealing a dark

180

shadow in the street. The two centurions started uneasily and there was a dry chuckle before the figure stepped into the warm glow of the fire. Macro recognised one of the officers from the Thracian cohort.

'Very cosy in here. And a small banquet besides!'

Severus swallowed nervously. 'Stellanus . . . What do you want?'

Stellanus laughed humourlessly. 'Thank you. I don't mind if I do.'

He shut the door behind him, crossed the room and pulled up a stool. 'No spare cup? Then I'll have to make do.' He grasped the jug and swung it into the air so that the spout was over his bearded lips and then poured a stream of the scarlet liquid into his mouth, swallowing greedily until he set the jug down heavily and smacked his lips. 'A nice drop, that!'

Severus glared back. 'Like I said, what do you want?'

'Just came to find the new commander of the Fourth Cohort.' He stuck out his hand towards Macro. 'Centurion Marcus Stellanus, seconded to the Second Thracian Cavalry. Greetings. I didn't have a chance to introduce myself earlier, at headquarters. Thought I'd come and track you down.'

'So you have,' Macro replied evenly, ignoring the outstretched hand. 'Though I have to say, you make an unlikely centurion.'

Stellanus grinned through his beard. 'This get-up? It's Quertus's idea. Makes us all look wild and terrifying. Grrrrrr!' He made a face and laughed.

Macro did not blink. 'Yes, I can imagine that might put the shits up some small kid on a dark night. But to me you look like a latrine brush.'

Stellanus frowned. 'Sorry?'

Macro smiled. 'The kind of thing I'd wipe my arse on.'

Stellanus's brow creased and he fixed Macro with a glare, and then suddenly he grinned once again. 'Ah, you're a hard case. Let's face it. Any man in the legions who lives long enough to command a cohort of his own has to be a hard case. You and I are cut from the same cloth, Macro. I was the commander of the Fourth before I volunteered to serve Quertus.'

'So I understand.' Macro casually reached over and took a fold of the other man's dark cloak between his thumb and forefinger and rubbed it gently. 'Somehow I doubt that we are cut from the same cloth. I wear the uniform of a Roman officer, not the rags of some barbarian dog.'

Stellanus pulled his cloak free and eased himself back out of reach. 'There's no call for that attitude, my friend. I just called in to welcome you to Bruccium. We need good men, now more than ever. Quertus says that the enemy is close to breaking point. Another month or two and they'll be finished. So I welcome your arrival, and the prefect, and the column of replacements that are due to arrive. Fresh blood. Just what we need to teach those Silurian cunts a lesson.'

'Sounds like they've been taught quite a few lessons already. Same goes for the men in the fort.'

Stellanus glanced at Severus who quickly looked down at his wine and kept his mouth shut. 'It seems that someone has been telling you stories, Centurion Macro. The truth is that we do things a little differently around here. Some have difficulty in accepting that and they'd be wise to keep their opinions to themselves. However, once you see things for yourself and understand, then I am sure you'll give Quertus your full support, like most of the rest of us. If not, then at least you'll not put any obstacles in his way. That's my advice.'

Macro forced himself to smile faintly. 'For which I thank you, Stellanus. Now, if you'll excuse me, I'm tired. I need to retire to my quarters, unpack and settle for the night. I want to be fresh for the inspection tomorrow, when the new prefect introduces himself to the garrison as their new commander.'

'Ah yes . . . Prefect Cato, commander of the fort at Bruccium. Fine titles indeed. But there's more to a title than mere words, Macro. Let that be the first lesson of your new appointment, if you know what's good for you. How well do you ride?'

The abrupt change in subject caught Macro by surprise. 'As well as any legionary needs to,' he replied awkwardly.

'That's good enough. Quertus could do with another good officer for the Thracian cohort.'

'Then thank him for the offer. But for now I am in command of the Fourth Cohort of the Fourteenth Legion.'

Stellanus smiled coldly. 'For now . . .'

'I intend to make the Fourth into the best cohort in the legion. Do me a favour, Stellanus. Tell the Romans that have joined Quertus that there is still a place for them here. At least until the replacement column arrives. After that, I'll be sending a report back to Glevum to the effect that any legionary serving with the Thracians has surrendered the privileges, pay and bonuses that go with service in the legions. You might want to consider that offer for yourself.'

'I don't think so.'

'No?' Macro stood up. 'A pity. I was sure there was a decent Roman hiding under all that spectacular growth of stinking hair. Seems I was wrong. I bid you goodnight . . . Thracian.'

Stellanus's eyes narrowed beneath his heavy brow but he said nothing as Macro left the mess. Outside he drew a deep breath and strode towards the barracks at the end of the street. When he had landed in Britannia he had been excited by the prospect of returning to his career in the legions. It had felt like coming home, he mused. All the once familiar sights, sounds, smells and routine of life in the service of Rome. Now that he was here in Bruccium, that dream taunted him cruelly. Instead he found himself in the darkest of nightmares where death was a constant shadow mere inches from his back.

# CHAPTER NINETEEN

There was a storm during the night and rain slashed down on to the wood shingle tiles and gushed in torrents down the narrow streets between the barrack blocks. But it eased and then stopped just before dawn and the sun rose into a sky that was a patchwork of blue and scattered cloud. The garrison marched out on to the levelled ground below the fort and formed up in front of the mound of earth that served as the commander's review stand. The ground was sodden and the boots and hoofs of the men and the cavalry mounts quickly turned the track leading from the gate into a quagmire. A handful of the stakes burdened by the heads had collapsed in to the mud and Quertus had set a small party to work putting them back up more securely.

Cato and Macro left the fort before Severus and the first century of legionaries marched out and made their way to the stand to watch proceedings closely. The legionaries, as was their privilege, formed up in their centuries, four ranks deep, at the centre of the parade ground. Even though he knew how few effectives remained in his new command, Macro felt a bitter disappointment as he looked out over the surviving pair of centuries. Their number made a mockery of the colour party where the six standards joined the cohort standard-bearer and the men carrying the curved brass horns over their shoulders.

By contrast, the Thracian cohort appeared to be at full strength and fielded ten squadrons of riders, forming five on each flank of the legionaries. The unit's standard-bearer advanced his mount to the right of the line and unfurled a red banner with a black crow clutching a small skull in its claws. Cato's force looked woefully unbalanced as it stood, formed up, in silence. The last man to reach the parade ground was Centurion Quertus. He rode down the length of the formation, sitting erect in his saddle and surveying them with a haughty air of ownership. Then he turned his horse and walked it slowly over to the review stand where he casually dismounted and handed the reins to an orderly before climbing the ramp.

'Good of you to join us,' said Macro as he stepped forward to the right of Cato.

The Thracian said nothing but took up his position on the prefect's left and stood with his hands loosely clasped behind his back. A light breeze was blowing and it stirred the manes of the horses, the dark cloaks of the Thracians, the banner of the Blood Crows and the crests of the officers' helmets.

Cato took out the leather tube and extracted the document authorising him to take command. After the conversation he had had with Quertus the previous night, and another with Macro before dawn, he felt anxious. If the Thracian centurion chose this moment to challenge him, in front of the men he had ruled for months with a rod of iron, then Cato had no illusions about his fate. If he was lucky he would be arrested and locked in the safe room below the headquarters. Accordingly he had decided to play it cautiously, until he had had a chance to establish himself at the fort; he would bide his time until he discovered Quertus's weak point.

Cato unrolled the document and began to read.

'I, Tiberius Claudius Drusus Germanicus, first citizen, chief priest, father of the nation, do hereby proclaim that Quintus Licinius Cato has been appointed Prefect of the Second Thracian Cavalry Cohort. The said Quintus Licinius Cato is entrusted to uphold the honour of the cohort, obey the officers placed over him, and swear to devote his life to the Emperor and the Senate and people of Rome.' Cato paused to add emphasis to what followed. 'This appointment is by imperial decree, and the officers and men over whom Quintus Licinius Cato has been placed in command are reminded that they are bound by the oath that they took on enlistment to obey those placed in authority over them as they would their Emperor, without question, upon pain of the full rigour of military law. By my hand I affirm this.'

Cato turned the document round and held it aloft so that all could see the imperial seal at the bottom. He waited a moment before lowering the authority, rolling it up again and placing it back in the leather tube. Then he surveyed the men before him for a moment before he began his address.

'You know my name. You know my rank. And you may know that I have come from Rome to take up this command. But that is all you know. Some of you will have served under a number of different commanders. Most of them will have been the sons of wealthy and well-connected noble families in Rome. Some of your commanders may have worked their way up the ranks. I come from the second tradition. I joined the Second Legion while it was stationed on the Rhine. That is where I fought my first battle, against German tribesmen. After that, the legion joined the army being formed to invade Britannia. I was there at the landing, and at every battle before Caratacus was defeated before his capital at Camulodunum. Since then I have fought the Durotriges, the Druids of the Dark Moon and many other enemies of Rome.

'So, gentlemen, you see before you a soldier who has earned the right to be your prefect and commander of the garrison at Bruccium. I am no pampered aristocrat. I have experienced the freezing cold of sentry duty on a winter's night, as you have. I have felt the lash of a centurion's vine cane, as you have. I know what it is to march day after day in full armour loaded down with my kit and rations, and then to have to build a fort each evening. I know what to expect from the men under my command, because I have been in your boots, I have lived and fought as you have and carry the scars to prove it.' He was silent for a moment before he continued. 'I expect the highest standards from the men I command and I will be satisfied with nothing less. The campaign against the Silures and the Ordovices has been bitterly fought over the last three years. Many thousands of our comrades have already given their lives to the struggle, but their sacrifice has not been in vain. Governor Ostorius has gathered a powerful army which will strike the decisive blow against the enemy before this year is out. We here today will play our part in that great struggle. We will play our part in that victory. We will win our share of the glory, the spoils and add garlands and

186

medals to our battle standards!' He drew his sword and thrust it into the air. 'Honour to the Second Thracian! Honour to the Fourteenth Legion!'

Macro echoed his cry, as did the legionaries standing on the parade ground, but the dark figures sitting in their saddles remained still and silent.

When the thin cheers of the legionaries had died away, Quertus stirred himself and drew his long-bladed cavalry sword and raised it directly towards the heavens, and his voice bellowed out over the parade ground.

'Honour to the Blood Crows!'

At once, all the riders punched their spears up, a wavering forest of gleaming points, and their cry rang in the ears of the three officers on the reviewing platform. Quertus repeated the cry over and over again, his men responding with frenzied roars. Macro glanced at Cato and saw the firm set of his jaw and the bitter look of resentment in his expression. They exchanged a quick look and Macro felt a stab of concern for his friend.

At length Quertus lowered his sword and sheathed the weapon, and at once his men fell eerily silent. As the Thracian resumed his place at the prefect's side, Cato swallowed, stepped forward and turned to face the other officers.

'That all but concludes the formalities, gentlemen. There only remains one final matter before I inspect the men.' Cato paused, knowing that what he was about to say would come as a shock to Macro, but it was a necessary step in the present circumstances. The cheering of the Thracians a moment earlier simply confirmed his decision. He cleared his throat. 'I have decided to appoint you as my second-in-command, Centurion Quertus. You have the ear of the men and know them well. Do you accept?'

He stared at Quertus, until at length the Thracian's lips curled in a slight smile and he said, 'I accept, sir.'

'Good. I trust you will carry out your responsibilities in an efficient, and obedient, manner.'

'Of course. You can rest assured that I will give you the benefit of my experience and advice, for as long as you command the garrison, sir.'

'I thank you. Now, I'd like to inspect the men. Have the Thracians dismount and form two lines.'

'Yes, sir.' Quertus offered a salute and then turned away to descend the platform and stride across to his men, bellowing orders.

Cato stared after him, acutely aware of the silent presence of Macro at his shoulder.

'I imagine that you are wondering about my decision.'

'Not my place to, sir,' Macro replied curtly. 'You are the commander of the garrison. You give the orders.'

Cato nodded to himself and felt a surge of irritation at the impulse to explain himself to Macro. His promotion to the rank of prefect after two years of temporary commands had made him superior in authority to his friend. He would have to be sparing with his moments of friendship and especially in seeking advice from the only man he had ever considered a close friend. Cato felt a brief sense of loss as he thought of the years in which he had shared the same rank as Macro. That sense of equality was lost to him now. Lost to both of them, he realised, understanding that Macro would rue its passing at least as much as himself. It was tempting to indulge himself in a moment of loneliness but Cato grimly suppressed his emotions, cursing himself for being weak enough to let them divert him from the obligations and dangers of the present. It had been a hard thing to do to choose Quertus as his second-in-command. He had considered confronting the man, removing him from his command and putting an end to his intolerable challenge to the discipline of the army. But if he tried to face Quertus down now, there was every chance that most of the men in the garrison would back the Thracian. If that happened, he and Macro would be in grave danger. Until the reinforcements arrived, Cato knew that he had to let Quertus think that he could exercise control over his new prefect. Once Cato had enough men at his back who owed no allegiance to the Thracian, then he could put Quertus back in his place.

'The men are ready for inspection, sir,' Macro prompted.

'Very well.' Cato drew himself up and marched down towards the lines of waiting men. Quertus stood with the colour party of his cohort, beneath the black crow on his standard. He waited until the prefect had passed by before falling into step beside Macro as they

188

followed the garrison commander along the front line of soldiers. Cato's experienced eyes took in every detail of the men before him. The troopers of the Thracian cohort would have broken the heart of any legionary centurion responsible for drilling these men. The black cloaks that they wore were spattered with mud and streaked with grime and no attempt had been made to repair any fraying edges or small tears. Their hair was wild and unkempt and most of them sported tattoos on their faces. Although Cato had seen some of these men the day before, the impact of viewing an entire cohort was unnerving from a professional point of view. He had been in the army long enough to have certain expectations about the appearance of soldiers, as well as their performance, and to recognise the link between the two. But the barbaric sight that the cohort presented was itself unnerving, and he could well understand the effect this might have on an enemy who had grown used to the spit and polish of the Roman army. Quertus and his men appearing out of the mists that wreathed the mountainous landscape would strike terror into the hearts of their victims.

He stopped in front of a tall, gaunt man. 'Show me your sword.'

'Yes, sir.' The man leaned his spear against his shoulder and drew the long blade from its scabbard. The spatha came out freely and the man flashed it up to the vertical for Cato to see it clearly. The metal gleamed and there was no sign of the pitting and specks of rust of a poorly maintained weapon. Cato raised his hand and tested the edge with his fingers and found it to be well honed and as sharp as could be expected. He nodded.

'That's fine. Now open your cloak.'

The trooper did as he was ordered and Cato saw that the iron rings of his body armour gleamed dully from a fresh application of sand and hard rubbing with a leather cloth. Despite the wild appearance of his men, Quertus clearly insisted that their weapons and armour were well looked after. He ordered the man to sheath his sword and examined a random handful of others and noted with approval that they took good care of their kit. Then he turned his attention to their mounts. The horses were large and powerfully built, typical of the stocks bred for the army in Gaul and Hispania. They had shed most of their winter coats, but the flanks of the horses had not been groomed so as to leave them matted with mud which obscured the identifying brands on their rumps. But it was in keeping with the savage look of the cohort. Even so, the saddles and tackle were well maintained and the horses appeared well fed and alert.

Cato turned to Quertus. 'They have been worked up to hard condition, I take it.'

'Yes, sir. I had 'em exercised and drilled from the end of winter. They're good and ready for battle. They've already had a fresh taste of it earlier this month.'

'I see. That's good. The men and mounts are in good shape, Centurion, despite their appearance. That may be a matter that requires attending to in due course.'

'What does it matter what they look like, as long as they kill the enemy . . . sir?'

Cato raised his voice so that the surrounding men would hear him clearly. 'It matters because I say so.'

Quertus frowned briefly. 'Very well, sir.'

Cato was conscious of the need not to push his authority too quickly and turned to Macro. 'And now the legionaries of your cohort.'

'Yes, sir.' Macro nodded.

They paced past the gap between the two units and were joined by Centurion Severus as they began their inspection of the legionaries. Cato saw that the majority of them had drawn features and he sensed their wariness as he passed slowly along each rank. In contrast to the Thracians they were neatly turned out and their helmets were polished, shields well maintained and their weapons every bit as lethal as those of their mounted comrades. But they failed to conceal their nervousness.

'You!' Cato pointed a finger at a man who was leaning forward slightly, resting his weight on the rim of his shield. 'Stand up straight.' He stopped in front of the man and stared hard at him. 'Name?'

'Caius Balbus, sir.'

'Is this how you present yourself on parade? Have you been drinking?'

'No, sir.'

'Then why are you standing there like a pickled old fart?'

Balbus grimaced and forced himself to straighten up, gritting his teeth. Severus stepped closer to Cato and spoke quietly. 'The man is sick, sir. Most of them are. Sick, or weak. Hardly surprising when they're on half-rations most of the time. Even less, when supplies grow short between the raids on enemy villages.'

Cato took a deep breath as he considered the situation. Another of the challenges he faced in dealing with Quertus. But perhaps this would be easier to resolve. It made no sense for Quertus and his cohort to ride out and leave the fort in the hands of men in poor condition to defend Bruccium. But then, the Thracian had probably calculated that the Silures would not dare to enter the valley guarded by the grisly trophies of the savage warriors who had thrust their way into the heart of the tribe's lands and built themselves an almost impregnable fort there.

'How many men are too sick to attend parade?' Cato asked.

Severus quickly consulted his wax tablet. 'Fifteen men from the First Century and twelve from the Second.'

'And none from the other centuries.'

'There are no other centuries, sir. I merged what was left of the cohort into two centuries ten days ago. The sick are on the rolls of the merged units. There should be ten or so more of 'em but I gave the order that every man who could still stand was to take part in the parade.'

Cato gestured towards Balbus. 'This one is having difficulty even standing. Get him off the parade ground and into the infirmary. He's to rest and be fed until his strength has returned. Same for the rest of them.'

Severus glanced towards Quertus who was standing with his officers, laughing and talking together informally. 'The standing orders are that legionaries are to be given no more than the specified ration, sir.'

'Then I'm specifying a new ration for them,' Cato responded irritably. 'We can't have men too weak to hold the walls of the fort.'

'Then can I have your order in writing, sir? I'll need to present my authority to draw extra rations to the quartermaster. He's one of the Thracians.'

191

'Fuck,' Macro muttered. 'This is getting too bloody much to bear. Those auxiliary bastards need to be put in their place, sir.'

Cato was silent for a moment, then he nodded. 'I'll deal with it, as soon as the parade is over. Centurion Severus!'

'Sir?'

'Send Balbus to the infirmary. Him and anyone else too weak to take their place in the battle line. Centurion Macro, you may dismiss your cohort.'

'Yes, sir.' Macro saluted and turned to the men and drew a deep breath. 'Second Cohort, Fourteenth Legion, dismissed!'

The legionaries stiffened to attention, then turned in unison and stamped down their right boots, before breaking ranks and turning towards the gate of the fort. Macro waited a moment before he spoke to Cato. 'I'll come to headquarters to collect the authorisation for the ration increase then, sir.'

'Of course. I'll join you there directly. Once I've dismissed Quertus and his men.'

Macro saluted and beckoned to Severus to join him as he made for the fort. Cato headed back to the Thracian cohort and gave Quertus permission to dismiss his men. As the men led their mounts away, Cato called their commander to join him.

'There's one other thing. The Silurian prisoner. He needs to be interrogated.'

'I've already seen to that, sir. My lads dealt with it last night.'

Cato gave him a cold look. 'I said Centurion Macro would handle the interrogation. I did not order you to do it.'

'I took the initiative, sir. Seemed to me that the sooner we made the bastard talk, the better.'

'I see. And did he reveal the location of his village?'

Quertus smiled. 'He was as good as gold. Gave us very precise directions as well as the number of men under arms.'

'Very good.' The anger Cato felt over the Thracian's taking on the interrogation faded as he contemplated the opportunity afforded by the information given up by the prisoner. 'Then we can prepare a punitive expedition as soon as possible.'

'I'll tell the men.'

'I will be leading the raid, and Centurion Macro will be joining us. I'm keen to see my new cohort in action.'

Quertus's smile faded quickly. 'That's not necessary, sir. My boys and I know the ropes. Leave it to me and we'll deal with the Silurians.'

'I've made my decision, Centurion. I'll see you at headquarters at noon to plan the raid. Bring the prisoner with you. He may be able to provide a few further details if they're needed.'

Quertus raised his eyebrows.

'Problem, Centurion?'

'It's just that we don't have the prisoner any more.'

'What do you mean? He's escaped?'

'No, he's still here. It's just that I decided we had got all the information that we needed from him.'

'I'll be the judge of that,' Cato said firmly. 'Just tell me where he is.'

Quertus raised a hand and pointed towards the track leading up to the fort. 'Just over there.'

Cato turned and glanced round. 'Why is he out here? I can't see him. Where is he?'

'There. Last stake.'

Cato felt a cold dread chill his flesh. He forced himself to look at the avenue of impaled heads, the nearest of which looked more freshly butchered than the rest. He felt his stomach knot as he recognised the bruised features of the young man they had captured two days earlier.

'Turrus . . .'

# CHAPTER TWENTY

Two days later, just before dawn, Cato was lying on a bed of bracken in a shallow fold in the ground on the side of a steep hill. It had been a cold night and the clammy damp of the dew had caused him to shiver in the last hour before the glow of the rising sun crept above the crest of the mountains to the east. For the first time in many days the sky was clear and a fine day lay ahead. Cato had left his scarlet cloak back with the rest of the men camped in the trees and donned one of the black cloaks so as not to stand out against the landscape when dawn came. At his side Quertus was silently scanning the peaceful scene below them. To their right and left sprawled the heavily forested slopes of the ridge. A wide vale, a mile across, was filled with gently rolling cultivated land, sown in strips and interspersed with stone pens in which herds of goats lay still on the ground, providing warmth for the kids that had been born in the spring and now slept pressed into their mothers. There were several clusters of round huts, the largest occupying a hillock in the centre of the vale overlooking the surrounding landscape. The main hut was more than fifty feet across, Cato calculated, and a thin trail of smoke lifted lazily from the opening in the thatched roof. Two men leaned against the daubed walls either side of the entrance that they were guarding. More men were asleep around the remains of the fires that still smouldered on the open ground in front of the hut. Several small buildings were close by.

'That's our first target,' Quertus said quietly as he pointed towards the main hut. 'The tribe's chief and his retinue. He's got at least a hundred men down there. That's quite a number for a village this size. He must have some visitors. Then there'll be more men in the farmsteads. Perhaps another hundred men in their prime, but I doubt many of them have ever wielded anything more dangerous than a club or a scythe.'

'Even a scythe can bring a tear to your eye.' Cato suppressed a bitter smile as he thought of the grievous wound that had once been inflicted on him by a scythe-wielding Druid. The scar still made the skin around the side of his chest feel tight from time to time. He thrust the memory aside. 'So, what is your usual plan of attack?'

Quertus studied the ground briefly before replying. 'The vale at the far end opens out on to that river valley. I've sent four squadrons round the back of the hills to cut across the open ground and block any escape in that direction.'

Cato looked at him sharply. 'This is the first I've heard about it. When did you give them their orders?'

'Last night. When you and Centurion Macro were asleep.'

'Why didn't you tell me when I woke? As the prefect of the cohort I should be told.'

Quertus met his glare calmly. 'As you said, sir, before we started out, you wanted to observe the tactics I have developed for my raids. Therefore I presumed that you wished to take no active part in the decisions of this operation. There was no need to tell you.'

Cato was silent for a moment. 'If I am to understand your tactics, Quertus, then I need to follow every detail. Make sure that I am informed of every decision in future. Is that clear?'

'Yes, sir.'

'Very well. Carry on.'

The Thracian sucked in a deep breath and continued. 'Once the main escape route is covered, we launch our attack against the chief and his retinue. We ride down from the trees and charge towards the hillock the moment the alarm is raised. When it is, my men will make as much noise as possible. Helps to put the shits up the enemy. We hit the chief and his retinue as swiftly as possible and go in hard and take no prisoners. With no one to lead them and no standard to rally around, the rest of the men in the vale usually try to surrender. Some villagers will try and make a break for it, but they will run into the four squadrons spread out across their path. Then we move in and kill everything and burn every building to the ground. There will be some who manage to evade us, and they'll bide their time until we have gone, and then emerge from their holes and run to the nearest tribes and relate what has happened to their allies. They in turn will send a patrol here to see for themselves and report back that the survivors were telling the truth.' Quertus's lips parted in a wolfish grin. 'And that is how I strike terror into the hearts of the enemy. That is how the legend of the Blood Crows spreads across the land of the Silures and fills the bastards with fear.'

There was a strained tone to his voice as he concluded and Cato shot him a quick look. There was hatred there, and something more. But there was no time to reflect on that. The enemy would be stirring soon and the Thracian cohort must launch its attack to make the most of the element of surprise. But there was one matter that Cato was determined to resolve before the attack began.

'Your plan is sound. There is only one change I want to make.'

Quertus looked at him sharply. 'You said you were here to observe. Not interfere.'

'Whatever I said, I am the commander of the cohort and I give the orders, and you will call me sir when you address me.'

Quertus stared back, struggling to keep his expression neutral. 'I know what I am doing, sir. I've used these tactics many times before without any problems. There's no need to change anything.'

'That is for me to decide,' Cato said firmly.

'Oh really?' Quertus shuffled back from the edge of the dip before raising himself up on to his knees. He moved with a sinuous grace for such a large man, Cato noted. Quertus casually flipped the side of his cloak across his shoulder to reveal his sword. Both men were still for a moment and Cato stared defiantly at the centurion. Then Quertus chuckled and rose to his feet so that he towered over the prone figure of his commander. 'So what is it that you think I should change, sir?'

Cato was propped up on his elbows, looking over his shoulder, and felt both uncomfortable and vulnerable. He eased himself back, out of sight of the huts in the vale below and scrambled to his feet before he addressed the Thracian on more level terms, while watching him for any sign of treachery.

'We'll carry out your plan as you've stated it, but at the end I want prisoners. Once we've broken their resistance, we'll take those that surrender alive.'

'And why would we do that?'

Cato knew that he did not need to explain himself to any subordinate, but there was a dangerous gleam in the other man's eyes and he did not want to force a confrontation while the two of them were alone.

'Prisoners provide intelligence on the enemy, and they are worth good money.' There was a third reason, that Cato did not hold with slaughtering women, children and other non-combatants. But he felt certain that to say this would only open him to Quertus's ridicule.

'They are the enemy, sir. Even the children. Savage barbarians, all of 'em!' He spat. 'Why let little nits grow up to become lice? Better put an end to them at one stroke.'

'We spare them because when this campaign is over they will be part of the empire, and paying their taxes. I suspect that the Emperor would not take kindly to the prospect of having those whom he will one day rule put to the sword.'

'The Emperor is not here. The Emperor does not know what savages these people are. They can never be civilised, only killed like the vermin they are.' Quertus spoke through gritted teeth, as if in pain, and his eyes blazed with rage. 'They deserve to be wiped out, every one of them! Village after village, man after man, even their cattle, their pigs, sheep and dogs. We must let nothing survive.'

Cato was momentarily shocked by his vehemence, and then he knew just how dangerous the Thracian was. He felt the hairs rise on the back of his neck as he stared at the man, and fear, ice-cold, spread through his guts. He swallowed and tried to speak as calmly as possible. 'Why? Why do you hate them so much?'

Quertus stared at Cato from under his thick brows. 'You don't know?'

'Why should I? If there's a reason, then tell me.'

The Thracian lowered his head so that Cato could no longer clearly see his expression. 'Roman, I know the Silures. I have lived amongst them. I was once their prisoner. They treated me worse than a dog. Bound me and tormented me with hunger and thirst, and beat me. Mocked me. Made fun of me . . . Humiliated me. Not just their warriors, but their women and children as well. You think children are innocent? Think again. Give them licence to do as they will and there is nothing they aren't capable of. Nothing. Look.' He rolled up his right sleeve and raised his arm. Cato saw that there was a crude lattice of white scar tissue. Quertus smiled grimly. 'They did that with spear tips heated in the heart of a fire. On my arms, my legs, my back and chest. Children . . . They must die along with the rest. I will have it no other way.'

Cato felt some sympathy for the other man's torment. Both Macro and Julia had once been prisoners of a rebel gladiator and his band of followers, and even though they had rarely spoken of it, he knew the experience had scarred them both. But experience does not justify behaviour, he firmly believed. There were no exceptions. He took half a step away from the Thracian and he responded gently, 'I am giving you an order, Centurion Quertus. We will take prisoners.'

'No!' Quertus lowered himself into a crouch, like a cornered beast, and his sword hand grasped the handle of his weapon. 'They die! And I will kill any man who shows them mercy.'

'Then you'll have to kill me.' Cato spoke without thinking and was horrified by his foolishness. His fingers crept up his thigh towards his sword.

'Kill you?' Quertus chuckled. 'Do you think I couldn't?'

Cato's heart was beating like a hammer inside his chest. 'I wouldn't be the first Roman you have killed, right?'

'Not by a long way, Prefect.' There was a faint scrape as he began to draw his blade.

Cato reached for his weapon but resisted the temptation to rip it from the scabbard. 'That's enough, Quertus. Think about what you're doing. You threaten me with a weapon and, by the gods, I swear I'll have you crucified.'

'What's going on here, then?' a gruff voice interrupted. Cato glanced to his left and saw Macro emerging from the gloom, picking his way through the stunted saplings growing along the edge of the hollow. There was a small growl of frustration in Quertus's throat before he sheathed his weapon and eased himself into a more erect posture. Cato followed suit, his heart still pounding inside his chest. In a wild moment of fancy he thought about calling on Macro to help him kill Quertus here and now while they had the chance. But there was the danger that he might fatally injure one of them. And what if they returned to the camp without the Thracian? How would his men react? Whatever story Cato made up, they would be suspicious and send someone to look for their leader. When they found the body, they would tear Cato and Macro apart. With bitter realisation he knew that this was not the time to act. He turned to his friend and tried to sound calm.

'Macro, what are you doing here?'

'You've been a long time, sir. I was worried. Came to make sure nothing had happened to you. Both of you.'

If his meaning was clear to Cato, it was just as clear to Quertus who glanced up at the sky and pressed his lips together before he spoke.

'We'd better get on with it, sir. Before the enemy stir.'

'Yes.' Cato nodded, keeping his gaze fixed on Quertus. 'Back to the camp. You lead the way.'

Quertus set off at once, striding up and out of the hollow, his bulky shoulders brushing through the slender limbs of the saplings, spraying dew in his wake. Cato hurried after him and Macro fell into step at his shoulder.

'You all right, sir?' he asked softly.

'Fine.'

'Looks like I turned up at the right moment just then. What was going on?'

'A difference of opinion. That's all.'

Macro was quiet for a moment. 'A difference of opinion with that Thracian cunt is likely to be the death of a man. You'd better keep a close watch on him.'

'I already am, believe me.'

They struggled to keep up with Quertus as they left the saplings and entered the tall pines that stretched up the slope. Already a pale light was spreading across the sky and filling the trees with a milky hue. Ahead Quertus strode swiftly, occasionally glancing back, but he neither slowed his pace to let them catch up nor tried to draw ahead and leave them behind. He seemed content to maintain a safe distance between them. A short while later they reached the clearing where the four squadrons of Thracian cavalry had spent the night without fires to warm them. The men had already saddled their mounts and stood in small groups, talking in undertones, their spears against their shoulders and their oval shields resting on the ground.

As soon as they spied their leader they hurried to their horses, took the reins and waited for their orders. Quertus swung himself up into the saddle and called out as loudly as he dared, 'Mount up!'

Cato and Macro took their horses from one of the handlers and mounted. They eased their horses into position amongst the standard-bearer and the horn-blowers. Quertus sat tall in his saddle, a short distance apart surveying the hundred and twenty men of his main force. When the last of them had steadied themselves in their saddles and the only sounds were the champing of the horses and the scrape of their hoofs on the ground, Quertus nodded with satisfaction.

'Prepare to move out!'

He turned his horse towards the narrow trail leading out of the clearing and clicked his tongue. His horse trotted forward and Cato, Macro and the others followed on. Behind them the squadrons followed in column, until the air was filled with the clatter and clop of hoofs and the chinkle of the iron bits and curbs. A hundred paces through the trees the trail emerged on to the ancient track that led into the valley and Quertus turned the column down the gentle slope. For a short distance the trees obscured the landscape ahead and then, suddenly, they were riding in the open with grazing land on either side, where a handful of hardy cattle turned and bolted at their sudden appearance.

A mile in the distance, Cato could see the hillock upon which the chief's hut dominated the vale. Ahead, the track passed close by one of the clusters of smaller huts that made up the tribal settlement. Beyond, the track led past some pens and the leather covers of grain pits before dropping down to a fast-flowing stream. On the other side of a ford the track led up the slope of the hillock.

Quertus raised his sword arm and called out, 'At the canter!'

He urged his horse on and the animal kicked down and reared slightly before lurching forward at a faster pace. The men behind him followed suit and the air around Cato filled with the muffled thunder of hundreds of hoofs. A face appeared at the entrance of a hut closest to the track and a man leaned out, his eyes wide with alarm. He shouted a warning and ducked back out of sight. An instant later the column pounded by the hut and Cato saw a woman emerge from another hut further off, an infant clutched to her chest. She glanced at the standard and turned and ran, away from the settlement towards the treeline. More figures appeared and fled, in all directions. One of the horsemen veered off and instantly drew the attention of an officer who bellowed at him to rejoin the column.

The ford appeared ahead and then Cato was plunging through the water, exploding in a chaos of silver spray as the horses churned through the current. Quertus slowed the pace on the far bank and thrust his arm to the side. 'Form line!'

The colour party, with Cato and Macro, formed the centre of the line and the squadrons alternated to the right and left.

'Up there!' Macro thrust out his arm and pointed up the slope. 'They've seen us.'

Several men had piled out of the huts and were gesticulating down the slope, calling their comrades to arms.

In a matter of moments the line was formed. As the last of the men on the flank edged their mounts into place, there was a sharp blare from a horn, and an instant later the sound was taken up by another horn further off.

'That's stirred them up,' Quertus growled. 'No time to waste. We strike now.' He drew his sword and thrust it into the air. 'Blood Crows! At the command! Charge!'

# CHAPTER TWENTY-ONE

Quertus swept his sword down and spurred his horse forward with an inchoate roar. His men took up the cry, as did Macro, while Cato clamped his jaw shut and breathed deeply and quickly through flaring nostrils as he urged his horse on, drawing his sword and using the flat of the blade to slap the animal's rump. The line of horsemen rapidly gathered speed as they surged away from the bank of the stream, over the rich calf-deep grass that was bejewelled with dewdrops and speckled with bright yellow flowers. The sun was rising above the hills behind the horsemen and the first rays flooded the valley, burnishing it with pale gold light.

As the horses built up their speed to a full gallop, Cato felt the wind roaring in his ears and his body swayed and jolted at the impact of the horse galloping beneath him. He tightened his grip on the reins, clamped his thighs against the flanks of his mount and leaned forward, keeping his sword hand low and out to the side where it could not accidentally wound him, or Macro to his right. On either side the Thracians kept their spears vertical for the same reason and Cato saw that they were holding to their discipline; not a man had lost his head and lowered his point yet. The din of Macro's excited shouts filled his ears. The faster horses began to pull ahead and Quertus bellowed above the din for his men to hold the line.

A hundred and fifty paces ahead, the Silurian warriors were hurrying towards the chief's hut to form a defensive perimeter. They snatched up the first pieces of armour and weapons that came to hand. Most had shields, large, flat and round, with elegantly painted faces depicting wild animals. In their other hands they gripped an assortment of spears, swords and axes. As the gentle slope began to flatten out, Cato saw the chief emerge from his hut, a tall, broad figure, the top of his head bald, with the red hair of the fringe tied back in two plaits. His men had bought him enough time to pull on a chain-mail vest and he clutched a long-handled battleaxe in his right hand as he shouted orders to them.

As the Blood Crows swept on to the crest of the hillock, the outer huts forced them to flow round and crowd together, causing the riders to curse and the horses to whinny as they pressed up against each other. There were still men emerging from the huts and as Cato approached an entrance, the leather curtain swept back and a Silurian stood behind his raised shield and thrust a hunting spear out at the passing riders. The point tore into the flank of the standard-bearer's horse, just ahead of Cato. A shrill neigh split the air as the animal jerked to the side, snatching the spear from the warrior's grasp. The butt caught against the side of the hut and snapped with a sharp report and the splintered end spun towards Cato's face. He ducked his head just in time and felt the impact as the wood glanced off the crown of his helmet. Then he looked up and twisted in his saddle to thrust his sword towards the man. The spatha he had drawn from the fort's stores had a longer reach than the gladius he was used to, and the warrior leaped back as the sword struck the wooden door frame. Cato snatched it back and then the hut was behind him.

To his right he saw Macro strike down a short Silurian wearing a brown tunic. The man half turned just in time to see Macro's blade slash through the air and into the side of his head, cutting flesh and shattering the jawbone. The warrior collapsed and was lost from view beneath the horses. There was a brief cry of pain, before it died, with him, crushed into the ground.

'Kill them all!' Quertus screamed, a manic expression etched into his features. His men echoed his cry as they cut down the handful of men who had responded too late to the alarm to join their comrades in front of the chief's hut. A second man emerged from the largest hut, tall and powerfully built. He was protected by armour and a helmet, beneath which his blond hair flowed over his shoulders. He carried a spear and a shield and thrust himself between two men to take his place in the battle line. There was something about his face that struck Cato. Something familiar. But there was no time to give the thought more than an instant.

The Blood Crows surged forward, thundering across the open space, kicking over the remains of the fires and sending swirls of ash and bright cinders into the air. Some of the Thracians surged in between Macro and Cato, forcing them apart, and Cato found himself twenty feet to the left of his friend and the rest of the command party, just as the first of the horsemen lowered the points of their spears and charged headlong into the line of Silurian warriors. There was a rippling clatter and thud as weapons clashed and struck shields. Battle cries died on men's lips as they locked in combat, furiously wielding their weapons as they hacked and thrust at each other. There was an opening between two horsemen ahead of Cato and he pulled on his reins to direct his mount into the gap, sword held up, ready to strike.

An enemy warrior sprang in front of him, baring his teeth through the thick dark hair of his beard. He raised his shield and stabbed a spear at the neck of Cato's horse. The beast reared away, front legs lashing out as Cato threw his weight forward and clutched the reins tightly to avoid toppling back out of his saddle. A hoof connected with the point of the warrior's spear, knocking it downwards, and the warrior retreated a few paces from the danger of the hoofs. Then the horse dropped forward and Cato struggled back into an erect position, just in time to parry another thrust from the Silurian. His long blade clanged and he twisted his arm to deflect the spear point, then spurred his horse forward, into the enemy warrior, thudding into his shield and knocking him back. Cato gave him no time to regain his balance and swung his sword down, reaching as far forward as he could. The edge hissed through the air and struck the man on the woad-patterned skin of his shoulder. The blade bit through his flesh and struck the man's collarbone, which snapped beneath the savage force of the blow. He uttered an agonised cry and staggered back, his shield slipping from his fingers. Yet he still had the wit to wield his spear, even through the red veil of his pain, and thrust the point up at Cato.

Cato pulled savagely on his reins and Hannibal turned sharply to the right, and the point of the spear clattered off the shield. Cato

204

twisted in the saddle and swung his sword again, unable to get much power into the blow. But it was enough to make the Silurian stumble back, blood streaming down his chest from the wound in his shoulder. He dropped his spear and clamped his hand over the torn flesh and turned to stagger away from the fight. Cato let him go, and seeing that there was no immediate threat, he looked round. The auxiliaries had driven into the loose ranks of the enemy and several small pockets of fighters were battling it out in front of the large hut. Macro was at the side of Quertus as both men charged into a loose pocket of Silurians and lay about them, scattering the enemy and cutting down another handful of warriors to add to those already lying on the ground, dead or wounded.

The chief, his tall companion and several of his men had formed a tight circle to hold off the Thracians. As Cato watched, one of the Blood Crows edged his horse in and thrust his spear. The tip clattered against a shield, and as he drew the weapon back, the tall man with the blond hair ran forward and piked the rider in his side. The impact was powerful enough to knock him out of the saddle and he fell to the ground on the other side of the horse. At once a burly Silurian armed with an axe leaped forward and swung his weapon down with both hands. The head of the axe smashed into the auxiliary's back, driving him into the soil. Another blow to the back of his head split the iron helmet and shattered the man's skull.

Then Cato saw the cohort's standard-bearer, off to one side, trapped against the hut by a group of Silurians who used their swords to frighten the horse as they closed in for the kill. The shame of letting the standard fall into enemy hands was ingrained into every soldier of the Roman army and Cato automatically turned his horse towards the hut and spurred it forwards. He brushed past some horsemen who had been hanging back a short distance from the fighting. Cato brandished his bloodied sword and shouted an order.

'Follow me!'

He did not wait to see if he had been obeyed as he concentrated his attention on the confrontation between the Silurians and the standard-bearer. Already one of them had injured the horse and blood flowed down its coat and spattered on to the ground. A second man feinted towards the rider, forcing him to turn and confront the danger. At once another darted forward on the other side and quickly stabbed him in the calf before leaping back. The standard-bearer cried out in pain and his lips parted in a grimace as he shifted from side to side, desperate to keep all of his opponents in view.

The sound of Cato's approach caused the nearest of the warriors to glance round and then turn to face the new threat, feet braced as he covered his body with his shield and raised his sword, aiming the point at the Roman bearing down on him. Beyond him, Cato saw the standard-bearer look up into his eyes. There was a strange expression in the man's face, cold and calculating. Then he released his grip on the shaft of the standard and the image of the black crow on the red cloth fluttered as it fell to the ground.

'What . . .'

Cato looked on in horror as the standard-bearer grasped the reins and urged his horse away from the side of the hut. One of the enemy fell upon the standard with a shout of triumph. He cast his shield aside and snatched up the standard before he saw Cato's horse racing towards him. With a quick cry and gesture to his companions he ran off with the standard.

Leaning forward in his saddle, Cato held his sword out to the side as he charged the nearest of the Silurians. He slashed his sword through the air, but his enemy nimbly stepped aside then forward to make his own attack, a powerfully directed thrust at Cato's waist. The nervous movement of his horse spoiled the attempt and the point glanced off the side of Cato's breastplate. Cato made another cut, battering the Silurian's shield and driving him off. Both men paused for an instant, sizing the other up, and then the Silurian's companion rushed forward to join the fight. Beyond, the third man made good his escape, clutching his trophy, and disappeared round the back of the hut. Cato heard the sound of hoofs behind him, the men he had ordered to follow him, and pressed his attack on the Silurian who had turned to face him. Steering his mount forward he slashed at the shield again and again, thudding blows cutting splinters out of the painted wooden surface, driving the man back, away from his companion.

'Deal with them!' Cato shouted, as he spurred his horse on,

making for the back of the hut. Only recovering the standard mattered at the moment. As his horse lurched into a gallop he heard the clatter of weapons behind him as the Thracians dealt with the two men. Cato's mount thundered round the curve of the hut and then he saw the Silurian, holding the standard in front of him like a cross-staff as he ran down the slope away from the fight. Fifty paces on was a large wicker enclosure containing twenty or thirty horses, some of which were already saddled. A young Silurian groom had emerged through the gate to stare anxiously up the slope towards the sound of fighting. At once he ducked back inside and re-emerged a moment later with a pitchfork. He lowered the points towards Cato. The man with the standard rushed on, glancing back at his pursuer, his expression shot through with alarm as he saw the Roman close behind him.

Cato gripped his legs to the flanks of his mount and readied his sword as he closed on his prey. The blade rose, paused, as Cato judged the timing of his blow, and then slashed down. At the last instant the Silurian threw himself to one side and rolled over in the grass, still holding tightly to the Blood Crows' standard.

'Shit . . .' Cato hissed, reining and turning his horse towards the warrior, who regained his feet and sprinted on towards the enclosure, screaming orders to the young man at the gate. Cato urged his mount into a steady canter, converging with the warrior, but it was too late to pick him off before he reached the gate and there he turned. His chest heaved from his exertions as he thrust the point of the standard towards Cato. The chase was over and Cato stopped his horse a short distance from the two men. He could see that the young man with the pitchfork was afraid. His eyes were wide and the points of his makeshift weapon were trembling. Cato edged his horse closer and pointed his sword at the youth and flicked the blade to the side.

'Go! Get out of here!'

Even though the words were not in his tongue, the meaning was clear enough and the Silurian began to shuffle to the side until a sharp word of command from his comrade stopped him. Cato heard the sound of hoofs behind him and glanced back up the slope to see the two Thracians riding down towards him. The sight lifted his spirits. There was no way the standard would be lost now. Then they slewed to a halt a hundred feet away.

'What are you waiting for?' Cato called out to them. 'On me! Now!'

They did not react, and their mounts stood in the long grass, tails swishing, as the two men watched silently.

Cato felt rage burn in his veins. So much for the vaunted reputation of the Blood Crows, he thought bitterly. He was about to shout at them again when the Silurian with the standard let out a roar and charged towards him. There was little time to react and Cato turned to present his shield, his sword held overhead. The warrior's eyes were wide and his lips were bared as he braced his shoulders and threw all his weight behind the thrust. The point struck the shield low, splintering the wood. The tip punched through the laminated strips and burst out the other side and struck the horse just in front of Cato's knee. The horse lurched to one side as Cato swung his sword at the warrior's head. The Silurian ducked, and wrenching the standard free he backed off and readied himself, then shouted at his comrade. The young man hesitantly moved forward, edging round to flank Cato.

'Fuck . . .' he muttered, turning from side to side as he tried to keep both men in view. He risked a glance back up the slope to where the two Thracians still waited and a cold tremor rippled down his spine. This was not right. He turned his attention back to the enemy. The main threat came from the warrior. If Cato could put him down he was certain the youth would turn and run. On the other hand, the young man's nervousness made him unpredictable. He could just as easily throw himself at Cato like a wild animal as flee from him. Instinctively Cato turned on him and leaned forward to strike at the pitchfork. The youth was not quick-witted enough to parry the blow and the blade snapped one of the prongs and knocked the tool down. At once Cato made a weak back-handed cut, the point of the sword ripping the man's tunic and scoring a light flesh wound across his chest. He shrieked more in surprise than pain and staggered back in terror, releasing his grip on the pitchfork. Then he stumbled round and ran off, away from Cato and the enclosure, towards some huts a few hundred paces away.

The other Silurian hurled a contemptuous insult after him and then surged forward again, stabbing out with the Blood Crows' standard. This time he aimed higher up and Cato lifted his shield to block the blow. At the last instant his opponent twisted the point aside so that the iron cross piece at the top of the standard swept past the edge of the shield. Then, with a powerful flick of the wrist, he hooked the crosspiece behind the shield and pulled with all his strength. The shield lurched in Cato's grip and the trim at the top caught him a jarring blow under the chin. He tasted blood in his mouth and then the shield was wrenched again, and he let go. The standard and shield flew back towards the warrior who lost his footing and tumbled on to the grass. Before he could recover, Cato leaned down from his saddle and thrust his sword into the Silurian's throat and pinned him to the ground, twisting the blade, before he wrenched it free. Blood pumped from the wound and the Silurian clamped his hands over his throat as he spat blood, gurgled, and struggled for breath. Certain that the man was finished, Cato eased himself down from the saddle to recover the Blood Crow standard and his shield. He slipped the shoulder strap of the shield over one of the saddle horns and then climbed back into the saddle, holding the standard aloft so that the weighted fall clearly revealed the image of the crow. His heart was filled with relief that the danger of the unit being shamed by the loss of the standard had been averted.

He turned his horse up the slope and saw the two Thracians flick their reins and steer their horses down the slope. Cato scowled at them and was about to berate them when he realised there was something in their expressions that wasn't right. They looked at him coldly as they drew closer, then lowered their spears and held them out to the side, ready to strike.

Ready to strike Cato down.

# CHAPTER TWENTY-TWO

Most of the enemy had fallen and the survivors clustered around their chief and the tall man with the blond hair, who fought as well as any man Macro had ever seen. He moved lightly on his feet and struck deft, lethal blows with his spear. He had already killed two of the Thracians and injured a third, without suffering a scratch in return. Around him were another ten or twelve Silurians, some injured, but all of them keeping their shields raised and their weapons pointed towards their foes.

There was a brief pause as the horsemen drew back and formed a crescent round the Silurians who were backed against the entrance to the chief's hut. Their chests heaved as they stared warily at the Thracians.

Macro found himself close to Quertus and called across, 'Time to tell 'em to give up. Do you know their tongue well enough to ask?'

Quertus glowered as he faced Macro. 'They'll fight to the end. There'll be no prisoners.'

Macro edged his horse alongside the Thracian. 'Yes, there will. You heard the prefect. We'll take any that surrender. Only those that don't are fair game.'

Quertus growled and glared towards the men in front of the hut.

'Those are the orders,' Macro said firmly. 'Tell them to lay down their arms.'

For a moment it seemed that the other man would refuse. Then he nodded and drew a breath and called out to the enemy. As the fair man made his reply, Macro sat tall in his saddle and looked round for Cato.

'Where the hell is he?' he muttered to himself. 'Sometimes I reckon it's not safe to let that lad out . . .'

Then he recalled the glimpse he had had of his friend chasing a man round the rear of the chief's hut. Macro turned back to Quertus who was still trading comments with the native. He could see that the Silurians were easing themselves into upright postures as the exchange continued. Macro sensed that their surrender was almost assured and that he was no longer needed at Quertus's side. He tugged on his reins and worked his way through the horsemen and then trotted towards the rear of the hut, in the direction he had seen his friend take a short time earlier. He passed a body lying sprawled on the ground and continued round. As he reached the top of the slope he felt a surge of relief as he spied the red crest of Cato's helmet and saw that the prefect had the standard of the Thracian cohort in one hand and his shield in the other. A short distance in front of Cato were two of the Thracians, casually riding towards him. Macro was about to call down to his friend when the words died in his throat. The two men spurred their horses into a canter and charged towards Cato with their spears lowered.

'What the fuck?' Macro muttered. The realisation that his friend was in great danger hit him like a blow and he jabbed his heels in and slapped the rump of his mount. 'Yah!'

The horse leaped forward, galloping down the slope. Ahead he could see the Thracians closing in. Cato watched them intently as he struggled with his shield, swinging it round to cover his body. Then, at the last moment, he lowered the standard, like a lance, and made for the man to his right. The three men came together with a thud as a spear glanced off the shield. There was a clatter of weapons as Cato and the man to his right wildly exchanged spear thrusts and parries. The standard was never designed for such work and was unwieldy in Cato's hand as he fought for his life. His chances of surviving were made worse by the need to keep glancing to his left and fending off the attacks of the other Thracian. Macro could see that his friend could not hold his own for much longer and savagely urged his horse on. Then there was a sharp cry of frustration as the standard lurched out of Cato's fingers and fell into the grass. He snatched his hand back and fumbled for his sword as his opponent moved in closer to his unprotected side to deliver the fatal blow. At the last moment Cato thrust his shield into the face of the man to his left and threw himself under the upraised spear of the other assailant and inside his shield to grab at his cloak and tunic in a desperate attempt to unseat the Thracian. The two writhed, with Cato half out of his saddle, while the other Thracian worked his horse towards the prefect's back to strike from the rear.

At the sound of Macro's horse the second man hesitated and looked round, then instinctively swerved his mount round to face the unexpected threat. Macro held his shield up and hunched down so that it covered him up to his cheek. There was no time to think and he simply clamped his jaw shut and rode directly towards the man. Only at the last instant did the Thracian understand Macro's intention and try to spur his horse out of the way. It was too late and Macro's horse collided heavily. With a shrill whinny of terror the other horse was knocked off its feet and it fell on to its side. It rolled on to its back, legs kicking wildly in the air. The rider let out a cry of panic before the weight of the horse above him drove the breath from his lungs and crushed his chest and limbs.

Cato was still struggling with the other man, one arm scrabbling for purchase around his torso while the other grasped the wrist of his spear hand and fought to keep the point away from his body.

'Hold on, lad!' Macro shouted as he took control of his frightened mount which was trying to shy away from the fight.

The remaining Thracian jerked hard on his reins, moving his horse away from Cato's and pulling the prefect out of his saddle. Cato held on desperately, knowing that he was finished if he released his grip and gave the man enough room to use his spear. Then, when he felt as if he must fall under the other man's horse, he released his grip on the man's wrist and snatched at the handle of his dagger. He drew it out as quickly as he could and stabbed at the Thracian's thigh and groin. The man let out howls of pain and rage and let his spear drop as he punched his fist into Cato's cheekguard, and then struck him hard on the bridge of his nose. Cato felt something crack with a sharp pain and then blood coursed from his nostrils. The Thracian grunted, his fist raised to strike again, and Cato looked up to see the edge of a sword buried in the angle of his neck and he felt the warm splatter of the man's blood on his face. The Thracian looked down at Cato, his mouth gaping, a look of surprise in his eyes, before they rolled up and he slumped in his saddle with a deep groan. Then the sword was wrenched back and the man uttered one more cry before his horse shimmied to one side, dragging Cato with it a short distance until he pulled his dagger from the Thracian's leg and released his grip on his cloak. He fell to the ground, thrusting his dagger to the side so that he would not land on it. The impact was hard, driving the air from his lungs and jarring his helmeted head, but Cato had the presence of mind to tuck up as he lay on the ground as hoofs thudded into the grass around him.

'It's over, lad,' Macro's anxious voice called down to him.

Cato risked a look up and saw the transverse crest of a centurion's helmet blocking out the strengthening light of the dawn sky. Reassured, he rolled on to his feet and rose unsteadily, wiping the blood from under his nose with the back of his hand. Macro retrieved the standard from where it was lying in the grass and planted the sharpened butt firmly into the ground. Then he turned and looked at the two Thracians. The horse which had been knocked over had struggled back on to its feet and stood a short distance from its rider who writhed feebly, gasping for breath. The other man swayed in his saddle for a moment and then slid off to one side and dropped to the ground. His mount skittered off a few steps before stopping and lowering his head to graze.

Macro turned to Cato. 'Mind explaining what the fuck that was all about?'

Cato was still catching his breath and dealing with the pain from his broken nose. He held up a hand, the blood in his nostrils making his voice sound thick. 'A . . . moment . . .'

'They were out to kill you, lad. I saw it all. No question.'

Cato nodded and paced over to the man Macro had felled. He leaned down and saw the terrible wound where Macro's sword had cut at an angle into his neck, shattering the collarbone and some ribs before coming to a stop six inches deep. The blood pulsed from the wound, pooling on his chest and overflowing on to the grass as the Thracian gritted his teeth and stared into the pale sky. Cato knelt down at his side.

213

'Why did you attack me?'

The Thracian's eyes flickered towards Cato but he did not reply. The prefect leaned closer. 'Tell me!'

The man's lips lifted in a faint, mocking smile.

'Bastard needs a bit of prompting,' said Macro. He moved round his friend and stood by the Thracian's head. Lifting his boot, Macro pressed it down on the wound, gently at first, then increased the pressure so that the Thracian cried out in agony and writhed. Macro ground his boot into the wound, the hobnails biting into the bloodied flesh and bone, before he eased up.

'You answer the prefect's question, or you get some more of that.'

'Why did you attack me?' Cato repeated.

The Thracian was panting as he fought against the waves of pain from his injury. He licked his lips as he summoned up the strength to reply. 'I did it . . . for the centurion.'

'The centurion? Quertus?'

The man nodded feebly. 'The cohort . . . belongs to him . . . Not you. Never you.'

'Did he order you to do this?'

The Thracian slumped back into the grass and began to tremble uncontrollably as he bled out. Cato grabbed his blood-saturated neckcloth and pulled his head up sharply. 'Did Quertus order you to kill me?' he growled at the man.

The man's eyes rolled up into his head as he choked on his blood. Then, as it dribbled from the corner of his mouth, he spoke again, faintly. 'Quertus . . .'

'What?' Cato demanded. 'What about Quertus? Speak!'

But it was too late. The Thracian's head lolled back lifelessly and Cato glared at him for a moment before releasing his grip on the neckcloth and withdrawing his hand angrily. 'Bastard!'

As he stood up, Macro removed his boot and wiped it in the grass nearby to get some of the blood off. The centurion stared down at the body and clicked his tongue. 'Have to hand it to Quertus, he inspires loyalty in his men.'

'Loyalty?' Cato spat the word out bitterly. 'Loyalty to what? Not Rome. Only to that sick bastard who wants to bathe himself in blood.'

214

Macro looked at his friend. 'I was being ironic.'

They stared at each other before Cato smiled nervously, glad to release the tension that had built up in his chest. Macro grinned. 'There you go. I think I must have known you for too long, Cato. Irony – now that's not something that used to come so easily to me. Anyway, what in Hades' name is going on? Do you think these bastards were acting on their own, or on the orders of Quertus?'

'What do you think? He's behind this. He wants me dead, just like the last prefect, so he can carry on running Bruccium like his own little kingdom.'

Macro puffed. 'He's taking a big risk. One dead prefect looks like bad luck. Two looks like a conspiracy.' He paused and shook his head. 'Fuck . . . Conspiracy. It hangs about us like a bloody cloud. I thought we'd be living the good life once we got back to the army. Not this . . . Are you sure Quertus is behind this?'

'I'm certain. I was set up, Macro. The standard–bearer must have been in on it. He let the Silurians take the standard, knowing that I would give chase and be led away from the fight. As soon as I was separated from the rest of the cohort, these two went after me. They gave the enemy a chance to do for me first, before they stepped in to finish the job. All very neat. I'd have died a good death trying to save the standard and Quertus would have a story he could sell to you, and report back to headquarters when the time came.' Cato nodded grimly. 'He's as cunning as a snake.'

Macro prodded the dead Thracian with the toe of his boot. 'What do we do? He's failed in his attempt, and you're still alive. What now? Stick a knife between Quertus's shoulder blades? Bastard deserves as much.'

Before Cato could reply, they heard the sound of approaching horses and looked up to see Quertus leading one of his squadrons down the slope towards them. Macro readied his sword as he turned to face them, his expression grim. Cato moved to his side, and placed his hand on top of the pommel of his sword.

'Macro,' he said quietly. 'We're in great danger. Let me do the speaking.'

His friend nodded, keeping a wary eye on the approaching riders.

Quertus reined in a short distance away and his men rumbled to a halt on either side. There was a brief stillness during which Cato scrutinised the face of the Thracian officer and saw the cold look of frustration there that confirmed his suspicions. Quertus gestured towards the standard.

'You saved it, then. Saved the cohort's honour.'

'I saved the standard,' Cato replied deliberately. Then he gestured to the bodies of the Thracians. 'But I could not save these men.'

Quertus glanced at the bodies and then his dark eyes fixed on Cato. 'What happened here?' he asked in a flat tone.

'They tried to take the standard from that Silurian. He slew them both before I could intervene.'

Macro stirred beside him; the explanation had taken him by surprise. Cato fervently prayed that Macro would hold his tongue for the next few moments. Quertus nodded slowly.

'Then they died heroes.'

'It would seem so.'

At length the Thracian gestured towards Cato's face. 'You're wounded, sir.'

'It's nothing.' Cato turned away and strode across to his horse and climbed into the saddle. Macro hesitated a moment, glaring at Quertus, before he followed suit. Cato looked round the valley and saw the distant figures of the men and women of the tribe running for their lives, clutching their children by the hand as they made for the trees each side of the valley. He wiped the blood from his lips. Already it was beginning to clot in his nose and the flow was no more than an oozing trickle. He cleared his throat.

'Centurion Quertus, order your men to round up prisoners. They are only to kill those who resist. The prisoners, and our casualties, are to be taken up to the chieftain's hut. Is that clear?'

Quertus nodded.

'I said, is that clear, Centurion?'

'Yes, sir.'

'That's better. Then see to it at once.'

'Yes, sir.' Quertus wheeled his horse round and barked out orders to his men. Riders set off at once to inform the other squadrons as Cato and Macro rode back up the slope. Quertus beckoned to the rest of his men and they fell in behind the prefect and his companion.

216

At the top of the slope, Cato made his way round to the open area in front of the large hut and saw twenty or so of the enemy sitting on the ground, guarded by several of the Thracian auxiliaries. Amongst the prisoners was the blond man, conspicuous by his stature and the lightness of his hair compared to the mostly dark-haired Silurians. He had been stripped of his weapons, his shield and his helmet, and now Cato had a clearer view of his features. He reined in a short distance away and stared at the man.

'Macro, see that one?' Cato pointed. 'He seems very familiar. Do you recognise him?'

Macro looked and shrugged. 'Can't say that I do.'

Cato frowned. 'I've seen him before. Recently. Sure of it . . .'

Cato steered his horse over towards the man and stopped six feet from where he sat. The native looked up defiantly.

'On your feet!' Cato ordered, gesturing with his hand.

The man did not move and Macro trotted up, red-faced. 'You heard the prefect! On your fucking feet, you mangy dog!'

Slowly, and with as much haughty dignity as he could manage, the warrior stood up and squared his shoulders, regarding his captors with a contemptuous expression.

'Who are you?' Cato demanded. 'You're not a Silurian.'

'I am of the Catuvellauni,' the man replied in lightly accented Latin.

'Then what are you doing here? Your tribe surrendered to us years ago.' Cato forced himself to sound cold. 'Which makes you an outlaw.'

'Outlaw? I am no outlaw. I pledged to fight Rome to my last breath. Like many in my tribe, I chose to follow Caratacus.'

At the mention of the enemy leader's name Cato felt a thrill of realisation flow through his mind. That was where he had seen him before. At the stone ring, standing amongst the entourage of the native king who had resisted Rome from the very first moment that the legions had landed on British soil. Like many of the Catuvellauni, he had light-coloured hair, but there was something more about him. His build and his face reminded Cato of Caratacus himself.

'What is your name?'

'My name?' The warrior's lips curled in a sneer. 'My name is for

217

my people and those men who fight at my side as brothers.'

'Is that so?' Macro smiled cruelly. 'Sir, if he won't give us his name, he has no need of his tongue any more. Let me cut the bastard's tongue out.'

Macro reached for his dagger and drew the blade, holding it up so that the warrior could see it clearly. Cato said nothing for a moment, allowing Macro's bloodthirsty request to do its work. He saw the warrior look away from the dagger as his mask slipped and he revealed a glimpse of the fear in his heart.

'Tell me your name,' Cato ordered. 'While you still have a tongue in your head.'

The warrior looked up, hurriedly composing himself, and stared back at his captors. 'Very well. I am Maridius.'

'Maridius,' Cato repeated. 'Warrior of the Catuvellauni and, if I am not mistaken, brother of King Caratacus.'

# CHAPTER TWENTY-THREE

'So what do we do with him, this Maridius?' Macro asked as he warmed his hands over the brazier. Even though summer was not far off, the Silurian mountains were wreathed with cold winds and frequent mists and rain. Outside the walls of the headquarters building a breeze gusted in the night, rattling the shuttered window of Cato's office. Decimus had brought them a simple meal of stew. Some of the horses injured in the recent attack had not been passed fit for any further service by the horsemaster of the Thracian cohort and had been slaughtered for their meat. The garrison of Bruccium relished the addition of fresh meat to their diet for a few days before the usual issue of gruel would resume.

Cato poured himself a cup of posca, the common legionary's drink of cheap wine, watered down. 'We were damned lucky to get our hands on him.'

'True,' Macro agreed with feeling. 'But what was he doing in that village in the first place?'

Cato took a sip, and thought a moment. 'It's likely he was sent there by Caratacus. Perhaps to recruit more men. Or perhaps to see at first hand the effect that Quertus was having on their allies and try to rally them. Unless he tells us, we can't be sure.'

'He hasn't said a word. I've had some of Severus's lads work him over, but the bastard is as tough as he looks. We haven't got anything useful out of him yet. Perhaps we'll have better luck this evening.'

'I hope so. I've told Quertus to send some of his men to do the interrogating tonight.'

Macro looked up sharply. 'Why involve him?'

'I am the prefect of the Thracian cohort as well as commander of the fort. I need to make sure I take every opportunity to remind him, and the rest of his . . . my men.'

Macro sighed wearily. 'I doubt the Thracians will have any more luck than my boys. Although the way they look might just give them an edge in putting the frighteners on Maridius. But I wouldn't get your hopes up.'

'Well, if we can't make him talk, then he might serve as a hostage – assuming there's any fraternal sentiment between him and Caratacus. In any case, he'll need to be taken to Glevum. He's too important to keep here.'

Macro nodded and then turned to another matter. 'What do we do with the rest of the prisoners? We can't keep 'em here.'

Only fifty or so of the Silurians had been captured in the valley eight days previously. Many more had chosen to die fighting, or had been cut down by the Thracians before they could make a choice. When the column had returned to Bruccium the captives had been herded into one of the empty barrack blocks and the doors locked behind them. They were fed meagre rations once a day and allowed to slop out their latrine tubs each morning. The garrison had already consumed much of the food looted from the village and would soon start eroding the limited reserves held inside the fort's granary.

'I've made a decision about them,' Cato replied from behind the simple trestle table that acted as his desk. He leaned back as Decimus lifted a bowl from his tray and set it down, along with a bronze spoon, in front of his commander. 'They'll be escorted back to Glevum. I'll send four squadrons of the Thracians along with them to guard the prisoners. Quertus will be in command.'

Macro looked up from his bowl at his friend. 'What makes you think he'll go along with that?'

'Because it'll be an order. I'll arrange it so that if he refuses, then he will have to do so in front of the entire garrison. Then we'll see who the men obey.'

Macro sighed. 'I hate to be the one to tell you, but the Thracians will back him, almost to a man.'

Cato nodded. 'I expect you're right. That's why we're waiting for the reinforcement column to turn up. Once your legionaries are

220

up to strength I'll have more than enough men to swing things our way. If I pick the right moment, Quertus will have to give in or fight against superior odds. He's stepped over the line, but not so far that he can't see a way back. I intend to give him a chance.'

Macro was silent for a moment before he replied in a strained voice, 'For the love of all the gods, Cato, why? That bastard tried to have you killed.'

Cato folded his hands together and rested his chin on them as he considered his friend's protest. Macro was right. The Thracian was dangerous, and driven by a madness Cato could barely understand. There was more to the extreme manner in which he waged war than simply the bloodthirsty proclivities of his race. He wanted revenge, consumed by the desire to destroy the Silures, right down to the last living creature that they possessed. And yet the effect on the enemy of the horror of the Thracian's campaign – the heads, the rotting corpses and the burned-out remains of villages – had been impressive. They feared the men of the cohort. The very sight of the Blood Crow banner had sent them running for their lives. Perhaps fear was the very best of weapons, Cato mused. Nothing could stand before it, neither the best armour nor the highest of ramparts. Only courage of equal intensity stood any chance against a strategy based on instilling such terror as Quertus and his men inflicted. Terror then, the supreme tool of war . . .

Part of Cato's mind recoiled from this line of thought. The cool calculation of a moment before made him despise himself. He was not Quertus. He never could be. But at the same time he knew he was perfectly capable of such ruthlessness. The difference between himself and the Thracian was that he chose not to be ruthless . . . Or perhaps that was merely the excuse he offered himself to justify his moral cowardice. He raised his eyes and looked at Macro, wondering if he should try to explain his doubts. As far as his friend was concerned, Quertus had condemned himself the moment he had tried to have Cato killed. Nothing else mattered. Macro was inclined to take a more direct route in his judgement of people.

'If Quertus can be persuaded to leave Bruccium and escort the prisoners back to Glevum,' Cato began, 'then he will be out of the way while we take full control of the situation and make sure that he cannot try to resume control when he returns. If he does try, I'll be able to play by the rules and have him arrested for insubordination, and even mutiny. Due legal process will be served.'

'What the fuck is wrong with you, Cato?' Macro groaned. 'Where was due legal bloody process when he tried to stab you in the back, eh? When your enemy fights dirty, you do the same. Say the word, and I'll stick a sword in the bastard's guts and I won't shed a fucking tear over the cunt. That's my kind of due legal process.'

Cato was momentarily taken aback by his friend's words. 'Er . . . Quite so.'

There was a brief silence in which Cato allowed his friend to simmer down a bit before he continued. Decimus took the chance to clear his throat. Cato glanced at him.

'Might I go now, sir?'

Cato nodded. 'Get yourself something to eat.'

'Thank you, sir.' Decimus turned towards the door and was about to leave the room when Macro called to him.

'Hey, Decimus, see if there's any of that Silurian bread left in the officers' stores. If there is, bring us a loaf each.'

'Yes, sir,' Decimus replied and left the office, shutting the latch quietly behind him.

Cato did not have much of an appetite, thanks to his concerns. 'I'll be fine with just the stew.'

'Suit yourself. If you don't want the bread, I'll eat yours.'

Macro fell on his stew, slurping the steaming liquid from the spoon as Cato stirred his thoughtfully and then spoke again.

'Macro, we must be careful. We have never been in a situation like this before.'

As he spoke, Cato recalled the march back from the Silurian village. He and Macro had made sure to stay within the column, day and night, always one watching while the other slept. Quertus had made one attempt on Cato's life, and he was bound to have more men amongst his followers who were prepared to do his bidding and murder a superior officer. As soon as they had returned to the fort Cato had given orders for the headquarters guards to be drawn from the legionary cohort alone. Men that Centurion Severus had hand-picked for their trustworthiness.

'Too right,' Macro responded. 'And I thought working for that slimy rat Narcissus was dangerous. The gods will have their fun with us.'

'I wonder who is laughing. Macro, I'm serious. We're in grave danger as long as Quertus remains here in the fort and challenges my authority. If we're going to deal with him, we must do it one step at a time. Right now, we bide our time until the reinforcements turn up. Once they're here, we can get things back to where they should be. Quertus will have little choice but to accept it.'

'And what? We let bygones be bygones? Sir, he tried to kill you.'

'What proof is there of that? Without proof what can I do?'

Macro opened his mouth to protest, then frowned, and shook his head. 'Bollocks. Due legal process again, I take it.'

Cato nodded. 'As things stand I cannot bring charges against Quertus. Not for the attempt on my life, nor for the murder of the previous prefect. Besides, there's more to this than dealing with Quertus. You remember I mentioned that being here might have something to do with Pallas? That he might have wanted to send us someplace where there was a good chance we might be killed?'

Macro waved his spoon around. 'You really think such a place is hard to find in this corner of the empire?'

'We're not in the empire. We're well over the frontier of the province. Far enough from any help if we get into trouble. And we *are* in trouble. If we try and take a short cut in dealing with Quertus, you can be sure that Pallas's man here in Britannia will have us charged with the crime. You don't just get away with murdering a senior centurion, or bringing disciplinary charges against him without adequate evidence. Anything like that is likely to rebound on us. Especially if someone is looking for any excuse to drop us in the shit. Like I said, we have to be extremely careful. If it's to be done, Quertus must be disposed of in a way that can be justified. You understand, Macro?'

The centurion sighed heavily. 'This ain't on, Cato. I thought we'd left all this sort of thing behind us. I thought we were going back to the legions to do some proper soldiering and leaving all the skulduggery to those with a taste for it.' He shook his head, then took another, joyless, spoon of stew before muttering, 'It ain't on, I'm telling you.'

Cato could not help a wry smile. 'Come now, did you ever think it would really be so simple?'

Decimus opened the door to the officers' mess and peered round before he crossed the threshold. There was no one there due to the late hour and a fire was burning low in the hearth, providing a warm glow that lit up the modest room. He breathed a sigh of relief that he would not have to be in the same room as any of the officers of the Thracian cohort. He quickly shut the door behind him and crossed to the doorway leading through to the storeroom where the officers' food was stored. General items were shelved on one side, with named shelves for each officer's private stores opposite. Not that there was much left on any of the shelves, Decimus tutted to himself. There had been little of worth taken from the village, just a few roundels of goat's cheese, some jugs of their sweet ale and the hard flat loaves of bread that tasted as unappetising as they looked. Decimus picked up two from the common stores and marked the wax slate hanging from a thong by the door. He heard the door open and close a moment later and swallowed anxiously as he emerged from the storeroom and saw the looming bulk of Centurion Quertus standing in front of the door. The glow from the fire cast a gently wavering shadow behind him and lit his dark features with a ruddy glow so that he looked even larger than he did in daylight. His eyes fixed on the prefect's servant but he said nothing.

Decimus approached hesitantly and nodded towards the door. 'If you'll excuse me, sir.'

'Not yet.' Quertus spoke in a rumbling undertone. 'I'm hungry. Fetch me some cheese and bread. And a jug of beer.'

'Sir, I was just taking these to headquarters.'

'Later.'

'The prefect and Centurion Macro are expecting me to return as soon as I can, sir.'

'Once I've finished with you, you can go. Now, build the fire up and then get me my food.'

Decimus hesitated a moment. The Thracian scowled and the

servant hurriedly turned about and set the loaves down on a table. He went over to the fire and took some logs from the pile in the corner and stacked them over the embers in tiers before picking up the fan and carefully stirring up some flames until they consumed the lowest logs. All the while he felt the presence of the Thracian officer who had sat down on the nearest bench and watched him work in silence.

'That'll do,' said Quertus. 'Now the food.'

Decimus scrambled up and made for the foodstore where he heaped a wooden platter with the requested items and returned to serve them to the centurion. 'There you are, sir. Now if there's nothing more . . .'

'There is something else.' Quertus tore off a corner of his bread and chewed steadily until his mouth was empty enough to speak. 'Your name is Decimus, isn't it?'

Decimus nodded, not happy that the Thracian officer knew even that much about him.

'Cat got your tongue?'

'N–no, sir.'

'That's better. Well then, Decimus, perhaps you can help me.'

'Of course, sir.'

'Are you happy serving the prefect?'

Decimus chewed his lip. 'Happy, sir? I hadn't given it any thought.'

'Oh, I'm sure that you have. I would find it hard to believe that you would be happy in a place as far flung and wild as Bruccium. You have the look of a former soldier about you. The limp suggests you were discharged unfit. Am I right?'

Decimus nodded, then as the Thracian officer's brow knitted he quickly spoke up. 'Yes, sir. I served in the Second Legion. Before I met the prefect I was in Londinium working the wharves.'

'And you gave up the comforts of Londinium to come here?'

'The prefect offered to pay me well to serve him, sir. It seemed like a good idea at the time.'

'But not so good now, I'll bet.' Quertus smiled thinly. 'I imagine that you are thinking that no amount of silver is worth being in a place like this.'

Decimus decided that it might be best to make light of the situation and get away from the Thracian officer as soon as possible. 'I'm sure I could imagine enough silver to make anything worth while, sir.'

Quertus responded quietly, 'I'm sure you could.'

Decimus coughed. 'If that's all, sir, I'd better be off. Can't afford to keep the prefect and Centurion Macro waiting.'

'Before you go, Decimus, there's something I'd like you to think about.' Quertus leaned forward and fixed his dark eyes on the veteran. Decimus felt his blood go cold.

'You like silver, so you're a man after my own heart. What if I was to offer you twice what the prefect is paying you to work for me instead?'

'Sir?'

'Come now, Decimus. You don't think that bread and beer are the only things that the Blood Crows take from the villages we raid. There are plenty of silver lodes in these mountains, that is one of the reasons why the Emperor is so keen to get his hands on the land of the Silures. We've collected quite a small hoard of silver. I've promised fair shares for all the officers and men in the know. Why shouldn't you be able to dip your beak in as well? As long as you serve my needs. I see you are tempted . . . Why don't I make it easier for you? What if I paid you three times what the prefect has promised you?'

'A thousand sestertii, that's what Cato said.'

'So little for a good man like you? The prefect is a skinflint. What do you say to three thousand sestertii?'

Decimus's eyes widened at the prospect of such a fortune and Quertus pressed on. 'Of course, you'd get to keep what he has promised to pay you as well. Should set you up nicely for the rest of your life. And the best of it is that all you have to do is keep on serving the prefect. As far as I am concerned, what you have to do for me is to keep your ears and eyes open and report back to me anything he says that relates to me or my cohort. That's all there is to it. What do you say, Decimus?'

The servant was silent, his mind racing. 'I need to think about it, sir.'

Quertus considered the other man for a moment before nodding. 'All right. But I'll have your answer tomorrow. One other thing you need to know. If I ever discover you have repeated any part of this conversation, I will have your head. You'll find that it is much safer, as well as more rewarding, to be loyal to me in this fort. Understand?'

'Yes, sir.' Decimus swallowed nervously.

'Then you may go. Remember, one word out of place and you're a dead man.'

'I understand, sir.' Decimus nodded and made his way out of the officers' mess as steadily as he could. Outside, he shut the door, his hand trembling as he slid the latch into place, and then hurried the short distance down the street back to headquarters.

# CHAPTER TWENTY-FOUR

Maridius had his arms bound behind his back when he was dragged out of his cell and into the small hall in the fort's guardroom. He had been stripped down to his leggings and his face and chest were heavily bruised. One eye was so badly swollen that he could hardly see out of it. He stank of his own dirt and his skin was streaked with filth and dried blood.

'Get him on the hook,' Quertus ordered and his men dragged the warrior beneath the beam in the centre of the room. An iron hook stuck out from the side of the beam. While one of the Thracians held Maridius in position, the other brought out a four-foot-long shaft of wood with a length of rope tightly bound to each end. He pulled the prisoner's arms back and shoved the wood up beneath them, as far as it would go, and then lifted the rope over the hook and adjusted it until the shaft was parallel to the ground. Maridius grimaced as his shoulders felt the strain.

Cato and Macro watched the preparations from a bench at the side of the room. Macro sat with his back against the wall, his legs stretched out and arms folded, apparently unmoved by the prisoner's suffering. Cato, however, was not so insouciant. The interrogation of the prisoner was a necessary evil as far as he was concerned and he was keen to see it over with as soon as possible.

One of the Thracian interrogators turned to Quertus and stated, 'He's ready, sir.'

Before Quertus could respond, Cato leaned forward and snapped, 'You will address your remarks to me, trooper, if you want to avoid a charge of insubordination.'

The Thracian glanced at Quertus, who nodded discreetly. The

man stood to attention. 'Yes, sir. The prisoner is prepared for interrogation, sir.'

Cato replied, 'Very good. You may begin.'

'Yes, sir!'

The trooper went round to the front of the prisoner while his comrade moved behind Maridius, and savagely kicked him just behind the knee joints. The prisoner slipped down and his shoulders took the full weight of his body. He let out a strained cry of agony and then rolled his head back, eyes clenched, as he fought the pain. The man in front of him squatted slightly, drew his fist back and slammed it into Maridius's gut, driving the air from his lungs and leaving him gasping for breath. Another blow followed, and another in a steady rhythm, working his stomach and chest, until the cries of pain gave way to muted groans and gasps.

Cato leaned closer to Macro and muttered, 'Is this strictly necessary? Again?'

Macro nodded. 'You saw how it was with that Silurian, Turrus. They breed 'em tough in Britannia. That's why we need to spend more time softening 'em up before we get to the questions. Works well enough in most cases, but Maridius is proving something of a challenge. Maybe Quertus and his boys will succeed where Severus failed.' Macro was silent for a moment and his stomach grumbled. 'Pity I didn't have time to finish that last loaf. Bloody Decimus took his own sweet time in fetching it for us. I'm hungry.'

'Hungry?' Cato wondered. The spectacle before him did little for his appetite, but then nothing ever put Macro off his food, he reflected.

The blows continued for a while longer, before Quertus stepped forward and waved his men aside. 'That'll do for now, lads. Give him a breather before we continue.'

The Thracian troopers backed off and sat at a table in the corner of the room, while Quertus pulled up a stool and sat down in front of the prisoner. All was still for a moment and the sound of Maridius's ragged breathing filled the room, above the faint moan of the wind gusting around the walls of the guardhouse.

Cato stood up and crossed the room and stood at the side of the

Thracian officer. He stared down at the top of the prisoner's head for a moment before he began.

'I know you can understand Latin. Like your brother. You both speak it fluently. Your teacher must have been good.'

'Our teacher was a Roman prisoner . . . We put him to death the moment we understood enough to do . . . without him.'

'Why did you choose to learn our tongue?'

Maridius drew a deep breath and looked up, his good eye glinting with malevolence. 'Our father taught us that the first step in defeating your enemy is to understand him. And I understand all I need to know about Rome.'

'Oh?' Cato smiled thinly. 'And what do you understand about us?'

Maridius ran his tongue along his dry lips and thought a moment before replying. 'That you have an insatiable hunger for the land, property and liberty of others. You scour the earth and create a wasteland and call it civilisation. Some civilisation!' He snorted. 'You are a greedy people. You are like a great, fat leech sucking the blood out of this world. Your soldiers kill, rape and burn everything before them. Like these Thracian scum who you pay to carry out your dirty work. They are not warriors, not even men, but scum.'

Quertus leaned forward and casually backhanded him with a powerful slap. Maridius groaned, blinked and shook his head.

'Keep a civil tongue in your head,' Quertus warned. 'Or my lads will see to it that your tongue parts company with your foul mouth.'

'Fuck you . . .'

Quertus balled his hand into a fist but Cato intervened before he could strike. 'No. That's enough, for the moment.'

He returned the prisoner's glare calmly and then spoke again. 'You say that we hunger for the lands of others, but tell me, Maridius, how is that different from the wars you, your brother, and your father fought to conquer the tribes that surrounded the Catuvellauni? Correct me if I'm mistaken but your tribe crushed the Trinovantes, and took their capital as your own. You've also taken land from the Cantiaci, the Atrebates, the Dobunni and the Coritani.' Cato paused and shrugged. 'Seems to me there's not that much difference between the ambitions of the Catuvellauni and Rome, only that my people happen to be rather better at it.'

Maridius curled his lip and spat a gobbet on to the toe of Cato's boot. 'Fuck you!'

Cato glanced at his boot. 'And we happen to be somewhat more refined and imaginative in our use of language and invective as well, it seems.'

'You fucking tell that cunt!' Macro added emphatically.

Cato stifled a wince, and focused his attention back on the prisoner. 'So, now we've dispensed with the pretence that there is any moral high ground in this conflict, there only remains the question of who is going to win. You must know by now that Rome will triumph. We have more men, better men, and greater resources than Caratacus can ever hope to command. He can only delay defeat. Every death, on both sides, that happens before he finally surrenders is on his hands. He cannot beat us, only prolong the suffering and destruction until the inevitable defeat. You must see that.'

Maridius shrugged. 'Better to be defeated and die as warriors than live as slaves.'

'Slaves? Hardly. You and your brothers will be treated no differently to King Cogidubnus who was wise enough to become our ally from the first.'

'That fat coward?' Maridius sneered. 'He has damned himself, his line and his people in the eyes of every other tribe in Britannia.'

'Hardly every tribe. The Atrebates are only one of twelve tribes who have made peace with Rome.'

'Then damn them too!' Maridius shouted.

No one spoke for a moment. Macro yawned. 'This is all very interesting, sir, but it's not helping us. He's as mad as the rest of 'em. Let's find out what we need and put an end to it.'

Cato raised a hand to silence his friend. 'I'll give you one last chance before the interrogation continues, Maridius. While I admire your courage and your pride, it is only helping to prolong the suffering of your people.'

The prisoner gave a dry laugh.

'What's so funny?'

'They are not my people. They are the Silures and the Ordovices. What do I care for their suffering?'

'That's nice,' Macro commented.

'They are still people,' Cato continued. 'They deserve better from those that lead them. They deserve peace.'

'Roman peace?'

Cato ignored the taunt. 'Peace. That is what we will give them once Caratacus is defeated. I need to know the location of his army, and how many men he has. I don't care how I get the information, but I will get it.'

The prisoner glowered and then thrust out his jaw defiantly. 'Fuck you.'

Macro sighed. 'What, again?'

With a tired expression Cato stepped aside and nodded to Quertus. 'Your men may continue.'

The Thracian moved his stool back a pace and then nodded to his men. The trooper tasked with beating the prisoner rose to his feet and moved round to the front of Maridius as he cracked his weathered knuckles and rolled his neck, like a boxer loosening up for a bout, thought Cato. He braced his boots on the floor as Maridius clenched his jaw and half closed his eyes, preparing himself for further blows.

The door to the guardroom opened suddenly and all eyes turned towards it as the duty officer, one of Severus's optios, stepped inside and saluted Cato.

'Sir, beg to report, one of the sentries says he has seen movement below the fort.'

'Movement?' Cato frowned. 'What do you mean? Be specific, man.'

The optio was a young man, only a year or two older than Cato had been when he first held the rank. His anxiety was clear to see as he opened his mouth and tried to marshal his thoughts.

'Just make your report, Optio.' Cato forced himself to speak calmly. 'What exactly has the sentry seen?'

'He says there are men in front of the fort.'

'He saw them? How many?'

'He heard voices, sir. And horses. Then he sent another man to find me.'

232

'And where were you?'

The optio took a quick breath. 'In the latrine, sir.'

Cato bit back on his irritation. No doubt the optio had been spending the time with some comrades, in the way that many men did, in the traditional cosy camaraderie of the latrine block. It was far more comfortable to enjoy the banter in the warm and dry of the latrine than spend the night patrolling the windy ramparts of the fort. But that was no excuse. The optio was on duty. If he needed to piss then he could do it at the foot of the rampart. If he needed a shit, then he'd have to wait until he went off duty.

'We'll deal with that later,' Cato said curtly. 'Did you hear or see anything yourself when you got to the wall?'

'I-I am not sure, sir.'

Macro's patience snapped. 'Either you did or you didn't. Which is it?'

'I thought I heard voices, sir.' The optio glanced from Cato to Macro and back to the prefect.

Quertus laughed. 'The fool's imagining things. The river's high. I've known men mistake the sound of a fast current flowing over the rocks for something else, and their imaginations do the rest. It's nothing. Optio, go back to your duty and discipline your sentry. Perhaps a week cleaning out your shit in the latrine will cure him of his nerves.'

'Wait,' Cato interrupted. 'You seem very sure of yourself, Centurion.'

'Why shouldn't I be? The Silurians are too frightened to show their faces in this valley. There's been no sign of them anywhere near the fort in months. Your man is jumping at shadows. I thought legionaries were made of tougher stuff.'

Macro bristled. 'There's no better fighting man than a legionary. You'd do well to remember that, Thracian.'

'Maybe, but there are clearly better sentries. Optio, tell your man to pull himself together and stop being a coward.'

'That's a word too far,' Macro growled, taking a step towards Quertus as his hand slipped down towards the handle of his sword. 'You bloody take that back or I'll knock your teeth so far down your throat you'll be shitting them for the next month.'

233

Quertus stood up and stared down at Macro with an amused smile twisting his lips. But there was a deadly coldness in his eyes that made Cato scared for the life of his friend. He stepped between them before the confrontation could go any further and addressed the optio, still standing nervously by the door. 'Optio, this fort is the furthest we have pushed into the enemy's territory. That means we don't take any chances. If you, or any of your men, even think there is any danger it is to be reported at once. Have you given the word for Severus's century to be called out?'

The junior officer shook his head. 'No, sir.'

Cato felt a sick feeling in his heart. It was too late to castigate the optio now. That would only cause further delay. 'Then do it now. I want Severus and his men on the wall at once. But tell him to do it quietly. Go.'

The optio dashed out, relieved to escape from the stern gaze of his commander. Cato turned to the other officers in the room. 'It's probably nothing, like you say, Quertus, but I'll take no risks over the fort's safety. Let's see what's happening for ourselves.' Cato paused and gestured towards the prisoner, still hanging by his arms from the iron hook in the beam. 'You men, return the prisoner to his cell.'

Outside, the fort was still and quiet and only the cool breeze brushed between the buildings. The sky was mostly clear and sprinkled with stars. A waxing moon was dimly visible behind a bank of ghostly silver cloud but would not provide much illumination for a while yet. Cato paused to listen briefly but there was no sound of the alarm being raised, and no sound of anything ominous from outside the fort. He allowed his spirits to rise for a moment as he led the other two officers towards the main gate that gave out on to the slope sweeping down towards the parade ground in the valley. He made himself walk at an unhurried pace in order to appear as cool-headed as possible in front of the Thracian. As they reached the gate they heard Severus issuing orders in a muted tone and the dull thud of boots as the legionaries hurried from their barrack block and made for their stations on the wall. The gatehouse was a timber and turf construction and a small brazier a short distance from the watchroom provided warmth and illumination for those on duty.

The officers entered the gatehouse and climbed the ladder that gave out on to the platform above the gate. Stout pine posts formed the breastwork and the sentry on duty turned towards the officers and stood to attention, grounding his javelin.

'You're the one who reported movement?' Cato asked brusquely.

'Yes, sir.'

'Make your report then.'

The sentry nodded and turned back to the breastwork and leaned his javelin against his shoulder as he gestured into the darkness beyond the defensive ditch. 'Down there, sir. I heard voices in the direction of the parade ground, and I saw someone moving.'

'You saw someone? You're sure of that?'

The sentry hesitated a moment and then committed himself. 'Yes, sir. It was definitely a man, crouched in the grass a short distance beyond the ditch.'

Quertus gave a dismissive snort as he leaned on the wooden rail running along the top of the breastwork and stared into the darkness. 'I can't see or hear anything . . . How long ago was it when you think you saw something?'

'Just before I told the optio, sir.'

'And nothing since then?'

'No, sir,' the legionary admitted.

Quertus tutted and turned to Cato. In the faint loom of the starlight Cato could see the sneer on the Thracian's face. 'Seems like I was right, after all . . . sir.'

Cato did not respond but stepped up to the breastwork and strained his eyes and ears as he stared down towards the parade ground. Beyond the ditch the ground seemed to merge into a dark mass; he could only just make out the dim outlines of the haystacks and only because he knew they were there. Macro stepped up beside him and was silent for a moment as he, too, searched for signs of danger.

'What do you think, sir?'

Cato looked round as he heard the sounds of the legionaries deploying along the wall on either side of the gatehouse. Even though they had been ordered to stand to as quietly as possible, the

235

thud of nailed boots on the wooden walkway and the dull clink and clatter of kit seemed very loud in the still night. Cato was torn between the need for caution and the fear of making himself look foolish in front of Quertus for calling Severus and his men out on the whim of a sentry. He glanced at the legionary and could make out his grim features. He was in his thirties and had the stern, lined face of a veteran. Not the kind of man to raise the alarm without good cause, Cato decided. He turned back to Macro.

'I can't see anything. But this man has and we'll keep the men at their posts until first light.'

'Yes, sir,' Macro replied in a relieved tone. 'What about the other century? And the Thracians?'

'You'd rouse my men just because of a nervous sentry?' Quertus shook his head.

'They are my men, Centurion,' Cato said firmly. 'Every man in this fort is under my command. Including you. I'll thank you to remember that.'

Quertus was silent for a moment before he shrugged his wide shoulders. 'As you wish. Though it is my duty to advise you that I know the men, the fort, and this valley far better than you, and I say there is nothing out there. The enemy are too cowardly to dare show their faces in front of Bruccium. A tendency that seems to be spreading to some in our own ranks, it seems.'

The remark was addressed at the sentry but the veteran did not show any sign of reacting to the insult.

'Your advice is noted, Centurion,' Cato said curtly. He turned to Macro. He had made his decision. 'Pass the word for the rest of the garrison to stand to.'

Macro nodded. 'Yes, sir.'

He crossed to the ladder and clambered down before trotting off towards the barrack blocks. Cato turned to the sentry. 'Give us some privacy, soldier.'

The veteran lifted his shield and moved to the opposite corner of the gatehouse platform. Once he was sure the man was out of earshot, Cato rounded on the Thracian.

'I will not have you question my orders again.'

'As I said, I was offering advice.'

'There's a world of difference between offering advice and the insolent, insubordinate comments you have grown accustomed to. That comes to an end now.' Cato spoke softly through gritted teeth, his face no more than a foot away from the Thracian's. Despite his earlier intention to play his hand carefully, something had snapped inside him and a cold, ruthless anger flowed through his veins. 'I have seen all I need to see of the fort, the men, the officers and the way you have been waging your campaign against the enemy. This is not the way of Rome. This is not the way of the Roman army. This is not my way. I am in command here and my orders will be obeyed without question from now on. If you overstep the mark again, Centurion Quertus, I will have you arrested and charges brought. Do you understand?'

The Thracian put his hands on his hips. 'Finally . . . I wondered how long it would be before it came to this. I was starting to doubt that you had any backbone at all. Just like that fool, Prefect Albius. Now, I'll have my say. I know your type. Young men who have caught the eye of a legate or governor and been promoted far beyond what they deserve. I was a fighting man while you were still sucking at your mother's tit. Sure, you've had your share of campaigns and battles, but you, and all the other stuck-up Roman officers, have been fighting to subdue Britannia for nearly ten years now. And the enemy are still out there, laughing at you.' He leaned closer and slapped his chest. 'They mock you but they fear me. I know how to break their will to fight. Your methods have failed. Mine are succeeding. And you'd do well to keep your nose out of it and leave the command of the garrison to me . . . sir.' He uttered the last word with undisguised irony and contempt.

Cato stared levelly back at him. 'Your methods? I don't see any method to what you have done here. The heads on pikes, the impaled bodies, the burned villages, the slaughtered women and children. There is no method in that. Just the bloodthirsty cruelty of a barbarian.'

'A barbarian who knows his enemy as intimately as his own men.'

'Oh?'

Quertus was quiet for a moment before he continued in a flat tone. 'You think me a barbarian . . . well, I learned my ways at the hands of the enemy. The enemy are a cruel people. Cruelty is the only language they understand, so I resolved to pay them back in kind, and with interest. And now it is their will that is breaking. I know what I am doing, Prefect. And I can do it with or without you. Understand that and perhaps you'll survive to return to Rome one day.'

Before Cato could respond, the sentry thrust his arm out. 'Sir! Down there!'

Cato turned and followed the direction indicated by the veteran. It took a moment for his eyes to catch the movement and then he saw a figure emerging from the gloom, a man on horseback steadily picking his way across the uneven ground to the avenue of heads before turning his mount up the track towards the gate. Any fleeting satisfaction that Cato felt over Quertus's misjudgement of the sentry vanished as he scrutinised the approaching rider. Then, when the man was no more than a hundred feet from the ditch, the moon finally broke free of the thin bank of clouds and bathed the night-time landscape in a thin wash of grey light. It was enough to make out some of the details of the approaching rider, and more men moving across the parade ground. Cato felt his heart lurch at the sight of the latter. Then his attention was drawn to the rider again as he reined in and raised something to his lips. A sharp note from a horn split the quiet of the night. The note was repeated again before the rider came on, having alerted the garrison of his intention to talk rather than spring a surprise.

Quertus chuckled and turned to the sentry. 'Soon as he gets in range, try him with your weapon.'

'No,' Cato intervened. 'He's played by the rules, so will we. Put aside your javelin.'

The sentry grounded the butt and turned his attention back to the rider.

'Rules?' Quertus breathed in deeply.

Cato ignored him and glanced back over the fort. The garrison was fully roused now and light glowed in the doors of the barrack blocks, illuminating men spilling out as they made adjustments to their kits on the way to their assigned stations. Small flames flared as men ran to light the braziers at the foot of each tower to prepare fires to light the tarred bundles of wood that would be thrown out to illuminate the approaches to the fort.

'You, in the fort!' a voice called out and Cato fixed his eyes on the rider, approaching the earth-covered trestle bridge that spanned the ditch.

Cato cupped a hand to his mouth. 'That's close enough! Stop there!'

The rider obediently reined in and sat tall in his saddle, staring up at the dark outlines of the men atop the gatehouse, black against the backdrop of the stars. Behind and below him, a torch flickered into life close to the parade ground. As the flame caught, other torches were lit and Cato could see a thin line of men stretching out across the ground facing the fort.

'Who are you and what do you want?' Cato called down.

There was a pause before the rider replied in a deep voice that carried the length of the wall on each side of the gate. 'I am King Caratacus, warlord of the free tribes of Britannia.'

Cato felt his blood chill. He leaned forward across the rail the better to make out the rider. In the torchlight the man's face was clear enough to prove the truth of his words.

'I have come to claim back what is mine,' he continued clearly in fluent Latin. 'You have my brother. I command you to give him up to me, if he still lives.'

Cato's mind was racing with surprise and the implications for the wider campaign now that the enemy leader was before him. If Caratacus had word of his brother's capture and rushed south to negotiate his release then the enemy army was without its commander. It presented a fine opportunity for Governor Ostorius to strike. The ladder creaked and a moment later Macro climbed on to the platform, breathing heavily from his exertions.

'You heard?' Cato asked him.

'Yes. Bastard has a fine pair of lungs on him. Doubt there's a man in the fort who doesn't know he's right on our doorstep.' Macro glanced over the breastwork and shook his head admiringly. 'Whatever else you say about him, the lad's got balls.'

'We should kill him. Now,' Quertus growled. 'Before the fool rides away.'

Macro sucked his teeth. 'He's right. Kill him.'

'No,' Cato replied decisively.

The enemy commander called up to them again. 'I asked if you had my brother, Maridius. Centurion Quertus, speak up and answer me!'

Before the Thracian could respond, Cato leaned forward. 'I am in command at Bruccium. Prefect of the Thracian Cohort.'

'Prefect? What happened to that vile cur Quertus?'

Cato answered as loudly as he could, so that the garrison would hear him. 'He serves me now.'

'And who are you, Roman? What is your name?'

There seemed no advantage to be gained from not answering and Cato drew a deep breath. 'Prefect Quintus Licinius Cato.'

'Prefect Cato . . .' There was a brief pause. 'Is my brother alive?'

'He is.'

'Good. Then I demand his release.'

'Demand?' Macro gave a light, dry laugh. 'The cheeky sod. Tell him to fuck off, sir.'

'Kill him,' Quertus muttered. 'Before it's too late.'

Cato ignored them both. 'Maridius is my prisoner. Why should I release him?'

Caratacus was silent for a moment. 'Because, if you do not, then I shall take this fort, and I swear by all the gods of my tribe that I will kill you and every man you command. Just as you have killed my allies. Every man taken alive will be impaled on the ramparts of Bruccium, and your heads will line the road from here to Gobannium . . . Release Maridius, and you have my word that I will spare the garrison, on the condition that you abandon the fort and march back to Glevum.'

'He's having a laugh,' Macro said softly to Cato. 'How is he going to take the fort? He'd need an army for the job.'

A cold sensation gripped Cato's guts as he replied to his enemy. 'I will not give up the fort, just as I will not give up Maridius, or any other prisoner.'

Caratacus sat silently in his saddle for a moment. 'So be it.'

Then he twisted round and called down into the valley in his native tongue and the men with the torches ran forward.

Macro craned his head and strained his eyes. 'What are they up to?'

'They're heading for the haystacks, I think.'

The warriors' torches cast a red glow over the haystacks as the men approached, then the first of the torches arced brightly through the air before landing on a haystack. More torches were thrust into the other haystacks and flames licked up from each, spreading quickly until they blazed in the darkness, casting great pools of light across the surrounding landscape. And revealing the dense ranks of warriors stretching across the floor of the valley where they stood in silence, by the thousand.

'By the gods . . .' the sentry muttered, staring out at the host.

Cato and the other officers said nothing as they grimly surveyed the enemy army. The earlier prospect of Ostorius taking advantage of the situation returned to mock Cato and he smiled bitterly at himself. The enemy commander had brought his enemy with him.

'Romans!' Caratacus called up to them. 'You see? I have more than enough men to crush Bruccium several times over. And I will. Unless you surrender Maridius and the others and throw down your weapons. You have until first light to decide.'

He turned his horse and rode back down between the rows of decaying heads. Behind him, the garrison of the fort looked down at the silent horde of warriors, bathed in the blood-red glow of the burning haystacks.

# CHAPTER TWENTY-FIVE

After Caratacus had ridden away to rejoin his army, Cato watched the blazing haystacks for a while, and the army waiting beyond, but there was no sign of any preparation for an immediate assault. He gave the order for the garrison to stand down while Severus and his century took the first watch. The rest of the men were permitted to rest at the foot of the rampart in case they were needed at short notice.

Once the orders were given, the senior officers were summoned to headquarters. No one talked as they waited for the last of the officers to arrive. Macro had given orders to Decimus to fetch food and watered wine and settled himself on a bench to one side of the hall while Quertus and his officers sat opposite. Cato paced slowly up and down between them while he waited for Severus and his fellow centurion, Petillius. The two legionary officers had stationed their men along the front wall, which was most at risk. The Thracians were assigned to the remaining three walls, which were protected by the river and the crags leading down from the fort.

Decimus arrived with a small cauldron of barley and lamb stew, mess tins and spoons, together with two jugs and Samian ware cups for the officers. As he set them down, the two legionary centurions arrived and took their place at Macro's side. Cato nodded to his servant.

'Serve the food, then draw some kit from stores and join Severus's century on the wall.'

Once Decimus had completed his duties and left, Cato began to address his officers as they supped on their stew. 'Enjoy it. I expect there will be little chance for a regular meal for the next few days.

By now you will all be aware of the situation. It seems that we have discovered the whereabouts of the army that Governor Ostorius has been trying to pin down for the last two years. Whether we live long enough to report that fact to him is another matter.' Cato paused, but there was no reaction to his attempt to lighten the sombre mood. He took a weary breath and continued to address his officers. 'Caratacus has demanded that we surrender the fort and hand over our prisoners. Of course, there is only one of them that really matters to him, his brother Maridius. If we concede then he gives us his word that we will be allowed to march back to Glevum unharmed.'

'His word?' Quertus interrupted. 'That's worth nothing. He's just like the rest of the savages who live in these mountains. He does not know the meaning of honour. We can't trust him.'

Cato nodded. 'And even if we could, I doubt very much whether the word of Caratacus would be enough to sway the hearts of the Silurians who follow him. After all the fine work that you have been doing in the valleys that surround Bruccium, they will be thirsting for revenge on you, your men, and the rest of us here in the fort. Whatever their commander says, they will not be satisfied unless every last Roman soldier is dead.'

'What goes round, comes round,' said Macro. He raised his cup to Quertus. 'A fine mess you've dropped us into, my friend.'

The Thracian scowled and one of his officers made to stand, his hand reaching for his sword until Quertus swept out an arm and thrust him back on to the bench. There was a brief, tense silence before Centurion Severus spoke up.

'What if we offered them Quertus, on the understanding the rest of us are permitted to leave the valley?'

Quertus glared at the legionary officer. 'Coward.'

Severus shook his head and answered angrily, 'It's because of you, playing the barbarian, that we're in this bloody situation. It's you the enemy want. Like Macro says, you're to blame and now you can reap what you sow.'

Macro turned to him. 'Now hang on, Severus. I was joking. There's no way we're handing one of our own over to those Silurian dogs to tear apart. Not even him.'

Severus glanced round at the others, and then fixed his gaze on Cato. 'Why should we give our lives for him, sir?'

'Because we are Roman officers. If you sacrifice Quertus to the enemy, then that will be a stain on your honour that will never fade. And not just you. It would be a stain on the honour of the legion, forever. I will not let that happen. In any case, I have made my decision. We defend the fort. That is our duty. It also happens to be our only chance of survival, Centurion Severus.'

The legionary officer opened his mouth to protest and then saw the cold expression on his commander's face and the mixed looks of contempt and anger on the faces of the other men and slumped back against the wall. 'Then we're all dead men,' he muttered despairingly.

'Not yet,' said Cato. 'First, Caratacus and his warriors have to get into the fort. It's our job to see that we keep them out. Bruccium is finely positioned. There's only one front they can attack us on easily and even though they greatly outnumber us, they'll not be able to throw their full weight at us at any one time. As long as we have enough men to fully man the gate and the wall on either side, we can hold the fort.'

'And how long do you think we can do that for, sir?'

'As long as necessary,' Cato replied, 'until we are relieved, or the enemy gives up their attempt to take the fort.'

Severus gave a mirthless laugh. 'We aren't going to be relieved. The fort is too far from any help.'

'Not true,' Macro chided his subordinate. 'As soon as there's enough light, we can put a flame to the signal fire. If the weather is good, the smoke will be seen from Gobannium. They'll raise the alarm and Legate Quintatus will send out a column. You'll see.'

'We can't use the signal fire,' said Cato.

Macro frowned. 'Why not?'

'Think about it. As far as Quintatus knows, the enemy is several days' march to the north, close to Ostorius and his army. Once the smoke from our signal fire is spotted and reported to him, he'll send out a relief column all right, and it'll march straight into a trap. Caratacus will pick his ground carefully and he has more than enough men to annihilate a detached force from the Fourteenth.' Cato shrugged. 'We daren't light the fire and lure our comrades to their deaths. Better that we fight it out, or find some way of getting a message through to the legate before he sends us any help.' As he concluded, Cato felt a sudden cold stab of horror. 'Shit . . .'

Macro cocked an eyebrow anxiously. 'What is it, sir?'

'The reinforcement column. They may already be on the road to Bruccium. If they arrive while Caratacus is still here . . .'

Every man in the room understood the danger well enough, and it was Macro who spoke up first. 'If they see the smoke from the alarm beacon, they'll know we're under attack and turn back.'

'Assuming the sky remains clear enough for them to see it.'

Macro pursed his lips. 'Either way, we have to warn them, sir. We have to get a message to the legate.'

'How?' asked Cato. 'Even now, I suspect that Caratacus has already closed the noose around us. It'd be a brave man who dared to try and find his way through the enemy lines. I'll not send a man to certain death.'

'Even if he volunteers?' Severus asked hopefully.

'Even if he is volunteered.'

Macro shook his head. 'Sir, it's a risk we have to take. Not just to save our necks. Ostorius needs to know what the situation is. If he learns that Caratacus and his army are here then he can march on Bruccium at once. It's the opportunity he's been waiting for. The chance to catch and destroy the enemy once and for all.'

'I'm aware of that,' Cato replied tersely. 'However, it would take several days to get a message to the governor, even if a man could find his way past the enemy and reach Glevum. By then, it's likely that the siege will have ended, one way or another.' Cato glanced round the room. 'Gentlemen, I've given you our situation as fully as I can. The blunt truth is we must make our stand here and hold Caratacus off for as long as possible.'

'What about Maridius?' asked Quertus. 'What do we do with him?'

'We try to use him. When dawn comes I'll have him taken to the gatehouse and show him to Caratacus. I will warn him that we will cut his brother's throat the instant any attack is made on the fort.'

Macro looked at his friend in surprise. 'You'd do that?'

'Make the threat, yes. Kill him, no. He's too important for that. Governor Ostorius will want him alive.'

Quertus leaned forward. 'And what if the fort is taken? What then?'

Cato was still for a moment before he replied. 'If it comes to that, then I'll give the order for him to be killed.'

'There is another path open to us, Prefect.'

'I'm open to suggestions, Quertus. Speak on.'

'We could cut our way out of the fort. March out closed up, and fight through their lines and make for Gobannium.'

Macro shook his head again. 'That's madness. There's too many of them. Our cavalry will have no room to deploy. They'll be hemmed in and cut down if they stay with the infantry.' He looked at Quertus with a knowing expression. 'Of course, it's possible that the infantry could open a gap and that would give the cavalry the chance to make a break for it. It'd mean sacrificing my men. But you might escape. That's about the size of it, am I right?'

Quertus showed no reaction for a moment. 'If we can save one unit, then that's better than losing two. It's a simple enough calculation, Centurion.'

Severus glared across the hall. 'And you call me a coward . . .'

Cato stepped forward and raised his voice. 'Gentlemen, quiet! No one is leaving the fort. We all stay here and fight. There is no other option. Caratacus has thousands of men at his back. I have, what? Quertus, what is the latest strength return on the Thracians?'

'Two hundred and thirty-eight.'

'And the wounded?'

'Twenty-seven, five seriously. The rest are walking wounded.'

'Not any more. I want every man who can stand ready to take his place on the wall. And you, Macro? Your cohort's strength?'

'One hundred and forty-eight, and nine walking wounded . . . A hundred and fifty-seven in all. Though most of them still need feeding up.'

Cato did a quick calculation. 'Four hundred and twenty, or so. Enough to hold the wall either side of the main gate.'

'Barely,' said Quertus. 'Once we start losing men, we'll be stretched thin.'

Cato shot him a withering look. 'Obviously. We'll deal with that if the time comes. Meanwhile, there's every reason to think we can hold out. We can make our food last for ten more days at least. More, if we cut the rations of the prisoners. The real problem is going to be the horses. With the loss of the haystacks, they'll have to make do with whatever feed we have inside the fort. Quertus?'

The Thracian officer scratched his jaw. 'There's a standing provision of three days in the stables.'

'Three days?' Cato thought briefly. 'Very well, keep one of the squadrons on full feed. The rest of the mounts go on half feed. After two days, cut it to a quarter. If we're still under siege when the supply is exhausted we'll have to start slaughtering them. At least that'll help with the rations for the men. Fresh meat will give them heart.'

Quertus's expression darkened and his officers stirred and exchanged angry glances. Quertus rose to his feet.

'No one is killing my horses. Not without my say-so.'

Cato casually clasped his hands behind his back so that no one might see the tense trembling of his fingers. The Thracian had challenged him in front of all the officers. Now was the moment to stand his ground, yet he was filled with fear that he had insufficient authority to compel Quertus and the officers of the auxiliary cohort to bow to his will. He forced himself to speak slowly, clearly and forcefully.

'I have tolerated your insubordinate manner for long enough, Centurion Quertus. The next time you address me in such a fashion I will have you arrested, regardless of the need for every man I can scrape together to defend the fort. It is because of you that every one of us in this room is in danger . . . Now, if I give the order to start slaughtering the horses then it will be done at once and without question, starting with your horse. Is that understood?'

There was a unbearable stillness in the room. Cato stared at his subordinate without blinking. For his part, the Thracian glowered, then at length gritted his teeth and nodded, before slowly easing himself back down on to his bench.

Cato felt a flush of relief flow through his limbs and allowed a moment for the other men to reflect on the Thracian's climbdown before he continued. 'If, or when, the enemy attack, Centurion

Severus will hold half his century in reserve behind the main gate. Centurion Stellanus will take fifty of the Thracians to cover the sides and rear of the fort. The rest will defend the wall facing the parade ground. Understood?' Cato glanced round at his officers and they nodded. 'You know your duty. You have your orders. There's no more that needs to be said, gentlemen. Centurion Quertus, see to it that your men are divided into two watches. You'll alternate with the legionaries. Make sure that you keep them on their toes.'

'My men know their duty, sir,' Quertus replied sourly.

'I'm glad to hear it.' Cato nodded his head towards the door. 'To your stations then, gentlemen.'

Quertus and his officers filed from the room, followed by Severus and Petillius. Cato caught Macro's eye and raised a hand to indicate his friend should remain. Macro closed the door and turned back.

'What is it?'

Cato spoke in a low voice. 'When the action starts, be sure to keep an eye on Quertus. After what happened in the Silurian village, who knows what he might try to do in the heat of battle.'

'Don't worry, lad,' Macro made himself smile. 'If he decides to play his little games, he's going to find out that I play for keeps.' He drew a finger across his throat and chuckled. 'Right now, I can't think of any better way of passing the time than sticking a blade between that bastard's ribs and giving it a none too gentle twist.'

Cato cocked an eyebrow. 'Charming thought. But let's not get ahead of ourselves. We need Quertus, for the present, given the hold he has over his men. We'll deal with him once the siege is over, assuming we're still around then.'

Macro frowned. 'An equally bloody charming thought. Thanks for that.'

Cato laughed, and then smiled at the momentary release of tension. He reached for his helmet liner and slipped it on before putting on his helmet and fastening the strap. Macro followed suit but finished before his friend, and noticed the clumsiness of his younger friend's fingers.

'Here,' he said gently. 'I'll do that.'

Cato took a step away, and shook his head, angry with himself for betraying the anxiety he felt inside. 'I can do it.'

He forced himself to continue steadily tying off the thick leather thongs.

'Do you think Caratacus is going to back down when you threaten his brother, come the morning?' Macro asked.

Cato lowered his hands and paused. 'I don't know. He has marched his army down here to put paid to Quertus and his raids just as much as he has come to rescue Maridius, I should think. If I were in his place, I'd put the need to shore up the support of my allies above the life of my brother. But then I've never had a brother so perhaps I cannot understand the depth of his feeling for Maridius.'

'I haven't got a brother either, but I think I would want to save one if I had the chance,' Macro mused. 'If I failed in that, then I'd not rest until I had avenged him.'

'Then you have something in common with Caratacus.' The thought caught Cato by surprise. Perhaps there was more truth in that than he would like to think. There was a kindred spirit between the likes of Macro and Caratacus, brothers in arms regardless of the causes for which they fought. They had certain attributes of valour, integrity and honesty of feeling that Cato felt he could only aspire to and never achieve. He was too questioning of things to allow himself the pleasure of such certainties. His heart ached as he felt a keen sense of loss over knowing that he could never share the sureness of sentiment enjoyed by Macro.

Macro looked outraged. 'Me? Share anything with that bastard? Never! Bollocks to that.' He reached for the latch. 'The very fucking idea . . . I have to get back to the wall.'

Before Cato could say another word his friend had strode out of the room, muttering darkly to himself.

'So much for the notion of the universal bond of the warrior.' Cato shrugged and set off after his friend.

Throughout the night the garrison of Bruccium kept watch over the approaches to the fort. Stocks of javelins were brought from the stores and stacked at the foot of the rampart, along with bundles of kindling, tightly bound and liberally doused with pitch so that they would readily catch fire when the time came to bundle them over the wall and illuminate the enemy. Flames flickered in a handful of small braziers spread around the inside of the ramparts and some of the soldiers were warming themselves by the meagre blazes, their faces washed in a ruddy hue. The watches changed as a horn sounded from headquarters, blowing a brief series of notes over the camp. The haystacks had burned fiercely for a while, bathing the ground and the enemy warriors below the fort in a lurid red. The flames died down after midnight and only pinpricks of red still glowed in the darkness.

Cato and Macro based themselves in the gatehouse, taking turns to walk the defences and ensure that the men were alert. Every so often Cato would pause and stare down into the night, straining his eyes and ears to detect any sign of enemy movement. But there was nothing save the occasional muted order or brief exchange of words from the direction of the parade ground. There was no sign of any activity beyond the other walls of the fort where, in any case, the rush of the river over the rocks made it impossible to pick out any faint sounds. On his return to the gatehouse, Cato laid his helmet to one side and sat against the side of the guardroom. He pulled his cloak tightly about him and closed his eyes. Opposite, Macro snored deeply, until he was roused at the appointed hour to take his turn around the defences. Cato could not sleep, but wanted to show the sentries in the gatehouse that he was confident enough to slumber in the presence of his enemies. It would create a good impression on the men, he knew, and word would quickly spread about the cool-mindedness of the fort's commander.

But although his head tilted in repose and his chest rose and fell with an easy rhythm, his mind was seething as he went over the layout of the fort and the ground upon which it stood. Then he tried to place himself in the mind of Caratacus and assess the weak points in the defences, and where and how he might assault the fort. For each possibility Cato considered his response and how he might deploy his meagre numbers to hold off the enemy horde. The greatest danger would be if Caratacus unleashed a rolling assault along two or three sides of the fort. That would soon force Cato to commit his reserves and inevitably leave some section of the wall vulnerable. There was one other issue to plague his thoughts. Caratacus would be determined to deal with the fort and its defenders as swiftly as possible, before Ostorius got wind of his location. The garrison could expect an assault at any moment.

As if in answer to his concerns, Cato heard the tramp of boots on the floorboards beside him and a hand shook his shoulder. He hesitated just long enough to give the impression that he was being roused from a deep sleep and then blinked his eyes open and looked up at the dark shape of the duty optio looming over him, barely visible in the wan loom of the single oil lamp burning inside the guardroom.

'What is it?'

'Begging your pardon, sir, but one of the lads says he's heard something in front of the gate.'

Cato gestured across the room to the bulky form of Macro, snorting and rumbling in his slumber. 'He heard anything above that? Amazing . . . I'll come.'

Cato rose stiffly and picked up his helmet. As he tied the straps he strode over to Macro and prodded him in the side with the tip of his boot.

Macro groaned and recoiled with a smack of his lips and a sleepy, 'Arrrrr.' Then his eyes opened and he sat up, rubbing his thick curls vigorously. 'What's up?'

'Seems the enemy are on the move.'

'Right,' Macro muttered decisively. He picked up his helmet and stood up. 'Let's have a look then.'

Up on the platform the section commanded by the optio was staring down the slope. The optio indicated a tall figure in the corner. 'That man, sir.'

A light drizzle was falling, just enough to impart the faintest of hisses as it fell on the timbers and turf of the fort. There was no sign of any stars, just a barely discernible mass of dark cloud weighing down the sky. The two officers approached the sentry quietly and took up position at his side.

'All right, lad,' Macro said softly. 'What's happening?'

The legionary replied without looking round. 'I heard a clatter a moment back. Like a spearshaft catching on the trim of a shield, sir.'

'That's a pretty precise description. You sure about it?'

'I've heard the sound enough to know, sir. I'm sure.'

'All right.' Macro nodded, then leaned forward to peer into the gloom alongside Cato. For a moment both men were still, then Macro eased himself back and shook his head. 'Whatever it was, there's nothing there now.'

Cato did not move. Even as he was listening his tired mind would not rest. He calculated that there was no more than an hour left before dawn. The light would begin to return to the world long before then. It was the best time to attack. The defenders of the fort were sure to have had a sleepless night for the most part. They would be weary and on edge so that the slightest thing would further shake their nerves and undermine morale.

'I said, there's nothing there,' Macro repeated patiently.

Cato turned towards him with an irritable expression. 'I heard you, Centurion. And I'll be obliged if you kept your opinions to yourself until I ask for them.'

Macro breathed in deeply and bowed his head. 'As you command, sir.'

'That's right.' Cato took one last look down the slope to satisfy himself that the fort was safe for the moment. Then he turned back to Macro. 'I want Maridius up here on the tower at first light so I can show him to Caratacus. Have him chained in one of the nearest stables so we can get him quickly, if need be.'

'Yes, sir.'

Macro saluted and made his way towards the optio who was waiting by the top of the ladder leading down into the guardroom. Cato watched his retreating back with regret. He had not meant to snap at his friend. His temper was not improved by being awake all night, ears and eyes straining to detect the slightest sign of danger. He was about to call Macro back on some pretext so that he might apologise when he heard a faint whirling noise from the direction of the parade ground. At once the sound grew in volume and seemed to come from a broad area directly in front of the fort. Other men heard it and craned their necks towards it. A word of command was barked from somewhere in the darkness and the noise intensified for an instant before ceasing, to the accompaniment of a swift ripple of grunts. Cato recognised the sound and immediately grasped the danger.

'Down!' He cupped his hands to his mouth and called to both sides of the gatehouse. 'Get down!'

An instant later the air was filled with the sharp crack of stone missiles striking the wooden stakes and boards of the parapet along the wall and atop the gatehouse. The terrible crack and rattle of shot striking home all but drowned out the zip of overshoots passing harmlessly over the wall and on into the camp. There was a handful of sharper sounding impacts and a few cries of agony as the more exposed of the sentries were struck by the slingshot.

Out in the darkness another order was shouted, and Cato recognised the voice at once – Caratacus. A great roar erupted and then the ground in front of the fort seemed to come alive as thousands of figures rose up from the knee-length grass and charged towards the ditch beyond the walls

'Sound the alarm!' Cato cried out as loudly as he could, his throat straining. 'Man the wall!'

# CHAPTER TWENTY-SIX

Mᵒʳᵉ slingshot rattled off the wooden palisades with a deafening clatter, drowning out the shrill sound of the long brass trumpet that blasted out across the fort, calling the men to arms. The shouting of the enemy had swiftly subsided as they charged up the slope towards the outer ditch. Only a few voices bellowed out of the darkness, urging their men on and no doubt heaping curses on the Roman defenders. Cato glanced round the tower and saw that one man was down. Macro was leaning over him, grasping the legionary by the armour on his shoulders.

'You all right, soldier?'

Cato crossed over to him, crouching low as the air was filled with the soft whip of shot flying overhead. A keening rattle was coming from the soldier's throat. Cato could just make out a shadow on the man's helmet and reached out to touch it. Sure enough, there was a shallow indentation, the depth of a spoon, where the helmet had taken the full impact of a slingshot. Even if the man's skull had not been shattered by the blow, the force would have rendered him senseless.

'Get him to the rear of the tower!' he ordered one of the legionaries crouching nearby, and then scurried to the back of the gatehouse and glanced down into the fort. The fires in the braziers had been stoked up to ensure that they weren't extinguished by the drizzle and by their flames he could see men streaming up the wooden steps set into the turf ramparts, before spreading out along the rampart. Their centurions and officers shouted at them to move quickly and keep their heads down as they took up their positions, on one knee behind their shields. The legionaries held the wall either side of the main gate, with the Thracians on each flank. Satisfied that the garrison had responded quickly, Cato turned to beckon to Macro and made his way to the front of the tower. The sound of shot still cracked against the timbers but Cato knew that he must observe the enemy's progress. Steeling himself, he rose up behind one of the boarded crenellations and looked down at an angle towards the ditch.

The dark slope seethed with shapes and the first of the enemy had already reached the edge of the ditch and were scrambling down towards the shadows that filled the bottom. At once there was the clatter of shards of broken pottery, which were commonly planted in the ditches of forts across the empire, along with other obstacles, to slow attackers down. Cries of pain told of those who had cut their feet or hands on sharp edges. Abruptly the slingshot ceased as the enemy feared hitting their comrades closing in on the defences.

Macro stood up and cupped a hand to his mouth and bellowed along the wall.

'Prepare the faggots!'

Several men heaved the bundles on to the rampart while others held torches to the braziers, and the moment they were alight their bearers hurried up to join their comrades.

'Light 'em up!' Macro ordered. 'Then over the wall!'

Despite the flammable combination of kindling and pitch, the drizzle made it difficult to set fire to some of them but a handful caught quickly, crackling furiously. The moment they were well ablaze two soldiers holding a long pitchfork between them pierced the bundles and swung them back, took up the strain and then on a grunted signal heaved them in an arc over the rampart. The flames roared ferociously as they plummeted down through the darkness, struck the ground in a fiery explosion of sparks and rolled on a short distance before coming to rest, casting a wavering red loom across the surrounding area. Some fell short and rolled back into the ditch amongst the attackers picking their way across to the scarp, causing some to cry out in panic as they thrust themselves out of the path of the blazing faggots. Some were not so lucky and were seared by the flames and howled in agony. By the glow of the faggots Cato could see small groups of men glistening in the drizzle as they struggled up the slope with crudely made assault ladders.

He filled his lungs and shouted, 'Loose javelins!'

The legionaries and Thracians stood up against the palisade and readied their throwing arms. The range was short and the iron points of the weapons angled down towards the wave of native warriors surging up the slope towards the fort. There was no need to aim and each man hurled his weapon forward with an explosive grunt. The lethal shafts, momentarily picked out by the fires below, flew through the air and plunged down amid the heaving mass of the enemy. Cato saw a man struck as he stood on the edge of the ditch to the right of the gatehouse, pierced through the stomach by the iron shaft at the head of the weapon. He doubled up, dropping his axe, and fell back, hands clutching the shaft.

More of the attackers went down. It was difficult to miss them as they clawed their way up towards the foot of the wall. Then the first of the ladder parties reached the ditch and carried their awkward burden down, across and up the other side. They planted the base on the sodden ground and swung the top of the ladder up against the palisade, close by the gatehouse. At once warriors swarmed up the rungs, urged on by a nobleman in a chain-mail vest, who was striking his sword and shield together in frenzied excitement. Cato turned to Macro and pointed down.

'See him?'

Macro nodded.

'Take him!' Cato ordered, trusting to his friend's far better talent with the javelin. For himself, he had never quite got over the danger he posed to his own side after once nearly impaling Macro with a javelin during his first combat on the Rhine frontier.

Macro snatched up one of the weapons stacked to the rear of the tower and stepped up to the parapet. He aimed with his left arm as he drew his right back, bicep powerfully bunched in readiness. Macro's eyes narrowed fractionally, and then he hurled his throwing arm forward with an animal grunt of effort. The javelin flew down in a flat trajectory, and passed harmlessly by the native leader who had just taken a step to one side to shout encouragement to his warriors, wholly oblivious to the weapon that slashed through the space where he had been standing an instant before.

'Bastard!' Macro yelled in frustration. 'Wait. I'll have you . . .'

He turned away to fetch another weapon but Cato caught his arm. 'Too late for that. Look!'

The first of the enemy warriors had reached the top of the ladder and was battling with a pair of legionaries blocking his way. The native carried a long-handled axe in his right hand which he swung wildly as he edged himself up another step. The heavy blade of the axe battered the shield of one of the defenders, splintering the surface and driving the man back. His comrade instinctively retreated a step at the sight of the fierce weapon slicing through the chilly air. At once the warrior threw a leg over the palisade and nimbly dropped on to the walkway. He slashed right and left with his axe, the head crashing off the heavy shields of the legionaries, holding them off, while a second man clambered to the top of the ladder. Further along the wall more ladders were being raised and the defenders were fully committed as they struggled to thrust the ladders back, and if that failed, desperately striking at the heads and shoulders of the men scaling the ladders. Cato saw Quertus, fifty paces away, hacking the arm off an enemy trying to clamber over the palisade. The Thracian let out a triumphant roar as the warrior fell off the ladder, and then he turned to look for another opponent.

Cato swallowed nervously and drew out his sword. 'Macro, on me! We're needed on the wall.'

He climbed down the ladder into the gatehouse, dropping the last few feet, and rushed towards the doorway giving out on to the wall. No more than ten feet away the comrade of the axeman dropped down into a crouch and turned to face Cato as he burst out of the gatehouse, sword held out to the side, ready to strike. Light from a brazier directly below cast a vivid glow on the near side of the man's face, revealing a wiry beard and wet locks of hair, beneath which his eyes blazed as he weighed up his Roman opponent. Then, with a snarl, he charged Cato, a long sword raised above his head, ready to slash down and cleave his opponent's skull. Cato was raising his sword ready to parry the blow when Macro barged out of the gatehouse behind him and knocked him towards his opponent. Half stumbling, half falling, he instinctively knew that he must use his forward momentum if he was to survive the next instant. Already the warrior's sword was sweeping round, glinting like molten bronze as it reflected the bright glow from the brazier.

'Shit!' Macro hissed as he leaped to the side.

Cato threw his weight forward, tumbled under the warrior's outstretched arm and crashed into the man's chest. An acrid sweaty odour filled Cato's nostrils. The impact drove the man back a step before his heel caught on the edge of a rough-hewn plank and he tripped and fell. Cato thrust out his leading foot and locked the knee to break his momentum and stumbled to a halt over his opponent. The Silurian was still holding his sword and he desperately swung it in an arc at Cato's shin. It would have been a crippling blow had the tip not struck the inside of the parapet with a thud. Both men exchanged a brief look before the native tried to snatch his sword back. But it was too late for him. Cato leaned forward and punched his short sword into the man's ribs, felt the impact ripple down his arm before a bone cracked and the blade sliced into his resisting flesh. Cato gave the sword a violent twist, just as he had been trained to do as a recruit. He placed his boot on his victim's chest and wrenched his sword out of the wound with a wet sucking noise. The Silurian gasped and slumped back, mouth agape.

Ahead of Cato was the ladder and the axeman a short distance further on. A hand appeared on top of the parapet and an instant later a head and shoulders and the tip of a sword. The man saw Cato at the same time and let out a cry of alarm. Cato grabbed the top of the ladder and tried to thrust it to the side, but the weight of the men on the rungs was too great. The Silurian, fearful of toppling, had clamped his sword hand to the ladder shaft to steady himself, but now saw that he was safe and grinned as he drew his sword back to thrust at Cato.

There was a blur of motion at the periphery of Cato's vision as Macro's sword punched forward into the man's face, shattering his cheekbone and knocking his head back. He cried out and snatched his hand away from the ladder to clutch at the wound and lost his balance, falling from the ladder into the unlit shadows below the wall. His cry alerted the axeman who glanced over his shoulder, his eyes wide with rage as he saw the two Roman officers.

'Take the ladder!' Macro snarled. 'He's mine!'

There was no time for Cato to respond as his friend thrust past him, lowering himself into a crouch as he sized up the tall, broad Silurian who was twirling his axe shaft as he turned, showing off his slick skills with the weapon.

Cato hurriedly sheathed his sword and grasped the ladder shafts. Bracing his boots, he wrenched the rough pieces of timber to the side, and felt the ladder give under its reduced burden. Slowly, then more easily, it tilted and Cato released his grip. It toppled against the angle of the gatehouse, shaking two men loose before it fell into the ditch.

Meanwhile Macro feinted at the axeman, testing his reactions. At once his opponent swirled his axe round and grasped the shaft in both hands to block the blow.

'Fast reflexes,' Macro complimented him in an undertone. Then he stepped forward to make a genuine attack, thrusting at the man's guts. The Silurian knocked the blade aside with a sneer and then blocked the next thrust at his face and let his right hand slip smoothly down the axe shaft as he made a diagonal cut towards Macro's shoulder. It was done so swiftly that Macro only just had time to leap to the side; the blade of the axe missed him by less than a finger's breadth. He fell against the palisade, a short distance in front of Cato, knocking the breath from his lungs. The axeman stepped forward and thrust the butt of his weapon into Macro's chest, striking one of the silver medallions on his harness and knocking him back a step. He made to punch the heavy shaft again but Cato leaped past his friend and thrust his sword into the warrior's chest. It was a blow struck at full stretch and resulted in a shallow flesh wound, but it halted the axeman in his tracks and he hurriedly faced the new threat. Macro snatched a breath and took his place at Cato's side.

'This one's beginning to annoy me.'

Cato nodded, teeth gritted, his eyes fixed on the axeman. Then he lunged again, his height and reach superior to Macro's, and he forced the axeman to give ground. Macro let out a roar and charged forward, and Cato followed suit. The sudden movement of the two officers caught the enemy warrior by surprise and he hesitated for less than a heartbeat, and that was the death of him. Macro struck first, stabbing into his right shoulder, jerking the man's hand from his weapon so that the axe dropped to the walkway. Cato followed up with a thrust just below his throat, shattering the collarbone and driving six inches through his windpipe. The axeman staggered back defenceless and then jerked to a stop, head thrown back as the tip of a pilum burst through his side. Behind him a legionary wrenched the point free and kicked him down the turf slope of the rampart where he rolled to a stop, hands clamped to his throat as he spluttered and bled out.

'Good work, soldier!' Macro grinned. 'Spitted him like a pig!'

The man smiled at the praise and turned back to face the parapet, bloodied javelin tip raised, ready to strike at the next man rash enough to attempt to scale the wall. Cato sheathed his blade, heedless of the blood that still stained it, and looked along the wall. A handful of duels were being fought at the top of the ladders but no more of the enemy had gained the walkway behind the parapet. He nodded with satisfaction.

'All well so far. Come on. Back to the tower.'

They climbed to the top where they could gain a clear overview of the attack. The men to the left of the gate were also holding their own against the natives swarming in front of the fort, lit from behind by the faggots blazing on the ground. As he watched, Cato could see that the flames were starting to die down earlier than he had expected and he glanced up at the heavy loom of the night sky; the rain was falling harder, pinging off the curve of his helmet and providing a light background hiss to the sounds of battle. In the open ground behind the main gate the men of the reserve stood waiting with spears and shields grounded. In front of them Cato could easily pick out Severus, pacing up and down, tapping his sword against his greave. He could practically smell the man's anxiety and despite himself Cato offered a brief prayer to the gods that the centurion would lead his men well if they were called upon to plug any gap in the line. Looking to his right, he saw Quertus shouting encouragement to his men. Every so often he would stand up, in full view of the enemy, and roar his defiance. Just the example the men needed at such a moment, Cato conceded with a touch of admiration.

He turned to Macro. 'This rain won't serve us well.'

'It's as bad for the enemy as us. Worse. At least we have shelter.'

Cato shook his head. 'You're missing the point. It's starting to put the faggots out. If it carries on like this we won't be able to light the signal beacon come the morning. Even if we could I'll wager the clouds will swallow up any smoke we make.'

Macro stared up at the sky, blinking away the raindrops. 'Is there nothing in this bloody land that isn't against us?'

Before Cato could reply, his attention was caught by a movement on the slope in front of the gatehouse. As he strained his eyes he could just make out a large party of men stealing up the track out of the gloom. He leaned forward in an effort to see better.

'Careful, sir!' Macro warned. 'You want to make an easy target for those bastard slingers?'

As if to underline his words, Cato heard a faint whup as a shot passed close overhead. He started guiltily and eased himself back behind the protective hoarding and watched from there. As the men approached, there was something about the way they clustered together that sent a ripple of anxiety through Cato's guts. Then he realised what it was.

'They've got a ram . . . Macro! Look there!' He pointed out the men climbing the track and making directly for the narrow causeway across the ditch.

Macro squinted through the dull shimmer of the rain and frowned. 'That's all we need.'

Cato turned to the other men on the tower. 'Gather up the javelins and get over here, now!'

The legionaries grabbed the bundles of javelins and formed up along the front of the tower.

'There's a party of men heading for the causeway,' Cato explained, speaking loudly to be heard above the din of the fighting and the rain. 'They've got a ram. Don't let them reach the gate.'

The legionaries grasped the danger at once. They hefted their javelins in an overhand grip and raised their shields to protect them from the slingers. Then taking aim on the approaching enemy they waited for Cato's order, Macro taking his place amongst them. Cato watched the warriors closely and could now make out the long, thick length of timber they carried between them. More than likely it was the trunk of a pine tree felled from one of the forests that grew

261

along the side of the valley. At least they would not have had the wherewithal to cap it with a heavy iron point, Cato reflected. But even though it was a blunt, roughly hewn weapon, it would still smash through the gate eventually. The head of the party was no more than thirty paces from the start of the causeway and Cato raised his arm.

'Make ready!'

The range was long, and in the rain it was likely that his men's grip would not be as good as it was in dry weather. Cato let the enemy come on. He wanted the first volley to be as devastating as possible.

There was a grunt as one of the legionaries swept his throwing arm forward and his javelin arced towards the enemy and fell several paces short.

'Who the fuck was that?' Macro raged, turning to stare along the parapet and glaring as his eyes located the culprit. 'You're on a charge. The moment this little fracas is over! Now pick up a fresh weapon and wait for the bloody order!'

The legionary snatched up a replacement javelin and took aim.

Cato saw that the enemy were escorted by men carrying large round shields. Beyond, he saw a smaller party of men led by a tall warrior who stopped well beyond javelin range to watch the progress of the men carrying the ram. Cato nodded to himself; it must be Caratacus. His enemy's intention was clear now. While the Romans were kept occupied along the wall the ram would batter the gate before the defenders realised Caratacus's intentions. It was a good plan, Cato conceded, except the Romans were ready and waiting.

The first men had reached the end of the causeway and Cato filled his lungs, swept his arm forward and roared, 'Loose javelins!'

There was a chorus of grunts as the legionaries hurled their weapons down from the tower, over the causeway to where the bunched ranks of the enemy formed an easy target. The iron-tipped javelins punched through flesh and bone with soft thuds and an instant later the cries and groans of the injured cut through darkness. The party stopped abruptly, the ram dropped to the ground and those with shields swung them up to cover themselves.

'Again!' Cato ordered his men. 'Pour it on, lads!'

The legionaries snatched up more weapons, took aim and hurled the javelins. More of the enemy went down, including those with shields – the wood and leather they were made of provided poor protection against the impact of the deadly iron points. Macro was shouting with glee as he threw one weapon after another and urged the legionaries on. Beyond the tangle of dead and wounded the survivors were breaking and running back down the track. Cato heard the enemy leader shouting angrily at them, and then breaking off to call out an order. A moment later more slingshot whirred out of the darkness, smashing into and splintering the hoardings, with a few shots cracking off the shields of the legionaries. One of the deflections caught Cato on his cheekguard with a loud ring. He felt the blow but luckily the small missile had lost most of its energy and did not injure him.

'Take cover!' he ordered as the sharp rattle of shot intensified, and another legionary was hit, the blow spinning him round. A further shot struck him in the face, pulverising his nose and eye socket in a spray of blood. He collapsed like a sack filled with stones and thudded on to the wooden boards, his shield clattering beside him. The other legionaries ducked down behind the parapet, their heavy rectangular shields adding further protection as the barrage of slingshot rattled against the tower. Cato took an anxious breath during a brief lull and glanced over the wall. The enemy had taken up the ram once more and were making their way across the causeway. A loud crack on the wood beside him sent splinters flying and he felt a hot stab in his cheek and ducked back down.

'Shit . . .' He reached a hand up and felt the blood pouring down his face, and then touched something hard protruding from his flesh. Gritting his teeth he pinched the end tightly and pulled it out and flung it away. The sharp, stinging pain intensified but Cato ignored it.

Macro crouched down beside him, breathing hard. 'The bastards have got us pinned down, sir.'

A voice shouted in front of the gate and a moment later began a short rhythmic chant. At the third beat there was a crash of wood on wood and Cato and Macro felt the tower tremble beneath them. The timbers of the gate were sturdy, as were the fastenings, hinges and the locking bar, but Cato knew that there was a limit to the punishment they could take.

'We have to hold them up as much as possible. I'll stay here and have the men continue with the javelins.'

'That'll be hot work.'

'Can't help that. We have to whittle them down and try to save the gate. If the outer gate goes, there's only the inner gate. If we lose that we're as good as dead.'

Macro nodded.

'I want you to take command of the reserve. Form up behind the gatehouse and open the inner gate. If they break the other one down, then you go in hard. Drive them out and take their ram. They'll produce another soon enough, but it'll buy us some time. Clear?'

'Yes, sir.'

'Then go.'

As Macro clambered down the ladder, Cato turned to the men crouching behind the hoardings. He raised his voice so that he would be heard above the clash of weapons, the cries of men and the steady pounding of the enemy's ram. 'Lads, we have to keep up the pace with the javelins. Use 'em quickly and don't fuck about or you'll make yourself an easy target. Get to it.' Cato knew the danger of exposing himself to slingshot, but equally he knew that he had to lead these men by example. He took a light javelin from the stack at the rear of the tower, deliberately making sure that he did not look at the two casualties that had been dragged to the rear. Then, bracing himself behind a hoarding, he readied the weapon, clamped his jaw tightly and sprang up, leaned forward and hurled the javelin down on the glistening backs of the men clasping the ram, their hair and clothes slick in the rain. He saw it strike a warrior between the shoulders before he dropped back down. A moment later two missiles struck the tower where he had been standing. He felt a rush of elation sweep through his body and he offered a triumphant thumbs-up to the men. 'One more barbarian sent to his gods!'

# CHAPTER TWENTY-SEVEN

Macro hefted his shield as he emerged from the gatehouse, striding over to the half century formed up a short distance away. At his approach Centurion Severus stopped pacing and turned towards him expectantly.

'Stand to!' Macro ordered and the legionaries hurriedly raised their shields and presented their javelins in a neat action, just as if they were on the drill ground. He nodded with approval before turning to their commander. He noted the nervous expression on the other man's face. Just then the ram crashed into the outer gate once again, causing Severus to flinch as his gaze shot towards the sound.

'They'll be through that soon,' he said anxiously, 'then the inner gate, and we won't be able to stop them.'

'Oh, I doubt that!' Macro said loudly enough for the other men to hear. 'Because we're the men who are going to give those barbarian cunts a good kicking. Now, you two.' He indicated the legionaries at the left end of the small formation. 'Get the inner gate open. Smartly does it.'

Severus's mouth gaped. 'Open the gate? What the . . . ?'

Macro made himself smile and continued evenly, 'Come now, those bastards are ruining one of the gates. Damned if I'm going to let them put a scratch on the other.'

Severus stared at Macro as if he were mad, but Macro gave him no chance to speak. He drew his sword and turned to the legionaries. 'Lay down the javelins. This is a job for swords, lads.'

They set their weapons down and stood ready, hands resting on the pommels of their short swords as they waited for his orders.

'Form column of fours! Close up and shields to the front!'

The rain had formed puddles on the ground and the men's boots splashed through them as they took up their positions. The two legionaries sent to open the gate had lifted the locking beam out of its brackets and were hauling the heavy timbers inwards. The wooden peg hinges groaned as the gate opened to reveal the dark maw of the short passage leading to the outer gate. Their work done they joined their comrades and Macro took his place at the head of the tight formation, gesturing to Severus to join him.

'Let's give 'em the wedge. You and I are taking point.' Macro grinned and muttered the centurion's credo, 'First into the fight, and last out!'

Severus nodded and smiled weakly. 'First in. Last out.'

Macro's expression hardened as he drew his sword and raised it into the damp air. 'First Century, Fourth Cohort draw your swords! We fight for the glory of the Fourteenth Legion!'

The legionaries thrust their blades up and let out a cheer. Up on the wall on either side, the men who were not engaged with the enemy glanced round at the noise and Macro's heart was warmed as he saw the men from the Blood Crows join in, echoing the cry from one end of the wall to the other. He lowered his sword and pointed the tip towards the passage. There was a sharp crack from the darkness as the ram shattered one of the timbers of the outer gate.

'At the slow step . . . advance!'

The legionaries paced towards the opening, shields raised to the front, covering all but the eyes of the men. As they entered the passage, the ram struck home again, smashing through the ruined timber and dislodging another length. As the ram was drawn back, Macro could make out the dim shapes of men through the jagged gap. He could also see that the locking beam was still intact. He halted his men, two paces back from the gate, far enough inside the passage so that the enemy would not see them in the darkness.

The ram struck again, accompanied by a raucous cheer from the Silurians as they sensed that it would break through in a matter of moments. Another length of timber gave way with a splintering crunch. The next blow struck the locking bar full on and it leaped in the iron brackets that held it against the inside of the gates. It fell

266

back into place, only to creak and begin to split at the next blow. Two more strikes were enough to complete the job; the bar shattered and one side of the gate burst in, revealing the packed ranks of the enemy warriors waiting to charge into the fort. As Macro braced his boots and snatched a deep breath he saw two javelins plunge down. A warrior jerked upright with a howl of agony as he groped for the shaft that had pierced his back and plunged into his vital organs. Then he toppled off the causeway into the ditch.

'For Rome!' Macro bellowed, his cry instantly echoing back to him off the interior of the gatehouse passage. 'Advance!'

Ahead of them the men clustered about the ram looked up, straining their eyes into the darkness. They were clearly outlined against the red hue of the faggots still burning outside. Before they could react, Macro and his legionaries thrust their way out of the passage. Macro punched his shield into the nearest man, knocking him back into his comrades, and followed up with a savage thrust of his short sword into the Silurian's chest. At his side, Severus slashed at a shoulder and opened up a deep cut down the length of the arm, before he pushed his shield forward and stepped in behind it. The legionaries following the officers pressed forward on each side, stabbing at their enemies. The Silurians had not expected to be counter-attacked at the moment of their triumph and those holding the ram released their grip and let it drop on to the causeway as they backed away from the danger, leaving their armed comrades to take up the fight. Some reacted quickly, raising their round shields and charging the Romans emerging through the broken gate.

This was the close-quarters fighting that the legions trained for and at which they excelled, and in the dense press of bodies covering the causeway the lethal points of their short swords flickered out from between their large curved shields, stabbing deeply into limbs and torsos before being ripped free, causing terrible, crippling injuries that bled freely. Macro grinned fiercely as he battered his way forward with his shield, thrusting his sword again and again. Sometimes his blows did not land. Sometimes they were parried aside, but most struck home and he felt the warm flow of blood trickle over the guard and on to his hand as he pressed on, leading his men step by step across the causeway. To his left he glimpsed the ditch, the slopes and bottom littered with the dead and dying of the enemy. More were crowded in the narrow strip of ground between the scarp and the wall, eager to climb ladders and hurl themselves at the defenders.

'Down your javelins!' he heard Cato shout from above. 'Those are our men!'

Macro had given no thought to the danger of being struck down by his comrades and mentally thanked his friend as he thrust his sword again, only for his opponent to desperately throw up his shield and deflect the blow. Suddenly there was a surge through the ranks of the Silurians and a large warrior, dressed in furs, thrust his way to the front, a huge war axe clasped in his powerful hands. His comrades glanced at him in awe and hurried out of reach as the axe swung round in a vicious arc over his head. With a savage roar the giant fixed his attention on the crested helmet of Severus, determined to slaughter the Roman officers and break the will of the men following them.

Severus stood his ground, shield raised and sword held back ready to strike. He had no choice. The ranks of the men behind him made retreat impossible. The giant planted a foot forward and swung his axe in a wide arc at chest height. Macro heard the whipping hiss of the axe head as it cut through the air, then the shattering crash as it tore through the edge of Severus's shield, shattering the bronze trim and the layers of wood and leather which exploded into fragments under the terrifying power of the blow. The ruined shield leaped from the centurion's numbed fingers and tumbled over the side of the causeway into the ditch. The giant let out a triumphant cry and continued his swing with bunched muscles. The axe swept round again, this time at a slightly greater height. Severus half turned to throw his sword up and try to block the blow, his mouth opening as a last cry tore from his lips. 'Noooo!'

The axe head clanged as it knocked the sword from the centurion's grip, sending the weapon cartwheeling through the air. An instant later the edge struck the centurion in the neck, cleaving through flesh and bone and sending the head, encased in its polished helmet, leaping from the officer's shoulders.

'Fuck me . . .' Macro was momentarily astonished by the deed, then, with a cold stab of reason, he knew that he would be the man's next victim.

'Not me, friend!' he growled as he turned towards the giant and powered forward, crouching to lower his centre of balance. Nothing could resist the impact of such a heavy axe, Macro knew. He had to get close to the giant, inside the range of his fearsome weapon. Already the Silurian warrior was turning towards him, wielding his axe and making ready to strike. Macro charged home, thrusting his shield up just before he crashed into the man. The trim at the top of the shield caught him under the chin, snapping his jaw shut and cutting off his bellowing war cry. At the same time Macro swung his sword arm out and stabbed in at an angle. It was not the most effective blow, lacking power, but it caught his man in the side, below the ribs; it penetrated the folds of his fur cloak and bit into his flesh before Macro fetched up hard against the inside of his shield, marvelling at the solidity of his opponent. He braced his boots and shoved as he snatched his sword out and stabbed again, and again, hearing the man's grunt as the blows drove the breath from his lungs.

Knowing that his axe would not serve him well in such a close struggle, the giant threw it down and grasped the sides of the shield and tried to rip it from Macro's grasp.

'No, you fucking don't!' Macro spat, tightening his grip on the handle. Above him he saw the furious face of the man looming over the top of the shield. Instinctively, Macro powered up from the balls of his feet and headbutted the giant with his helmet, the solid metal of the brim guard crushing the bridge of the man's nose. He released his grip and staggered away, blood pouring down over his beard and more soaking the tears in the folds of his cloak, matting the fur. Gasping for breath, Macro drew up, realising that he had reached the far side of the causeway. Before him the last of the party charged with breaking down the gate had turned to flee, leaving a score of bodies scattered over the packed earth in front of the ruined gate, most skewered by javelins.

'Macro!'

He turned and looked up and saw Cato pointing down.

'Macro, get the ram inside!'

'Yes, sir!'

He turned and ordered two of his sections to sheath their blades and take up the stumps of branches that the enemy had been using

269

as handles. The remaining men formed a shield wall at the end of the causeway to cover their comrades. Not a moment too soon. As the enemy drew away from the Romans, a hail of shot flew out of the darkness and clattered off the surface of the shields. The men carrying the ram struggled back inside the gatehouse, grunting under the load, as Macro steadily called the step for the shield wall to fall back inside the fort.

Above them Cato let out a sigh of relief. The capture of the ram would win them several hours at least. Although he had lost the outer gate, the inner gate still held and there would be time to seal up the passage with earth and rocks to render it impassible. Looking up at the sky, he detected the first hint of the coming dawn amid the rain and clouds, a thin skein of grey along the edge of the mountains to the east. Already he could pick out more detail in the fight on each side of the gatehouse, and the ground in front of it. There, he saw Caratacus again, fists clenched and resting on his hips as he glared up at the fort. Then the enemy commander turned to his followers and a moment later a war horn blared out, its deep notes carrying across the battlefield. One by one the men at the top of the ladders, struggling to gain a foothold on the wall, broke contact and eased themselves down rung by rung. Those below backed away cautiously, climbing down and then out of the ditch before hurrying back down the slope, some with sufficient presence of mind to carry their assault ladders away with them. For a moment Caratacus stood still, then it seemed to Cato that his enemy picked him out on top of the tower and he raised a finger and pointed directly at him, his threat clear enough. He would not give up. Not until the the fort of Bruccium, its garrison, and its commander were wiped out.

Caratacus turned away and paced slowly down the slope, along with the rest of his army.

Cato heard the ladder creak behind him as Macro climbed into the tower and came and stood at his side.

'Round one to us,' Cato said quietly.

Macro nodded. 'But we lost Severus, and a handful of others. Did you see?'

'I saw.' Cato's gaze flicked briefly down at the causeway where the centurion's headless corpse lay sprawled across the body of one of the Silurians killed by a javelin. Then he recalled his first duty in such a situation.

'Give the order for the men to stand down. The Thracians can take the first turn on the wall. Have the wounded taken to the surgeon and rations issued to the rest. Oh, and let them know that I'm proud of them. We've made certain that the enemy will remember the garrison of Bruccium for the right reasons now. They know we can put up a decent fight as well as burn and massacre.'

Macro nodded, then paused before he turned to leave. 'You sure you want to tell the lads that?'

Cato stroked his chin. 'Perhaps not the last bit. Just tell them I'm proud of them. Proud to be their commander. That should put some fire in their hearts . . . They'll need it, when Caratacus comes for us again.'

# CHAPTER TWENTY-EIGHT

Dawn broke over a very different scene to the previous morning. Nothing remained of the haystacks except blackened piles of smouldering ash. There were scorched patches on the slope in front of the fort where some of the faggots had burned out and bundles of charred kindling where the rain had extinguished others. Bodies lay scattered along the ditch and below the wall. The enemy had taken their worst losses before the main gate where bodies covered the ground and much of the causeway, amongst which the shafts of javelins poked up at all angles like a carelessly used pincushion. As soon as there was light enough to see that the enemy had retreated as far as the parade ground, some two hundred paces away, Cato sent out a patrol to retrieve the still serviceable javelins from amongst the corpses. At the approach of a group of slingers, the patrol hurried back through the ruined gate into the shelter of the fort, with salvaged javelins bundled up under their arms. Another section had brought in the bodies of two legionaries who had been killed in the attack on the ram, as well as the corpse of Severus. His head had not been found. One of the natives had probably taken it as a trophy before retreating down the slope, Cato decided as he stood in the tower and surveyed the scene.

The enemy camp sprawled across the floor of the valley. They had not yet built themselves any shelters and slept in the open, around the fires they had struggled to light in the hours since the sun had risen. The rain had stopped but the ground and the branches of the trees were soaked and only those who had ventured far enough into the valley's forests to penetrate the most sheltered parts had returned with readily combustible fuel. From the size of their camp,

Cato roughly estimated their number at close to ten thousand, perhaps several hundred of whom were mounted, judging from the horses grazing along the floor of the valley.

'Outnumbered at least twenty to one,' Cato muttered to himself. 'Even Macro wouldn't bet on those odds.'

Casting his eyes over the terrain surrounding the fort, Cato could see small parties of men camped on the far bank of the river that curled around the high ground on which the fort was constructed. There would be no escape in that direction. It would take a courageous man to swim the fast-flowing river, dodging the rocks around which the water swirled. Even if it was possible to swim the river, there was the enemy to evade before any attempt could be made to escape from the valley and reach the nearest Roman outpost and raise the alarm. It would be a suicide mission, he decided. But it might yet be necessary to send a man, if the overcast did not lift. The heavy clouds hung low in the sky, obscuring the tops of the hills that lined the valley, thicker since dawn had broken and visibility seemed to be steadily reducing. It would be pointless to light the signal beacon. There was no chance of the smoke being sighted from Gobannium, or any other outpost. For the present the garrison was on its own.

Cato stifled a yawn, determined not to show that he was tired, and turned to the nearest sentry. 'Let me know the moment the enemy makes a move.'

'Yes, sir.' The legionary saluted and turned his attention to Caratacus's army as the fort's commander descended the ladder into the gatehouse. At the bottom he saw that Macro was overseeing the blocking up of the passage between the smashed outer gate and the inner gate. The end of the nearest barrack block was being demolished and men were carrying the rubble across to the passage in wicker baskets and piling it up inside.

Macro nodded a greeting. 'Soon be finished here. They'll not get through that lot.'

'Very good,' Cato responded with satisfaction. That was one less weak point in the defences to worry about.

Macro lowered his voice as he continued, 'Do you know the butcher's bill yet?'

Cato sighed. A clerk had brought the report to him at the end of the first hour of the day. 'Twelve dead, eighteen injured. Most of them downed by slingshot. We're going to have to be careful not to expose ourselves on the wall unnecessarily from now on. It's too much of a risk.'

'What isn't in this situation?'

'True enough.' Cato rubbed his brow and then saw Decimus, still in legionary kit, limping from the direction of headquarters, carrying a mess tin and a cup, stepping carefully around the puddles and mud. As the servant looked up and saw his commander, he hurried over.

'Brought you something to eat, sir. Need to keep your strength up, so here's stew and some posca.'

Cato took the mess tin gratefully, realising just how hungry he was after the night's action. The stew was warmed through rather than hot and he spooned it down hurriedly.

Macro licked his lips. 'Any more of that about?'

Decimus glanced at him. 'All gone, I'm afraid, sir.'

'I see.' Macro tapped his nose. 'I hope you enjoyed it as much as the prefect seems to.'

Decimus looked down awkwardly. 'Seemed a shame to let it go cold, sir.'

'I'm sure,' Macro growled.

For a moment Decimus looked anxiously down at the ground, before he summoned up the nerve to speak. 'Sir, is there any hope of us getting out of this alive?'

Cato chewed on a morsel of meat and then swallowed. 'There's always hope.'

Decimus's shoulders sank and he nodded in a resigned fashion.

Cato was watching the expressions of the men passing by as he finished his snatched meal. They looked tired, but grimly determined. There were even some who were engaged in cheerful exchanges with their companions. This early success had boosted their morale. But that was hardly necessary. These men were legionaries, hardened professionals, used to hardship and danger and imbued with a firm sense of tradition and the need to uphold the honour of their legion. They would play their part well enough. It was the auxiliaries who concerned Cato. Their morale was more uncertain, a problem

274

exacerbated by the excesses of Centurion Quertus. Although their ranks had been leavened by those legionaries transferred in from the other cohort of the garrison, Cato sensed that their morale was more brittle. They were used to patrolling and raiding the enemy's territory. This kind of static, stand-up fight required firm resolve. Both units were bound to be tested to the limit in the days to come.

As if anticipating his thoughts, he saw Quertus approaching him along the open ground behind the wall.

'Here's trouble,' said Macro.

'Not necessarily.'

'With him, necessarily, I'd say.'

Cato drew himself up to his full height as the Thracian approached and nodded an informal salute to his superior. 'A tough night, sir. But we gave them a hiding and sent 'em packing.'

'Oh really?' Macro scratched the stubble on his jaw. 'You think we've won then?'

'For now. They won't dare to make another frontal assault in a hurry,' Quertus asserted confidently. 'Not now we've proved, once again, that they should be afraid of us.'

Macro glanced at Cato and cocked an eyebrow. 'Heroes all, eh?'

Cato ignored the comment and addressed the Thracian. 'I take it you have something to report?'

'Yes, sir. My horses. We've got oats to feed them for a few days as you know, but they'll need watering.'

'Of course they will. There's plenty in the fort's cistern. And there's plenty in the well.'

Quertus shook his head. 'They'll drain the cistern in a couple of days. And they'll run the well dry in even less time.'

'I see. Then we'll have to ration their water and their feed.'

'That's not possible, sir. The food we can restrict, but they can't do without water. Not if we want them in a fit state to ride.'

'What do you suggest?'

Quertus gestured towards the rear of the fort. 'There's a narrow track that winds down the cliff there. Wide enough for a man to lead a horse. My lads can take 'em down there to the river to be watered.'

Cato considered the suggestion. 'Best do it under cover of darkness.'

'Too dangerous, sir. If they put a foot wrong on the path they'll fall into the river. We can only use the path in daylight.'

Cato sighed in exasperation. 'Then see to it. Make sure you give the handlers an escort in case the Silurians try to spring a trap.'

He considered the exchange concluded, but Quertus did not move away.

'Is there something else, Centurion?'

'Just the question of what you intend to do next . . . sir.'

'Do?'

'I'm next in the chain of command. If you fall, then I will need to carry out your intentions.'

Cato smiled thinly. 'I intend to defend the fort.'

Quertus nodded in the direction of the enemy camp, his earlier bluster gone. 'We've beaten them off once, but we can't do it indefinitely. If we lose men at the rate we did earlier then it's only a question of a few more attacks before we're spread so thinly they'll overwhelm us.'

'I thank you for that assessment,' Cato responded curtly.

'We can't stay trapped in here. We have to get out.'

'That's not possible. We're surrounded, in case you hadn't noticed.'

'Then we'll have to break out. While we still have enough men to do it.' Quertus glanced up. 'If this weather holds, it'll be dark tonight. Dark enough to cover our escape.'

'And dark enough to have us blundering into each other, if not the enemy.'

'What if we use our prisoners as a shield? Caratacus would hardly let his men attack us if there was any danger to his brother and the others.'

Cato shook his head. 'He might not. But given the suffering you've visited on the local people in recent months, I dare say Caratacus will have trouble restraining his allies. They want nothing more than to butcher us all and take our heads as trophies. It's too dangerous. We've been over this, Quertus. Our best chance is to sit it out until we are relieved. That's my decision.'

The Thracian gave him a frosty look. 'It's the wrong decision.' Before Cato could respond, he turned and strode away, back towards his men resting on the slope leading up to the wall.

Macro glared after him. 'The enemy would be doing us a favour if they knocked that gobshite on the head.'

Cato was too tired to comment. He finished the last of his stew and drained his cup. Then he rubbed his jaw thoughtfully for a moment.

'I think it's time we brought Maridius and the other prisoners into play.'

It had started to rain again as scores of men stood along the wall looking on curiously as two legionaries lowered a ladder to the ground close to the causeway. Beside them Macro regarded Cato with concern.

'This ain't a good idea, lad.'

Cato gestured towards the prisoners pressed together behind the gatehouse under the watchful eyes of several legionaries. 'I think it might buy us a little more time.'

'What makes you think Caratacus will agree?'

'It's more than likely that he won't, but he will think it over. And every hour that he wastes pondering the problem improves our chances of getting through this alive.'

'Not by much. You said it yourself. We're out on a limb here and as long as this cloud stays above us then no one's the wiser in the rest of the army.' Macro hawked up some phlegm and spat over the wall. 'Fucking weather in this island is unbelievable. You'd have to be a mad dog or a Celt to venture out into the noonday gales in this dump, I tell you.'

Cato smiled as his friend continued in a more earnest tone.

'Watch yourself. If there's a hint of treachery then you turn and bolt back to the ladder. I'll have a party of men on hand with javelins to cover you.'

Cato was silent for a moment before he nodded. 'Fair enough. But keep them out of sight. This cuts both ways. If Caratacus suspects we might be trying to lure him into a trap we'll lose any chance of talking our way out of this. Right, I'd better get going.'

Cato nodded to the trumpeter and the Thracian lifted his curved instrument and blew a deep note out across the valley. As soon as Cato saw that some of the enemy had turned to look at the fort, he swung his leg over the wall and felt for the nearest rung. When he had a solid footing he began to descend. At the bottom he stepped back and raised his hands towards the parapet. Macro dropped the spare standard shaft down. A broad red pennant had been attached to it and Cato held it aloft and wafted it from side to side over his head. He would be spotted easily, and the red of the pennant and his military cloak would stand out against the tawny grass and heather of the slope. He climbed carefully down into the ditch, picking his way past the bodies lying there. Some still lived, groaning feebly and reaching out an imploring hand as he passed by. There was nothing he could do for them and he steeled himself to ignore their plight as he climbed the far side of the ditch and slowly descended the slope, waving his banner as the notes of the bucina continued to ring out. Around him the desultory hiss of the rain added to the gloom of the day.

'That's far enough, sir!' Macro called out. 'Stay in javelin range!'

Cato stopped. He continued to wave the pennant, in easy circles as it became soaked by the rain. Below him, only the nearest of the enemy were clearly visible, the rest becoming grey and indistinct in the mizzle that filled the valley. He watched as one of the screen of men guarding the camp turned and ran towards a large makeshift hut made from cut branches and heather that sat in the midst of those struggling to take shelter in the open. A moment later a handful of figures emerged from the hut and regarded the lone Roman officer a quarter of a mile away. After what seemed to be a swift exchange, Cato saw one of the men stride across to a horse line nearby and untether a white mount and vault on to its back. He turned the beast towards Cato and stirred it into a gentle canter. His army stood and some offered a cheer as he rode by and then through the line of sentries towards the fort. He slowed down as he approached Cato and walked his horse up to within ten paces before he reined in, casting a wary eye across the surrounding ground and the fort lined with soldiers.

Cato grounded his standard.

'You wish to speak, Roman?' Caratacus asked in his accented Latin.

'I do.' Cato gestured towards the nearest bodies lying on the slope. 'Last night's assault cost you dearly. I wish to discourage you from wasting any more of your men's lives in such futile attacks.'

'I thank you for your concern,' Caratacus responded flatly. 'But I have every intention of taking your fort and burning it to the ground.' He gestured towards the sky and a smile flickered across his lips. 'Weather permitting.'

'You cannot take the fort. It is too strong a position and you have no siege train, nor the expertise to make the weapons you require to batter down our defences.'

'All we need is a decent ram. Even an uncivilised barbarian has the wit to construct one of those, as you have seen.'

'Yes, I admired the rudimentary handiwork of the ram we captured. The gate has now been blocked up, so any more rams you decide to make will be useless. All that's left is to mount frontal assaults. And we have seen how that ends.'

'We took our losses,' Caratacus admitted. 'But so did you, and I rather suspect that I can afford to lose more men than you can. Besides, many of my followers have kin in these valleys and their hearts burn with desire to avenge themselves on those you have slaughtered. It is my intention to keep attacking Bruccium until it is destroyed and every Roman inside its walls is killed.'

For a moment Cato pondered explaining that this was the work of Quertus, but he realised that would make no difference to men who viewed all Romans as brutal oppressors. He sighed.

'I feared that is how you would respond, sir.' Cato raised the standard twice, the signal he had agreed with Macro earlier. Caratacus started suspiciously.

'What trickery is this?'

'No trick, I assure you. You know that we hold prisoners, your brother Maridius amongst them. If you look there, on the wall to the left of the gatehouse, you will see them in a moment.'

Both men watched as a line of men and a few women shuffled out along the parapet under the guard of Macro and some legionaries. Leading them was the tall, proud figure of Maridius. As soon as he saw Caratacus he called out, and Macro quickly strode across and slapped him hard across the face.

'Keep your barbarian mouth shut!'

Cato winced at the violent silencing of the man and saw Caratacus's expression darken. He cleared his throat and spoke loudly to the enemy commander. 'I want you to know that if you launch another assault on my fort, I will execute ten of my prisoners, out here, in full view of your army, and mount their heads on the gatehouse to remind you of your folly. If that fails to deter you, the next time it will be your brother. Only in his case I will be sure to make his death long and painful. He'll be crucified on top of the wall. I've heard that it can take a man three days to die on the cross. Maridius, as you know, is a fine warrior. Strong and tough. He'll be sure to go the distance before he's done.' Cato spoke in a cold, calculating tone, determined to conceal any hint of his disgust for the image he was painting.

'So, this is Roman civilisation,' Caratacus sneered. 'Your ways amount to little more than the enactment of cruel spectacles. Just as I had been taught.'

Cato shook his head. 'This is not civilisation. This is war. You threaten to slaughter me and my men. It is my duty to do whatever is necessary to prevent that. You leave me no choice.'

'I see.' Caratacus's eyes narrowed shrewdly and he stared at Cato for a moment. 'I sense that your heart does not stand behind your words, Roman. Would you really be prepared to carry out your threat?'

'If you attack us again, you'll discover that I act on my promises. This I swear. I will kill your people the instant the first Silurian reaches the ditch in front of my fort. They will die by my own hand.' Cato stared fixedly into his enemy's eyes, daring him to believe otherwise. Caratacus stared back and then glanced over Cato's shoulder towards his brother and the others on the wall.

'I doubt you have the heart for it.'

'That is your mistake.'

'Then let me make *you* a promise, Roman.' Caratacus raised his voice so that it carried clearly to those standing on the wall of the fort. 'If you do as you say and harm those you hold captive, then I swear by all my gods that I will show you and your men even less pity. We will take the fort and if you have killed just one of your prisoners, I will take as many of you alive as possible. Then

I will have you flayed alive, one each day, in front of his comrades. You last of all . . . Now, I will make you an offer. The same as before. Surrender your prisoners unharmed, and I will allow you free passage from this valley. I am not an unreasonable man. I will give you a day to consider. If you refuse my offer we will attack again. In that event, if you have harmed my brother or the others, you know the fate that awaits you. There will be no more words between us.' He tugged on his reins, and turned his horse about and trotted back down the slope. Cato watched him for a moment, seized with the urge to call out to Macro to have his men loose a volley of javelins at the enemy commander. With Caratacus dead, the coalition of tribes still resisting Rome would collapse. But the moment passed; Caratacus spurred his horse and was soon well out of range.

Cato sighed with frustration at his hesitation, even though he knew it was not in his nature to be so ruthless as to break the rules of parley. Caratacus had also sensed it, and Cato felt a leaden despair at his failure to conceal his true character. He put the standard against his shoulder and returned to the fort.

# CHAPTER TWENTY-NINE

The remaining hours of the day were spent preparing for the next attack. The sound of hammers ringing came from the fort's forge as Macro oversaw the production of caltrops, the small four-pointed iron weapons that were often strewn on the ground in front of Roman battle lines to break up enemy charges. A misplaced foot or hoof that was impaled on a caltrop was enough to cripple a man or horse and take them out of the conflict. There had been none of the devices in the fort's stores and Macro had to give orders to melt down the stock of spare javelin heads, bridles and the handful of iron bars intended for trading with natives, before Quertus had adopted a more forceful strategy. Smoke billowed from the forge but quickly dissipated in the breeze that accompanied the rain, even before it was swallowed up by the low clouds.

'The trouble is, we can't create enough of 'em to make much of a difference,' Macro explained to Cato as the latter checked on his progress late in the afternoon. The heat in the forge was intense and the farrier and his assistants were stripped down to their loincloths. They sweated over the furnace and took turns at the bellows used to keep the fire sufficiently hot. The melted iron was poured into a hastily prepared mould that produced V-shaped lengths that were joined and beaten together while still glowing red. The centurion mopped his brow and indicated a wooden tub, no more than a quarter full of the dark, spiked weapons. 'That'll cover barely a tenth of the length of the front ditch. We've got enough material to provide for the rest, but not the other ditches. And besides, what we have won't be finished for four, maybe five days.'

'Well, it's something,' said Cato. 'We'll spread them thin to start with and hope that we injure enough of them to slow the rest down the next time.'

'Then you think Caratacus will attack, regardless of your threat?'

'I'm certain he will. In his place I would.'

'And you'll go through with it? What you said you would do to the prisoners?'

Cato took a deep breath and nodded. 'I have to. In the first instance at least. Then he might be wary of causing the death of his brother. It'll be a bad business, Macro. A very bad business. But it will have to be done.'

'You don't have to be the one,' Macro said gently. 'Just give the order. Someone else can do it. I'll do it if you want. Or ask Quertus. He'll be happy to kill the prisoners since he never wanted them in the first place.'

'No. It has to be me,' Cato said in a resigned tone. 'Caratacus must see that I carry my threats through. It'll also do the men good to see that I am as ruthless as that Thracian. I want no one to be in doubt that when I say I'll kill someone, I will do it. Good for discipline.'

Macro raised his eyebrows in surprise. 'Well, if you're sure, lad . . .'

Cato smiled at his friend. 'I'm just glad Julia isn't here to see it.'

'Don't worry about her. She knows the meaning of being a soldier. Julia's seen more than her share of death. She'd understand.'

'Killing in the heat of battle is one thing. This is quite another.'

Macro shrugged. 'It's all the same in the end, however you dress it up.'

Cato looked at him searchingly. 'You really think so?'

'I know it.' Macro picked up a strip of cloth and dabbed his face. 'Killing is killing, whether you call it murder or war. It's just that when some high-up bastard has made a policy of dealing out death, it makes it more acceptable. Try telling that to the victims!' Macro laughed drily, then frowned as he saw one of the farrier's assistants slump down on a stool and reach for a canteen. 'Back on your feet, you! No slacking off! We see this through until I say we're done.'

The legionary rose stiffly and took up his hammer and tongs and reached for the next two hoops of glowing iron to fashion another caltrop.

'I had better get back to work, sir.'

'Very well. Make sure you rest tonight. If Caratacus makes another attempt before dawn, I want you fresh for the fight.'

'And you? Will you sleep?'

'I'll try.'

Macro shook his head with a sad smile, and returned to overseeing the production of the small but effective weapons.

Cato was relieved to leave the hot confines of the forge and enjoyed the cool bite of the breeze outside. The clouds still lowered overhead and although it would not be dusk for an hour or so the light already seemed to be fading. He turned towards the stable block being used to hold the prisoners and prepared himself for the tough task that lay ahead.

He had not gone more than a few paces before he saw Quertus emerging between the officers' mess and one of the barrack blocks assigned to the Thracians. The centurion spotted him at once and came striding across the street.

'Sir, a word.'

Cato stopped and replied tersely, 'What is it?'

'I need permission to water the horses, sir. As I mentioned earlier. I'll take them down to the river one squadron at a time, and have pickets posted upstream and downstream in case the Silurians try anything on.'

Cato nodded. It was a sensible enough plan. 'Very well. Make sure that you don't take any risks. At the first sign of trouble you pull your men back into the fort at once. If Caratacus tries to cut us off from the river and we get short of water then we may have to get rid of the mounts sooner than we thought.'

Quertus hesitated before he replied, 'As you command.'

The Thracian turned away and strode back in the direction of the officers' mess. Cato stared after him for a moment and muttered, 'Well, that's something of a change in attitude . . .' Perhaps the man was beginning to accept that he could no longer challenge authority. It was a pity that it had taken the present dire situation before Quertus had conceded, Cato thought. At least that was one problem less to vex his overburdened mind. Or one more thing to be suspicious about, a voice at the back of his mind warned. Cato chewed his lip as he watched the Thracian walk away. Damn the man, he thought.

'Get your people on their feet,' Cato ordered Maridius. The conditions in the stable were as tolerable as they could be for prisoners in a fort under siege. Every man was needed on the wall so half a section, four men, had been given the duty of guarding the Silurians. The latter were manacled with their hands behind their backs and then a chain was passed through the iron loop and they were fastened to the stout timbers that supported the stable's beams. There was no chance of the prisoners breaking loose and turning on the defenders of the fort. There was equally no chance of using the latrine and the air was foetid with the stench of human waste and the sour smell of sweat that became pronounced whenever people were constrained in close quarters for any length of time.

The Catuvellaunian prince sat with a straight back and returned Cato's gaze defiantly. He made no attempt to respond to the order. Cato turned to the legionaries who had entered the stable with him. 'Get 'em up.'

The legionaries strode forward and kicked the prisoners into action with their heavy boots and prods from the butts of their javelins. The sudden burst of violence caused the prisoners to cry out in protest and pain but they rose quickly enough and soon stood in a loose cluster in the middle of the stable, gradually falling silent under Cato's stern gaze, until only the clink of the chains swinging from the posts and the shuffling of feet in the straw could be heard. Cato looked them over, noting the filth caked on their clothes, skin and hair. There were a few older men and women amongst them and a handful of frightened children pressing themselves to their parents. Their wretched appearance instinctively provoked Cato's pity, but he forced himself to quash the sentiment.

He needed ten of them. Ten to execute the next day if Caratacus made any attempt to attack the fort. But who to choose? Cato felt a slight nausea in the pit of his stomach. This power over life and death appalled him. Yet it was his own words that had made the choice necessary. He must face up to the consequences of his promise to the enemy commander. But who should he pick? The old? They had led a full measure of life and had least to lose. The young? They would be easiest to lead to the slaughter and their deaths would have a far greater impact on the enemy than the loss of the old. But why should there be any greater sense of loss over a life hardly lived than the loss of a wealth of experience? Where was the logic in that? And what of the men of military age? In a war it was their deaths that should be felt most keenly, if only because they had most to contribute to the ability of their nation to wage war, yet their deaths would weigh least of all in the hearts and thoughts of their people.

One of the legionaries coughed and Cato realised that he had been staring at the prisoners for some time. He felt angry with himself for deliberating at length over the fates of these people. The simple truth was there was no right answer to the question of selecting who should die. He was a soldier with a job to carry out and there was no depth to the issue beyond that. Cato stepped forward and pointed to the nearest tribesman.

'Take him and nine others out of the stable. Chain them to the gatehouse.'

'Yes, sir,' said the optio in charge of the guard party.

'And have Maridius locked in the strongroom below head-quarters. Place one of your men outside. I want him watched. He's too precious to allow anything to happen to him. If he tries to take his life, your man will be answerable for the consequences. Is that understood, Optio?'

'Yes, sir.'

Cato took one last look at the prisoners. 'Carry on.' He turned and left. That was all it took to determine the fates of ten people, he reflected, an arbitrary decision and a single order. It should have felt like a liberation from the burden of responsibility, but it didn't. The decision weighed on his heart like a great rock, grinding his soul to dust.

The light was fading when Cato left the prisoners and made one last circuit of the fort to ensure that his men were ready to face whatever the enemy might throw at them during the second night. As he made his way along the wall that overlooked the river he saw some of the Thracians below, leading strings of horses down the last stretch of the path to the river. More men, dismounted, were spread out along the slopes, keeping watching for the approach of the enemy. The unmistakable figure of Quertus was already in the shallows, watering his beast. Looking across to the far bank, Cato could see that the tribesmen were powerless to intervene. That would change soon enough, he mused. Caratacus was sure to post slingers along the bank to harry any further attempt by the defenders to lead their mounts to drink at the river.

When he completed his tour of the wall, Cato climbed into the gatehouse tower once again to check on the activity of the enemy before he returned to his quarters for a quick meal. Then once he had decided on the night's password he would rest for a few hours. He had decided to entrust the second watch of the night to Macro, who could be depended upon to raise the alarm in good time if Caratacus decided to make another night attack. The climb up the ladder seemed exhausting and Cato realised he had had no sleep for nearly two days. Now that he thought of it, nothing seemed more welcoming than the prospect of his simple cot in the modest living quarters of the garrison commander.

The rain had stopped and down in the valley the evening gloom was pricked by the red glow of campfires. Cato could see a party hard at work trimming several tree trunks at the edge of the parade ground. The sight did not unduly unsettle him until his gaze came to rest upon another party of warriors busy bundling slender saplings together and binding them tightly. They were too big for faggots and then he realised that Caratacus had given orders to make fascines to bridge the ditch. The enemy would start dragging them forward as soon as night fell. They would tumble them into the ditch and slowly build up more causeways across the defences to enable them to bring the rams to bear against other sections of the wall. It was clear that the Silurians were determined to carry through their attack. Nothing was going to stop them taking Bruccium, Cato reflected. So much for his new command. It had lasted less than a month.

'What the fuck am I thinking?' Cato suddenly demanded of himself with a fierce whisper. He had no right to be defeatist, not while the lives of hundreds of men depended on his leadership. It was the most woeful and shaming self-indulgence and he felt disgust and loathing for himself. Not for the first time, Cato felt as if he was just playing the part of being a prefect and the real fear was that he would be found out. Other men, the real professional soldiers, would see through his façade. Worst of all was the prospect of Macro at last recognising him for what he was. To lose Macro's respect would break his heart. It had been an odd friendship from the outset, Cato reflected. At first Macro had despaired of his efforts to learn the soldier's trade, but in time he had shown enough courage and ingenuity to win the veteran over. It was Macro's seal of approval that had given Cato the heart to fight on, up through the ranks, to surpass even his mentor. Macro had been more of a father to him than his own father, more than a brother. That was the peculiar bond of soldiers, he realised. A bond more powerful than family ties, not love perhaps, but something even more essential, and more demanding.

Cato let out an exasperated sigh. He was doing it again! The endless round of self-investigation that served no purpose. His mind was wandering because he was tired, he concluded. Rest was what he needed. Very badly.

Turning away from the enemy camp, Cato left the gatehouse and trudged back to his quarters where Decimus brought him what was left of the bread, stale and hard, and a wedge of the local goat's cheese. It was a poor meal and Cato had little appetite but he made himself eat, knowing that he needed to sustain himself through the coming trials of the siege. The evening briefing of his officers was perfunctory as each knew his duties and had little to report. Cato dismissed them swiftly and retired to his quarters, removed his sword belt and cuirass but left his boots on in case he was roused by an emergency, and slumped down on his bed. He reached across to extinguish the wick on the small oil lamp that provided the room with a dim light and lay back on the straw-filled bolster. He stared up towards the barely discernible rafters and wood shingle tiles. Once again he mentally went over the defences of the fort but before he had got very far he had fallen into a deep and dreamless sleep and for once began to snore as loudly as his friend Macro.

The blare of the horn took a moment to wake Cato, and there was an instant of foggy incomprehension as he stirred. Then, with a stab of panic, he bolted upright and was instantly alert. Swinging his boots over the side of the cot he snatched up his sword belt and ran for the door. As he went through the small courtyard he saw the clerks emerging from their quarters, faces bleary by the light of the sentry's brazier. There was already a hint of the coming dawn in the distant sky and Cato felt a surge of anger. Why hadn't Decimus come to wake him over an hour earlier, as ordered? Cato looked for Decimus, meaning to order him to fetch his helmet and armour and come to find him, but there was no sign of his servant and no time to look for him. Outside in the street the first men were already spilling from their barracks, kit in hand as they raced to take up their positions on the wall. There was no sound of fighting, no war cries from outside the fort, just the hurried tramping of boots and shouted orders from the officers of the garrison's two cohorts.

Cato stopped, not sure in which direction to head. His instinct told him to run to the wall overlooking the enemy camp, but the horn was sounding from the rear wall. It seemed that Caratacus was trying a different approach, and Cato ran down the street leading to the rear gatehouse. It was a common feature of Roman camps to build four gates, regardless of their functionality. Bruccium was no different, even though three of the gates opened on to steep slopes. He heard shouts ahead, and then the ringing clatter and scrape of weapons.

'To the rear gate!' Cato shouted as he ran. 'To the rear!'

The cry was taken up and boots pounded through the darkness behind him and to the side as men raced between the barrack blocks towards the rear gate. Cato could see the gatehouse looming at the end of the street, the top of the tower illuminated by the glow of a small brazier. Below it dark shapes swirled about, and Cato felt an icy dread as he realised the enemy must have broken in. How was that possible? This was Macro's watch. He would not have let such a thing happen.

Then he heard his friend shouting above the fray. 'Hold the bastards back!'

Cato tore his sword from the scabbard and slung the latter aside as he ran hard towards the fight. Bursting out from between the last pair of barracks he glimpsed two or three men holding horses to one side and a score of others, Thracians, around the inner gate engaged with a handful of men defending the passage. Then he saw that the smaller group were carrying legionary shields and wearing Roman helmets. One even had the crest of a centurion. So that was it. Caratacus had used some captured kit to trick his way into the fort.

Macro called out again. 'Don't let 'em get out, lads!'

Out? Cato abruptly scrambled to a halt. What was this? What was happening? More men were emerging all around the gatehouse, some bearing torches they had hastily snatched up from the watch fires that burned through the night. By their light the scene became clear. Quertus and a band of his men were trying to cut their way through the section of legionaries manning the gatehouse, and the duty officer, Macro. As more men arrived on the scene, they hesitated as they saw the skirmish, not sure what to do, which side to take in the unequal fight. The Thracian commander looked up, his expression wild and fearful.

'Kill them!' he shouted to his followers. 'Now, or we're dead men!'

Cato strode forward, sword held ready. 'Quertus!' he bellowed. 'Throw down your weapons, you and your men. Do it now!'

The Thracians at the gate backed away from the legionaries uncertainly, turning towards the approaching prefect. Around them, in a growing ring, stood the legionaries and auxiliaries roused from their sleep by the alarm. Cato grasped what must have happened and he stopped a safe distance from Quertus.

'You're trying to desert . . . Centurion Petillius!'

'Sir?' the officer responded from the gathering crowd.

'Get your men over to the gate at once!'

'Yes, sir! Legionaries! On me!'

Men surged forward and took position between the Thracians and the gate. There was enough light now for Cato to see the horse holders clearly and he gave a start.

'Decimus? What in the name of the gods are you doing?'

His servant shrank before his superior's gaze, and then released the reins of the horses he was tending and edged forward, glancing from Cato to Quertus and back again. Then he hurried across to join the ranks on either side of the Thracian officer. The other handlers followed his cue and ran across to join their leader. In amongst them he saw Maridius, arms bound to his side. Cato glared at them all, still unwilling to believe the evidence of the treachery before his eyes. Then he turned to the gate. 'Macro!'

There was no reply. Cato edged round and joined Petillius and his men. 'Macro! Speak up, man!'

'He's here, sir!' a legionary replied and Cato thrust his way through to the foot of the gatehouse. In the gloom he saw a legionary spreadeagled on the ground, lying still. Another was sitting with his back to the gate, nursing an injured arm, one hand clamped over the wound to stem the blood. One of the men was kneeling beside a figure lying on his side. Cato felt his heart leap as he crouched down. Macro's eyes were flickering and he groaned feebly, but there was no sign of blood on his body.

'He took a blow to the head,' said one of the sentries. 'Saw it happen just after you arrived, sir.'

Cato felt relief, then the rage flowed back and he stood and turned to Quertus, his sword thrust out towards the Thracian. 'Arrest that man! Arrest all of them!'

'Sir?' Centurion Petillius looked confused.

'Cowards!' Cato spat. 'Cowards and deserters! Do as I order. Arrest them!'

Petillius took a step towards them. 'Drop your weapons!'

Quertus laughed harshly. 'I don't think so. If you take on me then you take on all my men. Isn't that right, boys? We've had enough of this Roman puppy! He has not earned the right to command you. This fort is mine. This fort belongs to Thracians!' He punched his sword into the air and the men around him cheered uncertainly, then again with more heart. Cato noticed that some of those who stood in the ring of men around the gatehouse joined in, and began to cross the open ground to join their commander. A chill of fear trickled down his spine at the growing danger of the situation. He stepped forward and addressed the ring of men.

'Hear me! Hear me!'

The cries of the other men died away and Cato thrust his finger at Quertus. 'This man, this coward, was about to abandon the fort and leave us to our fate!'

'Liar!' Quertus shot back. 'I was sending my men to raise the alarm since this Roman refused to give the order! He would have us die here! I would save us.'

Cato pointed at Maridius. 'Then what is the enemy prince doing here? You were going to use him as a hostage to get through the enemy lines. Is that not so?'

Quertus's eyes narrowed craftily. 'Of course. What chance would my men have without him? Better to put him to some good use than let him rot in chains.'

'And you were going to remain here, I suppose,' Cato asked cynically. 'After you sent these men on their way?'

'Of course. My place is here, beside my comrades. Leading them into battle.'

Cato's lip curled. 'You liar! You coward. The proof of your treachery is there by the gate. The men you attacked in order to escape from the fort. You would have killed them all and ridden off leaving the gate open to the enemy. No doubt you hoped that we'd be wiped out, and you could return to Glevum and claim to have cut your way free, with a valuable prisoner to hand over to the legate. I can see it all.'

'You can see nothing!' Quertus shouted back. He swept his arms out as if to embrace his men. 'My brothers, now is the time to take our fort back from this arrogant fool! It is he who should be arrested! He is the coward, the prefect without the heart to kill his enemy right down to the last hunting dog. He is not worthy of your loyalty. I have proved myself to you time and again. Follow me, my brothers! Follow me! And put this dog in chains with the Silurian scum!'

Quertus thrust his sword up with a deep roar which was echoed by his most ardent followers in the gathering crowd. Cato's heart pounded in his chest. He felt his authority slipping from his grasp with every passing moment. He must act while there was still a chance to sway the Thracian auxiliaries. He could count on the loyalty of the legionaries, but they were outnumbered. If it came to a fight, they would lose. There was only one thing he could do to save the situation. He must grasp the opportunity that Quertus had unwittingly offered him.

Drawing himself up, Cato stepped forward, out into the open between the legionaries and Quertus and his band, where all could clearly see him. He raised his arms and slowly the noise began to die down.

'Centurion Quertus accuses me of being a coward. You all heard him. I will not take such an insult from any man! You are all brave soldiers. Only a brave officer deserves your loyalty. So let us put it to the test. Let us see who is fit to command the Blood Crows!' He pointed his sword directly at Quertus. 'I challenge him to fight me for the right to command. If he refuses then it proves he is the coward I say he is!'

There was a stunned silence before Quertus stepped forward and confronted Cato with a cold smile. 'You would fight me?' He lowered his voice so that only Cato might hear his next words. 'You're a damned fool, Prefect Cato . . . and now you'll die because of it.'

Quertus shrugged off his fur coat and unfastened the straps at the side of his breastplate and let it drop to the ground so that he stood in his tunic, like Cato. Except that he was nearly a head taller and broad in proportion. He let the blade of his sword rest against his shoulder. 'Do you want to settle this with the spatha or the gladius?'

Cato thought swiftly. The cavalry sword had greater reach and weight, but he had trained to use the legionary weapon and had wielded one through every campaign he had fought in. 'I was a legionary before I was ever a prefect. And I'll fight as a legionary should.'

Quertus gave a wolfish grin. 'As you wish. Then let us begin. Clear the ground there!' he bellowed and the Thracians stepped back to create an open space twenty paces across, lit by the wavering glow of the torches held by several of their number. Above them a pallid hue was already bleeding across the sky, and Cato could see that the clouds were thinner than in the previous days, and there was even a patch that looked as if it might break to reveal the heavens. He felt a strange calmness come over him now that he was committed. Then he turned his attention to the Thracian and lowered himself into a crouch and held his sword ready.

'There can only be one commander at Bruccium,' he said calmly. 'There can be no quarter asked or given. This is a fight to the death.'

Quertus nodded. 'To the death.'

Cato swallowed, took a last deep breath and called out, 'Then begin!'

# CHAPTER THIRTY

The last word was still on Cato's breath when Quertus charged at him, mouth agape as he let out a deafening, savage roar. If it was supposed to terrify Cato, the tactic failed. He did not flinch as he held his sword out with a solid grip and a firm arm. The Thracian swung his longer blade in a sweeping diagonal arc towards Cato's neck and Cato thrust his weapon to the side to deflect the blow. Metal struck metal with a shrill ring and a bright spark that instantly died as the tip of Quertus's sword buried itself harmlessly in the ground. Cato whipped his blade back across his opponent's chest in an effort to draw first blood and he was rewarded with a ripping sound as the point tore open the folds of the centurion's tunic just below the neck hem. Quertus scrambled back and raised his sword to block any further blows.

Cato knew that he must keep close to his opponent if he was to use his weapon to best effect and pressed forward, thrusting and making small, vicious cuts that forced the other man to parry and block desperately as the onslaught drove him back towards the ring of spectators. The latter hurried out of the way, parting to reveal the grassy bank of the rampart to one side of the gatehouse. Then, swiftly summoning up his powerful strength, Quertus smashed Cato's sword aside and swung wildly at his head. Now it was Cato's turn to retreat and he stepped back easily, poised on the balls of his feet so that he could use his leg muscles to spring in whichever direction he needed. A gap opened up between the two fighters, and Cato edged back yet further to give himself space to consider his next move. Both men were breathing quickly, and Cato felt blood pounding in his skull, as if he had been running for some distance. His limbs felt light and eager, as if they had a life of their own, and there was a burst of exhilaration in his heart as he kept his eyes fixed on the Thracian.

Quertus gritted his teeth and the corners of his mouth lifted in a wry expression of amusement.

'Quite the warrior, aren't you, Prefect? You have more backbone than I thought,' the Thracian growled. 'But it won't save you.'

Cato leaped forward a step and feinted, partly to test his opponent's reflexes, and partly to shut him up. Quertus retreated nimbly and held his sword out, the point aimed at Cato's face, taking advantage of his greater reach to stop Cato in his tracks.

'Not so fast!'

Cato returned to a safe distance and weighed up his enemy. The man was quick as well as strong, a dangerous combination indeed. Yet there was also a swaggering arrogance that might yet play into Cato's hands – if he lived long enough to exploit it. At the same time he was aware of the anxious excitement in the faces of the men watching the duel. At first there had been silence but now a voice called out, 'Finish the Roman brat!'

A handful of other Thracians called out their support for their leader and clenched their hands into fists and shook them at Cato. At once the smaller number of legionaries responded with cries of support for Cato. More joined in and the air was thick with shouts. Cato was reminded of the atmosphere of a gladiator spectacle and was thankful that he had never had to endure the fear and shame of those forced to fight for the entertainment of the mob.

Keeping a wary eye on his opponent, Quertus steadily paced his way round the ring of spectators until he had his supporters at his back and Cato was forced to gaze into their hostile expressions. The encouragement from the legionaries struggled to make itself heard over the din of the Thracians but one voice rang out.

'Get stuck in, sir! Kill that Thracian dog!'

'Quiet, you fool!' another voice cut in behind Cato's back. 'You want that Thracian dog to come looking for you afterwards?'

Cato smiled bitterly to himself. So, even the legionaries, much as they feared and disliked Quertus, were cautious about their commander's chances of winning the fight. Well, he would show them, Cato resolved. He would prove them wrong, and prove that he had the right to command the garrison by force of arms as well as by the Emperor's authority.

Quertus stood, calm and relaxed, as if in contempt for his foe, and then he turned his back on Cato and faced his men, arms raised to acknowledge their acclaim. The sound of their cheering rose in response and Quertus punched both fists into the air repeatedly.

Cato gritted his teeth and moved towards the man's back, momentarily visualising the point of his sword plunging in, cutting through his spine and angling into his black heart. The auxiliaries shouted a warning to their officer and Quertus spun round and lowered himself into a crouch. He forced a laugh for the benefit of his men and called out in a loud voice, 'Attack me while my back's turned, would you? And you call me a coward!'

As his men responded excitedly to his taunt, Quertus paced forward confidently, swinging his blade in a broad ellipse. Cato did not stop, did not hesitate, but moved directly into contact, viciously striking the spatha aside and lunging for the other man's chest. Quertus parried the blow firmly and stepped forward, punching the guard into Cato's chest and knocking him back. Cato rode the blow to lessen its impact but even so the air was driven from his lungs and pain burned across his ribs. At the same time he was forced to throw his sword up to block a rushed chop to his head as Quertus tried to take advantage of the winding blow he had struck. The blade clattered to the side, but a moment later there was a searing pain in Cato's thigh, just above the knee, as the point of the Thracian's sword tore a shallow wound across his flesh.

The two men parted and Quertus let out a triumphant cry as he saw the crimson streak across the prefect's knee. His supporters cheered while the legionaries fell silent, staring anxiously at their commander, trying to determine the seriousness of his injury. Cato risked a quick glance down and saw the blood running down his shin and over the top of his leather boots. He lowered and raised himself cautiously but felt no increase in the pain and no telltale twinge that would indicate serious damage to his muscles. Even so, he was bleeding, and it would sap his strength the longer the fight lasted. Gritting his teeth, he stepped forward again and feigned a slight stumble, letting out a genuine groan.

Quertus laughed drily. 'I'm disappointed, Prefect Cato. I'd have hoped for more of a contest. But look at you. Thin and weak and bleeding like a stuck pig. I could let you bleed out but I want a good kill. Something that will show all the men that I am fit to be their commander.'

Cato leaned over his injured leg and looked up from under his dark fringe, breathing deeply. He licked his lips and rasped, 'You're not fit to be in the Roman army, let alone command one of its forts.'

'We'll see about that.' Quertus lowered himself slightly and approached cautiously. Cato let him come and raised his sword, the point wavering as he straightened his back and prepared to fight for his life once again. As Quertus raised his sword to strike and lifted his right foot to swing forward, Cato launched himself forward with a throat-tearing roar. There was just enough time for the Thracian's eyes to widen in surprise before the point of Cato's sword flashed up, forward and into the other man's left shoulder. The blade tore through cloth, skin and muscle before jarring against a bone. Quertus grunted explosively under the impetus of the blow and staggered. Cato pressed on, throwing his weight behind the sword, twisting the handle as he drove forward.

But Quertus's fearsome reputation on the battlefield was well-earned and he recovered swiftly, tearing himself free of the blade then twisting away from Cato so that the prefect's momentum carried him a few paces past before he scrabbled to a halt and turned to face Quertus. At once Cato threw himself forward and there was a desperate exchange of blows. The men began to cheer again, each side urging their officer on, and now the legionaries were shouting almost as loudly as the auxiliaries. With a last ringing clatter of blades, both men retreated from each other and crouched, chests heaving as they exchanged hostile glares.

'You're a crafty bastard . . .' Quertus growled. 'I'll give you . . . that.'

Cato kept his silence and began to circle slowly. The wound in his opponent's shoulder was deep but it was hard to make out the blood seeping into the folds of Quertus's black tunic, save for the glistening where the cloth had become saturated. Cato nodded with

297

satisfaction. While it was not a mortal wound, it was bleeding badly and would get worse if the Thracian exerted himself.

'What the fuck is this?' a groggy voice demanded.

Out of the corner of his eye Cato was aware of Macro rising unsteadily to his feet, a hand clutched to his head. He stared at the two officers and quickly sized up the situation. 'Gut him, lad!' he bellowed. 'Kill the bastard!'

With an angry growl Quertus came on again, slashing left and right with his longer blade, driving Cato back as he parried each blow, feeling the force of the blows jar his sword arm with a tingling pain that threatened to loosen his grasp of the handle.

Then it happened.

The full, savage weight of the Thracian's cavalry sword smashed against the hilt of Cato's gladius. His fingers spasmed and he felt the blade slip from his grasp. At once Quertus let out a triumphant roar and moved in for the kill. Cato leaped to the side and heard the swish of the blade as the sword swept down behind him and struck the ground with a dull metallic note. He sidestepped quickly as his opponent drew his sword back and came on with the point at waist height, ready to strike a final, killing blow.

'You can't run from me,' Quertus sneered. 'Stand and take your death like a man, not like a cowardly Roman!'

Cato kept his arms wide, his legs braced, ready to spring in any direction the moment he detected his foe was about to strike. At the same time he knew he was being manoeuvred back against the gatehouse. Around him the air was thick with the cries of the Thracian's supporters, baying raucously for his blood. The calmness that had filled his mind had shattered. Now his senses vied with his racing mind in a desperate jumble of glimpses of the faces in front of him, the pureness of the patch of blue sky in the clouds above, the vision of Julia as he smiled down at her the morning after their marriage, Macro laughing heartily as he cast a winning throw of dice, and the sweet smell of the air after a summer shower . . . A man snatching at the myriad treasures of his life for that last taste of their delight before he was claimed by oblivion.

Something glittered briefly before it fell to the sand close by Cato's feet. He glanced down and saw a cavalry sword by his boots and instinctively snatched the weapon up, his senses registering the difference in weight and balance to the short sword of the legions. His arm muscles tensed under the burden and he saw Quertus's face harden as the triumphant victory that had been so certain only moments before began to slip from his grasp.

'No more fucking about,' the Thracian snarled as he hefted his weapon. 'Now you die, Roman scum.'

His lips drew back to reveal his clenched teeth as he charged straight at Cato, sword arm outstretched and the point flying towards the prefect's throat. Cato fell back. His heel struck the timbers of the gate and pain flared up his calf. There was no retreat, no chance of dodging to the side. He knew he could do nothing now but stand his ground. He raised the spatha, as if to try and parry the blade cutting through the air towards him with the full weight of the Thracian behind it. Cato swallowed hard, and felt the muscles of his throat tighten in fear, and then dived for the ground directly at the feet of his opponent. The sword flashed overhead and splintered the gate as the blow struck. A heavy boot kicked Cato in the side of his head, jarring his neck. Then he hit the ground and rolled on to his shoulder and the handle of the spatha lurched in his grip as the point bit deeply into Quertus's flesh. Cato held the weapon tightly as the sword was wrenched down in his hand, forcing his wrist to twist the blade. Boots scuffed the ground and there was a deep groan from the Thracian and then stillness.

Cato's head was ringing, yet he was aware that the shouting had stopped. He was dazed by the blow to his skull and it was a moment before he saw Quertus's features no more than a pace away. His eyes were wild and staring and his jaw sagged, gasping for breath. Then nausea filled Cato's guts as his head spun, forcing him to clench his eyes shut briefly.

'He's done for,' a voice muttered thickly, and Cato tried to nod, thinking to accept his fate. He felt hands reach under his arms and draw him up, away from the ground. His head began to clear and the nausea passed so he risked opening his eyes. A familiar face was anxiously looking at him.

'Cato . . . sir?'

He blinked and forced himself to reply, slowly and clearly. 'Macro. You all right?'

'Am I all right?' Macro let out a deep laugh and tapped the side of his head. 'Ain't been a weapon yet made that'll get through this skull!'

Cato nodded. 'I dare say. What . . . Quertus?'

'Like I said. Done for.' Macro nodded towards the ground and Cato looked down and saw the Thracian lying on his side, the cavalry sword buried almost to the hilt in his groin and angled up into his vital organs. He rocked from side to side as a pool of blood expanded beneath him, a low keening note in his voice as he gasped for breath.

Cato's mind quickly cleared. 'Good.'

He looked up at the faces of the men surrounding the rear gatehouse of the fort. Some of the Thracians seemed stunned. Others were clearly angry, their expressions darkening as the legionaries began to cheer Cato's name.

'Better get that leg seen to, sir,' Macro was saying. He took off his neckcloth and bent down and carefully dressed the wound.

Cato struggled to keep his mind focused. He had done it. He had bested the Thracian. In front of the whole garrison. He had taken a terrible risk, gambled his life, in order to put an end to the struggle for supremacy over the garrison and now he stared at the auxiliaries with cold authority. A figure stepped forward and Cato's eyes flickered towards the man and he recognised Centurion Stellanus.

'Excuse me, sir.'

'What is it?'

Stellanus gestured towards the dying man. 'My sword, sir. I'll take it back now.'

'Your sword?' Cato arched an eyebrow. 'Yes . . . Yes, of course.'

Stellanus nodded and approached. He hesitated as he stood over Quertus, and then rolled the Thracian on to his back and reached down to grasp the sword handle. Bracing a boot on the man's groin, Stellanus worked his sword free. A rush of dark, almost black, blood gushed out after the blade came free with a sucking sound. Quertus's body tensed and he let out a last, rasping gasp, and sagged slowly as the light went out of his eyes and he died. Stellanus wiped the blood from the blade and sheathed his weapon before he stood stiffly in front of Cato.

'At your command, sir.'

Cato nodded, then spoke softly. 'Why?'

'Sir?'

'Why did you throw me your sword?'

Stellanus frowned. 'He called you a cowardly Roman, sir. It ain't true. It ain't true of any Roman officer. In any case, you had the right to die with a sword in your hand.'

'I thank you.'

Stellanus stared back in silence for a moment before he responded flatly, 'I'd have done the same for him, sir.'

'Him?' Macro intervened scornfully. 'That bastard?'

Stellanus nodded. 'Whatever you may think of him, he had a warrior's heart, and deserved a warrior's death.'

He was interrupted by the sound of the horn at the front gate. The alarm was being raised. Every man turned towards the sound, a series of strident notes carrying across the fort. It was Cato who recovered first. 'To your positions! Every man on the wall!'

Macro jerked his thumb towards the group who had supported Quertus. 'What about them? Bloody deserters.'

Cato glanced at the men. 'We'll deal with that later. For now I need every single man. Send 'em back to their units.'

'Even Decimus?'

Cato turned and stared at his servant. The man was trembling under the withering gaze of the two officers. Cato felt a stab of pity for a man, any man, who was in the thrall of fear to such an extent. Pity, and a degree of empathy. But it was the greater fear of being found out that caused Cato to force himself to carry out the deeds that Macro ascribed to courage. So it was with a mixture of pity and guilt that Cato shook his head. 'Send him back to my quarters.'

When he reached the tower above the main gate Cato could see the full length of the valley as the rising sun burnished the rim of the hills to the east. The sky was clearing and the coming day promised to be dry and warm with only the mildest of breezes. Perfect conditions to light the signal fire. The smoke would be clearly seen for ten or twenty miles. Down below, the enemy camp was bristling with activity as men hurriedly formed into war bands and the thickly coated ponies favoured by the mountain tribes were saddled and mounted. Already, the first bands were moving towards the head of the valley in the direction of Gobannium. A small force advanced towards the fort and halted at the foot of the slope. Its purpose was clear enough to Cato: to contain the garrison while the main body dealt with whatever had roused them. It could only be the presence of Roman soldiers nearby. For an instant Cato felt his heart soar at the prospect, and then his fierce joy turned to an icy dread as he realised what that must mean. There might still be time to avert the disaster.

Cato whirled round and rushed across the tower and leaned over the rail into the fort. He thrust his arm towards the optio in charge of the signal beacon, a large iron basket filled with kindling dipped in pitch. To one side lay the dried leaves that would make plenty of smoke when the flames had taken hold. 'Light the signal fire! At once!'

Turning his attention back towards the head of the valley while the optio carried out his orders, Cato cursed whatever gods had seen fit to sweep back the cloud and rain from the sky only on the very morning that the column of reinforcements marching from Glevum were nearing the fort, too close for the signal beacon to warn them off in time. The enemy's intention was clear. Caratacus was preparing to ambush the Roman column. The reinforcements would be surrounded by the native warriors and cut to pieces. The Romans were blissfully ignorant of the danger. As far as they were aware, the enemy commander and his host were far to the north, their attention fixed on the ponderous advance of Governor Ostorius and his army. They would discover the truth soon enough, Cato mused bitterly.

There was only the slimmest of chances to save the column, Cato knew, but he was not going to simply stand by and watch his comrades massacred.

# CHAPTER THIRTY-ONE

'Why not let me go?' Macro asked bluntly. 'You've been wounded, sir. And the men need you here in the fort.'

Cato shook his head as he finished strapping his greaves on. He straightened up and smiled at his friend. 'I was appointed Prefect of the Second Thracian Cohort as well as commander of the garrison. I think it's time I exercised my rank now that Quertus is out of the way.'

They stood beside the side gate opening on to the slope nearest the track that led to the head of the valley. Two squadrons of the cavalry cohort were hurriedly mounting up in the open space between the wall and the barracks and stables of the fort. Sixty riders were all that could be spared for the task that Cato had in mind. Any more would leave Macro with too few men to defend Bruccium. Cato could see the thick column of smoke billowing into the air from the signal fire. It rose steadily enough for a short distance but a light breeze had come with the dawn and the smoke soon dispersed into distant wisps of grey. If the men in the reinforcement column were alert, there was a chance they might see the signal and have the sense to turn back while they still had a remote chance of escape.

Macro looked round at the Thracians and clicked his tongue. 'What do you think you can achieve with sixty men?' He looked anxiously at his friend. 'It's nothing short of suicide.'

'I hope it's something short of that,' Cato replied with a thin smile. 'We are better mounted than the enemy, and we have the element of surprise. They won't be expecting us to ride out to support the reinforcement column.'

'Really? I wonder why?' Macro responded drily.

Cato's smile vanished and he lowered his voice so that only Macro would hear him. 'Would you have me stand by while our comrades are massacred? I have to try and help them cut a way out of the trap. You'd do the same if you were in my position, and you know it.'

Macro could not deny the truth of that but he persisted with his argument. 'Where's the logic of it, Cato? You charge out there and try to rescue our lads and it's fifty to one against that you come through it. You'll just be throwing away your life, and the lives of the Thracian lads. The reinforcement column hasn't got a chance.'

'Not so. You're prepared to offer odds of fifty to one.'

'Only a fool would place a stake on that.'

Cato held out his hand. 'Then call me a fool. I'll put ten sestertii on it.'

Macro grasped his hand and tried to sound light-hearted. 'Done! Easiest ten sestertii I ever made . . .'

There was a brief, awkward silence as they clasped hands and silently said their farewells. Then Cato withdrew his hand and looked over Macro's shoulder. 'The men are ready. We have to get going. Make sure that you have one of your centuries ready to hold the gate open for us if – when – we return with the reinforcements.'

'They'll be ready. I'll lead 'em myself.'

'Good. Then I'll look forward to seeing you shortly.' Cato tested the fit of his helmet, took a calming breath and walked stiffly over to his horse which was being held for him by one of the Thracians. He took the reins and patted Hannibal gently on his broad cheek and muttered up towards his dagger-like ears, 'Behave for me today, and when I give the word, run like the wind.'

The horse snorted and jerked its head fractionally and Cato smiled quickly before he took the reins and vaulted into the saddle, trying not to wince at the sharp pain his leg rewarded him with. Taking a firm grasp of the reins, he took the large oval shield that the handler offered up to him and slipped the strap over his shoulder. Despite the custom for senior officers to carry a sword, Cato had chosen to be armed with a long, heavy spear like the rest of his men and he shifted his grip on the weapon to find its balance point. He settled the butt into the small leather holster hanging from the saddle and wheeled

Hannibal round to face his men. The squadrons were formed up two deep behind their officers, Centurion Stellanus and a Thracian, Decurion Kastos, stern-faced as they regarded their prefect, waiting for the traditional short speech of encouragement before they were led into battle.

Short it would be, Cato thought; there was little time to spare. He would have preferred to dispense with formalities altogether and simply give the order to quit the fort, but he knew that the men would need to be addressed following on so closely from the death of Quertus.

'Blood Crows!' he began. 'Our comrades are in the gravest of danger. Caratacus means to cut them down and take their heads as trophies to offer to his Druid allies. That is no fit fate for any soldier. The enemy means to humiliate them, before our eyes, and therefore humiliate us for being powerless to intervene. But we shall not be humbled, and nor shall our comrades. That is all that matters to us this day. Our task is simple. We shall ride to their rescue and clear a path through the enemy so that our comrades can gain the fort . . . What has gone before cannot be changed. We have in our grasp the chance to win undying glory for the Blood Crows. Those who live to remember this day will never forget the honour they have shared with their brothers, nor the honour in which they will be held by the rest of the army.' He paused, vaguely frustrated by his failure to deliver the kind of stirring speech he had read of in the history books of his youth. But there was no time for that kind of carefully rehearsed rhetoric. He grasped his spear and raised it aloft.

'For the glory of Rome! For the honour of the Blood Crows!'

Centurion Stellanus took his cue and thrust his spear overhead. 'For the honour of the Blood Crows!'

The rest of the men took up the cheer and their horses stamped and scraped their hoofs eagerly, caught up in the excitement of their riders. Cato turned to Macro and nodded.

'Open the gates!' Macro bellowed and the two legionaries waiting beside the locking bar instantly heaved it out of the sturdy iron brackets and set it down to one side before drawing the gates apart.

Cato steered his mount round and urged Hannibal towards the arch under the gatehouse with the cry, 'Advance!'

Stellanus gave the order to his men and they followed their prefect, walking their horses forward two abreast. As Cato passed Macro, they exchanged a brief bow of heads. The other squadron followed, passing through the gate, across the bridge over the narrow ditch and on to the track that led diagonally down the slope at the side of the fort. Cato knew that they would not be seen until they rounded the corner of the small hill upon which the fort stood and was content to let the column walk that far before increasing the pace. He felt his heartbeat quicken and had to force himself not to look back towards the gatehouse and the safety of the fort. In the distance, a mile away, he could see the rear of the enemy force heading to intercept the reinforcement column. As he rode at a steady pace, determined to give the impression of being calm and in control, Cato's mind was filled with anxiety over the danger that lay before him.

With luck, the officer leading the column would have a few men screening the main body and the moment they became aware of the enemy, the reinforcements would close up and trust to their heavy shields and iron discipline to carve their way through to the fort. On the other hand, Cato reflected, the officer might well be one of the freshly minted tribunes who had reached the frontier with his confidence in Roman supremacy and contempt for the barbarian undented. The kind of man who blundered forward until tripped up by experience. Some struggled back on to their feet, others paid the price of their arrogance in full.

The rough track leading down across the slope began to level out and now Cato could see the edge of the parade ground and the enemy camp beyond. They would be spotted at any moment, if they had not already been. He tapped his heels to get his horse's attention. 'On, Hannibal. On!'

The beast stirred and increased his pace to a gentle trot. Behind, Stellanus and then Kastos repeated the order and a faint rumble took the place of the gentle clop and scrape of walking horses. Cato had scrutinised the ground in the valley before leaving the fort and had chosen to head for a bare ledge overlooking the head of the pass. The ground up to it offered little cover and seemed open enough to be usable by cavalry. He gently pulled on the reins to steer Hannibal in its direction and then looked towards the enemy. The horsemen had been seen by those still in the camp who were gesticulating and pointing at the two squadrons setting out from the fort. A moment later the first of the horns sounded the alarm to alert their comrades further up the valley. It took only a moment for the rearmost of the war bands, just over half a mile ahead, to stop and turn about. For a moment they hesitated and then Cato watched them fan out into a line facing his men. Most of the enemy carried shields and spears, but some carried more basic weapons and had no armour.

Cato led the Thracians towards the enemy line at a steady trot. More had stopped to turn and look back, uncertain how to react to the unexpected response from the garrison at Bruccium. Cato felt a moment's satisfaction at the sight. Any seeds of confusion that he could sow would serve to hinder the enemy's attack on the reinforcement column. Caratacus's warriors would arrive piecemeal and there would be a chance for the reinforcements to deploy for battle rather than be caught strung out along the line of march. With luck, they might already have seen the smoke from the signal fire and paid heed to the warning.

Three more of the war bands had turned back to confront the Thracians and were hurrying across the open ground to take up position on the flanks of the line. The sight did not unsettle Cato as he had no intention of engaging with them. It would be suicide for such a small force of cavalry, well mounted and armed as they were, to charge headlong into an overwhelming mass of infantry. That was not Cato's plan. The real danger was presented by the enemy horsemen. They heavily outnumbered the two squadrons and, more worryingly, would be able to outpace them. If they managed to attack and pin down the Thracians long enough for the infantry to intervene then it would all be over very swiftly and the destruction of the two squadrons would simply be the first Roman casualties of the day.

The enemy line was no more than a quarter of a mile distant and Cato quickly estimated their number at five hundred. He lifted his spear and pointed to the right of the line, towards the ledge on the side of the mountain overlooking the pass. 'Wheel right!'

He struck out in the new direction and his men turned their

mounts to follow him. The enemy, fearing an attempt to outflank their line, were thrown into confusion before their leaders pushed and cajoled them into forming a crude ellipse, bristling with spears and other weapons. The Roman cavalrymen continued along their line of advance and passed close enough to the Silurian warriors to clearly hear their war cries and insults. A number of the Thracians returned the shouts in kind until Centurion Stellanus rounded on them furiously.

'Keep your bloody mouths shut or I'll have you on a charge the moment we get back to the fort!'

They trotted on and reached the rising ground below the ledge. To their left was the track leading up the valley, passing through a thin belt of fir trees before it climbed to the saddle between the two mountains. Cato could see parties of enemy warriors picking their way up either side of the track to take up position to attack the reinforcement column. Ahead of them rode Caratacus's cavalry. At their head was a small group of brightly cloaked riders, clustered about the long rippling standard of their commander. The enemy horsemen were far enough away to present no immediate danger to the Thracians, Cato calculated. Glancing back he saw that the warriors they had passed shortly before were once again spreading out, marching across the route the Thracians had taken from the fort in order to cut off their line of retreat. They were committed now, Cato thought sombrely.

Hannibal's flanks were heaving with the effort of climbing the slope but Cato urged him on, keeping up the pace, until at length they reached the ledge and the ground levelled out into a narrow strip of grass tussocks and patches of peat. He turned and looked down into the valley. The enemy infantry who were intent on cutting the Romans off from the fort were steadily picking their way up the slope towards them. Beyond the fir trees Cato could see over the saddle and his heartbeat quickened as he caught sight of the reinforcement column – a slender ribbon of scarlet shimmering with reflections from highly polished helmets. A small force of cavalry marched at the rear, protecting the carts and waggons of the baggage train. Seven or eight hundred men in all, Cato estimated with a sinking heart. He had anticipated that Legate Quintatus would send at least twice as many legionaries or auxiliaries to escort the reinforcements to the fort before turning back to Glevum. As it was, the slender hope that he had entertained that they would be strong enough to cut their way through to Bruccium was dashed.

Cato calculated that the reinforcements had been marching for nearly two hours and had covered perhaps five miles from their camp of the previous night. It was as well that they had not attempted to march on into the darkness to reach Bruccium. Otherwise they would have blundered into Caratacus's army and been wiped out within earshot of the fort. As yet they seemed not to have seen the smoke rising from the fort, or at least they had not reacted to it. Nor had they seen the war bands hidden in the folds of the ground at the edge of the broad saddle, nor those waiting for them across the track leading down into the valley. They were marching blindly into the trap that Caratacus was laying for them.

Stellanus edged his horse forwards alongside the prefect and glanced briefly at the scene spread out before them before turning to Cato.

'What are your orders, sir?'

'We have to warn them of the danger.' Cato twisted in the saddle. 'Trumpets! Sound the attack! As loudly as you can!'

The men carrying the long hooked cavalry horns drew breath and raised their instruments to their lips. An instant later the short sequence of notes blasted out across the valley, echoing off the rocky crags above the Thracians. Cato pointed along the ledge.

'We'll ride out along there and skirt round the enemy ambush before we make for the column. Have the horns keep sounding as we advance.'

'Yes, sir!' Stellanus saluted.

Cato raised his spear and tilted it forward. 'Second Thracian! Follow me!'

The mounts rumbled into a gentle trot along the ledge and then followed the line of the slope. As they made their way towards the pass, Cato was relieved to see that the column had halted. Now he could make out a century of legionaries at the front; the rest of the soldiers carried the oval shields of auxiliaries. There was no sign of any deployment. He silently cursed their commander for not being more cautious and urged Hannibal on. A few hundred paces ahead and further down the slope he could see the first of Caratacus's men gathering themselves for the assault. They, too, had been alerted by the trumpet signals and Cato could see the pale dots of faces looking up the slope. His mind was working through the disposition of the enemy forces and the ground over which the coming battle would be fought. It was already clear that there would be little chance of breaking through to the fort. All that was left was the possibility of a fighting retreat towards Gobannium. If they reached the outpost and Caratacus chose to lay siege to that as well then his force would be stretched to cover both Roman fortifications. To that extent Macro and the rest of the garrison would have a better chance of survival, Cato reflected.

His thoughts were interrupted by the blare of Celtic horns from the group of riders clustered around Caratacus. The note was quickly taken up by the other war bands and then the sound of their wild cheers crashed up the slope towards Cato and his men like the roar of a wave. Warriors erupted from the ground and surged towards the front and flanks of the Roman column. Cato felt his guts tighten with a terrible anxiety as he saw that none of the men was moving.

'What the fuck are they waiting for?' Stellanus demanded.

Then, as if in answer to his words, the soldiers in the column began to form up around the baggage train and the escort's cavalry squadron trotted out to one side to form a line. The men were well drilled, Cato knew, but it was clear that there was little chance of them completing their manoeuvre before the warriors charged in amongst them.

'Shit,' he muttered to himself, then turned in his saddle to issue an order. His hand had been forced. There was only one thing to do now. 'Halt! Deploy in line and make ready to charge!'

# CHAPTER THIRTY-TWO

'Charge?' Centurion Stellanus repeated, wheeling his horse round to face his superior. 'Sir, we cannot charge down the slope. It's too steep. Half our men would fall before we reached the pass.'

'I know that, damn you,' Cato snapped. 'I'll thank you not to question my orders, Centurion. Now have the men form up. And watch the pace I set. I will not have any man race ahead, nor lag behind. We will reach the battlefield as one. It's our best chance of survival. Is that clear?'

Stellanus gritted his teeth and nodded, before turning to repeat the order. 'Form line!'

The two squadrons wheeled to the left and spread out along the slope. Cato looked down and saw that there were perhaps three hundred paces of steep ground to negotiate before it was sufficiently level to give the order for the charge. There would be no mad scramble across the open ground as with the cavalry charges of less disciplined armies. Roman cavalry were strictly drilled and the charge was a carefully graduated build-up in speed. They would only unleash their mounts and let them gallop the last fifty paces to contact with the enemy. Even so, the advance down the slope would need to be carefully handled to keep the formation together.

Glancing to both sides, Cato saw that the two squadrons were ready, the men clutching their spears and holding their shields close. The tails of their mounts flicked and some of the horses tossed their heads, sensing the tension of the riders. Cato held his spear aloft. 'Hold the line. When the order is given to charge, don't stop until you reach the column . . . Blood Crows, forward!'

Hannibal started down the slope at a walk. As they descended,

Cato looked ahead to see that the swiftest of the enemy had reached the reinforcements while they were still deploying into a box around the baggage train. The first Silurians were easily dealt with, but as more and more charged home, the legionaries at the front of the column were not able to complete their change of formation and a disordered battle line rapidly fringed the carts and wagons huddled in the middle. The cavalry squadron, a short distance away, spurred forward into the fight and was engulfed by the horde of Silurian warriors closing round the Roman column.

At the foot of the slope the infantry who had been shadowing the Thracians stopped and turned to face their opponents. In amongst them Cato could see some of the dark cloaks of the Druids who shouted encouragement to the warriors and hurled curses and spells at the oncoming horsemen. As the slope began to ease, Cato called over his shoulder, 'Form wedge on me!'

The squadron commanders relayed the command and the troopers adjusted their pace so that the line quickly transformed into an arrowhead, with ten men riding at the rear, ready to fill any gaps as their comrades fell. They would have to break through the enemy line in order to make for the embattled column and Cato gradually changed the direction and made for the warrior's right flank. The enemy were now no more than a hundred paces away and the more undisciplined of them were loosing arrows in their direction. The shafts fell well short and Cato tapped his spurs and gave the order, 'At the canter!'

Hannibal lurched beneath him and surged forward at an easy run. The ground rumbled and the air filled with the chink of bits, the slap and thud of shields and the creak of leather. The gap between the two sides narrowed swiftly and Cato tightened his grip on the handle of his shield and raised his spear over his head, ready to strike down at the enemy. Ahead he could see their faces and read their expressions: fear, excitement and grim determination. He snatched a breath and cried out as loud as he could to be heard above the din, 'Blood Crows . . . Charge!'

The Thracians took up the cry as they spurred their mounts forward and braced themselves in their saddles. The sharp notes of the trumpets cut through the cacophony of hoofs and bellowed war cries. Cato hunched forward, the left of his body covered by the shield, the muscles of his right arm bunched and ready to strike at the first Silurian who stood before him. The distance closed in what seemed an instant and he saw two men leap aside immediately in front of him. He thrust his spear at the nearest of them but the Silurian was too quick and the point found only thin air. Cato snatched the spear back as Hannibal plunged on, into the enemy ranks. Another man, braver this time, stood his ground directly ahead and Cato angled his spear tip round. The Silurian carried a kite shield bearing a swirling design, and he held a long sword above his head. Snatching at his reins with his shield hand, Cato dragged Hannibal's head round and the horse whinnied as the iron curb bit caught in its mouth. Hannibal swerved and his breast smashed into the warrior's shield, knocking him back. Cato stabbed his spear and this time the point struck the man in the thigh. A flesh wound, but deep enough to cause him to cry out in agony and stumble away. Cato pressed his heel into the horse's flank to straighten him and continued forward. On either side the Thracians crashed into and through the enemy line. Cato saw one of his men turn and start to chase after a fleeing tribesman and bellowed, 'Leave them! On! On!'

He spurred Hannibal forward and continued up the gentle rise to the pass where he could just make out the flicker of weapons and a handful of standards weaving above the grass crest of the slope. The Thracian squadrons had burst through the right of the enemy line and scattered the warriors. Glancing back over his shoulder, Cato was relieved to see that the formation was intact, though less clearly defined than it had been before the impact of the charge. There were no gaps and he could not see any men caught in a fight with the enemy infantry. He felt a surge of elation that they had broken through so easily, then he braced himself for the real fight that was to come.

The wedge pounded up into the pass and the bitter struggle ahead of them was revealed in all its desperate savagery. Thousands of enemy warriors surged around the beleaguered column. There was no sign of any survivors of the squadron that had made their forlorn charge a short time before. On a small rise Caratacus and his retinue sat on their horses watching the fight. For an instant Cato was tempted by the idea of leading his men against the enemy general. If he could be killed then the heart, and brains, would be knocked out of the coalition of tribes still opposing Rome. Then, at last, there might be peace in the new province of Britannia. But before he could act on his impulse and issue the order, he saw Caratacus and his followers ride down to join the battle on the opposite side of the hard-pressed Roman perimeter.

Ahead of him the nearest of the enemy warriors had turned towards the sound of the approaching Thracians. The wild appearance that Quertus had encouraged and their reputation for savagery seemed to ride ahead of them and some of the tribesmen fled from their path, leaving only hardened warriors to stand their ground. Looking beyond them Cato saw a seething mass of the enemy he and his men would have to cut through to reach the column. And then what? Escape from the pass seemed impossible. He thrust the thought aside. For him there must only be the here and now. He must lead his men and fight on for as long as possible. If the gods favoured him, he might live through this yet. Otherwise he briefly prayed that his end would be swift and relatively painless.

Hannibal's flanks heaved from the exertion of the charge but the horse gamely charged on, knocking aside two men before a third slashed a blade at the bronze chamfron guarding the horse's forehead and eyes. Fortunately it was only a glancing blow but the ringing impact startled the horse into rearing up and lashing out with its hoofs. Cato threw his weight forward and struggled to regain control.

'Easy, lad! Easy . . .' Cato spoke tenderly and Hannibal dropped forward and Cato urged him on. Around him the wedge formation had been blunted as the Thracians ploughed into the ranks of the enemy infantry, shouting their war cries as they stabbed left and right with their long spears, thrusting into the limbs and bodies of the Silurians. Cato looked round and saw that some of the saddles were empty, and close by, another man was surrounded by warriors stabbing at him as he attempted to keep moving and not present his foes with an easy target. But there were too many of them and as he raised his arm to strike with his spear an axe thudded into his back, not cutting through the chain-link armour but still shattering the bones beneath. The spear tumbled from his fingers and a moment later he was dragged from his saddle and out of Cato's sight.

Centurion Stellanus's voice carried above the fighting, raw and strained. 'Keep on, boys! Keep going forward!'

Cato pressed on, his shield held high as he braced his spear arm. An older warrior, sinewy with matted grey hair, sprang out of the throng wielding an axe, his teeth bared in a savage snarl as he saw the Roman officer and charged. Cato leaned forward and thrust his spear. The point struck true, deep into the man's groin. He doubled over and dropped his axe and slumped down on to his hands and knees, and then Cato had charged past him and was looking for his next foe. So intent was he on the fighting that he was almost upon the Roman line before he was aware of it. A gap opened between the Silurians and there stood men brandishing the heavy rectangular shields of the legions. Cato drew up sharply and called out, 'Open ranks! Let us through!'

There was no reaction; the narrowed eyes of the legionaries peered suspiciously over the rim of their shields. To one side was the slender crest of an optio and Cato pointed his spear towards the man.

'You! Tell your men to open ranks!'

The optio regarded him briefly and then bellowed the order to his men. To his relief Cato saw the shields part and he spurred Hannibal through the gap and into the space behind the backs of the Roman soldiers. At once he wheeled round and brandished his spear. 'Blood Crows! Blood Crows! On me!'

More men surged through the gap, singly and in small groups as they fought their way free of the Silurians. Cato saw that most of the two squadrons had made it through. A handful of individuals had become separated from the formation and he saw the last of them, no more than thirty paces away, savagely hauled off his horse into a swirl of enemy warriors. Their bloodied weapons rose and fell before they turned back to renew their assault on the reinforcement column.

Cato holstered the butt of his spear and called out, 'Centurion Stellanus! Decurion Kastos! On me!'

'Here, sir!' Stellanus thrust his horse through the riders milling in the gap between the legionaries and the wagons.

'Where's Kastos?'

'He took a spear to the chest and went down back there.'

Cato nodded. 'Then I'll take direct command of his squadron.'

'Who in Hades' name are you?' a voice interrupted them and Cato turned to see a tribune standing on one of the wagons close by. A tall, broad man, a few years older than himself. Cato turned his horse and edged towards the wagon.

'Prefect Quintus Licinius Cato, commander at Bruccium.'

The officer nodded a greeting. 'Tribune Mancinus, sir. Of the Fourteenth. What are you doing here?'

Cato ignored the abrupt tone. 'I had hoped to help you cut your way through to the fort. But it seems you are somewhat under strength for the job.'

Mancinus shook his head wryly. 'My thoughts exactly. But the legate said the escort would be adequate. Not his wisest decision.'

'I'll say. What is your plan?'

'Plan?' The tribune gestured to the fight raging around the wagons. Wounded men were being dragged back from the fighting line and propped up against the wheels of the wagons. 'What do you think?' The tribune's voice was strained. 'We're fighting for our lives.'

There was a brief hesitation before he conceded command. 'What are your orders, sir?'

Cato looked round and saw that for the moment the Roman soldiers were holding their own. He turned back to Mancinus. 'We have to fight our way out of this. We can't go forward, there's even more of the enemy in the direction of the fort. We'll have to make for Gobannium.'

The tribune pursed his lips. 'Might not be so easy, sir. We were being followed by a war band soon after we left Gobannium. They stayed with us until this morning and then vanished. Or so I thought.'

'Well, that's the only direction open to us now.' Cato winced as an arrow glanced off his shield and deflected into the air over his helmet. 'I'll use my men to clear a path. Have the infantry close up and we'll get moving. Empty three of the wagons for the wounded. The rest will have to be abandoned. The prospect of easy spoils will slow some of the enemy down.'

Mancinus nodded, and turned to shout orders to one of the sections waiting in his small reserve. The men laid down their shields and began to unload the last three wagons, dumping the spare kit

316

and rations on the ground which was slick with churned mud from the heavy wheels, hoofs and boots of the column. The injured men were hauled up and roughly deposited on the bed of the first wagon. Cato knew that the wagon would soon be filled by more of the wounded, and the same would be true of the other vehicles.

While the legionaries prepared the wagons, Cato ordered Stellanus to form the Thracians across the track towards the rear of the perimeter.

The optio in charge of the reserve approached and saluted. 'Sir, what about the draught animals? Do we take 'em with us or kill 'em?'

Cato glanced at the mules and oxen harnessed to the wagons that were being left behind. There was no sense in letting the enemy make use of them. It was standard practice to destroy them rather than let them be captured. Yet they might serve a useful purpose. He refined his plan a moment and then addressed the optio.

'Have them taken out of harness and placed in front of the Thracians. You have feed nets?'

'Yes, sir.'

'Then fix one to the harness of each animal.'

'Sir?' The optio looked surprised and then nodded obediently. 'Yes, sir.'

'See to it. Quick as you can.'

The optio hurried off to carry out his orders and Cato paused to take stock of the battle. He had lost a third of his men. No more than forty Thracians remained. The reinforcement column was faring better, thanks to the shield wall they were able to present to the enemy. They would take far fewer losses than the lightly armed Silurians, but that would not last. The price of heavy armour was the exhaustion that it inflicted on the soldiers. That was why the legionaries fought in relays in great set-piece battles. There would be no respite for them on the road back to Gobannium, Cato realised. A few hours from now, they would be worn out and become easy pickings for their nimble enemy.

As he waited for his orders to be carried out, Cato mentally retraced the route out of the valley. The track led through the pass and descended into another valley beyond. There the pass narrowed and was lined with a thick forest of pine trees. If they could reach that then a rearguard might hold the enemy off long enough for the rest of the column to get away. Or at least gain enough of a lead to reach Gobannium.

Over the heads of the men fighting he could see Caratacus and his escort, urging their warriors on. For a brief instant Cato sensed that the enemy commander was looking straight at him, still as resolutely determined to obliterate every last man of the garrison of Bruccium and every other Roman who stood in his path. Then Caratacus spurred his horse and moved to another section of his army and dismounted to wade into the fight.

Tribune Mancinus approached and stood at his side to watch the progress of the uneven struggle raging about them.

'What do you want the draught animals for?' Mancinus asked.

'If you've read your Livy, then you should be able to guess.'

'Livy?' Mancinus shrugged. 'Not on my syllabus, I regret to say, sir.'

'Too bad. He has his uses.' Cato saw that the animals and the Thracians were in position and the last of the three wagons had been turned about and was ready to move off. 'We're ready, Tribune. When I give the word the animals will cause something of a diversion. My cavalry will follow them up and try to open the way for the column. Get your men moving at once. Keep 'em closed up and their shields presented to the enemy. If you can save the wounded, do so. But if they fall out of line and can't be rescued, leave them. Is that clear?'

'Clear, but hard to stomach, sir.'

'That's too bad. We can't afford to slow the column down for anything. Not if there's going to be any chance of saving some of the men at least.'

'I understand, sir.'

'Good. Then let's be about our business.' Cato clicked his tongue and steered Hannibal past the abandoned wagons to the front of the tightly packed ranks of the Thracians. He saw the optio overseeing the tying of the last feed bags to the nervous mules and oxen herded together behind the line of auxiliaries holding the rear of the perimeter.

'Optio, you have your tinderbox with you?'

318

The man patted the leather pouch hanging from a strap across his shoulder. 'Yes, sir.'

'Then get a flame going at once. Soon as you have, get your men to light some twists of straw and set the feed bags alight.'

The optio raised his eyebrows in surprise but nodded obediently and got to work. Cato made his way towards the centurion in command of the rearguard.

'What's your unit, Centurion?'

The officer, tough-looking and swarthy, saluted. 'Fourth Hispanic Cohort, sir.'

'And you?'

'Centurion Fernandus, sir.'

'When I give the word, I want your men to draw aside to let the animals pass. They'll need to move quickly if they want to avoid being trampled.'

'Yes, sir.'

All was set and Cato returned to his position at the head of the Thracians. In front of him the optio had lit a small fire, fed with handfuls of dry feed. As soon as the flames had taken he waved his men forward and they lit their tightly twisted lengths of straw and hurried to their places behind the animals, where they waited for the order. Cato settled himself in his saddle and took hold of his spear.

'Light them up!'

At his command the legionaries thrust their makeshift torches into the feed nets and at once the dry, combustible material was set alight. Thin trails of smoke curled into the air and the flames spread rapidly. The heat and the glare alarmed the animals and they began to jostle against each other. Cato held off a moment longer, to ensure that they were agitated enough to rush forward when the opening was made for them. One of the oxen let out a loud bellow of fear and pain and stamped a foreleg.

'Now, Fernandus!'

The auxiliary centurion snatched a breath and yelled, 'Fourth Hispanic! Open ranks!'

The fighting line parted as the men in the centre section fell back and drew aside. They moved quickly enough to surprise the enemy who stood facing the gap, weapons raised and eyes staring. The ox bellowed again and the flames from the feed bag began to scorch its hide. With a snort it charged for the gap, trying to escape the burning hay on its rump. The other animals began to rush forward to get away from the same torment, straight at the closely packed ranks of the Silurians. There was no chance to get out of the path of the stampeding animals and the men were borne back by the impetus of the terrified brutes. With a scream the first of them fell under the hoofs and then more were trampled as the draught animals surged out of the Roman formation. Nothing could stand in the path of the panicked mules and oxen. Their bellows and braying filled the air as the flames, fanned by their frantic efforts to flee, flared behind them, adding to their terror.

Cato waited until the last of the animals had stampeded away and then advanced his spear. 'Blood Crows! Stick it to 'em!'

Not the formal command, he knew, but one that would be unmistakable, and his men spurred their mounts and charged out of the square, through the gap. Cato and the squadron of the late Kastos charged to the left, Stellanus and the others to the right, bursting through the scattered and terrified Silures, thrusting their spears again and again, cutting down the routing enemy. As the last of the cavalry cleared the column, Tribune Mancinus gave the command to advance and the men behind the wall of shields steadily began to move back along the track leading over the pass towards Gobannium. The Silurians kept pace, wildly hacking at the shields and risking an occasional lunge at an exposed leg or gap that opened between the shields. For their part the Romans stabbed their swords at the enemy. There were still some who retained their javelins and used their greater reach to good effect, skewering any tribesmen who ventured too close to the line of shields. The men of the column left a trail of bodies, dead and dying, in their wake, mostly tribesmen but some Romans among them, who were butchered as they fell behind.

The animals had scattered, running blindly on in a futile effort to get away from the flames that scorched their backs, and it was then left to Cato and the Thracians to keep the line of march open. They charged to and fro across the track, breaking up any groups of enemy warriors attempting to make a stand in front of the box formation crawling through the pass. As Cato had hoped, the enemy fell on the abandoned wagons and ransacked them looking for valuables, armour and weapons. It was not until Caratacus rode down on his followers and drove them forwards again that the battle was renewed in earnest.

They had covered nearly a mile with little loss when they approached the slight rise before the valley narrowed. Cato was rallying his men for another rush at the enemy when Centurion Stellanus, who had ridden a short distance further ahead, suddenly reined in and stood staring down the far slope. He turned and beckoned frantically to Cato.

'Sir! Over here!'

The enemy war bands had drawn back and were watching the Thracians warily, so in the brief lull before they came on again Cato spurred his horse ahead to join Stellanus. As he drew up beside the centurion the reason for the latter's consternation was immediately apparent. The track was blocked by a hastily thrown up breastwork of rocks and felled trees. A line of roughly sharpened stakes angled out of the ground in front of the barricade and the trees on either side, which spread across the narrow width of the valley, right up to the crags. Behind the defences stood the enemy, weapons held ready, hurling challenges. As Cato and then a handful of Thracians joined the centurion, their jeering increased until it echoed mockingly off the mountains on either side.

For a moment, Cato was confused. He had not seen any war bands hurrying past to get ahead of the column. Then it hit him. These were the men who had been following Mancinus. Far from disappearing, they had dogged his footsteps just long enough to ensure that he walked into the trap, and then set about putting in place the last element of their commander's plan. Cato could not help but admire the shrewd intelligence of the Catuvellaunian king. Once again he had outwitted his Roman opponents.

The moment passed and Cato's admiration turned to cold dread. There was only the most slender chance of survival now. They must break through, or they would most certainly die where they stood.

# CHAPTER THIRTY-THREE

'You must hold this ground until the job is done,' Cato explained to Mancinus. 'A third of the men are already down. I'll need a century of the Gaulish auxiliaries to cut through the barricade. That leaves you short-handed. Stellanus will do what he can to cover the flanks but it'll be down to the rest of the escort and the garrison replacements to hold the enemy back.'

The tribune nodded and adjusted his grip on the handle of his shield. 'We'll do our duty, sir.'

Back in the direction of Bruccium, the Silurians were massing across the width of the valley, building themselves up for another rush at the shields of the Romans with a rising chorus of battle cries.

Cato smiled at the tribune. 'In this instance duty is not enough. I need you and the men to be bloody heroes.'

Mancinus smiled back. 'Those who are about to die . . .'

Cato shook his head. 'That's not quite what I had in mind. I'll see you and your men on the far side of the barricade once we're through.'

'Yes, sir. Good luck.'

Cato nodded and strode off to join the auxiliaries of the First Century of Fernandus's cohort. They had formed up in a blunt column, eight abreast and ten deep, in close order. Cato had left his spear and Hannibal in the hands of one of the walking wounded and drew his sword as he took his place in the front rank of the century. The commander of the cohort looked at him uncertainly.

'Sir, I should be leading this attack. These are my men.'

'And it is my order they are carrying out. I will not ask them to risk a danger I wouldn't face myself.'

Fernandus shrugged. 'As you wish.'

Cato nodded. 'Get back to the rest of your cohort. Something tells me the enemy won't wait much longer before they come on again.'

The centurion bowed his head and turned to trot back towards his men, lined up to the right of the legionaries who were holding the centre, while the replacements intended for the fort held the left. Beyond that there were barely ten men in each of the remaining Thracian squadrons at the end of each line. They would hold Caratacus and his horde back for the first charge, but after that it was in the lap of the gods. Cato cleared his mind and shifted his shield round in front of his left shoulder and drew his sword level.

'Advance, at my pace!' he ordered. The auxiliaries tensed around and behind him, faces set in determined expressions. They knew as well as he that their survival and that of their comrades depended on them breaking through the barricade and then holding the breach open long enough for the rest of the column to retreat along the track between the pine trees.

'One! Two!' Cato intoned repeatedly, and the tight formation tramped forward towards the line of stakes less than a hundred paces ahead. Beyond, the enemy warriors lining the makeshift defences brandished their weapons and dared their enemy to come on and do battle. Behind him Cato could hear the blast of war horns and a great roar as the rest of the Silurians rushed towards the thin Roman line covering the retreat.

Step by step the auxiliaries made their way along the track towards the enemy and then Cato saw a man clamber atop the barricade and whirl a leather thong above his head.

'Shields up! Form tortoise!'

The inner ranks of the formation lifted their shields, rank by rank, from the front, and behind the shields the century became a crowded world of gloom, panted breath, the smell of sweat and muttered prayers to the gods. The muffled sounds from beyond were suddenly drowned out by the loud rattle of slingshot striking home, battering the leather surface of the shields. Cato lowered his head so that he was just able to see over the rim of his shield and raised his voice as he continued to intone the pace. 'One! Two!'

There was a cry of pain as one of the auxiliaries was struck on the shin, the shot smashing the bone. He fell out of formation and covered his body with his shield as another man took his place. The bombardment intensified as they reached the line of stakes and Cato called the formation to a halt. He ordered two men to work the first of the stakes free. Another auxiliary was struck as a stone glanced off a shield and hit him in the face, breaking his cheek and blinding him in one eye. He let out a brief groan but kept his place.

'Good lad,' Cato called across to him.

The first stake came out and then another. And all the time slingshot, accompanied by rocks, smashed against the shields. Then there was a shout and the blare of a horn and Cato risked a look over his shield and saw enemy warriors clambering over the barricade and rushing forward to engage the auxiliaries.

'Here they come! Brace yourselves!'

A moment later Cato felt his shield crash against him. He staggered back a pace before thrusting savagely forward and restoring the line at the front of the formation. More blows landed and hands tried to rip away the shield as the tribesmen attempted to get at their enemy. But the auxiliaries held their ground and punched their swords out, stabbing at the warriors surrounding them. The two men working the stakes continued their task, grunting as they wrenched them from the ground.

Suddenly there was a deafening crack and splinters shot through the confines behind the shields and a broad shaft of light pierced the gloom. Cato glanced round and saw that a huge Silurian warrior, stripped to a loincloth, his powerful body covered with swirling tattoos, was swinging a heavy war hammer back for another blow. His first had shattered the shield and caved in the chest of the man holding it. He now lay on the ground blinking as blood gurgled and sprayed from his lips. The hammer whirled round in a vicious arc and struck again, sending another man flying into his comrades.

'Shit!' Cato muttered as two warriors forced themselves into the gap. One carried a hunting spear and thrust it into the stomach of an auxiliary. The second tribesman darted in, clutching a small axe which he swung into the forearm of another of the auxiliaries. The formation was breaking up as the other men instinctively backed away.

'Hold your positions!' Cato bellowed. Then fingers closed round the edge of his shield and tried to wrench it from him. Cato hacked at the knuckles with his sword and was rewarded with a sharp cry of agony as two digits went flying and the warrior snatched his ruined hand back. Cato saw the giant with the war hammer smash another man down using an overhead blow that crushed the auxiliary's helmet and the skull beneath it. Blood exploded from the face and ears of his victim. More of the enemy had thrust their way into the formation. Cato could see at once that it would not hold and it would be suicide to continue with his original plan.

With a bitter stab of frustration he sucked in a deep breath. 'Fall back! Fall back!'

He kept his shield up as he cautiously retreated step by step. The other men closed ranks and fell into step as Cato called out the timing. The enemy stayed with them, the giant leading the attack, his weapon whirling and crushing one auxiliary after another. Cato knew that he had to be dealt with before he broke the spirit of the surviving men of the century. He halted the formation, then waited for the hammer to rise up again, ready for another overhead blow. Cato launched himself forward, slamming his shield up and into the giant's face. His nose broke with a soft crack and Cato swung his sword in a short arc round the edge of the shield and stabbed him in the armpit. There was not enough power in the blow to break through the man's ribs and the blade carved a shallow tear across his tattoed flesh. Cato did not wait to finish the job but fell back and continued to order the retreat of the century. He saw blood streaming down the giant's face as the man staggered back, dazed. His comrades let out a groan of anxiety at the sight and fell back from the shields of the auxiliaries, long enough for a gap to open up between the two sides. There were far more Silurians lying on the ground than Romans and the sight of the wall of shields, and the lethal points of the swords pricking out between them, was enough to deter the enemy from renewing their attack. They contented themselves with jeering at the retreating Romans before one of their chiefs had the wit to bellow at his men to replant the stakes that had been torn up.

Cato led the men back out of slingshot range and then ordered them to form line to cover the rear of the rest of the column. By the

325

time he could turn his attention to the fight across the main battle line, the enemy were already falling back. But they had exacted as heavy a price as they had paid and the line was no more than one deep across most of its length. The next attack would undoubtedly break it, Cato realised. He hurried across to Tribune Mancinus who was having a wound to his arm dressed by an orderly.

'We can't get through,' Cato informed him.

'I saw.' Mancinus puffed his cheeks. 'Can't fight our way through to Bruccium. Can't retreat to Gobannium. Not much of a choice left, sir.'

'No.' Cato pointed to a small knoll near the middle of the pass. 'That's the spot for us.'

The tribune considered the position and shrugged. 'As good as any place for a last stand.'

'We'd better take up position before Caratacus comes for us again.'

Mancinus nodded and waved the orderly away as soon as the dressing was tied off. The three wagons were driven up to the top of the knoll and the teams of beasts were led a short distance away before the drivers cut their throats. Cato ordered Stellanus to gather the Thracians, of whom twelve still lived, though they had saved three more of the mounts.

'We'll stay by the wagons and plug any gaps if the enemy cut through.'

Stellanus cocked an eyebrow. 'If?'

Cato ignored the comment and watched the legionaries and auxiliaries begin to fall back around the hillock. The enemy knew that the end was near and began to edge forward as Caratacus beckoned to the men of his blocking force to join in the kill. The bloodied giant had recovered from the blow to his head and nimbly climbed over the barricades and threaded his way through the stakes to lead his party, somewhat larger in number than the surviving Romans, swinging his hammer as he came.

The last of the men trudged into place on the knoll and turned to face the enemy. Many were already wounded and had bloodied rags hastily tied about their limbs. Shields had been battered and some shield trims had split under the impact of swords and axes. Stellanus held Hannibal for him and Cato climbed into the saddle. From his vantage point he looked round the small ring of soldiers standing shoulder to shoulder in silence as they waited. The injured in the wagons could only look on helplessly. Some held swords or daggers, though Cato was not sure if they meant to fight until the last breath or end their lives rather than face the possibility of torment from the Silurians. The standard-bearers of the two cohorts stood on the drivers' benches of one of the wagons where the units' colours would fly above the heads of the men until the end.

Mancinus made his way over to Cato and offered his hand. 'It's a shame that it has been such a short acquaintance, sir. A pity you didn't remain in the fort.'

Cato sighed and gestured towards the reinforcement contingent. 'They were to join my command. I couldn't stand by and let them be cut down.'

Mancinus smiled. 'You have a rather old-fashioned view of what the duty of a commander is.'

'That may be, but rank comes with burdens as well as privileges.' Cato cupped a hand to his mouth. 'Lads! It's too bad we're here, but there's one duty left to us now. Take as many of the bastards down with us as we can. Every one who dies by our hand is one less for Rome to deal with. We will be avenged. You can be sure of that. That's work for our comrades. Let's do 'em proud! As for the enemy, let's show them how Romans die!' He drew his sword and thrust it above his head. 'For Rome, and for the Emperor!'

'For Rome!' Mancinus repeated, in part, and the cry spread around the knoll as the men prepared to sell their lives dearly.

Cato saw the enemy commander and his companions riding at the head of the oncoming ranks of the Silurians and he wondered if Caratacus might offer them a chance to surrender. If so, he knew he could not accept. After the cruel destruction that Quertus had visited on the kinfolk of the tribesmen, there would be no mercy shown to Roman prisoners, and they could only expect to live long enough to be given a pitiless and painful end. But Caratacus gave no sign that he intended to offer them terms. As he called out to his men, there was a distinct note of triumph in the words he spoke in his native tongue. The enemy warriors flowed round the knoll until they completely encircled it and only then began to close in. Their shouts were deafening and their faces etched with hate and triumph as they waved their fists and pumped their shields and weapons at the Romans. It was only at the last moment, when they were no more than a few paces away, that some instinct spread through the Silurian ranks and they charged home, slamming into the shields and desperately trying to work gaps between them to strike at the men behind.

For a while the line held and the Romans fought with a desperate savagery that matched that of their opponents. Bodies fell in front of the shields and the Silurians had to clamber over their comrades to get at the legionaries and auxiliaries. But one by one the defenders of the knoll began to fall, and with each casualty the ring closed tighter about the wagons and the handful of horsemen beside them. Cato resolved to lead them in one final dash towards Caratacus, hoping by some miracle to get close enough to make an attempt on the life of the enemy commander. But Caratacus held back, with his men, watching the destruction of the last of the relief column.

Cato snatched a brief moment to think about the manner of his death. It was true that it had been foolhardy to ride to the aid of the men around him, yet he could not have lived with himself if he had not. And there was the euphoria following his defeat of Quertus. It was not just the Thracian who had been defeated, but Cato's fear of certain death. It had been liberating to trust his life to his courage and skill at arms. Perhaps it was that sense of triumph that had led him to this end. That, and the hope that his actions might help save these men. Now that they were doomed, he resolved that he would make his sacrifice of value to Macro at least. If they killed enough of the Silurians, that might undermine their will to continue attacking the fort. There was some comfort in the thought that his last service in life would be to help the truest friend he had ever known.

A short distance away the giant who had battered the tortoise formation apart thrust his way forward to take a swing at a legionary. The soldier raised his shield to block the blow and it shattered under the impact and drove him down on to his knees. The Silurian kicked out and sent his opponent sprawling. One more blow caved in his chest and he fell motionless on the bloodstained grass.

'Stellanus!' Cato called out. 'Take that one down.'

The centurion nodded, lowered his spear and urged his mount forward. The Silurian looked up with a brutal snarl as he spied another victim and raised his hammer. It blurred through the air and struck the horse on the side of the head. At the same time Stellanus thrust his spear and the point pierced the giant's thick neck and burst out above his shoulder blade. He let out a roar of pain and rage, cut off abruptly as blood filled his windpipe and mouth. The horse staggered to one side and fell, rolling over the centurion and into the backs of three more legionaries locked in combat. The animal's legs kicked out, sweeping two more men down, and left an opening in the Roman line. At once the Silurians rushed forward, bursting in amongst the defenders of the knoll. The giant staggered over to the horse, still twitching, and bent down to grasp Stellanus by the neck. The centurion could only move one arm and he beat it against the giant's jaw, but for all the effect it had he might have been patting a hound. A moment later, powerful hands gave his head a sharp twist, breaking his neck. Then, blood coursing from his mouth, the Silurian's eyes rolled up and he collapsed over his victim.

More tribesmen scrambled over the bodies and poured up the slope, spreading out as they threw themselves at the Romans. With the perimeter collapsing, the soldiers fought individually. Others went back to back or formed small clusters and hacked ferociously at the warriors swirling round them.

'The standards!' Mancinus cried out as he backed up towards the wagons. He turned and looked at Cato. 'Save the standards!'

Cato hesitated for an instant, torn between his duty to fight alongside his comrades and the shame that would befall them all if the standards were taken by the enemy. Then he turned to the standard-bearers on the wagon and sheathed his sword. 'Give them to me!'

The two men handed them over and Cato passed the auxiliary standard to one of the Thracians and kept hold of the legionary standard, ramming the base down into his spear holster. A small group of Silurian warriors broke away from the fight below and began to sprint up the slope towards the wagons.

'Get out of here!' Mancinus shouted to Cato and then ran to

meet the enemy, knocking one man down with his shield and stabbing another in the stomach. He wrenched the blade free and struck again before he was borne back by three more men and thrown to the ground. He called out one last time. 'Go!'

Cato kicked in his heels. 'Blood Crows! Follow me!'

He charged down towards the melee, intending to cut his way free and make for the shelter of the trees now that the enemy blocking force had abandoned its position to join in with the destruction of the Roman column. The horsemen held together and those on the ground before them hurried out of their way and turned to slash and stab at them as they pounded by. The sounds of battle filled the air, while around them a raging sea of weapons flickered and blood spurted. A wild-eyed youth sprang at Cato, hands clawing for the shaft of the standard, and he lashed out with his boot, the nailed sole striking the tribesman in the face and sending him flying. They passed through what was left of the Roman line and plunged on through the ranks of the Silurians.

Ahead, a shrewder warrior stepped to the side of the oncoming horses and thrust his hunting spear out. Cato swerved aside but the rider following him did not see the danger and the spear got caught between the horse's legs and it pitched forward, hurling its rider from his saddle. He landed in a group of warriors, knocking them over, and then they fell on him like wild dogs. Another Thracian was struck by an axe that nearly severed him at the knee, but he let out a defiant roar and then clenched his jaw shut, pressed his thigh tightly against the saddle and rode on. The enemy were thinning out and Cato saw that they were almost free of the melee. Ahead there was open ground at the end of the line of obstacles where the pine trees met the rock-strewn side of the pass. His heels nudged Hannibal's flanks and the horse turned in that direction. The Thracians raced after him, knocking aside the last of the enemy, and then they were on open ground, hoofs thudding on the peaty soil as they desperately made their bid to save the standards and salvage some honour from the massacre taking place behind them.

They reached the end of the line of stakes and slowed down as they entered the trees. Cato reined in and looked back towards the knoll. The fight was almost over. Silurians were swarming over the wagons, hacking at the helpless injured who lay within. Only a few pockets of resistance still held out. Cato urged Hannibal in amongst the trees and out of sight before the enemy turned their attention towards the small party of horseman who had broken out. The thick pine branches overhead filtered the light into a dull green, pierced here and there by shafts of a golden hue. The sound of the fighting was muffled and birdsong chirruped above. The ground was covered with many years of fallen needles and twigs and the horses padded through the straight tree trunks, weaving their way into the forest. Cato knew that they had to regain the track as soon as possible and stay ahead of the enemy. If they remained in the trees, Caratacus would soon be able to throw a screen of his warriors round them and close in for the kill.

'Sir.' One of the men broke into his thoughts and Cato looked up.

The Thracian gestured to the man who had been wounded in the knee. 'We have to see to Eumenes. He can't go far with his leg in that shape.'

Cato saw that the injured trooper was in terrible agony, and his leg hung uselessly from the tissue that still held the shattered joint together. Blood dripped from his boot on to the forest floor. He shook his head. 'We can't stop. He'll have to cope until we put some distance between us and the enemy.'

'Sir, he can't ride much further in his condition.'

Cato knew that was true. Just as he knew that they would be taking a great risk if they halted to attend to the wounded man. It was too bad. They had to save the standards and reach Glevum. It was vital that Governor Ostorius was made aware of the location of Caratacus and his army as soon as possible. He hardened his heart as he replied to the trooper.

'Bind it up and then catch up with us. He has to ride on. If he can't then he must be left behind.'

The Thracian saluted bitterly and turned to help his comrade. The order given, Cato flicked his reins and waved the other men on and headed in the direction of the road to Gobannium.

# CHAPTER THIRTY-FOUR

By late afternoon the sky had cleared of clouds and the sun shone over the fort at Bruccium. Macro had given orders for the signal beacon to be kept burning and the grey plume of smoke rose high above the valley now that the breeze had dropped. In the hours that had passed since Cato had led the two squadrons out of the side gate Macro had remained in the tower above the main gate, the highest viewpoint in the fort. He had watched the riders climb up to the ledge and along the side of the mountain until they were out of sight. The last of the war bands had disappeared over the crest at the head of the pass and after that the rest of the enemy camp had settled down to continue their vigil. Scouts watched the fort from a safe distance while their comrades set about the daily business of foraging for food, firewood and timber for the construction of shelters. They were also busy constructing a number of screens to protect them from the defenders' javelins when the order was given to attack the fort again.

'It seems that these barbarian lads can be taught,' Macro muttered wryly to himself. Then his expression resumed its stern fixedness as he turned his gaze back towards the pass. He was tormented by not knowing how his friend's desperate act was playing out. The garrison badly needed the men of the reinforcement column, together with their escort. Bruccium could easily withstand any number of assaults by the enemy once the two cohorts were brought up to strength, together with whatever forces had been sent to ensure the reinforcements arrived safely. Looking round the line of the wall Macro was painfully aware of how thinly the remaining men were stretched. He had less than two hundred effectives. If Caratacus ordered an attack before Cato returned, there was a good chance that the Silurians would overrun the defenders. Straining his eyes towards the pass, he admitted to himself that it was possible that Cato might not return. It seemed like a long time since his friend had left the fort and Macro could not help fearing the worst.

He clenched his fist and smacked it against his thigh in frustration. Anything could have happened. Caratacus might have been driven off. The reinforcement column might have been forced to retreat. The battle might still be raging in the confines of the pass. There was still no indication of which of those three possibilities was most likely. He leaned against the wooden rail and closed his aching eyes to rest them for a moment, aware that he felt light-headed due to the lack of sleep over recent days. His limbs felt stiff and heavy and for the first time he began to wonder how many more years of soldiering he had in him. Macro had known many veterans who had served far longer than the twenty-five years they had signed on for. Longer than was good for them, frankly. But the army was inclined to overlook the handicap of their advanced years due to the invaluable experience they had accrued while serving in the legions.

As for himself, Macro, like many old sweats, had dreamed of retiring to a small Etruscan farm, with a handful of slaves to work it for him, and spending the evenings in a local tavern reliving experiences with other veterans. Now that prospect was growing ever more imminent, he realised that he regarded the idea with disdain . . . quiet despair even. Soldiering was all he knew. All he cared about. All he really loved. What was life without the routine, camaraderie and excitement that encased him like a second skin?

His mind wandered for a moment, losing itself in the warm fug of pleasing memories, and then he was jolted into wakefulness by a sharp pressure on his chin and he stirred quickly, eyes blinking open. His head had drooped so that the flesh under his chin had caught on a splinter on the rail. He bolted upright, horrified at the idea that he had allowed himself to fall asleep, even for a moment. The penalty for doing so while on sentry duty could be death. That he was not on duty was no excuse, Macro chided himself bitterly. It was unforgivable and he glanced round the tower to see if either of the two men keeping watch had noticed. Fortunately their attention was on the enemy camp and he allowed himself a brief sigh of relief. Nothing he could do would affect the outcome of the action in the pass. It would be better to allow himself a rest and get something to eat while the situation was calm around the fort. He would surely need his strength later in the day.

Casually stretching his shoulders, Macro crossed to the ladder. 'I'll be at headquarters. If there's any sign of the prefect, or our column, or anything else, send for me at once.'

'Yes, sir.' One of the sentries bowed his head.

Macro climbed down the ladder and reached up to untie the chinstrap of his helmet as he left the gatehouse. He tucked the helmet under one arm and removed the padded liner, giving the matted hair plastering his scalp a good scratch. The legionaries had been relieved during the morning and were lying or sitting on the slope of the rampart. Some were managing to sleep while others conversed in muted tones. There was only one group playing at dice, by the corner tower, where their noise would not disturb their resting comrades.

As he entered the courtyard of the headquarters block Macro exchanged a salute with the sentry. Even with every man required to defend the walls, it was still necessary to ensure that the garrison's pay chest was kept under guard. Inside the commander's quarters Macro set his helmet down on a table and called for Decimus.

There was no reply, no sound of footsteps, and Macro frowned. Cato's servant had been ordered to return here after the fight with Quertus.

'Decimus! Damn you, man. Where are you?' Macro's shouts carried clearly through the building. With an irritable growl Macro glanced into the prefect's office, found no sign of life, and decided to make for the kitchen to see what food might be had for a hurried meal. As he entered the room with its heavy scent of woodsmoke, Macro was aware of a shadow in the far corner and turned for a better look.

'Fuck me . . .' he whispered, standing still.

A body was hanging from a length of chain with two links looped over a meat hook in one of the beams. The man's face was puffed up, his eyes bulged and a purple tongue poked out of his mouth. It was a moment before Macro recognised him and he shook his head in pity. 'Decimus. You stupid bastard.'

Macro's pity did not extend to sympathy as he stared at the body swinging slowly in the gloom of the corner. He felt a weary sense of disappointment in the servant for taking his own life. Why had the man chosen to do this? Fear of punishment for betraying Cato? Fear of being taken by the enemy when Bruccium fell? Whatever the reason, Macro was sure it was not good enough for Decimus to take his own life. That was no way for a man to die, particularly a man who had once been a soldier. There was no justification for such an end. Macro had no time for all those tales of noble Romans taking their own lives for the good of Rome, or their family line. Far better to die with a sword in your hand, facing the enemy and screaming curses into their face as you fell. This? Macro let out a long sigh. This was the choice of a coward . . . For a moment, without willing it, he imagined the servant's last moments and an inkling of the man's desperation found purchase in Macro's thoughts.

He dismissed the notion swiftly. That sort of thing was better left to the likes of Cato. Macro turned towards what was left of the rations on the shelf above the scored worktop. There was a chunk of the local cheese left and some brittle roundels of hard-baked bread. He took them down and pulled up a stool and ate stolidly, refusing to spare another look at Decimus's body.

He was halfway through the cheese when he heard footsteps hurrying down the corridor that ran the length of the prefect's quarters, ending at the kitchen.

'Sir! Sir!'

Macro chewed quickly to empty his mouth and swallowed. 'In here!'

A moment later the sentry appeared in the doorway, breathless. 'Sir, the enemy are coming back.'

Macro felt his guts tighten. 'Any sign of our lads?'

'No, sir. Noth—' The sentry's response died in his throat as he saw the body. He stared at it, oblivious of Macro's glare.

'Finish making your damn report!' Macro barked.

'What?' The legionary looked at the centurion, the horrified spell broken. 'Yes, sorry, sir. Beg to report that the tribesmen are coming down from the pass. I saw Caratacus amongst 'em, sir.'

'And no Romans. You're certain?'

'Yes, sir.'

'No prisoners?' There was still that hope to clutch at.

'I couldn't make any out. Not before I came to report, sir.'

Macro stood up and gathered up what was left of his makeshift meal. He nodded towards the body. 'Take that down and get it out of here.'

He made for the door to the corridor and stopped at the threshold. 'Put Decimus with the other bodies. Might as well give the poor bastard a decent grave when it's all over.'

'Yes, sir.' The legionary nodded.

Macro stared at him. 'Well, what are you waiting for? Want him to start stinking the kitchen out? And make sure you clean up the mess underneath him.'

The legionary grimaced as he set his javelin and shield beside the counter Macro had been sitting at and headed for the slop bucket. Macro took a last look at the corpse, shook his head, and strode off.

As he made his way back to the main gate his face settled into a sombre expression. If Caratacus and his forces were returning from the pass then it was almost certainly because they had given the reinforcement column a hiding. Which meant the garrison was on its own again. With fewer men to defend the fort than ever. Not a happy prospect, Macro mused. The only hopeful aspect of the whole affair was that the beacon signal might have been seen further afield and a message had been carried to Legate Quintatus to alert him that the Bruccium garrison was in trouble. Even so, Glevum was over sixty miles away. It would take the Fourteenth Legion at least three days to march to the rescue of the garrison. Macro knew that they could not hold out for that long.

Macro's muscles were aching by the time he climbed to the top of the tower and crossed to the parapet. The remaining sentry was staring along the valley where a large column of enemy warriors, several thousand strong, was marching down the track to the camp. The banner of Caratacus rippled above the group of horsemen at the front, and behind them the war bands came one after another. At their approach the men left in the camp surged forward to cheer their comrades' return. The sun was dipping low over the rim of the mountains to the west as the warriors entered the camp. The valley was bathed in its red glow and long shadows spilled out across the grass and heather surrounding the fort.

The front wall was lined with the men from the garrison watching in silence. Macro could make out a number of horses being led beside the enemy force. The clipped manes and saddles were of Roman design, and he knew then that Cato's attempt to assist the men of the reinforcement column had been in vain. Macro's heart sank like a rock at the thought that his friend had perished along with the other men of the two squadrons of Thracians. He strained his eyes along the columns of warriors and saw men being supported by their comrades, and others being carried on makeshift stretchers fashioned out of pine branches and the red cloaks of legionaries. Finally, he saw what he hoped to see. A file of prisoners towards the rear of the column. Twenty or so men, hands bound behind their backs and linked together by loops of rope round their necks. They still wore their armour and as Macro stared he saw that one of them wore the breastplate and cloak of an officer, though the distance was too great to be sure of his identity. His heart quickened at the prospect that it might be Cato. But then the brief moment of hope chilled as he considered what fate Caratacus might have in store for his prisoners. If the prisoner was Cato, then it would have been better for him to have died in battle, Macro told himself bitterly.

As dusk closed in over the valley Macro gave the order for the garrison to be issued with full rations. He saw no point in letting the men go hungry. They would fight better on full stomachs when the morning came. Down in the enemy camp they had already begun to celebrate their victory and Macro decided that the enemy commander would be likely to indulge his men and there was little risk of another night attack. Even so, he had the men bring their bedrolls to the foot of the rampart so that they would be on hand if there was an attempt made to rush the fort.

One by one fires were lit across the floor of the valley. By the light of the flames Macro saw the enemy warriors drinking, and snatches of singing and laughter carried up to the garrison of Bruccium. The biggest fire burned in front of Caratacus's shelter and Macro could easily pick him out where he sat with his comrades on the raised ground of the reviewing platform overlooking the parade ground. As the night wore on, there was no sign that the celebrations were coming to an end and a new moon rose over the mountains and took its place among the stars. Then there was a commotion down on the parade ground and Macro saw figures massing around the fire. More fuel was added until great tongues of yellow and red licked up into the night. Soon thousands thronged around the fire.

'Centurion Macro!'

He turned towards the voice and leaned over the side of the tower. In the moonlight he could just make out Petillius on the wall.

'Sir, do you see? They're going to attack. Shall I sound the alarm?'

Macro looked back down the slope. The enemy were making very little attempt to conceal their preparations if they were about to make an attack. He looked back towards the waiting centurion.

'No need to sound the alarm. Caratacus and his lads are just having a bit of fun. Let our boys rest. At least they'll be more ready to face what the morning brings than the enemy will.'

Petillius was silent for a moment before he replied in a reluctant tone, 'As you wish, sir. I hope you're right.'

The last words stung Macro's pride and he was about to snap at his subordinate when he realised that Petillius's nerves were even more strained than his own. It would do the man no good to have his superior bawl him out. Macro sighed. 'Get some sleep, Centurion. I'll keep watch on them for a while.'

'Yes, sir.' Petillius nodded, took one last look over the wall, and then descended the wooden steps to the foot of the ramp and sat down, crossed his arms over his knees and lowered his head.

Macro leaned on the rail and watched the crowd gathering around the fire. It was clear that something was about to happen, something to mark the height of their celebrations. Then he saw a small party emerge from the darkness, and the crowd parted before it. A tall figure in dark robes led the way. Behind him came clusters of three men, each with a prisoner pinned between two of them. The prisoners were thrust on to the ground close to the fire, five in all.

338

More of the tribesmen arrived carrying wooden frames in the shape of an A. They bound the first of the prisoners to the frame with his head at the apex and his limbs tied firmly to the lengths of timber stretching out at an angle. When the preparations were complete, the figure in the dark robe gestured towards the fire and the frame was raised off the ground and set upright. The prisoner started writhing as he saw the fire and knew, as Macro did at the same time, what fate was to befall him. Several men strained on a rope fixed to the top of the frame and began to slowly pay it out so that the frame tipped towards the fire. For a moment the crowd fell silent and then the man's cries of pain, quickly followed by screams, sounded. The natives let out a cruel roar at his agonies. The soldier twitched uselessly against the ropes that bound him to the frame. His tunic caught alight and he was engulfed in fire as his screams reached a new pitch of torment and terror.

Macro turned away, not wishing to see any more. He slumped down inside the tower, resting his back against the hard timber of the palisade, but he could not escape the chilling sounds from below. He stared up at the cold stars and prayed to the gods for deliverance.

# CHAPTER THIRTY-FIVE

'I didn't expect to find you here, sir.'

Legate Quintatus regarded the exhausted mud-spattered individual who had been brought to his quarters shortly after he had retired to his bed for the night. He had hurriedly put on a tunic and gone to the office of the commander of the fort at Isca to confront the man who had demanded he be awakened at such a late hour.

'Prefect Cato . . . You look as if you have been through the mill.'

Cato was too tired to appreciate the legate's laconic comment. He was so exhausted that he could barely stand, yet he must make his report as swiftly as possible if there was still a chance that Macro and the others could be saved. He had been in the saddle since leaving the mountain pass that morning. Together with the surviving Thracians, he had ridden out of the forest a short distance ahead of a party of Silurian horsemen who had pursued them as far as Gobannium. Along the way they had been forced to leave the wounded man behind. He was in too much pain to continue and they could not take him on without slowing down and risk being caught by the enemy. He understood the situation well enough and made his farewells to his comrades before drawing his sword and walking his horse back along the track towards their pursuers.

At Gobannium Cato was informed that Legate Quintatus and his column had advanced to Isca. Cato rested the horses for an hour before continuing on, riding hard through the afternoon and on into the dusk, then darkness, before they had seen the distant campfires of the Fourteenth Legion and the auxiliary cohorts attached to the legate's command. They had been picked up by a cavalry patrol whose immediate reaction to the appearance of the Thracians was to take them for the enemy. Only the prefect's presence had persuaded them otherwise. Cato demanded to see the legate at once and they were escorted to the fort at Isca around which the small army was camped. Leaving the standards with a tribune on the legate's staff, Cato immediately made his way to the private quarters of Quintatus to make his report.

'It has been a fraught day, sir,' Cato replied wryly. 'I had assumed you were at Glevum.'

'We received orders from Ostorius two days ago to march into Silurian territory. It seems that the governor has lost contact with Caratacus's army and his patrols can find no trace of him. He's either made his way north to link up with his Brigantian allies, or he's marched south. That's what Ostorius wants me to find out.'

'He went south, sir. He's besieging Bruccium. That's what I have come to report. That and the loss of the column sent to reinforce me.'

Quintatus stared at him. 'What's that? And what of the escort? Tribune Mancinus?'

'All lost, sir.'

'Impossible!'

'They were ambushed in the pass near the fort. I took some of my cavalry out to try and cut a way through for Mancinus's men, but we were caught in the trap along with them. I only just managed to get out with the standards, sir.'

'They're safe? Well, that's something. But, by the gods, I've lost nigh on a thousand men.'

'And you'll lose the fort as well, sir, unless you bring your column up at once.'

Quintatus thought for a moment. 'The fort is a side issue. The real opportunity is to catch up with Caratacus and force him to give battle. Failing that, I can hang on to his heels until Ostorius arrives with his army and we can catch and crush him between us.' His eyes gleamed at the prospect. Then he regarded Cato again. 'Are you certain that it is Caratacus and that he has his entire army with him?'

'It's him all right, sir. I've seen him before. I recognise him well enough. And there are at least ten thousand men with him.'

'Then it must be true. But why would he want to take Bruccium?'

'Two reasons, sir. Firstly, the Thracians have been carving up Silurian territory for the last few months.'

'That will be the work of Centurion Quertus.' The legate nodded. 'A fine officer, that.'

Cato pursed his lips briefly. 'His methods were . . . unusual, but it seems they helped to provoke Caratacus into action.'

'I assume that you are claiming the lion's share of the credit for that?'

'I would never claim any credit for the work of Quertus, I assure you, sir. But the reason Caratacus came after the garrison was more likely down to the fact that we captured his brother, Maridius. He is our prisoner at the fort.'

The legate smiled. 'You have been busy, Prefect. It appears that you and Centurion Quertus have done very well indeed. I am sure that the governor will be the first to reward you both handsomely if this results in the defeat of Caratacus. Of course, Ostorius will be the main beneficiary. The Emperor will give him a public ovation at the very least. A suitable triumph for a long career in the service of Rome.'

'I seek no reward, sir. And Quertus will not be able to accept one either.'

'Oh? Why not?'

'Centurion Quertus is dead, sir.'

'Dead. How?'

Cato hesitated for an instant. 'He died fighting, sir.'

The legate nodded. 'I would expect nothing less of the man. He will be avenged. But first we must lose no time in marching on Bruccium. Wait here, Prefect. I'll issue orders to my staff to have the men ready to break camp at first light.' He scratched the stubble on his chin. 'It's thirty miles. Nearly two days' march. Who have you left in command at the the fort?'

'Centurion Macro, sir.'

'A good man?'

'The best, sir.'

'Then I pray that we arrive in time to save him, and the others. We can't afford to lose good officers like him, and Quertus.'

'No, sir.'

The legate gestured towards a jar of wine on his desk. 'Help yourself while I set things in motion. I'll be back as soon as I can. I will need more details from you.'

'Thank you, sir.'

Once he was alone, Cato stood still for a moment, his mind dulled by tiredness, but he could not allow himself to rest yet. He took one of the legate's finely decorated silver cups and poured himself a generous amount of wine. With the cup in hand, he eased himself down on to a couch with a horsehair cushion and took a sip. It was a sweet wine, not quite to Cato's taste but it warmed his insides as it flowed into his stomach. He resisted the temptation to drain the cup and pour another. He needed to keep his wits about him. There were certain matters that he still had to resolve with the legate before he could let go and rest. He felt his eyelids drooping and instantly stood up, the wine slopping from his cup. Setting the cup down, Cato made himself pace steadily up and down the length of the office, not trusting himself to stop, let alone sit again. His head felt as if it was stuffed with wool and he worried that his mind would not be able to function as sharply as it needed to. The rhythmic pounding of a headache made matters worse.

It was almost an hour before Quintatus returned, fully dressed and freshly shaven, and Cato mentally cursed him for taking the time for the latter when he should have returned here to continue his conversation.

'Glad to see you are still awake, Prefect. You can get some rest soon. I've told my body slave to have a bed prepared for you in the tribune's mess. There'll be hot food and drink as well.'

Cato nodded his thanks and the legate returned to his desk and sat. He waved Cato towards the couch. 'Please.'

'I'll stand, sir.'

Quintatus cocked an eyebrow and shrugged. 'As you wish. Now, there are a few details I need to settle. You say Caratacus had ten thousand men, or thereabouts.'

'That's my estimate.'

'How many of those are cavalry?'

Cato struggled to organise his thoughts. 'No more than five hundred.'

'And the infantry? What quality?'

'A quarter have armour. More now since the loss of the column. The rest are lightly equipped. But they are well motivated, sir. I've rarely seen men fight so hard. They've suffered losses attacking the fort and Tribune Mancinus's column but I doubt it will hold them back. Caratacus knows how to get the best from his men.'

'That may be so, but they'll be no match for the Fourteenth Legion. I just hope that they remain in front of Bruccium long enough for me to arrive on the scene. Then I'll put paid to Caratacus. The man has been a thorn in the side of Rome for too long. If I am the one chosen by the gods to complete the task then maybe I can share an ovation with Ostorius, eh?' Quintatus smiled self-consciously. 'It is never a bad thing to win favour at the imperial court, Cato.'

'In my experience, it is wiser still to have nothing to do with the imperial court, sir.'

Quintatus gave him a calculating look. 'You speak from experience?'

'Yes, sir.'

'I see. Then that's a story that is worth hearing.'

Cato did not respond at first but stared back with an inscrutable expression. 'Let me just say that it is easy to make enemies simply through serving the Emperor loyally and protecting his interests. My promotion to prefect was my reward for such service. However, life seems to give with one hand and then take with the other. My promotion was balanced by incurring the enmity of a powerful element at court.'

'No doubt you crossed the path of one of those infernal freedmen of his. That, or his new wife and that son of hers, Nero.'

Cato ignored the prompt for further information. 'It was out of regard for that enmity that I took the first opportunity to leave Rome and take up command of a unit on a distant frontier. It was my hope that I might devote myself to a military career and be forgotten. But it seems that I was hoping for too much. Why else

344

would I be given the command of the garrison at Bruccium?'

Quintatus settled back in his chair and folded his hands. 'I'm not sure I follow your line of thought, Prefect.'

'It's straightforward enough, sir. The previous prefect was killed in suspicious circumstances. Murdered most likely.'

'That is a serious thing to suggest.'

'Murder is always a serious matter. But you were content not to investigate the matter too closely, while you gave Centurion Quertus a free hand in how he chose to wage war against the Silurians.'

'I'm not sure that I am pleased with the direction this conversation is taking.'

Cato rubbed his brow, wincing at the headache that was starting to make him feel nauseous. 'Sir, I am not trying to make trouble. I just wish to make matters clear. If you are unhappy with what I say then I can only assure you that I am unhappier still to be pursued by the ill will of an enemy far away in Rome. Please do me the courtesy of being honest, as I am being.'

The legate considered this for a moment and then nodded. 'Very well. Continue. But I may not wish to confirm or deny any suggestion you put to me.'

'I understand.' Cato struggled a moment to think clearly before he continued. 'My posting to Bruccium was intended to solve two problems. Firstly, it was hoped that I would be disposed of by being sent there. If the enemy didn't see to that, then Centurion Quertus had shown himself willing and able to dispose of commanders. Secondly, you calculated that his . . . methods would provoke Caratacus. He could hardly carry on operations against Ostorius while his allies were being forced to endure the wholesale massacres that Quertus took to with such enthusiasm. The Silures would either be forced to sue for peace, or they would threaten to withdraw their warriors to protect their own lands. Neither of which Caratacus could permit. So he was forced to make for Bruccium, where in due course he would present you with an opportunity to confront him.' Cato nodded. 'I congratulate you, sir. It is a neat solution. Your talents are wasted here on the frontier. I am sure that they would be better employed in Rome.'

'I take it that was intended as an insult.'

Cato sighed. 'Merely a statement of fact.'

The legate's face twitched, and then he composed his features and regarded Cato closely. 'And what do you propose to do about it? You must know that I can easily brush aside such accusations. It would be your word against mine.'

'I know that.'

'Then what do you want from me?'

'To be left alone, sir,' Cato replied flatly. 'It is through no fault of my own that I have an enemy in the palace. Since I joined the army I have never wanted to do anything more than be a good soldier. I managed it for some years, before I, and my friend, Centurion Macro, were forced to undertake some tasks for one of the imperial secretaries. Now, for the first time in years, we had hoped to be free of his influence, and to return to soldiering. And we're good soldiers. Experienced soldiers. We don't deserve to be played like pieces in some game. It's a waste of our talent, and our loyalty to Rome. I don't want to live my life worrying if someone is going to stick a knife in my back.' Cato paused a moment. 'So this is my plea. You have played your part. You have done the favour asked of you by someone in Rome. You don't owe them anything else. That being the case, give me your word that you will not try to harm me, or Macro. I have no objection to being placed in danger's way. That is the duty of a soldier. Leave us be, and we will serve Rome, and you, loyally. And you will have cause to thank us. If you plot against us, then it is not only dishonourable, it is something worse. It is a waste of good men.'

When Cato concluded, there was a silence in the room before Quintatus cleared his throat. 'Is that the deal you offer me?'

'It's not a deal, sir. What would be the point of that? I have nothing to bargain with. As I said, it's simply a plea. If you give me your word that you will treat us as soldiers then that is good enough for me.'

'And you would trust my word?'

'Yes. What choice do I have? You, however, do have a choice, sir. You can choose to be a man of honour, a professional soldier, or you can choose to be no better than the rest of that nest of vipers back in Rome.' Cato forced himself to stand up straight and meet the legate's gaze head on. 'Do I have your word?'

Quintatus scratched his chin thoughtfully. 'Very well. I give you my word that I will treat you no differently to any other man under my command. Is that good enough for you?'

Cato reflected a moment and nodded. 'I don't think there's anything else to be said, sir. May I go and find that bed you mentioned?'

'Be my guest.'

Cato bowed his head and turned to half walk, half stumble from the room. The legate watched him go and was silent for a moment before he shook his head and muttered to himself, 'What a remarkable young man . . . A pity he has earned himself such powerful enemies.'

# CHAPTER THIRTY-SIX

For most of the following day the enemy were content to remain in their camp and the men of the garrison of Bruccium looked on with a sense of relief. The screams of the men who had been burned alive had unnerved many in the fort and even Macro, tired as he was, had been unable to get much sleep. It was long after midnight before the Silurians finished celebrating their victory and began to settle for the night, leaving their fires to die down. When the sun rose and there was no sign of any pending attack, Macro allowed most of the men to return to barracks to rest. A quarter of their number remained on duty, manning the wall and keeping watch for any sign of enemy activity. Orders given, Macro curled up on the floor of the tower and surrendered to the leaden weariness that weighed so heavily on his limbs.

He was woken at midday by one of the sentries, as he had ordered, and stirred stiffly to regard the enemy still sleeping off their festivities of the night before. Some small parties of younger men and boys were scouring the valley for firewood. Food was evidently running short, as a small herd of cattle and another of goats were driven into the camp from a nearby valley and were being slaughtered a short distance away from Caratacus's shelter. The first of the carcasses was dragged over to the parade ground and cut into chunks for roasting on a spit over a freshly lit fire. More cooking fires were lit as the remainder of the slaughtered animals were distributed to the rest of the camp. As the afternoon wore on, the smell of roasting meat drifted up to the defenders

Macro felt his stomach rumbling and contemplated just how good a roast leg of beef would taste after the meagre rations he had

348

been enduring in the fort. He even considered having some of the horses slaughtered but put the notion aside. It would be bad for the morale of the surviving Thracians. If it seemed inevitable that the fort would fall then Macro resolved to have the animals killed to deny them to the enemy. But only then. In the meantime there was only thin gruel and the last chunks of dried-out cheese and stale bread to look forward to. Thankfully, he mused, hunger had a way of making even the most unappetisingly bland food seem like a banquet.

Late in the afternoon, as the enemy feasting came to an end, a small party headed up the slope towards the main gate. They announced their approach with blaring horns and Macro saw that it was Caratacus, together with four men. One of them wore the black cloak of a Druid, while another was one of the prisoners. He had been stripped of his armour and boots and wore only a torn tunic. He was held firmly in the grip of two burly warriors and his head hung on his chest as they dragged him towards the fort. At the sound of the horns, Centurion Petillius climbed the tower and joined Macro. They exchanged a nod before Petillius gestured over the rail.

'What are they playing at now?'

'We'll know soon enough.'

Caratacus stopped beyond javelin range and put his hands on his hips as he addressed the defenders.

'Romans! Last night you witnessed the fate of some of your comrades. It is a pity that you had to watch the entertainment from afar. If you had shared the warmth of our fires you would have been there to see their flesh burn and hear the prayers they offered to your gods, begging for mercy.' Caratacus paused and looked round theatrically. 'Where are they now? Where is your Jupiter? Your Mars? It seems that your gods lack any interest in you. Or is it that they fear the power of our deities? In any case, the words of the dying fell on deaf ears. As I say, it is a shame you could not share such entertainment with us. To that end, I have come to offer you a small spectacle of your own. Here, where you can see and hear clearly.' He stepped up to the prisoner and roughly raised his chin so that his face was visible to the defenders.

349

'This is the commander of the Roman column we annihilated yesterday,' Caratacus announced.

Petillius cursed 'Shit. That puts paid to the prefect and the Thracians.'

The enemy commander continued addressing the garrison. 'This man is Tribune Gaius Mancinus, a proud and haughty aristocrat. No doubt one of those Romans who can trace his family line all the way back to Aeneas. Let us see how a Roman aristocrat dies. A simple execution would be too merciful. I have never been too proud to learn from my enemies, and the Blood Crows have proved to be excellent teachers. You have terrified my Silurian friends and I must show them that you are, after all, just mortal men. Not demons. So, when we take the fort I shall hand any survivors over to the Silurians to do with as they wish. The purpose of this afternoon's lesson is to show you that you will reap what you have sowed . . .' The enemy general stared at the faces watching him from the wall and then stepped aside and gestured to the Druid to continue.

The dark-robed figure approached Mancinus and took out a knife. He cut into the neckline of the tunic and then ripped it down as far as the tribune's groin. Then he made another cut until the cloth was rent top to bottom, exposing the front of the Roman officer.

'Sweet Mithras . . .' Petillius muttered. 'They're going to gut the poor bastard.'

Macro quickly turned to him. 'Get Maridius up here, fast as you can!'

Petillius ran back to the ladder and descended two rungs at a time. A moment later Macro heard his boots pounding towards the barracks where the Catuvellaunian prince was imprisoned. In front of the fort the Druid scored a shallow cut across Mancinus's chest. The tribune strained to free himself from the grip of the two warriors but they were strong men and held him firmly and his efforts came to nothing. The blood flowed down over his pale skin. The Druid waited for a moment before he cut into Mancinus's flesh again, an inch or so higher up where the Druid could see his handiwork more clearly. This time the Roman could not help crying out and the sound cut into Macro's heart. He raged against his enemy and his inability to do anything to help Mancinus.

As the Druid began to make a third cut, Macro turned away and hurried across to the rear of the tower and looked down into the fort, willing Petillius to appear with the prisoner. Another cry sounded from in front of the fort and Macro clenched his jaw in a silent grimace. Then he saw Petillius appear between two of the stable blocks, thrusting Maridius before him. The prisoner wore only the baggy breeches he had been left with after his questioning some days earlier. Although his face and body were bruised, the swelling around his eyes and lips had subsided.

'Bring the bastard up, quick!' Macro bellowed.

He turned and ran across the tower and waved his hands to attract the attention of Caratacus. 'Enough! Tell your Druid to put aside his blade!'

The enemy commander and his companions looked up at Macro while Mancinus's head rolled back and he let out a faint groan.

'What is it?' Caratacus called back. 'Do you think to try and stop our entertainment? I thought Romans were used to this. I thought you had stronger stomachs. Are you so easily unmanned by the sight of blood?'

Macro did not respond to the taunt. He knew he had to delay Mancinus's torment long enough for Maridius to reach the top of the tower. His mind struggled to outline a means of saving Mancinus.

'Listen, you fucking savage, I've had enough of your game. You want to play rough with your prisoners? Then so can we. If your Druid puts that knife to the tribune again then I swear to all the gods that you will regret it for what's left of your miserable bloody life.'

Caratacus laughed. 'Don't waste your breath on empty threats! Besides, my army would be most disappointed if I put an end to this spectacle. I have promised the tribune to the Druids to make a blood offering to our gods. Nothing can save him now!'

Macro heard sounds on the ladder behind him and saw Maridius being bundled up the ladder. He crossed to him and hauled him up on to the platform before dragging him across to the wooden rail. Clenching his fist in the long hair of the prisoner, Macro jerked his head up so that his face would be clearly visible to Caratacus and the others.

'Do you recognise your brother, Caratacus?' Macro shouted down the slope. 'If you do any more harm to Tribune Mancinus, then I'll match you cut for cut.' He drew his dagger from its scabbard and held it up for the enemy commander to see.

There was a tense stillness before Caratacus responded. 'You wouldn't dare. He is too valuable a hostage to Rome.'

'We are not in Rome!' Macro called back. 'We are in the arse end of the world. There is you, me and the two men we hold prisoner. If you harm the tribune, then I will harm Maridius. That is what will happen. Understand?'

Caratacus did not reply for a moment as he stared up at his younger brother and the Roman officer standing at his side. Then he spoke again. 'If you harm my brother, then I swear that you, and any of your men I take alive when the fort falls will be subject to every cruelty, every torture, every humiliation before you are allowed to die. And I will do the same for every Roman prisoner that my army takes until we have driven you Roman scum from our lands. This I swear!'

Macro ignored the threat and kept his silence. Behind him, Centurion Petillius muttered, 'He means it.'

'So do I.'

The Druid turned to Caratacus and there was a brief exchange before the Druid raised his voice and turned back to the prisoner and cut him again, this time opening up his cheek with a swift slash of the blade. Macro did not hesistate. He turned to Maridius and stabbed him in the jaw. Blood splattered down on to the floorboards of the tower. Maridius let out a deep bellow of pain.

'Hold him still!' Macro commanded.

Petillius and the two sentries closed round the prisoner and grasped his shoulders as vivid red blood coursed down his neck and into the hairs on his chest.

Caratacus hurled a wild curse at the fort and took several steps forward, his hand making to draw his sword. Then he stopped abruptly, slowly let the blade settle back in its scabbard and thrust his finger towards Macro.

'I will kill you! Kill you with my bare hands, and take your heart and feed it to my hounds!'

Macro smiled grimly. 'First you will have to take the fort.'

'The fort will be mine! You cannot hold out against me.'

'We'll see. Until then, take the tribune back to your camp and look after him. I shall want to see him alive every morning. If not, I will execute your brother.'

Caratacus let out a pained animal growl. 'It is out of my hands, Roman. The tribune belongs to the Druids now.'

'Then take him back.'

'I can't!'

'Who is in command? You, or that clown in the black cloak?'

Caratacus struggled to choke back his outrage. 'He is the High Druid of the Silurians, the chosen man of our gods. He is not mine to command.'

'I don't give a shit. Tell him to step away from the tribune!'

Caratacus turned to the Druid and they spoke again in heated tones. Then, with an impatient flick of his spare hand, the Druid turned back to Mancinus and stabbed him deep in the side and ripped the blade diagonally across his stomach. The tribune half groaned, half screamed, as his intestines bulged out of the wound and slid down over his groin. Raising his bloodied blade again, the Druid plunged it into Mancinus's heart, then stood back and raised his arms to the sky and began a shrill chant. The warriors released his arms and the body of the tribune collapsed to the ground.

'No!' Macro lurched at the wooden rail in the tower. 'You bastards! Fucking barbarians! Bastards!' Then he snatched out his sword and thrust the point towards Maridius's throat. His eyes blazed down at Caratacus. 'See this, and remember!'

Then, with all the brute strength he could muster, Macro rammed his sword up into the prisoner's skull and his crown erupted as scalp, bone and brains burst into the air. The body tensed like stone, veins standing out, before jerking savagely and then collapsing on to the floor of the tower as Macro wrenched his sword free.

There was a wild cry of rage from Caratacus and a moment later the rest of his army who had been watching from their camp let out a roar of fury.

Macro turned back and saw Caratacus take out his sword and stand over Mancinus's body. Then he rained down blows, hacking

353

the flesh like a frenzied butcher. Macro tore his gaze away, steeling himself for what he must do. Taking a deep breath he hacked through Maridius's neck. It took several blows before the final bit of gristle parted. Switching his sword to his left hand, he picked up the head by the hair and swung it at arm's length before sending it sailing through the air. It bounced on the slope and then rolled before coming to rest a short distance from Caratacus.

Still with his bloodied blade in hand, Caratacus stared at the head, his body trembling, then he thrust his sword directly at Macro and screamed, 'I will kill you! Kill you all! Kill every Roman! Every man, woman and child! I will tear down this cursed fort with my own hands! You will not live to see another day! None of you!' He swept his sword across the wall of the fort, then turned away, clumsily sheathed his blade and began to stride down the slope towards the camp, his hands clasped to his face as his shoulders heaved with grief. One of his men stooped to pick up the head of Maridius and joined the others who kept their distance from their commander as they followed him.

'Now we're for it,' Petillius said quietly.

Macro nodded. 'They'll be coming for us as soon as it's dark. I want every man on the wall, fed and ready for the fight of their lives.'

He looked down at the headless body in its pool of spreading blood. 'First, get rid of that.'

Macro took a last look at Mancinus, though there was nothing left to recognise of the young man. Now the same fate threatened him. Macro's lips pressed together tightly and he shook his head. No. He would deny Caratacus his sport. When the end came, he would go down fighting, sword in hand, spitting curses at the enemy until the very last beat of his heart.

They came even before the final glimmer of the setting sun had faded in the western sky. As soon as Caratacus had returned to his camp the enemy had begun to assemble, and fresh bundles of faggots were hastily prepared and piled high on the parade ground. The tribesmen went about their work with a sullen quietness that was out of character and it was clear to Macro that they were determined to

354

avenge the death of Maridius. In the failing light of dusk, Macro sent for his surviving officers. The small group of men faced him him behind the main gate.

Macro stared at them and was gratified that none seemed to show any sign of fear. 'You all know what's coming. Caratacus means to take the fort with the next attack. The enemy's blood is up and we can expect that they will take heavy casualties and still keep going. Once they get over the wall and establish a foothold, then the game is up for us. If it happens then it would be better to die than risk capture. Make certain your men understand that. We need to match their resolve if we are to stand any chance of surviving this. I won't lie to you. We may hold off the first attack, but after that it's anyone's guess. If the fort falls, then we're dead men. And it will fall. There's too few of us to hold the wall. Too many of them, and no prospect of help from outside. The only choice that concerns us now is how we die: like soldiers, or like dogs.' Macro paused and softened his tone as he turned to the fort's surgeon. 'I don't want any men taken alive. If the wall is taken I'll have the trumpeter sound five long notes. That is the signal. You and your orderlies will deal with the wounded. Understand?'

The surgeon nodded. 'Yes, sir. I'll see to it that it's quick.'

'Good man.' Macro looked at the senior officer of the Thracian cohort. 'The same goes for the horses. Have some of your men ready. The moment the signal is given they are to lame them. It'll be quicker than killing them and just as effective.'

'Why not kill them now, sir? While there's time.'

Macro shook his head and smiled. 'Despite everything, I never give in. Never. Even now, there may be a way out of this. I'll not admit defeat until the end. And if that's the fate the gods have decided for us, then and only then do we accept it. Now, lads, to your posts.' He held out his hand and clasped forearms with each officer before they left to rejoin their men. Then, with a heavy sigh, Macro climbed back up to the tower and strapped on his helmet and waited for the enemy.

In the dying light the Silurians formed up in front of their camp, a dark mass of men and weapons set against the glow of their fires. For a time there was silence, and then a horn sounded a deep note

355

that echoed off the surrounding hills and the tribesmen surged forward without a sound.

Macro cupped his hands to his mouth and called out to the garrison, 'Here they come! Stand to!'

Along the wall the legionaries and Thracians stepped up to the parapet. Macro watched as the tribesmen swarmed up the slope. There was another blast from the horn and this time it was met with a deafening roar from the warriors. He could not help a cruel smile. Even though Caratacus had chosen to attack from the darkness, his men would arrive in a wave and be hard to miss. Especially as they neared the outer ditch.

He called out again. 'Torches!'

All along the wall fire glittered in shallow arcs as the defenders hurled small blazing bundles of kindling tied to lengths of wood. The torches struck the slope and rolled a short distance. Their flames cast pools of light by which Macro could see the first of the attackers loom out of the darkness. Their cheering had died down as they struggled up the incline towards the fort.

'Ready javelins!'

The defenders raised their weapons, throwing arms drawn back, waiting for the order.

Macro waited until he could see men all along the line of the slope, clambering up towards the outer ditch. He calmly waited a moment longer until he was certain they were within range so that not a single weapon would be wasted.

'Loose!'

A chorus of grunts greeted the order as the men hurled their weapons out into the darkness. Then the shafts flickered into view of the glow of the torches as they rained down into the packed ranks of the enemy. Macro saw several of the tribesmen struck down and there were cries of pain from the horde racing towards the ditch.

'Continue, at will!'

His men snatched up more javelins and launched them into the oncoming enemy. The last of the fort's stock would quickly be exhausted, but Macro had decided that it would be better to use up the weapons while his men still could. Scores of warriors were felled by the deadly missiles before the first of them reached the ditch and rushed down the slope. Now Macro could see the enemy's intention. Each man carried a small bundle of sticks. The warriors crossed the ditch and climbed the inner slope before placing their burdens at the foot of the wall and rushing away. And out of the gloom came the first of the wicker shelters, carried up to the edge of the ditch and set down, side by side, to form lengths of a makeshift wall to protect the attackers. The steady flow of javelins continued to claim casualties and the bodies of the dead and the wounded lay strewn across the top of the slope and in the ditch in front of the fort. And still they came on, dashing out from behind their shelters to add more combustible material to the steadily growing piles ranged along the wall. Most of the warriors' efforts were concentrated on the outside of the gatehouse, thrusting faggots into the gaps left where the garrison had hurriedly blocked the ruined outer gate.

A sharp, splintering crack caused Macro to duck down. The were more impacts on either side and he hissed a curse. The enemy had brought forward some slingers who were loosing their shot at close range from behind the shelters. Risking a quick glance along the wall to the right of the gatehouse, he could see one man was already down, sprawled on his back on the inner slope of the turf rampart. Another man was struck as he took aim with his javelin, his head snapping back with a sharp clang, his weapon dropping from his fingers as he collapsed and lay still. It was too dangerous to keep it up with the slingers so close to the wall, Macro decided. He snatched a deep breath and bellowed, 'Cease javelins! Take cover!'

The other officers repeated the order and the defenders lowered their weapons and crouched down behind the palisade as more shot zipped over and rattled off the timbers of the wall. The fort's medical orderlies hurried forward to pick up the casualties and carry them away to the infirmary and Macro wondered how many more men would fall during the night.

For the first hour of the night the enemy continued to pile their combustibles against the fort and their slingers were watchful for any sign of movement along the wall, loosing off their deadly shot at any Roman who dared to show himself. Macro risked the occasional glance to follow the enemy's progress and for a time he saw Caratacus and his shield bearer striding behind the shelters, surveying the work of his men. At length Caratacus called down to the camp and a short while later small flames flickered as they approached the fort and Macro saw teams of men scurry up to the piled wood with buckets. The sharp smell of pitch reached his nose and he knew that time was running out for the garrison. Then the stench of acrid smoke caught in his throat. The crackling sound of burning timber spread along the wall as one pile of wood after another was ignited. The rim of the parapet and hoardings were sharply defined against the loom of the fire burning at the foot of the gatehouse. A yellow tongue of fire licked up into Macro's field of vision.

'Shit. Shit. Shit,' he hissed through clenched teeth.

There was a cry of alarm from below. 'There's smoke in here! Get out! Get out!'

Macro turned and saw that the handful of men with him on the tower were looking at him anxiously. He smiled calmly. 'Time to move, lads. I don't fancy being a burned offering to some fucking barbarian god.'

The legionaries scrambled over to the ladder and descended out of sight. As Macro rose to follow suit, he felt the stinging heat of the flames rising up in front of the gatehouse. He swung himself on to the ladder and stepped down the rungs, immediately aware of the smoke starting to fill the watchroom. The doors leading out on to the walkway behind the wall were both open and there was a light breeze as air was sucked inside to feed the flames. Thin slivers of brilliant light were visible through the chinks in the gatehouse's timbers, and the roar of flames and crackle of burning wood filled Macro's ears. He breathed in and abruptly doubled over, coughing violently, and his eyes smarted. Making for the nearest door, he emerged from the gatehouse and staggered a short distance along the wall before crouching down.

It took a moment to clear his lungs and blink away the tears from his stinging eyes before he could take in the situation. Several fires were burning along the length of the wall facing the slope down to the parade ground, the biggest of which was the blaze raging up the front of the gatehouse.

'Sir!'

Macro looked round to see Centurion Petillius standing below him at the foot of the rampart, his face lit by the flames. Petillius was pointing towards the gatehouse. 'Shall I get one of the centuries to fetch water?'

Macro thought a moment and shook his head. 'They'd be too exposed to the slingers. Besides, there's too little left in the cistern to make a difference. Just pull the men back from those sections on fire. The rest can stay in place.'

Petillius saluted and hurried away to carry out Macro's order. He stayed on the wall for a short while longer, until the pain in his lungs had passed off, and then descended into the fort and stood back by the end of the nearest barrack block. The fires had established themselves now and flames licked around the angle of the gatehouse. There was nothing that could be done to save the structure, Macro realised. It would be gradually consumed by the flames and eventually collapse. The fire would burn on for a few hours before it died down. Come the dawn, it would be a smouldering ruin, and there would be nothing to prevent Caratacus and his army from picking their way over the charred remains and falling on the waiting men of the garrison.

When Petillius returned to his side, Macro told him to leave a handful of men on watch and order the others to come down and rest between the barrack blocks.

'And what of the horses and the men in the hospital, sir?' Petillius asked quietly.

Macro stared at the flames for a moment before he answered. 'We'll deal with it at the last moment. Best not to lower the men's spirits before then. I'll give the order when the time comes.'

'Yes, sir.'

'Once you've seen to the men, get some rest yourself, Petillius.'

'So should you, sir.'

Macro patted him on the shoulder. 'I'm fine.' He jerked his thumb towards the fires. 'Until that lot burns out, we're not going to be troubled. I'll be at headquarters for a while, if anything comes up.'

Petillius nodded, then strode away to the nearest section of men hunched down behind the wall. Macro turned towards the heart of the fort and saw the resigned expressions in the faces of the men he passed, lit by the ruddy hue of the flames. There was no doubting the fate that would face them the following morning and Macro felt too tired to humour them with any words of false hope as he trudged past. Back in the garrison commander's office, he sat down and took out a blank waxed tablet. Picking up a stylus, he composed a letter to his mother. The sentiments he offered were simple and honest; regret for the events of the past, and hope that she would be proud that he had died with honour. It was a short farwell, and when he had finished the handful of lines pressed into the wax, Macro read them over, then shut the tablet and bound it together. He took it down to the underground strongroom and placed it carefully under one of the chests of records. As he emerged from headquarters, he felt a calmness in his heart, a sense that all but one of his duties had been carried out.

The fires burned on through the hours of night, the flames peaking and then slowly beginning to subside. Just after midnight the tower groaned and slowly lurched out towards the slope before crashing across the causeway and into the ditch, provoking a cheer from the enemy beyond. After a while the cheering faded and the only sound was the crackle of the flames, steadily diminishing. For a while a few of the timber frames of the gatehouse still stood to remind Macro of its outline. Then they, too, collapsed on to the shrinking mass beneath the flames. As the first smear of grey light spread along the eastern horizon, Macro donned his helmet, took up his shield and climbed the rampart to join one of the legionaries tasked with keeping watch on the enemy. Glancing warily over the parapet, Macro could see the wicker shelters and a handful of the enemy looking on from behind.

'Rest of 'em fell back a while ago, sir,' the sentry reported. 'Resting up while the fires burned out.'

Macro nodded. 'They'll be back soon enough.'

The sentry was quiet for a moment before he responded. 'Better that it's over with quickly.'

'Just as long as you take a few of the bastards with you, eh?'

They exchanged a weary smile before continuing to watch for any sign of the enemy stirring to make their final assault on the fort.

Little by little dawn stole across the horizon and the darkness began to withdraw, revealing the slope below the fort, and then the parade ground, and the valley beyond. A landscape almost devoid of life and movement. Only a handful of figures were visible, picking over the ground before hurrying away towards the far end of the valley. At length even those behind the wicker shelters fell back, formed a small column and marched off

'What the fuck are they playing at?' Macro growled suspiciously, the hairs on the back of his neck tingling.

'Sir!' The sentry stood up and pointed to the east, towards the head of the valley. Macro turned and saw the head of a column of horsemen cresting the pass and descending the track that led to the fort. For a moment he dared not give in to hope. He uttered no word, not even as the other sentries strung out along those sections of the wall still standing started to shout in excited voices, calling the other men up on to the wall to see for themselves. Centurion Petillius ran up to join Macro, squinting towards the column edging towards them like a giant centipede.

'Ours?'

'Ours?' Macro laughed harshly. 'Of course they're fucking ours.'

# CHAPTER THIRTY-SEVEN

Legate Quintatus surveyed the bodies scattered across the ground and in the ditch before turning his gaze towards the gaping ruins where the gatehouse and several sections of the wall had burned down. His nose wrinkled at the acrid stench of charred timber as he turned to face Macro.

'Must have been quite a fight, Centurion.'

'Yes, sir,' Macro replied flatly.

'This is the kind of action that makes heroes out of the men who fought it,' the legate continued. 'I'm sure there will be something in it for you when my report reaches Governor Ostorius, and he sends it on to Rome. The garrison at Bruccium has distinguished itself and there will be awards to fix to the standards of your cohort, and your Thracians as well.' He turned and flashed a smile at Cato. 'The Blood Crows have won themselves something of a fierce reputation. Of course much of that was down to the efforts of Centurion Quertus. It is a shame he did not live to see this day.'

'Yes, sir. It is a shame.'

'Never mind. I'm sure his name will live on.'

Cato nodded. 'I'm certain of it.'

Quintatus turned his attention back to Macro. 'You have your orders. Make sure that the fort is completely destroyed. I don't want any of the enemy occupying this position after we leave the valley. That will be all, Centurion.'

Macro saluted and turned away to make his way back through the breach and into the fort. The legate stared after him for a moment and shrugged.

'A hard fighter, that man, but something of a surly character.'

Cato stifled his anger at this description of his friend. 'The centurion is exhausted, sir. He can hardly be expected to provide stimulating conversation in his state.'

Quintatus rounded on him sharply. 'By all means defend your officers, but I'll thank you not to express yourself in such an insubordinate manner. You, and the centurion, may have come out of this heroes but I advise you not to test my good will too far. Do we understand each other?'

'Yes, sir. Clearly.'

'Very well. Once your men have completed the destruction of Bruccium, have them join the rearguard. There'll be no time to rest them, I'm afraid. We have to march fast if we are to keep up with Caratacus. We can't afford to lose contact and let him give us the slip again. Ostorius would not be very forgiving.' Quintatus smiled. 'Even though it was the governor who lost track of him the first time. It would be gratifying to put an end to Caratacus before Ostorius reached the scene. Most gratifying indeed.'

Cato felt a stab of irritation. The commanders of armies had no right to pursue their political rivalries in the field. Men's lives were at stake, and a general owed it to those whose fates he controlled to focus his thoughts on the successful outcome of the campaign. The defeat of the enemy was all that mattered. Who claimed the credit for it was irrelevant. Or at least it should be. But there were times when it seemed that war was only ever a continuation of politics, Cato mused. No more so than in Rome where the two fields so frequently overlapped in the careers of those at the highest levels of society.

Legate Quintatus was surveying the column of his army marching past the ruined fort, thousands of men, mules, horses and wagons heavily laden with the accoutrements of war.

'We have wasted too many years trying to bring peace to this province. There has been little chance to win glory thanks to the Emperor claiming that the place was conquered a few months after we first landed. But there's a world of difference between the official view and the reality on the ground, eh? I'll be glad to be posted to a frontier where a reputation can be made. But I am getting ahead of myself.' Quintatus made a self-deprecating gesture with his hand. 'First we must complete the destruction of the enemy. With

Caratacus beaten we can finally put an end to native resistance on this miserable island.'

'I hope so, sir.'

The legate turned to frown at Cato. 'You doubt it?'

Cato framed his reply carefully. 'We have to defeat Caratacus first, sir. We'll only know if it is all over after that has happened. Even then, he has proved to be a resourceful enemy. Who knows? He may still have plenty of surprises up his sleeve. There are other tribes who haven't paid homage to Rome. And then there's the Druids, always ready to stir up hatred towards us.' He shrugged. 'I fear that it will be a while yet before Britannia knows peace.'

Quintatus let out an impatient sigh. 'Your spirit of optimism is somewhat less than awe-inspiring, Prefect Cato. I am sure you are a delight to have around when the morale of the men needs a lift.'

'Optimism is a commendable enough quality, sir, but the hard realities of a situation seldom pay heed to good humour, in my experience.'

'In your experience?' The legate's lips curled slightly in amusement. 'I trust that you will live long enough to do justice to the term.'

Cato met his gaze steadily. 'So do I, sir.'

Quintatus beckoned to the soldier holding his horse and the man hurriedly led the beast over and handed the reins to the legate, before bowing and offering his hands to give the officer an easy step up into the saddle. He looked down at Cato and his voice took on a curt tone of command.

'Destroy the fort, assemble what's left of your command and join the column.'

'Yes, sir.'

They exchanged a salute and Quintatus urged his mount into a trot, down the track towards the parade ground over which a column of legionaries was marching. Cato watched him for a moment, wondering if he could share the legate's optimism about the imminent end to the war against Caratacus and those who still resisted the brute power of Rome. Despite his reservations, he wanted to hope that the long campaign would soon be over. With Britannia at peace, he could safely send for Julia to join him. In time, many of the units of the island's garrison would be redeployed and a better posting could be found. Somewhere warmer, more civilised. He looked up at the grey crags on the mountains on either side of the valley and shivered. This was wild, hostile country and it was hard to see how it could ever be tamed. It would be better never to bring Julia to these shores. When the natives eventually gave in, it would be best to request a new command closer to Rome. He did not yet dare to hope for a position in the capital. Not while there were still those at the palace who bore him ill will. But that would not last forever, Cato reflected wryly. Those who plotted the fate of Rome at the emperor's side seldom lasted the distance. Soon there would be a new Emperor. More than likely it would be Nero, the adopted son of Claudius, and Cato had once saved the young prince's life. If the spirited youth became Emperor, there would be a purge of the old guard and Cato would be free to return to Rome, and Julia, and live in peace.

With that warm thought in his heart, he turned away from the passing column of infantry and picked his way through the breach beside the ruined gatehouse and went to find Macro.

The interior of the fort was heavy with the stench of burned timber and the more acrid odour of pitch. Small parties of men were preparing piles of combustible materials in the doorways of the barrack blocks and stables. Cato could not help observing the irony that Roman soldiers would complete the destruction that their enemies had failed to achieve.

He found Macro at headquarters, supervising the loading of the garrison's pay chest and records into a wagon. A section of legionaries had been assigned the duty. It seemed that Macro still did not trust the Thracians.

'How is it going, Macro?'

The centurion saluted as his friend approached and ran a hand through his hair and scratched the back of his neck as he collected his thoughts.

'The sick and wounded have already joined the baggage train. Along with the Silurian prisoners. The cavalry mounts have been removed from the stables, along with all the equipment we can carry in the remaining wagons.' He nodded towards the chests being loaded. 'Once that lot's sorted then we're done.'

'And our own kit?'

He gestured towards the wagon in the courtyard. 'Already loaded.'

Cato nodded. 'Good. Once the wagon is out of the fort you can give the order for the fires to be lit.'

'I'll be glad to do it.'

Cato glanced at his friend with a curious expression. 'You're pleased by the prospect?'

'Why not? Why feel sorry for the loss of this place?' Macro cast his eyes around the courtyard in front of the headquarters building. 'It has too much of the feel of Quertus about it. It's as if his shadow still lingers here. No surprise in that, I guess. He was not the kind of bastard who would be welcomed into the afterlife. Quertus deserves an underworld all of his own, to my mind.'

Cato was taken aback. It was unlike Macro to be in such low spirits. He addressed his friend in a gentle tone.

'Macro. Quertus is dead. I killed him. It's over.'

Macro shook his head slowly. 'Not for me, lad. I've served for twenty years in the legions, seen plenty of sights in my time and known some bad characters, but nothing like Quertus. His heart was touched by darkness.'

'Darkness?' Cato pursed his lips and thought a moment before he continued. 'I suppose so.'

'Suppose?' Macro chuckled humourlessly. 'Fuck that. He was insane. Quertus had an evil streak in him as wide as the Tiber. He was little better than a wild animal and cunning as a snake. He needed to be put down. I only wish I had been the one to do it. Not you.' He regarded Cato anxiously. 'I hope there's going to be no repercussions.'

'Not for a while, at least. The legate assumes from what I said that he died in battle. If I'm required to write a full report then the truth will be known. As I'm sure it will in any case. There were witnesses. Word will get out.'

'True, but there'll be few of them spoken in praise of Quertus, given that he was about to abandon the rest of us to Caratacus. I won't be the only one to back up your account. Not by a long way.'

366

Cato smiled gratefully. 'I know. I have no worries on that account.' His expression became more thoughtful. 'It's a pity that it had to happen. There was some merit in Quertus's tactics.'

'You're not serious?'

'Why not? Fear is the best weapon that can be deployed in war. And he put fear into the hearts of the enemy sure enough. His mistake was in putting fear into the hearts of his own men.'

'You do him too much credit, Cato. He was a bad 'un. That's all. Bad, and mad, to the core, and he touched others with it. His men, the Silurians . . . even me.' Macro's gaze slid away from Cato as he vividly recalled the deaths of Mancinus and Maridius. He winced, as if in pain. 'Don't make the mistake of speaking well of the dead. Some don't deserve it.' Macro glanced past Cato towards the wagon and called out, 'All right, the bloody thing's loaded so what are you waiting for? Get the wagon out of the fort and down to the parade ground and make sure no thieving bastards get their hands on it. Move!'

The driver of the wagon cracked his whip and the heavy wheels rumbled into motion as the vehicle and its escort left the courtyard and made for the side gate and the track leading round the fort to the parade ground. The melancholy spell of a moment earlier was broken and both men assumed the veneer of their rank as they turned back to each other.

'That's the lot.' Macro drew himself up. 'Fort's ready to be fired, sir.'

Cato nodded. 'Then I'll wait for you with the rest of the men outside. Carry on.'

As Cato made his way back towards the burned remains of the wall facing the parade ground he heard Macro's voice barking out the orders to the incendiary parties. By the time Cato reached the bottom of the slope and turned to look up, dark columns of smoke were swirling into the sky. Macro and a handful of his men emerged from one of the breaches in the wall and descended the track to join their comrades. Cato waved aside the man holding his horse. He felt that he wanted to walk for a while. The survivors of the garrison formed up and Cato waved his arm forward to signal them to advance and they fell into line at the rear of the column.

Far ahead, Legate Quintatus's cavalry were snapping at the heels of Caratacus and his warriors. Soon they would be forced to turn and fight. There would be a great battle which would test the courage and skill of the men of both armies, Cato knew. If Rome triumphed, there was a chance for peace in the new province. If not, the bitter war would drag on year after year. The prospect depressed Cato. More death. More suffering. The natives would desperately cling to the hope that they would ultimately humble Rome. That would never happen, Cato mused. No emperor of Rome would allow it to happen, whatever the cost. That was what Caratacus and his followers should really fear.

Again, it came back to fear. Perhaps, in that regard, Quertus had been right all along.

'We're a bit thin on the ground,' Macro said, breaking Cato's thoughts. He turned to gesture at the small column of men and horses behind them. 'Both cohorts have suffered heavy losses.'

'True, but the legate has promised us first call on the replacements coming up from Londinium. We'll return to the front line soon enough.'

Macro smiled at the prospect of breaking in some new recruits. 'Back to straightforward, proper soldiering. At last.'

'That's the spirit!' Cato grinned at his friend. 'We'll drill them until they drop and when we do go up against the enemy, they'll do us proud. Your men and the Blood Crows will be the best cohorts in the army. There won't be a tribe in Britannia that can stand against us.'

Macro nodded. 'I'll drink to that.'

'The first jar is on me, as soon as we make camp tonight.'

'Why wait?' Macro flipped his cloak back and drew out his canteen. 'Took the liberty of helping myself to what was left of the Falernian. Not bad stuff.' He offered the canteen to Cato. 'You first. Rank has its privileges.'

Cato shook his head. 'So does friendship. After you.'

Macro laughed, pulled out the stopper and took a healthy swig before he passed the canteen over to Cato. The prefect thought for a moment before he raised the canteen in a toast.

'To Rome, to honour and, above all, to friendship!'

# AUTHOR'S NOTE

History books often refer to the Claudian 'conquest' of Britain in AD43 whereas the more accurate word would be 'invasion'. There's a world of difference between the two terms. Rome, the ancient world's longest enduring superpower, had set its eyes on Britain a hundred years before the Claudian campaign when Julius Caesar was brutally busy carving his name into posterity by massacring the Gauls and seizing their lands for the then republic. The invasion of Britain, a land long considered the acme of barbarism and savagery, would cement his reputation in the minds of the Roman public. As it did, despite the fact that neither of his two incursions amounted to more than a brief reconnaissance of the southern part of the island. By picking up where Caesar had left off, Emperor Claudius was attempting to add lustre to a reign that had got off to a very shaky start after the murder of his predecessor and his own elevation only taking place when the Praetorian Guard recognised that returning Rome to a republic would rob them of their rather extensive perks.

In any case, the invasion went ahead and with the defeat of the native army led by Caratacus outside his own capital the Emperor was content to declare the 'mission accomplished', with the same temerity, inaccuracy and trimming that was deployed by President Bush in 2003 with regard to Iraq. There was a celebration in Rome and the Emperor, basking in the approval of his subjects, moved on to other matters, leaving the army in Britain to put the seal on the conquest and settle the province so that it could pay its way.

But the conquest of the island was very far from complete and it took a few years to create a frontier from the Wash to the Severn, and then more years to push it farther north and west, at least as far as the mountains of modern Wales. And that is where the Roman advance stalled. The legions and the auxiliaries were confronted with two of the most determined and courageous of tribes, the Ordovices and the Silures, led by a commander who had eventually worked out the appropriate tactics to use against the Roman war machine. Rather than confront his enemy in set-piece battles, Caratacus adopted the time-honoured expedient of 'guerrilla' warfare against a more powerful opponent, striking at isolated forts and columns and melting away before the concentrated strength of the legions. In this he was aided by the geography of Wales which at the time was heavily forested as well as possessing a mountainous interior. Perfect terrain for the kind of war he now waged against the Romans.

As is usual in such conflicts, the guerrilla has the initiative, and as long as he can evade situations where the enemy can deploy overwhelming force, the resistance can be continued. By striking at the most vulnerable element of the native forces led by Caratacus, in the manner in which Centurion Quertus carried the war to the Silurian villages, the Romans could retake the initiative and force the natives on to the back foot, as happens with my novel's depiction of Caratacus being obliged to counter the attacks of the Blood Crows.

Such tactics might work well in a world where there was no mass media on hand to report the 'collateral' damage, and it is interesting to ponder the fact that the effectiveness of conventional military power is inversely proportional to the breadth and duration of the mass, and increasingly social, media that reports on its activities. Conversely, the measure of success of the enemy guerrilla forces is directly proportional to the same media. How modern generals must envy the free hand that was dealt to their ancient predecessors!

Meanwhile, back to Cato and Macro. Having driven off Caratacus and his army they must now march with Legate Quintatus and attempt to chase down the native army and force it to turn and give battle. Despite the legate's optimism, Caratacus has defied Rome more than once when her generals had thought they had finally crushed the natives' will to resist. The conquest of Britannia is still some way off, and the struggle faced by Macro, Cato and the soldiers

370

of Rome must continue. There are great challenges ahead that will test our two heroes to the utmost – and they will return to confront Caratacus in the next novel in the series!

# IT'S A SOLDIER'S LIFE

## EXCLUSIVE WATERSTONES
## INTERVIEW WITH
## SIMON SCARROW

*Q: It's on Cato's mind in THE BLOOD CROWS that his relationship with Macro has changed because he has been promoted above his old friend. Do you know of any individuals who've experienced this situation, and how have they handled it? Can a friendship survive this kind of change?*

A: Due to the natures of Cato and Macro it was inevitable that Cato would overtake his friend in military rank one day, provided he lived long enough – no easy feat given the trouble they frequently find themselves in! I knew from the outset that the day would come and had been mentally preparing for the moment. I had wondered how each might cope with the new situation.

I realise that it might sound a bit odd, but to me the two men are very real characters, almost like old friends. They have grown in depth across the last eleven books and these days the exchanges they have take place in real time in my head and I feel like I am simply there as a glorified amanuensis at times, struggling to keep up with the lines tossed to and fro between the young, idealistic Cato and his plain-thinking, world-weary one-timer mentor. So I think I know these two individuals better than most.

For Cato it is something of a struggle. For many years he has been accustomed to the comfort of relying on Macro's vast experience and expertise in military matters. Macro has indulged him in the manner of a father, or older brother. At times Cato has had to rein in Macro's impulsive tendencies but he has always respected and had affection for his older friend. The first novel in which Cato exercised superior rank to Macro was THE LEGION and right from the outset there was a delicacy in the new arrangement. Cato was not wholly ready to issue orders to Macro and from to time needed, and still needs, the tacit approval of the veteran. This has become less of a burden as time has passed and Cato has adjusted to the reversal in their rank. Though it is not necessarily a reversal in their roles. How could it be, with the wealth of knowledge Macro has about soldiering?

From Macro's perspective, the new development in their relation-ship is bittersweet. When he first met Cato, the young recruit was about as green as a recruit can be, and yet early on Macro recognised Cato's courage, determination and intelligence and took it upon himself to act as mentor to the new recruit. This act of faith has paid off handsomely as Cato has become a fine officer with the ability to go far in the Roman army.

To my mind, the nearest equivalent in the modern army, albeit over a far shorter span of time, is the relationship between the NCOs and the cadets at Sandhurst. There is no question that the former are towering figures of authority in the minds of those who aspire to become officers. Behind the barked orders and streams of invective lies a world of experience that commands the respect of young men. Even after they receive their commissions, any officer worth their salt knows that he or she would be a fool to ignore the respectfully offered advice of NCOs. For their part, though they would seldom admit it, the NCOs take a fatherly pride in those they have led through the tough training regime to the point where they can take command of a body of soldiers and prove themselves worthy of their rank.

Q: *As we read this novel, Rome's grip on Britannia seems very tenuous. Yet the Romans held a substantial chunk of the island for another 300 years. What were the key elements in Rome's success in consolidating their victories and pacifying the tribes?*

A: The first point that needs to be made is that the Roman conquest of Britannia was very much a political decision. Nearly a hundred years before the Claudian campaign Julius Caesar had made two attempts to invade the island. He did this to enhance his reputation, since in the Roman mind Britannia was an island of mysteries, and the channel which separates her from the continent was seen by the Romans as the natural oceanic boundary of the known world. Therefore to cross that stretch of water was to go where no Roman had dared to go before. That Caesar had failed to complete the job meant that any Roman emperor who managed to subdue Britannia would be outdoing the achievements of the greatest individual in Roman history. It fell to Claudius to carry out the deed, a man desperately in need of a signal success to shore up his shaky grip on the throne he had only just inherited following the assassination of his predecessor, Caligula.

The ancient Britons were in no way a united people. The island was divided into tribal kingdoms that were frequently at war with one another. Even when faced by the imminent prospect of a Roman invasion only a handful of tribes allied with the powerful Catuvellauni to resist the invaders. Other tribes either negotiated alliances with Rome or sat on their hands once the legions stepped ashore and awaited the outcome. There was little love lost between the native kingdoms. Indeed, one of the tribes which was at the forefront of the Boudiccan revolt, the Trinovantes, had only recently been conquered by the Catuvellauni before the invasion. When the revolt broke out, their rage was as much directed against their former native overlords as it was against the Romans.

This, of course, made it somewhat easier for the Romans, who could play the game of tribal politics for their own ends much of the time. In order to consolidate their hold over the tribal lands they assimilated, the Romans built a network of forts linked by roads so that they might police the areas under their control. Generally, this proved to be a successful strategy since any simmering discontent could be nipped in the bud by the swift concentration of forces in the affected area.

At the same time the Romans were adept in co-opting native rulers by showering them with honours, gifts and easy credit (though some of them will have rued not reading the small print when the loans were called in. Witness the ire of the Iceni when the Roman bailiffs came calling). Along with the titles and gold, there was no question that the native leaders were seduced by the luxuries of the Roman lifestyle: wine, baths, under-floor heating and sundry other refinements that made living in Britannia somewhat more bearable.

Whether the Romans managed to win over the majority of the native population is open to doubt, as Stuart Laycock has argued in his recent and fascinating book, BRITANNIA: THE FAILED STATE.

*Q: Macro and Cato have fought in many a battle, and Macro is not a young man any more. What might happen to him as he approaches the end of his career? Have your researches revealed the average lifespan of an army regular in the Roman army of the time? And are there statistics to show what percentage of soldiers survived to enjoy a golden retirement?*

A: Macro is in his mid-forties at the time THE BLOOD CROWS is set. That would mean he is close to completing his period of enlistment. Many casual sources about the Roman army suggest that the men served for twenty-five years and received a bonus and plot of land on discharge. In reality, discharges happened every other year so a soldier might serve twenty-four or twenty-six years. In some cases they served far longer. When General Germanicus arrived on the Rhine to take up command he was accosted by wizened soldiers who put his fingers in their mouths to show that they had no teeth left. So the story goes. In any case, it would seem that the period of service was somewhat more flexible than some historians allow.

For centurions, like Macro, there were other options to taking an honourable discharge. Since it would have been a shame to lose such valuable experience, re-enlistment was encouraged for the best centurions. Some would stay on and take up the post of Camp Prefect, acting in place of a legion's legate whenever the other was called away from their command.

It is next to impossible to indicate the average lifespan of a soldier, or how many reached retirement. So much depended on whether a soldier served out his time on a relatively peaceful frontier, or was committed to a campaign, such as the conquest of Britannia. What we can be reasonably sure about was that the life expectancy of a soldier, combat permitting, was somewhat longer than his civilian counterpart. Regular exercise, decent pay (with the possibility of imperial bonuses, or booty), a healthy diet and good quality medical facilities set him apart from those living in the crowded, filthy tenements of Rome. That is why a career in the army remained an attractive option for a very long time.

*Q: Do accounts of modern-day heroism in the army inspire your descriptions of characters and actions in the novels? Or are the forms of warfare so far apart that there's little to draw on?*

A: The nature of warfare has changed tremendously over the centuries. Perhaps the key aspect has been the physical distance between combatants in most encounters. In the days of Macro and Cato you would be close enough to the man you were fighting to see every detail of his features, and to register your enemy through all your senses. Today, much of the killing is carried out at a distance. What Cato and Macro would have made of drone pilots sitting in darkened bunkers in England launching their weapons at enemies several thousand miles away is anyone's guess!

But that does not mean that heroism is dying out. All through history, and no doubt in the future, there will always be examples of outstanding heroism. Just as there will be episodes of close combat every bit as physical and perilous as the encounters that Macro and Cato find themselves in. While there is much to admire in real-world examples, I am occasionally disturbed to see young men aspire to heroism as an end in itself. Rather it should be regarded as the courageous response to an unavoidable situation.

The term 'hero' derives from the Greek *heros*, which referred to an individual with superhuman powers who was regarded as a demigod after their death. It's easy to see the allure of such a concept, but it rather overlooks the contradiction: you may want to be a (super)hero, but wherefore genuine heroism if you have superhuman powers? Too many young men confuse real heroism with a desire to win some measure of immortal fame.

For me the heroism of Macro and Cato is entirely rooted in their reaction to the situations that befall them. They do not set out to be heroes, but when the situation demands it they will respond according to the soldier's code. In that, they are no different to the genuine military heroes of the modern age, such as Johnson Beharry VC.

Q: *How easily could a modern-day soldier adapt to life in the Roman army? If a fit young man in his twenties was transported from Afghanistan to Britannia, AD 51, would he be of the necessary fitness level and could he quickly learn Roman military tactics? Would he be able to teach the Romans anything, given that so much of his expertise would be based on sophisticated twenty-first-century weapons and technological advances?*

A: There's no way of knowing. There are so many differences between the two eras. However, if we focus on the question of fitness then perhaps we can begin to make a comparison. It's well known that the men of the legions were required to march some 15–18 miles a day bearing a substantial weight of kit, and construct a marching fort at the end of the day's march, and then repeat the process throughout the campaign. That requires a considerable degree of fitness that many modern soldiers would struggle to match. That said, there are quite a few exceptionally fit soldiers in modern armies. Recently I was talking to a retired SAS officer who was telling me about his selection process. It culminated in a 50-mile march across mountains carrying a 50lb pack to be completed in 20 hours. And when you read of some of the exploits of such men, it's clear that they would have been more than a match for most legionaries!

Q: *There's a really strong element of humour in the novels, which make a great contrast to scenes of violence and slaughter. To what extent do you think this reflects the way soldiers have dealt with the hardships of war throughout the ages?*

A: Humour is a vital component of a soldier's life. It has to be, given the hardships they frequently endure. I recall one exercise in my Officer Training Corps days when we were on patrol during a freezing downpour. At length a voice piped up: 'Are we happy?' to which we all roared back in unison: 'Are we fuck!' Lifted the mood no end, I can tell you.

Humour serves as a useful relief mechanism for the build-up of stress and tension. I recently saw the terrific play *Black Watch* which brought home to me how vital humour is to soldiers, particularly when they are deployed in a theatre of war. Humour is also useful in deflecting away sentimentality and a tendency towards too much reflection. For many soldiers humour provides an extra layer of armour, against the danger from within, and soldiers understand this. That is not to say that they are unfeeling. Far from it. There is a gentleness to soldiers that, when it finds expression, is profoundly moving to witness. This, in part, derives from the nature of what they experience together. I have met many soldiers who say that they feel a closer bond with their comrades than with their families. But they'd make a joke about that too, rather than admit as much in company!

*Q: THE BLOOD CROWS is your twelfth novel featuring Macro and Cato, and Macro plays a substantial role in your novel ARENA, set around gladiator combat in ancient Rome. Could you direct readers to one novel for each of the two heroes that contains an achievement that they'd be particularly proud of?*

A: Macro's finest achievement, from his perspective, would, I think, be the defeat of Bannus, the fanatical leader of the Judaean rebels, in THE EAGLE IN THE SAND. The final showdown is a hand-to-hand fight in the depths of Wadi Rhum – a desolate wilderness of towering rocks and blood-red sand. There is a great deal at stake. If Macro had lost then he, along with Cato, would have been killed, and Bannus would remain at liberty to foment another bloody rebellion against Rome. After a desperate duel with the curved daggers of the Sicarii Macro finally emerges victorious and saves the day.

The event that Cato would be most proud of would be his promotion to centurion at the end of WHEN THE EAGLE HUNTS. Up until then he was labouring under the burden of having to prove himself worthy of being a soldier of the Second Legion and keenly aware of the example set by his friend Macro. With his promotion Cato entered the ranks of the centurionate, the body of officers who were the very core of the legion. If the Roman legions were the most formidable military force of the ancient world, then their reputation was founded on the courage, determination and unswerving loyalty to Rome, of the centurions.

Q: *Alongside your novels about the Roman army, you have written four novels about Wellington and Napoleon, and more recently you wrote about the Siege of Malta in SWORD AND SCIMITAR. Is your approach to writing novels set in other historical periods very different? And do you have plans to write about yet another period?*

A: The French Revolution novels were my first foray outside writing about Rome, and I was determined that they should feel quite different to readers. Aside from all the details in the background I wanted to try out a different style of representation. I have been very pleased by those reviews that said it was almost as if the quartet of novels had been written by a different author. I'd hate to be tagged as a one-trick pony. That experience gave me the confidence to try out different settings. The trouble is that there are so many great stories from the past that provide fantastic material for historical novelists. I have a stack of ideas and detailed notes for a range of projects, only a fraction of which will ever be completed before I shuffle off this mortal coil.

The very next novel I shall be writing will be set during the Second World War. Obviously I cannot go into much detail at this stage. What I can say is that it is a very interesting setting and it goes right to the heart of history and the nature of those who are fascinated by it. Hopefully it will also be a moving tale as well!